# Baby SEALs
# PART 7

J. W. Bloomfield

WESTBOW
PRESS®
A DIVISION OF THOMAS NELSON
& ZONDERVAN

Scripture quotations are taken from the Holy Bible, New Living Translation, copyright ©1996, 2004, 2015 by Tyndale House Foundation. Used by permission of Tyndale House Publishers, Inc., Carol Stream, Illinois 60188. All rights reserved.

This is a work of fiction. All of the characters, names, incidents, organizations, and dialogue in this novel are either the products of the author's imagination or are used fictitiously.

WestBow Press books may be ordered through booksellers or by contacting:

WestBow Press
A Division of Thomas Nelson & Zondervan
1663 Liberty Drive
Bloomington, IN 47403
www.westbowpress.com
1 (866) 928-1240

Because of the dynamic nature of the Internet, any web addresses or links contained in this book may have changed since publication and may no longer be valid. The views expressed in this work are solely those of the author and do not necessarily reflect the views of the publisher, and the publisher hereby disclaims any responsibility for them.

Any people depicted in stock imagery provided by Getty Images are models, and such images are being used for illustrative purposes only. Certain stock imagery © Getty Images.

ISBN: 978-1-9736-5947-1 (sc)
ISBN: 978-1-9736-5946-4 (e)

Print information available on the last page.

WestBow Press rev. date: 4/26/2019

Publisher's Cataloging-In-Publication Data
(Prepared by The Donohue Group, Inc.)

Names: Bloomfield, J. W., 1953- author.
Title: Baby SEALs. Part 7 / J.W. Bloomfield.
Description: Bloomington, IN : WestBow Press, a division of Thomas Nelson & Zondervan, [2019] | Interest age level: 013-019. | Summary: "Jeff and Danielle spend their senior year in high school in Australia, leaving all their worries in the US behind. Right? Apparently not–Australia is keeping them as active as all their years at home. Adjusting to a new school system proves easier than expected, but unanticipated challenges arise ... On the good side, Danielle has a boyfriend, her first. And Jeff has a girlfriend, not his first, but perhaps his next love ... Has Jeff found his forever love? Will the true story of Jeff and Danielle's relationship come out? What about their pilot certificates? And the movie they want to make? University decisions loom ... And is crime boss Owen getting involved in their lives too much–way too much?"–Provided by publisher.

Identifiers: ISBN 9781973659471 (softcover) | ISBN 9781973659464 (ebook)
Subjects: LCSH: Brothers and sisters–Australia–Juvenile fiction. | United States. Navy. SEALs–Juvenile fiction. | Man-woman relationships–Juvenile fiction. | Motion pictures–Production and direction–Juvenile fiction. | Organized crime–Juvenile fiction. | Christian fiction. | CYAC: Brothers and sisters–Australia–Fiction. | United States. Navy. SEALs–Fiction. | Man-woman relationships–Fiction. | Motion pictures–Production and direction–Fiction. | Organized crime–Fiction. | LCGFT: Action and adventure fiction.

Classification: LCC PZ7.1.B642 Bat 2019 (print) | LCC PZ7.1.B642 (ebook) | DDC [Fic]–dc23

# Other books in the Baby SEALs series

# Dedication

This book is dedicated with love to my wife, Christy, who encouraged, advised, and supported me in the writing of this book.

# Acknowledgements

Many thanks to all of you who gave me feedback and information during the writing of this book. Special thanks to my sister who proofread the book and made suggestions. Also, to her and her husband, the Ambassador, who gave me vital information and feedback on the Africa section. And to my family for their encouragement, feedback, and suggestions.

For the Australia section, I asked for help on my Facebook page and received incredible support. Many thanks to Richard and Linda Buchanan who were kind enough to answer even more questions about Australia. Thanks to my high school friend, Diane's, daughter Myesa, for her information regarding university life in Australia.

Any errors are mine. I may have (definitely) changed a few things after my sister edited it.

Follow me on my website, www.jwbloomfield.com, on Facebook at JW Bloomfield, and on Instagram at jw_bloomfield.

# Author's Note

Many series contain books that can be read more or less independently of each other. This series is not one of those. Each book builds on the one before and references people and events that occurred in the past. I didn't plan it that way; it's just the way the story developed. Before the first book was written, I already knew the major events in each book, and discussed them with my editor before the first word was written. At some point, I lost control, and the story took off on its own; I just tried to keep up. New characters appeared as they were needed, and then disappeared or grew. Past events shaped future events.

The books contain almost four hundred characters, not counting the ones who don't even have names. It has taken some spreadsheet legerdemain to keep track of their ages. With the adults in their middle ages, it wasn't so tough, but kids grow quickly and change a lot. Older people grow more fragile. Since the books follow Jeff and Danielle from age six through at least age eighteen, this was important. Hopefully none of my readers will find a character who is eighteen acting like a ten-year-old.

# Chapter 1

Jeff and Danielle Freedman soared through the clear, warm, December Australian air, dropping from fifteen thousand feet, wingsuits extended, bodies tilted for maximum distance as they aimed toward the drop zone several miles to the southeast. Jeff's mainly blue suit with black and white trim registered nicely in Danielle's camera as her green suit with black and white trim did in his when she took the lead. They passed over farmland, towns, small forests, and a river. Anyone looking up from far below would probably think they were birds unless for some reason they were peering through binoculars.

Nearing the point where they would deploy their parachutes, the twins spotted a Ute (Utility vehicle) traveling at a reckless speed over rugged landscape a moment before it rolled over and over, scattering its occupants in its path before it crashed to a stop, upside down and smoking. By unspoken agreement, the twins flared their wingsuits in the air, killing all forward speed, and popped their chutes, unzipped their arm wings, and circled around the crashed Ute, landing feet away from the body farthest from the vehicle and collapsing their chutes. Danielle rushed to the side of this one while Jeff moved to the next in line, tugging his radio earpiece out and letting it dangle as he inserted his cellphone Bluetooth in its place, tersely saying the words that would connect him to emergency services. He described the situation to the operator, giving the rough location northwest of the drop zone and the GPS information from his phone.

After a brief inspection, Danielle left the first body and hurried to the third one, giving Jeff a quick sitrep as she overtook him. He passed the information on, and after a quick examination and update to the emergency operator, rushed to the last victim. Soon the operator had an evaluation of the injuries, which, considering how the crash appeared from the air, weren't too bad: some broken bones, cuts and scrapes, but all four of the passengers had survived with no major injuries as far as the twins could tell; no compound fractures, no internal injuries. Not even a concussion among them.

The emergency operator said in her calm, professional voice, "We have reports of parachutes landing near your location." Jeff agreed. "That would be us. We were nearly to our drop zone at Skymasters when we spotted the crash." The operator acknowledged his reply, and soon they could hear sirens approaching. Just before the emergency vehicles rolled into sight, the owner of the property appeared in his own four-wheel drive vehicle, face red with anger, yelling from the moment he stepped out onto the field. He reminded Danielle of a rat terrier, scurrying around, barking to protect its turf. If Jeff and Danielle hadn't been present, he might well have kicked the four lying on the ground, even as the twins administered first aid, cleaning and bandaging and stabilizing breaks using the kits from their jump suits and makeshift supplies from items lying in the field. However, when Jeff unfolded from his position by one of the victims and towered by a head over the man, he suddenly calmed down, if by calm one meant no longer trying to kick the injured. The yelling continued.

Jeff let him rant as Danielle finished adding a last bandage, peering past the man at the heavy-duty vehicles rolling across the field, led by a police car that might have to be towed back out before it was all said and done. She stood beside her twin as the vehicles pulled to a stop in a circle around the group. The police officer barely had time to step out of his car before the small man was in his face, jabbing his finger toward the wreck and demanding everyone, including Jeff and Danielle, be arrested and locked up forever, longer if possible.

As the officer spoke calmly with the irate landowner, writing in his notebook, letting the man's wrath flow by him like water around a rock, the ambulance and firetruck crews set to work. Jeff and Danielle had already performed much of the preliminary work. The worst injured would be taken to the hospital in the ambulance, the other three in the back of the police car.

Finished for the moment with the angry man, the officer approached Jeff and Danielle, who were bundling their parachutes and stuffing them back in the packs, efficiently and neatly but not jump quality. They would repack them after they returned to the drop zone. Danielle's phone was already buzzing as the ground crew called to see where they were; by now they were several minutes overdue.

As Jeff explained what they had seen from the air and how they had happened on the scene, Danielle told Barb, their friendly liaison at Skymasters, what had occurred and asked if someone could possibly pick them up. They would walk out if necessary, but it would be cumbersome with the parachute packs. Barb yelled something into the room, and after a moment said, "JR is on his way. He can't wait to hear this story. Neither can I." Danielle sighed.

The ambulance and police car had both departed when JR drove up, again sending the land owner into a frenzy, screaming about "blokes driving all over his property". Jeff was seriously concerned about his heart and blood pressure. Curious, he asked, "Why don't you put up a fence and post it 'No Trespassing'?" If anything, this seemed to make the man even angrier, and he began a rant which involved, first, he shouldn't have to pay for a fence; and second, the trespassers knew it wasn't their land. Jeff left the fuming man who was now walking over to yell at the tow truck driver who had just arrived.

Ignoring the landowner, who he seemed familiar with, the driver joined Jeff, Danielle, JR, and the two men from the paramedic vehicle at the overturned Ute and asked, "Shall we flip it over so it will roll onto the tow truck easier?" Danielle replied, "Why not?" but the others stared at him. Danielle said, "You're all a bunch of burly men. It will be easy." She and Jeff positioned themselves on one side and lifted it some to show it could be done. After exchanging a look, the other three men walked over and were quickly joined by the tow truck driver who seemed anxious to stay away from the angry land owner.

The six positioned themselves evenly along one side of the vehicle, and on Jeff's count, lifted. The side climbed into the air, and after reaching a tipping point, crashed over onto its tires. One of them was already flat, a blowout being the reason for the disaster in the first place. A second one went as well when it hit the ground. Still, the tow truck driver agreed it would be easier to load this way. Soon, the Ute was chained in place on the bed of the tow truck, and with a wave of his hand, the driver made his escape, followed by the firemen in their truck. JR was edging toward his car as Jeff and Danielle made a final appeal to the angry land owner.

Danielle asked, "Why are you so angry? It's like being mad at bees because they're attracted to nectar. Why don't you do something like plant a hedge around your property if you don't want to put up a fence?" The man yelled, "Because I shouldn't have to. They know they're not supposed to be driving on my land." The twins gave up and climbed in the car with JR. As he drove away, he asked, "So, did you really have to land here instead of at the drop zone?" Jeff answered, "It's kind of automatic. We see trouble, and we go toward it." JR sniffed. "You may have to work on that, mate."

Back at the drop zone, the twins explained to Barb and the

others in the waiting room what had happened. Fortunately for them, no news crews had appeared, and no one seemed interested in filming video on their phones. This one incident, if it did make the news casts, would be without pictures. Except for the video on the twins' bodycams, of course. Which they had no plans to share. At least it had occurred on their last jump, and the other ones had been spectacular! They repacked their parachutes properly, strapped them on the backs of their motorcycles, and started home.

The day had mostly been a fun one, filled with phone and video calls from their friends and family back in the states where it was just now their birthday. While they wouldn't need to tell anyone except family about the accident, there would still be some explaining to do to their host family. This began as soon as they walked in the back door with their parachute packs, and Lucy ran to greet them, yelling, "You're on the news again, mates!" Jeff and Danielle exchanged looks and continued into the kitchen after storing the parachutes.

Jeff asked Lucy, "What did we do this time?" From her place by his side, she answered, "You rescued some people from an overturned car!" The rest of the Armstrong family was sitting in various spots around the kitchen, and turned to stare at the twins as they entered. Danielle asked, "What are they saying?" Jake said, "Something about the two of you parachuting to an overturned car and saving the lives of the passengers." Jeff rolled his eyes. "Well, that's just wrong. We called emergency services like anyone would do and stuck on some bandages. How did the news even hear about it? There weren't any news crews there." Sean said, "Maybe some of the people there called the news, although I wouldn't think it would be the people in the wreck. What happened?"

Jeff and Danielle spent the next few minutes describing the accident and their part in it. When they finished, Jake said, "Well, the bad news is the land owner is saying he's filing trespass charges against everyone, including you. I've already called Oliver. He says you're covered because it's legal to enter property to rescue someone. Besides, the land owner is also threatening the police, ambulance, and everyone else who was there. He may have a case against the four in the car that you gave aid to, but he's barking up the wrong tree on the rest." Danielle's phone rang then, and the twins left to receive more birthday wishes and clean up for dinner.

# Chapter 2

The next afternoon, the twins lounged cross-legged on the table in the Armstrong back yard, watching five-year-old Lucy (I am practically six) pirouette on the grass, attempting to perform the kata Jeff had taught her. The older young people had grown a bit in the past year, although their major growth spurt appeared to be completed. Both were six feet tall. Jeff was perhaps five pounds heavier than Danielle, but she was also heavily muscled from the constant training, especially now that their new gym was up and functional. The young man's hair was military short as it had been since he was seven. Hers was shoulder length, usually in a single braid.

In addition to watching Lucy, they were deep in discussion about the church they had joined when they arrived in Australia, Victory Bible Church. The discussion involved the potential growth of the church and how to deal with it. To be accurate, the growth had started after Jeff and Danielle visited the hospital soon after their arrival, and some of the patients and their families attended their new church the following day. That, however, was more of a one-off. What they were currently thinking of might begin a more sustained growth.

The reason for the possible growth? Danielle's connect-the-dots pictures. Well, that and the notebook the twins planned to create for Lucy. And Pastor Shane's dynamic Bible preaching on Sunday mornings and evenings as well as the Wednesday evening gatherings and the home Bible study groups. These all encouraged and sustained the growth. But the reason more people might visit was the pictures and the notebook.

The process was well established in the past, if two churches made a relevant data set. Jeff and Danielle produced the notebook with Danielle's connect-the-dots picture inside. Other children saw it and wanted one. Their older siblings and parents grew interested in the notebook, and, if they weren't already attending the church, visited. The dynamics of the church swept them up, and the family joined. They told their friends, neighbors, and co-workers about the church and showed them the notebook. Those people visited and joined as well, and so on.

The notebook itself wasn't extraordinarily special. It was divided into sections with the first one being a place for the pictures. Following were sections for notes from the Sunday School lessons each week, followed by one for notes from the two Sunday and one Wednesday sermons. Then there were sections for prayer requests, daily Bible reading, and daily Bible study. Eye-catching, though, were the pictures since they contained local scenes and people from the church. Members would anticipate the pictures, hoping they would be in one.

The twins debated for quite a while on whether or not to introduce the pictures and the notebooks. They had caused growth before and some notoriety, and they were trying to keep a lower profile this year. However, the deciding factor was Lucy. As they sat in the backyard watching the soon to be six-year-old flit around the open space, Jeff said, "She should have them. What happens, happens."

Jeff had been working with the young girl ever since their arrival in December, and her reading skill had improved dramatically. She had been quite a handful when she entered school the end of January, and it was only growing worse as Jeff continued to work with her, boredom being the biggest problem. With Jeff and Danielle's encouragement, her mother would probably begin homeschooling her within the next few weeks, assisted by the twins and Zoe. Her developing reading and writing skills made the binder more practical.

Back to the moment, Jeff produced a three-ring binder, and Danielle rolled her eyes. "You knew I would agree to this." He smiled. "Of course. I know what you're going to think before you do." She smiled back, although her smile perhaps had more teeth. She asked, "What am I thinking now?" He shrugged. "Perhaps you should discuss that with Pastor Shane." She aimed a mock punch at him, which he dodged.

Zoe stepped through the back door and dropped into a chair behind them. "What are you up to?" The eighteen-year-old had her Australian parents' ruddy complexion and blond hair, with her father's height but her mother's slighter build. Jeff leaned his head back to observe her upside down. "We're about to do something that may cause the church to grow." She smiled. "Isn't that a good thing?" Danielle said, "Yes, except it leads to logistic problems as the Sunday School classes run out of space. You can always go to two services, but class space can be an issue. And parking." Zoe commented, "Hmmm," as Lucy yelled, "Watch, Mom," and began her kata again.

After watching her for a moment, Zoe called, "Well done, mate!" and Lucy beamed, running over to plop in Jeff's lap. He hugged her until she squealed, and the three older ones continued the conversation. Zoe said, "You know, the building next door is empty and has been for sale for a while. It's big enough to be a home for Pastor Shane and his family and hold some Sunday School classes, too. It's too bad the church can't afford to buy it." Jeff and Danielle shared a look and determined to have Jake check into it.

Zoe noticed the binder in Jeff's hands. "What's that?" Jeff handed it to her, and she stared at the picture on the cover. After a moment, she recognized it as Lucy, and exclaimed, "It's Lucy! This is a ripper of a picture!" Next, she opened the binder and

9

gazed curiously at the connect-the-dots picture. Knowing what she was wondering, Danielle handed her a pencil, and Zoe drew a line from number to number, exclaiming when she finished, "It's Lucy again!" Lucy immediately left Jeff's lap to stand by her mother, gazing at the picture. Then she, too, yelled, "It is me!" Zoe, ears ringing, immediately said, "Lucy, inside voice," which earned her a reproving glare from the young girl, who proclaimed, "Mom, we're outside!" Zoe closed the binder and showed the girl the picture on the cover. Now she had to fight for possession of the binder, and Lucy finally agreed to stand by her as they paged through the binder together.

Zoe leafed through the other sections and said, "This is nice. For Lucy?" Danielle answered, "The first one is for Lucy, but it won't stop there. Probably everyone in her class will want one, and then the other youth classes, and then the adult classes. That's what happened at our other churches, anyway. We assume it will be the same here." Zoe noted, "You don't seem happy about that." Jeff sighed. "It's not that. We just don't have time to set up all the notebooks like we did at home." Zoe shrugged. "That's not a problem. Mom and I can handle it. Can't we, Mom?"

This last was aimed at Sophie who had just appeared beside the group, setting a tray of fruit on the table. "Pre-dinner snack, anyone? Can't we what?" Zoe explained about the notebook as she handed it to her to examine. Lucy followed the notebook and pointed out her picture among the dots. Sophie laughed. "This is really clever. Is it something that continues?" Zoe said, "That's what we were just discussing. Jeff and Danielle are willing to provide the material for Lucy's binder, but they don't have time to create them for all the other kids and everyone else if they want one."

Sophie continued through the various sections, ending with, "I want one. Jake will, too. So will our Bible study group." Zoe said, "You and I can make any additional ones, right, once the first one is ready?" Sophie nodded. "We'll need to buy binders and dividers and make copies, but certainly." Jeff said, "Danielle and I will pay for the materials if you two can put them together. It might be worth it to rent a nice copy/scanner/fax machine for Jake's office." Zoe and Sophie shared a look. Then, Sophie stood up to leave, with "Dinner will be ready in an hour. You should probably get ready for church, especially you, young lady." This was to Lucy who did indeed need a certain amount of cleaning up from her afternoon in the yard.

Lucy grabbed the notebook and ran inside to show Poppop. Jake was big, 6'3" and 200 lbs., muscle beginning to turn to fat despite his spare time spent with a local cricket team. This was beginning to change a bit as he spent time at Jeff and Danielle's gym. His ruddy complexion was topped by a balding head, the remaining blond hair turning gray and clipped short. Rushing to where he sat in the lounge room, she shoved the book into his lap.

He stared at the picture on the cover for a second, then exclaimed, "That's you! That's a ripper of a picture! Did Danielle draw it?" She confirmed this and waited impatiently for him to open the binder and spot the connect-the-dots picture inside. When he finished admiring the picture on the cover, he flipped the book open and peered inside. "Why, this one is you, too! You're a famous little wallaby, aren't you?" She giggled as he continued to page through the sections. "This is very nice. I guess it's yours, isn't it? I want one, too." She took the book back and said, "Talk to mom and Mummmum," and ran off.

The conversation at the dinner table was the binder and the logistics of creating more. The project had begun.

# Chapter 3

That evening on the walk to church, the group stopped by the large white building next door to the church. It had originally been a large house, almost a McMansion, that had been converted into business suites. The building was single story, but it contained a tall attic, large enough for additional rooms or quite a bit of storage. The For Sale sign had been visible at the street for at least as long as Jeff and Danielle had been in the city. Jeff and Danielle gave Jake a significant look, and he nodded, adding it to his mental list of things to do. Then the group continued to church.

At the evening service, the binder was received with the enthusiasm Jeff and Danielle had predicted. First to notice it were Jake and Sophie's friends who asked the small girl politely what she was carrying. When they spotted the picture on the cover, however, everything changed. There were exclamations of delight followed by more of the same when the binder was opened to the connect-the-dots picture. Notes from the morning's Sunday School lesson and the church sermon were in their sections along with the Bible Study plan. Immediately the requests for their own binder began, and by the time the family returned home, Zoe had a list of several names. Not a bad beginning.

Later, as they sat around the lounge discussing the day, Jake asked Jeff and Danielle, "What's your interest in the building?" Jeff explained that they thought the church might begin growing, and Zoe had suggested it was a possible place for the Sunday School classes to expand into, and even as a place for the pastor to live." Sophie said, "That's an interesting idea. I don't think the church can afford it, though, even if it grows." Danielle said, "There would be a way," and Jake and Sophie glanced at each other. The man said, "I'll check into it. Do you want to inspect it?" Jeff said, "Let's find the price and do a basic walk through to see if it's suitable at all. We don't need to proceed unless the church outgrows the current building." And so, the project was on the table.

Sunday led to Monday, and their second week of school. The four were met at the door by students who had caught the news of the weekend rescue on the telly or heard about it from their friends. There were sociable calls of "Good on you, mates!" and sarcastic "Oooo. There are the heroes," as well. Jeff and Danielle smiled at the first and ignored the second. They explained that they had been at the end of their jump anyway, almost to the drop zone, and had merely landed a bit early, applied some basic first aid, and called emergency services.

They also received another call to visit the principal. This was a congratulatory visit as he expressed his delight at the good publicity the school received when it became known Jeff and Danielle attended his school; a bit of a change from their earlier visit and a pleasant surprise. Zoe and her friends rolled their eyes when the twins told them about the conversation, but Jeff and Danielle, respectful of authority, even when they disagreed with certain people, said, "It is good for the school. Good news reflects well on everyone here, the same as bad news." This began a lively discussion regarding authority and respect, which carried on through lunch and even into the breaks between classes.

Jeff and Danielle explained their theory about experience. Jeff said, "Think of the person in our class who you think is the most clueless." He could tell some were considering one person, and some, another. Danielle continued, "Now match them against

13

those students beginning their first year here. Which is more likely to lose their way or not know how to act." There were scowls of concentration as the group considered their person of choice compared to a new student. Jeff said, "As clueless as they might be, their experience at this school still gives them a leg up over someone new. Experience matters. It matters with the staff here as well. They might be socially inept or not as interesting as someone else, but they still, for the most part, have more life experience than we do, and experience deserves respect. You could say it's respecting the age, but it's more than that." There were some nods of understanding as well as head shakes of disagreement, and the subject dropped for the time being.

Lunch was busy with barely time for Jeff and Danielle to put a bite in their mouths as students and even teachers stopped by to discuss the rescue and ask for details that were not mentioned on the news programs. Sean and Zoe answered the questions they could, but people wanted to hear from the twins. From their training with Mike, they were able to finish the meal despite the interruptions, which was good because they had packed some really nice Caesar salads with Romaine lettuce, homemade Caesar dressing, and grilled chicken.

Some of the visitors to their table expressed skepticism that the two had really parachuted into the situation, but Danielle didn't mind showing the video from their cameras as they sailed from the exit point to the drop zone. She stopped it before the accident, however, knowing it would somehow end up on the news or YouTube and would not help their attempt to stay under the radar, feeble though it now appeared.

Some of the older guys attempted to flirt with Danielle, but she kindly where possible, brusquely where necessary, brushed them off. Zoe brought up Henry, whom some had seen on Jeff and Danielle's birthday when he picked the Armstrong group up from school, and implied that he was Danielle's boyfriend, which cooled the jets of all but the most clueless ones. Zoe, sitting beside Jeff, didn't mind that the guys for the most part paid little attention to her. Some of the girls and guys asked about Lucy, and Zoe was happy to talk about her. She even recognized the change in her toward her daughter that made the discussion enjoyable.

# Chapter 4

The following Sunday, Danielle's second connect-the-dots picture was introduced in church by way of Lucy's binder, which she carried proudly in her arms and displayed to the crowd of Sunday School classmates and teachers. Her classmates were soon swarming around her, demanding their own and asking how they could get one. Lucy carefully wrote their names in her binder and said she would bring one as soon as she could, and everyone had to be impatiently content. In church that morning word had also spread by way of those who had examined the binder at the previous Sunday night's church service, and children brought their parents or siblings to Lucy, and the little girl sat surrounded by people until the service began, again carefully writing names in her binder. Jeff and Danielle had told her anyone who wanted one could have one, and if perhaps some asked more for the free binder and the three-stroke sketch than for an organized place to take notes and store prayer requests, they still had a tool in their hands that could help them grow in their spiritual journey if they let it.

As the family walked home, discussing the various Sunday School lessons and the binder, the sermon and the binder, the building next door to the church and the binder, Sophie asked Danielle, "Will you be able to do a drawing for the front of each binder like you did for Lucy's? That's a lot of sketches." Danielle shrugged. "I'll need to see the people, but the sketches don't take any time at all. I drew them for fund raisers back home." She added as the Armstrong family's eyes lit up, "Although I don't think I'll have time for that here. There is too much going on." She didn't mention that the movie project would hopefully soon begin taking up a great deal of their time.

She began working from Lucy's list of names that afternoon, and before dinner, sketches for all the names were complete. She and Jeff could connect every name on the list to a face since in this case they had met all the people. That might not always be true, and they would need either an introduction or a picture, but an introduction would be preferable. Sometimes what stood out in a picture was not what stood out if you knew the person.

Each sketch was scanned into her laptop. Some people were sure to lose their sketch if not the entire binder. Each binder contained the original sketch. If the owners were smart, they would make a copy of the sketch and store it somewhere safe, possibly behind a frame on their wall. For the most part, it would be the only one they would receive. If they lost it, Danielle would print a copy from the scan.

In the week since their original discussion, Jake had dug into the history of the building next door to the church. His research showed there was no particular reason Jeff and Danielle shouldn't purchase it if they so desired and it proved suitable to the church's requirements. He made an appointment for the following Tuesday after school, and after changing clothes, the entire Armstrong crew trooped over to the building to meet the realtor.

While Jake discussed the history and cost of the building, Jeff and Danielle examined it inch by inch, making note of its condition and the age of the supporting equipment such as the water heater, noting it did not have central air conditioning and heating. The building did indeed have a large attic that could easily be made into additional rooms, and it wouldn't be too much trouble to add a connection to the church next door. The twins liked it and continued their examination, from the sturdiness of the wood floors to the beams in the attic. The building was over a hundred years old and very well constructed. An examination of the electrical panel revealed that both the panel and the wiring were new, as were the plumbing fixtures.

When they mentioned it to the realtor, he said, "I think that is why the owner wants to sell it. He spent so much renovating the building that he had to set his rents high trying to recover the cost. No one wanted to pay it when there are cheaper locations that will do the job. He decided to sell and has the same problem. That's why the building has been on the market so long. I think now he just wants to recover what he can."

Jeff and Danielle nodded in agreement. They'd seen that before back home. The group left with Jake saying he'd be in touch. On the walk home, Lucy, riding on Jeff's shoulders, asked, "Are you going to buy it, mate?" Jeff tilted his head up at her. "How would we afford a whole building?" She giggled and shrugged. "You tell Poppop, and his foundation buys it." Danielle asked, "Why would the foundation want it? How would it help them?" Now the little girl was stumped. "I don't know, but the church could use it." Zoe asked, "Shouldn't the church buy it, then?" Lucy frowned. "I don't think the church can afford it. It's awfully big." Sean said, "Maybe someone else will buy it and rent it to the church for something they could afford."

The group pondered this as they made their way up the front steps and into the house. Everyone scattered to work on different tasks, but not before Jeff and Danielle nodded to Jake, and he set the wheels in motion to purchase the building. The owner was anxious to get his money back out of the building, the twins transferred the money into the foundation account, and in a couple of weeks, ownership of the building changed hands.

# Chapter 5

The remainder of the week was just as busy, with swimming or running, trips to the gym and shooting club, and, Sean and Zoe's birthday party on Friday. As with Jeff and Danielle's party a couple of weeks earlier, everyone was very "What birthday party?" and "Are you sure it's your birthday?" Behind the scenes, their friends were being invited, food was being planned, presents were being created or purchased.

Harry and Henry were able to attend, and once again the younger man was parked on the street outside the school when classes ended for the day. He was greeted warmly, and Danielle even went so far as to give him a brief hug, causing Jeff to make a quick, "I'm watching you!" gesture. The ice cream explanation was given again, and the group arrived home to find the surprise party in full swing. Friends from church and school were everywhere, along with the Happy Birthday banners in every room which Lucy proudly proclaimed to have helped make, explaining the excess of glitter on all of them.

Presents were piled in the middle of the dining room table, which also contained stacks of plates, cups, and plasticware, and a gorgeous cake with Zoe and Sean's faces outlined with icing. Various snacks and drinks lined the kitchen counter, and different forms of entertainment were set up in the game room, lounge room, and back yard. Some of the ones in the back yard involved water guns and water balloons, and a stack of hand towels waited by the back door for the unfortunate losers, and sometimes the winners, of these wet extravaganzas.

About the time the sun was setting in the west, all the guests moved from the inside and outside games to the dining room where the cake was served to many jokes as the faces were cut into pieces, "No nose piece for me, please!" and the presents were opened. The gifts were a mixture of practical, thoughtful, beautiful, and comic. Not unexpectantly, Danielle gave Zoe a sketch, one of her in her school uniform laughing with friends, although the friends weren't in the sketch.

What she discovered to be missing, though, was a gift from Jeff. Her first thought was that for some reason he hadn't given her one. Second was that the sketch was from both Jeff and Danielle although the label had only said from Danielle to Zoe. No Jeff. She was a little hurt even though he hadn't given one to Sean either. And he had given one to Lucy. Not only that, but he and Lucy seemed to be sharing some joke that didn't include her.

She sighed, knowing she shouldn't care. He had only been there two months, and he would be gone in ten more. Still, she thought they had bonded at the beach when they discussed Lucy. And it seemed to her that he was giving her as much help as he gave her daughter, although it wasn't as direct.

The party wrapped up, and when the last guest was out the door, including Harry and Henry, and the house was back in order, Zoe was surprised when Lucy called for her to come to the lounge room. When she entered, she found the rest of the family sitting in various chairs or on the sofas, except for Jeff, Danielle, and Lucy, who were gathered in what had come to be called the music corner. Jeff sat at his keyboard, and Danielle and Lucy had guitars slung over their shoulders. Lucy gestured for her mom to sit in a chair in front of them.

When she was seated, Lucy handed her a gift-wrapped box with a label that read, "From Jeff, For Zoe." He said, "It's a song. You can share it or not. We're going to play it for you now. It's called *Growing*." He began a piano intro, followed by Lucy on her small, acoustic guitar, then Danielle on her larger one. The song was all about Zoe, her growth, what she was becoming. When the song ended, Jeff and Danielle were both smiling at her, Lucy was beaming, Zoe and her mom were both crying happily, and even Jake and Sean were a bit teary eyed.

Zoe walked over to the keyboard and hugged Jeff and gave him a quiet "Thank you." She also hugged Danielle and squeezed Lucy until she squeaked. Sean said jokingly, "I want a song, too!" Lucy yelled, "They wrote one for you, too! Do you want to hear it?" Those seated in the room all clapped and exclaimed, "More! Let's hear it, mates!" Jeff nodded at Lucy, who said, "Do your hands like this," and clapped her hands once, followed by what would have been a finger snap if she had a little more practice. When the audience was doing as she directed, she bobbed her head in time with the claps and snaps and started, followed by Danielle and then Jeff.

This song was about all the pressure Sean had been complaining about suffering under since school began and his days of fun and leisure had changed to homework. It was half fun, half serious, and although the listeners laughed a great deal during the song, there were also some nods at the serious message underlying it all. Sean was touched, but in his boyish way, the most he could say was, "Great song, mates! Thanks! Do I get a copy, too?" Jeff picked up a rolled sheaf of papers tied in a ribbon from the top of his keyboard and tossed it to the young man who snatched it out of the air, asking, "Can I get a copy of the audio, too?" Jeff laughed and tossed him a flash drive also sitting on top of the keyboard.

Before Zoe could ask, Danielle said, "Your flash drive is in the box with the music." Zoe smiled and nodded, picked up her box and left the room. Everyone headed to bed. The next day, a trip was planned to Newcastle to visit a hospital there. They would be leaving early for the two-hour drive.

Zoe joined Jeff for the nightly tucking Lucy in routine. The little girl asked, "Did you like the song, mom? Was I good? Danielle practiced with me a lot!" Zoe asked, "How long have you been working on it, mate?" Lucy waved her hands. "Ever since Danielle gave me the guitar. It was the first song she taught me to play. You didn't know that's what it was did you? She taught me the one for Uncle Sean next. It was easier."

Zoe stared at Jeff. "When did you write it?" He smiled. "The day after the trip to the beach." She asked, "Who did the rest of the soundtrack?" He explained about Terry's band, and she asked, "My song is going to be on an album?" Jeff shook his head. "No. Not unless you want it to. It's your song. If it does go on an album, you'll earn royalties from it."

Lucy was bouncing up and down in her bed. "Mom! Your song could be on an album!" Zoe smiled down at her, kissed the girl goodnight, and said, "I'll think about it." Once in the hall, she told Jeff thank you again, entered her room, and closed the door. Inside the room, Danielle sat cross-legged on her bed, reading her Bible.

"Did you get Lucy to sleep?" Zoe shook her head ruefully. "I suppose she will doze off eventually. There is a lot of sugar in that girl from the party. And excitement. She is going to be a musician on a stage one day." Danielle laughed at the thought. As she changed into the shorts and t-shirt she slept in, Zoe said over her shoulder, "Jeff said my song could go on an album if I want. What do you think?"

Danielle cocked her head to one side as she considered the question. "Well, Terry's band has already recorded the song. It's on the flash drive in your gift box. You can decide what you want to do; keep it for yourself or whomever you choose to play it for or let them release it on an album. You don't have to decide tonight. Or anytime soon. If it is released, though, it will earn you royalties if you're interested in that."

Zoe paused in her clothes changing. "Do you think that's why

Jeff wrote it?" Danielle laughed. "I can tell you with absolute assurance that isn't the reason he wrote it." Zoe continued pulling the t-shirt over her head. "Sean will want his song released. He'll want everyone in the world to hear it. He won't mind royalties, either." Danielle said, "Maybe he'll want to wait for the school talent show. We could play it then; you and Jeff on keyboards, me on lead guitar. We would need another guitar and a drummer. Unless you think we could sneak Lucy in. Then we'd just need a drummer." The two girls stared at each other for a moment before bursting into laughter.

Early the next morning after brekkie, the family was on the road, driving to the hospital in Newcastle. They passed through a number of small towns along the way. Definitely not the outback; lots of trees, farms, and buildings. It was a pleasant drive. They arrived in the city about 9:30am and made their way to the hospital, where Jeff and Danielle, with the assistance of the Armstrongs, spent the next several hours in their usual routine.

Their first stop after the hospital was the beach. The twins wanted to experience every Australian beach they could and were constantly amazed at the clarity of the water. The middle of February was almost the end of summer, and the air and sea temperatures were perfect. The entire family was brown from time spent in the sun, and they spent most of their time swimming and snorkeling or towing Lucy along on a boogie board as she clung to the back and watched the underwater activity through her mask.

The remainder of the day was spent on a walking tour of Australia's second oldest city. The trip had been planned a few weeks in advance, and one of the doctors from the hospital, an amateur history buff, was delighted to guide their way through the eclectic streets to find hidden architecture, art and laneways.[1] After dinner at a restaurant near the seashore and a quick taxi ride back to the hospital, the family was on its way home by 8:00pm, in bed by 11:00pm, and ready for church the next day.

# Chapter 6

On Tuesday of the following week, Henry called Danielle, a not uncommon occurrence these days. Both were busy, although of the two, Danielle's schedule was the more crowded, with physical training, projects, homework, and preparing for the movie. While Henry was in country at the base, he spent most evenings in the barracks with the rest of the team.

During this evening's conversation, he mentioned that a friend of Harry's had invited him to bring his entire team to his farm to rid it of his feral hog problem. They were killing game and destroying crops, and his occasional killing of a pig or two seemed to be making the problem worse by ridding the herd of the stupid pigs and making the others more clever. He would arrange for a meat packing facility to show up with a refrigerated truck to process the meat for sell around the state to restaurants that specialized in bush meat if Harry would come.

When Danielle asked if they were going, Henry said, "Thinking about it. Leave Friday as soon as we're done for the day, drive all night, hunt Saturday, drive back Sunday." Danielle was silent for a moment, then said, "What if you flew?" He laughed. "You do know we're in the army, right, mate? We can barely afford to drive."

Danielle considered. One of the first things she and Jeff had done after they received their parachute qualifications, was to ask if their jump pilot would be interested in flying them places, specifically to cities with hospitals that were a little far to drive to timewise, but just as far by air travel by the time they cleared airport security. What they wanted was the convenience they had had back in the US with Mark, Mike's friend and their jump pilot, who had flown them to many destinations with no questions asked.

On a hunch, they had asked their current jump pilot, who flew the same single engine, fourteen passenger aircraft as Mark, if he would be interested in some ferry work, taking them and the Armstrong family to various nearby cities. He had named a price, she and Jeff had agreed, and they had their plane and pilot. Now, she asked Henry, "What if it didn't cost you anything? Jeff and I know a pilot who would fly us down."

Henry was silent for a moment. Then he said, "For free?" She said, "For you, Harry, and the men it would be. We could also throw in the ammunition, although one of you would have to pick it up. Oh, and you would have to bring weapons for me and Jeff. Henry was silent for another moment. "How many men?" She said, "Eight. Actually, seven if Jake wants to or needs to come. We're not supposed to go anywhere without our sponsor family. I'm not sure Harry qualifies, even if he is Sophie's brother. And, we haven't asked anyone if we can go. So, it's sort of an idea in progress." Henry laughed. "I'll check with the captain. You check with Jake and Sophie." They said goodbye and hung up.

The following morning, Jeff and Danielle brought up the hunt at the breakfast table. Sophie raised an eyebrow. "My brother wants to take the two of you on a pig hunt?" Jeff said, "Well, Harry's friend invited him and his team down. Harry was kind enough to ask us along." Jake said, "And you want to go on this hunt?" Danielle said, "Yes, sir. We like hunting wild pigs, and we're quite good at it." Sean asked, "What will you do with the pigs you kill?" Jeff explained about the meat packing facility that would be sending people and a refrigerated truck to handle the meat.

Jake asked, "What would you hunt with?" Danielle said, "Harry would bring something for us." Zoe asked, "Would you be bringing anything home with you?" Jeff said, "We were thinking some hams to smoke and some bacon. Maybe some pork chops." Sean asked, "Won't it taste weird?" Danielle laughed. "According to Harry's friend, these pigs have been eating up his garden and farm, so they have been eating better food than domestic pigs are fed. We'll see."

Jake shared a look with Sophie. "I guess I'll need to go. You're not supposed to roam around the country without someone from your host family accompanying you. How were you planning on traveling, by the way?" Jeff said, "Our jump pilot would fly us."

Jake and Sophie shared another look. She asked, "Is Harry paying for this? I assume the pilot and plane are not free." Danielle said, "Jeff and I would. It's a chance to see some of Victoria, and Harry and his team don't have a lot of time. While Jeff and I wouldn't mind driving, we'd rather have more time on the ground hunting this trip. It would be a shame to go all that way and not get all the pigs cleaned out. And, we haven't spoken with the pilot yet. He may not be available. We needed your permission to even begin."

Jake said, "We'll talk about it and let you know tomorrow. How's that?" The twins both nodded, and Lucy immediately said, "I want to go, too, mates!" Jeff shook his head. "Not this trip, sweetie." She pouted and said, "I never get to do anything," face down but looking up through her eyelashes. The others at the table stared at her a moment before bursting into laughter. After a moment, she joined in. It was hard to play the mistreated card when her life had exploded in activity since Jeff and Danielle had arrived on the scene.

That evening as they prepared for bed, Jake and Sophie discussed the trip. She asked, "What do you think?" He bowed his head in thought, then said, "Why not? It isn't as though they haven't done it before. Obviously, Robert and Michelle allow it.

I trust Harry to keep an eye on them." Sophie nodded her head in agreement. "We'll have to remind Harry to keep an eye on Henry. I trust Danielle, but it would be a shame for Henry to end up in the hospital because he treated her like a normal girl. Hopefully he knows better."

While the adults were discussing Jeff and Danielle, they were making their own phone call to the jump pilot to see if he would be interested in flying the group down. He jumped at the chance. Not only was it an opportunity to make some extra income, but his sister lived near the airport the twins wanted to fly to, and her birthday was Saturday. He was planning on flying down anyway, and now he would be paid to do so. Win/win. Pilot secured. The next morning over breakfast when Jake gave them permission for the trip, plans for the weekend seemed to be coming together.

Friday after school, the twins changed into camouflage gear and packed the clothing and personal items they would need for the trip. When Harry called to say they were almost there, Sophie drove Jake, Jeff, and Danielle to the shooting club. A car pulled up as they arrived, and the doors opened to eject Harry, who was driving, Lachlan, who was riding shotgun, Henry, Ned, and Angus from the back seat. Jeff and Danielle exchanged greetings with the men while Harry walked inside, returning a few minutes later with a .50 cal. ammo can. Soon, the two cars arrived at the airfield where they loaded all the gear on board and, in half an hour, were airborne.

As soon as the plane reached cruising altitude, Henry pulled one of the rifle cases into his lap and opened it. Inside was an Australian main battle rifle. He disassembled it slowly, showing Jeff and Danielle all the pieces. Then he quickly reassembled it. Handing the case over to Danielle, he nodded for her to repeat what he had just done. Slowly but smoothly, she repeated his actions. Then a second time, and a third. She passed the rifle case on to Jeff, who repeated what she had done. The other soldiers watched as the two young people worked, nodding to each other, unsurprised by how quickly they had learned.

The flight took about four and a half hours. Jeff joked with all the members of the team. Danielle spoke mainly with Henry. The plane landed on a well-groomed pasture on Harry's friend's property only a short distance from the large house. The airstrip was obviously used for night time flying as the entire length was well lit. A spotlight shone on a windsock. Jeff went forward to sit beside the pilot as he lined up for the landing, and the man cheerfully discussed the flight decisions, instruments, and weather conditions involved. Although he had never landed at night, Jeff was fairly confident that he or Danielle could have landed the plane, and he felt no qualms about performing the task if called upon.

Once on the ground, they were met by a Ute and a deuce-and-a-half truck. Harry and Jake climbed in the Ute while the others boarded the truck with all the gear and weapons. It was a short drive to the house, really a compound with a large, two-story frame house, barn, sheep-shearing shed, metal-framed building for working on farm equipment, and a bunkhouse for the hired hands. Harry and Jake would be staying in the house; the others would be setting up sleeping bags in the barn. The farmer's wife met them in the barnyard, and when she saw Danielle, tried to insist that she stay in the house as well. Danielle politely refused but did agree to take her shower in the house. Jeff and the team would use the communal shower in the bunk house.

As soon as the group cleared the plane, their pilot lifted off again to fly the short distance to the airfield nearest his sister's home. They would not see him again until Sunday morning. Everyone had eaten a meal of MRE's on the flight down, so all that was left for the evening was setting up their sleeping bags in the sweet-smelling hay from a stack in the barn, chatting for a while as they checked the area for poisonous spiders or snakes, and dropping off to sleep. Henry set his sleeping bag up on one side of

Danielle with Jeff on the other. As they prepared to sleep, Jeff said, loud enough for Henry to hear, "If you have to kill him during the night, do it quietly so you don't wake everyone." There were chuckles all around. Henry wasn't the only one to hear.

The next morning at daylight, everyone was up, gear packed, weapons loaded but no rounds in the chamber. A buffet style brekkie was served in the large dining room of the house. Ten hired hands were present, and from their conversation, it seemed they were a bit resentful that the farmer had brought in the soldiers to clear out the pigs instead of utilizing them. Jeff and Danielle had the greatest part in diffusing this situation by laughingly saying, "We weren't brought in because you couldn't do the job! We were brought in as a training exercise for us!"

The hired men accepted this with pride and jesting, although if they had thought about it, if they could have done the job, the pigs would already be gone, and much of the damage could have been avoided. They had been out more than once on roundups, but had been unable to hit most of the running animals they found, preferring a longer range shot at a standing animal. The soldiers, Jeff, and Danielle had spent much more time training on moving targets.

After breakfast, they again loaded into the Ute and truck and drove to a field which would be their starting point, followed closely by the refrigerated truck and the butchers who would process any pigs they killed. Also in the truck were three dogs and their handlers. This was the first time the twins had worked alongside dogs, and they were curious about how well it would go. The farmer let the way to an area of brush and trees alongside a field. Everyone could see the destruction levied by the pigs; a large area appeared to have been plowed by a tractor determined to turn all the crops under. Everyone exited the vehicles, and the farmer explained that there were manmade ponds all over his property, but many of them exhibited hoof prints, so there was none of them in particular that seemed to be the pigs' favorite.

The dogs were released. They were all trackers. None of them were one of the heavier breeds that could hold a pig until the hunters arrived since they weren't after an individual pig, but herds of them, and they wanted to find the herds. While Jake and the farmer stayed with the vehicles, the others spread out in a line following the dogs and moved through the tree and brush. Henry was in line on one side of Danielle, Jeff on the other. He noticed that while everyone in the line except the three dog handlers glided silently along, Jeff and Danielle seemed to be holding back to stay even with the rest. While he had to watch where he placed his feet to make sure no sticks were snapped or leaves rustled, the twins watched ahead and still made no sound.

Baying rose from their right, and the line shifted. In moments, they broke through into a field and spotted more than twenty pigs racing toward the opposite side of the clear area, perhaps one hundred yards distant. The five soldiers, Jeff, and Danielle opened fire, and none of the pigs reached the other side. The twins fired five rounds each for a total of ten pigs killed. The soldiers killed the other ten with several rounds fired, some due to misses of the wildly scrambling pigs, some due to the first round not being fatal. It would have been difficult to prove for sure who exactly did what, but everyone knew. The five men were effusive in their praise to the two youngest members of their group.

Leaving the pigs for the butchers who had just arrived with their truck, the handlers set the dogs in motion again. By the end of the day, as far as anyone could tell, there were no more pigs on the farmer's property. Dinner that evening was all the pork anyone could eat grilled on the barbie. Jeff and Danielle threw together barbeque sauce for the event, some mild(ish) and some hot. Most of the group, including the farmer and his family, preferred the hot. The soldiers, accustomed to squirting hot sauce on their MRE's to make them more palatable, loved the spicy condiment.

Afterwards, everyone sat around, stuffed and chatting. Henry took the opportunity to have a semi-private conversation with Danielle, something they were seldom able to do. They chatted about this and that, likes and dislikes, plans for the future; nothing romantic, but a time of learning more about each other. Jeff, Harry, and his team kept an eye on the two of them; more supervision than Jeff had ever been under, not counting the "sisters", of course.

The two set up a square of wood ten feet away and took turns throwing knives at it. Danielle let Henry throw first, and wherever he stuck the knife in the wood, she placed hers an inch to the left. Henry's knife always hit the wood, but that was the extent of his skill. When one of his throws landed less than an inch from the left edge of the wood, there was a pause in the conversation around them. The other members of the team had been watching the action, and now they waited to see how Danielle would handle this. She couldn't place her knife an inch to left as she had been; only air was there.

After a brief pause, she threw, and the knife landed an inch to the right of Henry's. Laughter erupted, and the others returned to their conversation. Henry asked, "What are you going to do after you graduate in December?" After a glance at his face, she answered, "Don't know. More of what we have been. Probably spend some time in the US and some time here. I don't see Lucy letting Jeff go." Henry laughed. "If Lucy has her way, you will be her aunt before the year is done." Danielle shook her head. "That won't happen; at least, not this year. Next year, who knows."

He said, "What about you? Family someday?" She shrugged. "I can't have one of my own. I have a lot of foster kids, though." He stared at her. "What do you mean you can't have a family of your own?" She didn't look at him. "I can't have children." His stare changed to disbelief, then softened. "Even if that is true, there are a lot of kids who would be lucky to have you for a mom." She laughed. "I know, but how would I choose?" He nudged her. "I think when the time comes, you'll know." Then he moved a bit away from her before the next sound he heard was Jeff's knife thunking into his own heart.

Around 11:00pm, the soldiers and Jeff left for the bunkhouse to take showers and stow their gear for the flight home the next day. Harry, Jake, and Danielle walked to the house, the girl returning to the barn a few minutes later after her usual quick shower.

The next morning, goodbyes were said, gear was loaded in the newly arrived plane, and it taxied down the pasture. Once in the air, the group decided the trip had been a total success. As far as they knew, the pigs were gone. Henry thought his relationship with Danielle had moved forward. Danielle agreed in her mind. Then the bee stung their pilot.

# Chapter 7

Shortly after sunrise on Sunday morning, their pilot coasted down on the farm airstrip, pulling to a stop near the group standing with their gear. Unnoticed by anyone, a bee landed on Harry's duffle bag and crawled inside. It was trapped when Harry lifted the bag and carried it inside the plane and remained stuck until half an hour from their destination when a bump of turbulence resettled the bag and opened a path for the bee to exit. It crawled toward the light of the opening, stepped onto the outer covering, and flew toward the sunlight streaming in through the front windshield.

Along the way, it landed on the pilot's neck, who swatted it absently with one hand; the bee stung him. Almost immediately, he was gasping for air as his windpipe began to rapidly swell closed. One hand clutched at his throat while the other groped for his pocket where the EpiPen was stored; or rather, where the EpiPen was usually stored. Murphy raised his ugly head. While visiting his sister, he had spilled coffee on his pants. As she washed them for him, he had stored the EpiPen in his travel bag. When the pants were clean and dry, he had meant to return the EpiPen to its usual spot but been sidetracked. He had thought of it as he boarded the plane for the return flight, but hadn't bothered to retrieve it, considering the chances of encountering a bee before he landed at home a very remote possibility. Now, the EpiPen was securely stored in his bag behind the seat.

As his hands left the controls, his feet pushed erratically on the foot pedals, and the plane fell into an unpredictable sliding dive. Jeff, using the flight home to log some air time and acting as co-pilot, immediately grabbed the control wheel which the pilot had released, but he had to fight to override the foot pedals. The plane leveled but continued to yaw. He yelled over his shoulder back into the cabin where chaos reigned. "Danielle! Ned! I need help up here." Danielle immediately fought her way forward, followed by the team medic. Jeff had not seen the bee, but the symptoms, assuming no one had poisoned their pilot, certainly resembled an allergic reaction. When Danielle reached the front, he told her, "Get him out of his seat!" This was spoken in a grunt as he wrestled with the controls."

Danielle immediately released the pilot's seat harness, and, with her head tucked between her shoulders to avoid his thrashing, pulled him back into the aisle, dropping him at the feet of the medic. She said, "There must be an EpiPen somewhere near!" While the two did a quick search of his body, Jeff brought the plane back under control. The search did not produce the expected device. Danielle yelled, "Where's his carryon bag?" After a quick look around, she spotted the bag near the pilot's seat and ripped it open. Quickly emptying the bag, she found the cartridge and tossed it to Ned, who jabbed it into the pilot's leg; meanwhile, Danielle climbed into the empty pilot's seat.

Slipping on the dangling headset, she asked Jeff, "Do you know where we are?" He glared at her. "Well, duh, of course." She asked, "So, who gets to land the plane?" He said, "Rock, paper, scissors?" Harry arrived then and demanded, "Sitrep!" Jeff answered, "For some reason, our pilot has gone into anaphylactic shock. We're about twenty minutes from our destination. I don't think he'll be landing the plane." Harry said calmly, "I don't suppose you two know how to fly?" Danielle said, "Yes. We're just deciding who gets to land the plane." Harry stared at her. "Seriously? That's the most important thing right now?" She stared back at him. "Well, yes." In his mind, he rolled his eyes, but all he said was, "Well, carry on then."

The pilot was coming around, but because of the time it had taken to locate the EpiPen, he was disoriented and confused; obviously in no shape to fly. As he stood over him, Harry heard Jeff identifying the plane and saying, "We are declaring an emergency. The pilot is out, and student pilots will be landing the aircraft." The lieutenant stopped beside the captain, stared at the pilot laid out in the aisle, and asked, "What happened? Who's flying the plane?" Harry said, "Anaphylactic shock. Jeff and Danielle." Lachlan stared at him. "Can they fly?" and Harry gave him a grim smile. "I hope so. They seem to think they can. We aren't crashing at the moment."

Jeff leaned around his seat and called, "Everybody strap in. They're diverting us straight in." Harry and Lachlan pulled the pilot into a seat and fastened his seat belt, then dropped into their own seats and did the same. Ned asked Henry, "Can those kids fly this plane?" Henry gave him a look and answered, "Of course they can," praying that he wasn't lying. In a few minutes, the plane was over the city, dropping lower and lower. Soon after that, it settled to a gentle, no bounce landing and rolled toward the hanger from which they had departed, followed by a firetruck and an ambulance. Pulling to a stop, Jeff and Danielle shut down the engine and began running through the final sequence.

As the ambulance pulled up alongside, Henry opened the door, and he and Ned helped the pilot navigate the stairs to the ground where two ambulance men took over. Through the windshield, Jeff and Danielle spotted Sophie running toward the plane. They sighed at the same time. Harry, who had once again stuck his head into the pilot space, said, "The pilot is with the ambulance crew. They say he should be fine. I'll calm my sister. By the way, nice landing, mates. Why don't you have your pilot certificates?" Danielle said, "Thanks. For both. We're working on the certificates. Lots going on." Harry laughed and turned to meet Sophie, who had arrived at the aircraft, anxiety written all over her face.

As the twins continued their checklist and the other men moved all the gear to their vehicle, Harry and Henry explained what had happened on the return flight. Sophie was dumbstruck. "Jeff and Danielle landed the plane?" Harry said, "That's right, mate." She stared at the sky as if in prayer, then said, "I have to get them out of here before the news people arrive." Harry turned his head to glance in the open door of the pilot's compartment. "How long before you can scarper?" Jeff looked over to say, "Another minute. We'll lock the plane and see where he wants us to leave the keys.

They finished shutting everything down, climbed out, locked all the plane doors, grabbed their bags off the ground and tossed them in the back of Sophie's vehicle, and turned to say goodbye to the soldiers. Jeff muttered to Danielle in elvish, "You can hug him goodbye, you know." She gave him a look, not a glare, more of a questioning look. Then they walked down the line, shaking hands and exchanging insults with the men, starting with Harry. When they reached Henry, Jeff gave him a fist bump and a friendly smile. Danielle paused in front of him for a moment, then reached up and pulled him into a quick hug. Not sure how to respond, he gave her a quick, light hug in return. She gave him a crooked smile, then turned and strode quickly toward the vehicles where the others were waiting. Thankfully, the soldiers didn't hoot or make any remarks during the hug, just climbed into their own vehicle for the ride back to the base.

Jake said, "That looks like a news van headed this way," gesturing toward a van with a satellite dish mounted on the top moving swiftly toward them. Jeff said, "Let me drive," and climbed into the driver's seat. The other three swiftly climbed in, making sure their seat belts were securely fastened. The soldiers headed in one direction, and Jeff took the other, making a roundabout dash toward the airport exit. The van, with a 50/50 choice, made the correct decision and followed Jeff. They were behind him as he left the airport and entered the freeway, although once he exited, it only took him four turns to lose them.

From beside him, Danielle said, "They probably have the license tag number and the means to track down who owns the car. We need to call Linda." The twins had met Linda the previous year after the incident with the abused girl in the grocery store, and after discussing it with Jake and Sophie, Robert and Michelle, and even Oliver, had decided it wouldn't be a bad idea to have a reporter in their court. They had begun giving her first shot at the story about their escapades, although there hadn't been that many since the girl; just the rescue earlier in the year when they were parachuting. This one would probably be bigger.

Before Danielle had a chance to call, her phone rang. Glancing at the display, she laughed and said, "It's her." When Danielle said, "Hello, Linda," there was no hello in return, just, "Was that you?" Danielle said, "Was what me?" Linda exclaimed, "Don't mess with me! Did you and Jeff land that plane?" Danielle said teasingly, "Oh, that. Yes, we did." Linda said, "I need details." Smiling, Danielle told her about the flight and their pilot going into anaphylactic shock, probably from an insect bite, although they weren't certain since no one had seen the culprit.

Linda said, "So you and Jeff landed the plane?" When Danielle said yes again, she asked, "Are you certified pilots?" Danielle explained no, but they had a fair amount of experience flying that particular aircraft and were working on their certificates. Linda laughed and said, "I heard through the grapevine that another news crew followed you out of the airport, but lost you." She continued seriously, "They know who you are, though." Danielle said, "We figured as much. I was about to call you so you would have first chance at the story. We'll stay out of sight until after the early evening news." Linda said, "I will play it down as much as I can. I know you don't want publicity."

Jeff pulled the vehicle into the garage at the rear of the house, and the door was down before the news van drove slowly down the road. Next there was knocking on the door and the telephone began ringing. Jake answered the door and told the reporters the twins would not be available until after church that evening. They weren't happy with this and tried to question Jake, who had grown quite good at stating, "I can't say, mate." Eventually, they gave up. The phone calls were allowed to go straight to voicemail.

The family ate a dinner of baked pork loin. Jeff and Danielle told them about Saturday and hunting the herds of pigs while Lucy stared at him, torn between being upset that he hadn't taken her along and happy that he was back. When the family walked to church, Jeff and Danielle ghosted through yards, streets, and alleys to arrive unseen in the church sanctuary, where they suddenly appeared beside the others. Most of the congregation had not heard anything about the incident with the plane, and to those who had, the twins simply said, "It was no big deal. We landed a plane." Shane welcomed them back, saying they had been missed at the morning service.

Afterwards, as they left the church, the family found news crews waiting to talk to them. By then, Linda's station had aired the story, and these stations hoped to have an update for the later news programs. Jeff and Danielle patiently answered their questions about the incident, although they were non-committal about the purpose of the flight, saying only that they had a chance to visit a farm in Victoria and took it, and that they hoped to earn their pilot certificates while they were in Australia. The day finally ended, and life moved on. And then Sebastian texted.

# Chapter 8

Just after lunch on the following Tuesday, Jeff received a text from Sebastian saying he thought he had found the main actors for their movie, and could they stop by after school. After confirming with Danielle, Jeff texted back an affirmative. Then they had to explain to Zoe and Sean why they wouldn't be going home with them without actually telling them anything. By now, the Armstrongs were all familiar with the twins and their secrets, and they were satisfied with Danielle's cryptic, "We'll explain when we get home."

As soon as the final bell chimed, Jeff and Danielle walked the 2.7 kilometers to the movie studio. The now green-haired receptionist greeted them warmly and called Sebastian, who opened the door to his hallway moments later and waved them toward his office. Once inside and seated, he began. "I have found some families that I think will work. It wasn't easy, and I almost thought we were going to have to make major changes to the script or go with some drastic changes as the young people grew older, but suddenly, the pieces started falling into place. I would almost call it a miracle.

He began displaying pictures on his office television, describing what the twins were seeing. "We'll do Danielle first. This family has four daughters, ages six, eight, ten, and twelve. They all enjoy sports and are athletic. They obviously aren't in the same physical shape as you two, but if we begin training as soon as they're hired, it should be apparent in the movie. The family enjoys snorkeling and SCUBA diving. The fight scenes will either need to be implied, use stunt doubles, or employ special effects. Age wise, we will make the transitions from actor to actor with makeup. You can see from the size of their parents that the oldest girl will probably be as large as you were at that age."

Sebastian changed to a different set of pictures, this time of boys. "The situation is the same with this family: four boys ages six, eight, ten, and twelve. You'll notice that the two groups are near enough in appearance that it isn't unfeasible that they are brother and sister. Neither group has any movie experience, but both groups have participated in theater, and some of them are musicians. We'll deal with the eye color using contact lenses. I feel really good about these two families.

Amazingly, I also found the same sort of situation for Cindy and Elizabeth. Those were the other major challenges. I also have candidates for the additional characters in the film. The crew is lined up. If you are serious about this film, I believe we're ready to proceed."

Jeff and Danielle exchanged a look. Jeff said, "It looks like you have done amazing work. I guess for us, we just need to break the news to our host family. Jake is also the lawyer for our foundation here in Australia, and he will set up the account to pay for the film. Whatever the family says, we will pay you for the work you've done so far. Just give us an invoice." Sebastian nodded. "I'll wait to hear the verdict. If it's a go, I'll begin invoicing the project. If not, I'll give you a final bill for my work."

They discussed next steps for another hour as all three made notes. Finally, glancing at the time, Jeff announced they needed to get home, and Danielle summoned an Uber ride on her phone. The receptionist paged Sebastian upon its arrival, and the three parted, with another meeting planned for the following week where work would begin in earnest if the Armstrongs gave the okay.

Minutes later, the twins stepped out of the car in front of the Armstrong home, and with a significant look at each other, entered the front door. Lucy met them with the thousand question torture. "Where have you been, mates? We were wondering whether or not to have dinner without you. Do you know what we're having for dinner? I helped cook it. I stirred things. How did you get home? Did you walk?"

As she chattered, the twins followed her down the hall, stopping long enough to say hello to Sophie in the kitchen and Jake at his office desk before splitting off to their bedrooms to change out of their school uniforms. Danielle grabbed Lucy by the arm as she started to enter Jeff's room behind him. "You come with me, little lady, so Jeff can change." The small girl broke away to enter the door to the older girls' room ahead of her.

Zoe was at her desk, hunched over her computer, scowling at a homework assignment. Lucy marched over to say, "You shouldn't look like that, mate. Your face could freeze that way." Zoe turned the scowl on her with a mock growl, and the small girl ran screaming to Danielle, begging for protection. Danielle picked her up, hugged her, then set her down to begin the one-minute process of changing into casual clothes.

This always fascinated Lucy, who never seemed to grow tired of it. She would stand in one of the desk chairs and poke at Danielle's arm or back muscles, sometimes running a finger over the scars or the tattoo, making exaggerated ooh and aah sounds until Danielle finished and tucked her under one arm, leaving Zoe to her homework and joining Jeff in the hall as they went to ask Sophie if she needed any help with dinner.

Presently, everyone was seated at the table, the blessing had been given, and all eyes turned to Jeff and Danielle in anticipation. Jeff began. "When we came to Australia, one of the projects we wanted to complete while we were here is a movie of our early years, from when we met until we turned twelve. While mom and dad were here, we found a movie studio and asked them to begin research. Today, our contact texted to say the main characters had been located, and he was ready to proceed. We went to see him after school, and Danielle and I agree. Now we just need your permission." He gave Jake and Sophie a questioning look.

The others at the table stared at the twins in stunned silence. Then Sean gave a whoop and yelled, "You're going to be movie stars?" Danielle shook her head no. "If we have our way, not that many people will know who the story is about." Jake asked more matter of factly, "Who's paying for this movie?" Jeff said, "Danielle and I." That earned some more stares. The family had some theories concerning how much Jeff and Danielle were worth, but paying for their own sky diving, SCUBA diving, and other hobbies was a far cry from the expense of financing a movie.

Sophie asked, "What do Robert and Michelle think?" Danielle answered, "They're behind us. They probably have the same concerns as you do. We just don't want this family to be negatively impacted by the movie production." Zoe asked, "Where will it be filmed?" Jeff said, "At the studio. Around the city. Maybe a little in the outback." He gave Jake the name of the studio and the address.

Lucy sat through most of this discussion with her chin in her hands. Once she heard that Jeff and Danielle wouldn't be movie stars, her interest waned. Roller skating at the gym sounded more interesting. Jake said, "We'll talk it over and give your folks a call. Then we'll let you know. Okay, mates?" Jeff and Danielle nodded. It wasn't as though their lives would end if they couldn't make the movie while they were here, and there were plenty of other things going on to occupy their time. More than enough, in fact, not even counting the unforeseen events that were normal in their lives.

True to his word, Jake and Sophie set up a video call with Robert and Michelle late that evening. The twins' parents had been expecting the call, having been updated on the meeting with Sebastian. The four spoke for half an hour, and when the call ended, Jake and Sophie told the twins all four parents were okay with them continuing the project.

This earned them beaming smiles from Jeff and Danielle, and they called Sebastian the next morning with the news. He set up a meeting for them to meet the primary actors and actresses on Saturday morning, and at 10:00am they were sitting in the company's conference room waiting for the first family to appear. The now red-haired receptionist led them in, and the twins got their first look at Danielle's counterparts.

They did not strongly resemble Danielle, which was not surprising, but they did resemble each other. It was easy to tell they were sisters, and the twins could see why Sebastian had picked them appearance wise. This should make for a smooth transition from age to age. For the next hour, Sebastian, Jeff, and Danielle chatted with the girls and their parents, getting to know them, asking about their likes and dislikes, acting experience, athletic preferences, and having them run some lines from the script.

The girls all liked sports, but not the same ones. Six-year-old Bobbie was in her second year of martial arts and made a very good young Danielle. Her memory was excellent, and she seemed to have just the right attitude. Eight-year-old Merit belonged to a gymnastics team. She would be perfect for the next stage. Abigail was the swimmer and loved to run. Finally, Caroline played in a girl's rugby league.

Next, they discussed language skills. Only Abigail had much experience with any because one of her friends spoke Japanese, and she enjoyed learning it. All the girls were intelligent, though, and obviously quick studies to be able to learn their lines, so it shouldn't be a problem memorizing enough for the movie.

All four girls were studying music in one way or another. Bobbie was beginning piano, Merit played acoustic guitar, Abigail piano and keyboards, and Caroline the flute. All could read music. It would probably be necessary to use a double for the guitar playing required, and they might even be able to cut in video of Danielle playing herself. There was a lot of video, especially of her playing at the giant 4<sup>th</sup> of July concert when she was seven.

By the end of the interview and after a brief, private meeting between the family members in the conference room and Jeff, Danielle, and Sebastian in his office, all four of the young actresses and their parents agreed to the movie. They were, if not acting, very excited about the story line. Sebastian would set up the contracts with input from Jeff and Danielle, they would be reviewed by Jake to make sure the twins were protected, and the project would officially begin. The family would be given access to the gym, and Jeff and Danielle would commence working with them, with other physical trainers to be hired as needed, as well as tutors. The four girls would not be spending much time at school for the next few months.

After lunch, the Leighton family arrived and were escorted back to the conference room. The boys did not resemble Jeff in any of the stages of his life, but they were obviously brothers, and by coincidence, they were enough like the Steinfield girls that it wasn't a reach to call them brothers and sisters in the same family. Jeff, Danielle, and Sebastian went through the same procedure of chatting and discussing acting experience, language proficiency, musical skills, and athletic preferences.

Ashton and Asa, the two middle boys, were both enrolled in martial arts. Alexander, the youngest, was a swimmer, and Alec, the oldest, was a member of a youth rugby league. If hired, they, too, would be spending considerable time at the gym. Both groups were a bit intimidated by Jeff and Danielle, especially Danielle, sitting there in her sleeveless tank top. Abigail had asked, "Are we supposed to look like you?" Asa asked the same of Jeff. Both times, the twins answered, "You will look however you look after you've spent some time in our gym."

The two younger boys played the guitar; the two older, keyboards. All four could read music. Even the two youngest had taken some piano lessons, so keyboards were not unknown. Only Alec had studied a foreign language. He had spent the last year with a crush on a girl who spoke French and had learned it to impress her. The twins admired his dedication. All four loved the stage and had acted in both school and local productions.

As before, the family stayed in the conference room to discuss the project while Jeff, Danielle, and Sebastian retired to his office to discuss the boys. The twins were impressed with Sebastian's choices and told him so. He nodded, pleased. Jeff said, "You seem to have a talent for finding, well, talent. If you do as well with the remainder of the cast, I have a lot of hope for this movie." Danielle added, "Just be aware, we want this to be a Christian film. That means there will be attacks on it, from people who don't want it made and from unseen forces trying to stop it. There will be problems you expect and some you cannot imagine."

Sebastian nodded. "The easiest way to stop the movie would be for something to happen to the two of you. So do take care of yourselves, mates. I have seen you on the telly more than once, and you haven't been here very long. You do seem to take risks, some of which might see you uninjured, but still sent home. That would be a problem, I imagine." Jeff and Danielle nodded.

They returned to the conference room where the family let them know they wanted to be part of the project. Hands were shaken all around. Then, as Jeff and Danielle spoke with the group, Sebastian left, but soon returned with the Steinfield family; the two groups met their costars for the first time. For an initial meeting, things seemed to go well. Only time would tell if they worked well together, but no problems immediately raised alarms.

Caroline said, "We've told you all about ourselves. What about the two of you? We've seen you on the telly over the past couple of months, and we're going to make a movie about your early years, but what can you tell us today?" Jeff and Danielle had expected this question to come up sooner or later, and they handed a flash drive to Sebastian, who plugged it into his laptop which he then connected to the conference room flat screen. Soon the two families were watching with wide eyes the thirty-minute version of Jeff and Danielle's lives, cleaned up for the youngest viewers.

When it finished, Asa asked, "Will we be doing all that? Parachuting? SCUBA diving? Shooting?" All eight young people began exclaiming, "Oh, please, oh, please, oh, please!" while both sets of parents said at once, "I don't think you'll be jumping out of any planes." When the room was quiet again, Danielle said, "We'll do what we can with you, but I think a great deal will be performed with special effects or stunt doubles."

Back at the house, Jeff and Danielle told the Armstrong family about the young actors and actresses. Zoe asked, "What about school for them?" Jeff explained that they would have tutors for the duration of the movie and would fit in classes and homework between videoing. Sophie was concerned about that. Danielle said, "You know it doesn't take six hours of classes a day when you're one on one with your teacher. Look at Lucy." Lucy perked up at this. Danielle continued, "Also, they'll be getting way more PE than most of their peers. And learning skills that many of their peers won't."

Jake asked, "And how are the two of you going to keep up with everything else you've got going? The movie is going to take a lot of your time." Danielle said, "Not as much as you'd think. They have the screenplay, we'll show them what we can do, and the crew will figure out a way to duplicate it. Jeff and I will review what they've done once a week or so. You'll see." She laughed. "Or we'll find out we're wrong."

# Chapter 9

The first attack from the enemy came immediately as the Armstrong family was sitting around the kitchen table the following Monday, enjoying brekkie before heading off to school, work, and other pursuits. Jeff and Danielle had begun the morning with the feeling that something was wrong, and they were waiting with patience but a heightened sense of urgency to find out what it was.

Danielle had just raised a spoonful of oatmeal to her mouth when her phone rang. Ordinarily, no one answered the phone during meals, and she glanced at the screen, prepared to send it to voicemail. Instead, recognizing the name, she answered. After listening for a moment, she said, "We'll be home as soon as possible." After another few moments, she shook her head and repeated, "We'll be home as soon as we can. We'll fly straight there."

She disconnected and glanced around the table before saying to Jeff, "Lily has come out of remission. She's in the hospital." Turning to Jake and Sophie, she said, "We need to fly home. Can you take care of the paperwork? They won't be happy since they want a four-week notice. We'll keep up with the classwork if we can." Jake nodded. "I'll submit the paperwork and speak with the school and the DE International[2] rep. There shouldn't be any issues. If there is, we'll deal with them when you return. How long do you think you'll be gone?"

Jeff shook his head. "I don't know. I'm sure they'll be trying new treatments, and hopefully it will begin working quickly." Lucy had been gazing between all the speakers during this conversation, and now she said, "We'll pray for her. I'll ask my Sunday School class to pray for her, too." Zoe added, "All of us will." The twins nodded, and having gulped their food, stowed their bowls and spoons in the dishwasher before heading off to pack and make flight reservations.

In less than an hour, backpacks and passports in hand, Jake was driving them to the airport. Their flight was in the air before lunch. On the long flight over, they prayed and read Bible verses about hope. Lily had been in remission so long, the chances that she might come out were just a small background worry, not even noticeable. Their daily prayers for her always included a 'Please let Lily stay in remission', but it had become almost an afterthought. Not anymore.

As they flew, the prayer network in Australia grew. It spread from the Armstrong family through their Bible study and Sunday School groups through the entire church, through their family and friends, through their families and friends and churches. By the time Jeff and Danielle landed in Phoenix, hundreds of people in Australia and America were praying for Lily. Sometimes God answers yes. But sometimes, He answers no.

The twins discussed thankfulness. Ever since Pastor John had proposed his congregation keep a thankful journal, they had both started one, and they had stayed with it for the past three plus years, adding three items every day for which they were thankful.

It was really fairly simple to come up with the items. Truly feeling thankful for them was something else entirely, especially when they were part of your everyday life. Yes, they could write that they were thankful for the abundance of clean water in their lives, but it was the trip to the village in Africa where it was a daily, painstaking exercise to obtain any water at all, much less clean water, that brought it home. Similarly, there were gasoline stations on every corner, and it was easy to write in the journals about the stations themselves and the people who worked there or brought the gasoline to the stations or refined it, but it was something else to be without or to wait in line for hours for a few gallons during a shortage brought on by storms or ice.

The same was true for Lily's remission. It was easy to write in the journals, thanking God for the doctors and nurses and hospitals and people who created the life-saving drugs, but it didn't mean the same as it did when Lily came out of remission. That made it more real, and their past casual thank you's seemed insulting somehow, as if they had just been going through the motions.

Then there were the even more problematic thank you's. Jeff was absolutely and whole heartedly thankful for Lucy. Every day was a new experience in thankfulness for the young girl. But her very life had been brought about by a traumatic experience for Zoe. He was glad Lucy's father was dead so he didn't even have to consider what he would do to the man if he ever met him, the least of which would be to end his life. But how could he thank God for what had happened to Zoe even if it had resulted in Lucy. Sometimes it felt like his head was about to explode, and he just had to let it go.

Eighteen hours later, after a short layover in LA, their plane was landing in Phoenix, the same day they left, and they carried their backpacks out to the passenger pickup up area where Cindy was waiting in one of the Avery's cars. They tossed their backpacks in the trunk and slid into the vehicle, Danielle claiming shotgun, and in the right side for a change. Cindy brought them up to speed as she drove to the Avery home to drop off their bags and then to the hospital.

Lily had awakened two days earlier with a temperature and pain. Her family had thought and hoped it was the flu or something similar, but a trip to the doctor had led to tests which had shown her cancer had returned. She was on new medication, and the doctor was hopeful, but so far in the short time since the new treatment had begun, there had been no response. Which in a way was good, because at least things hadn't gotten worse.

The twins entered the room. Mia and Elizabeth were there and received hugs of greeting. Mia commented that Preston was in the cafeteria picking up cups of coffee. Lily was lying in her hospital bed, IV attached along with monitoring wires, torso slightly elevated, eyes closed. When Jeff and Danielle approached the bed, she smiled, and without opening her eyes, she said, "G'day, mates!"

Jeff and Danielle hugged her gently around the various tubes and wires. Lily asked, "What time is it in Australia?" Jeff laughed. "The same day and time as when we left. We get to live the day over again." This caused everyone in the room to chuckle, and the twins settled down to tell everyone about life down under. There were the presentations they were making to different grades at the schools and even to service organizations. Their notoriety with the various rescues was making them more popular than they would have liked. Thanks to Officer Cameron, even various police groups were calling on them.

They told about the hunt Harry had taken them on to help a friend of his rid his farm of feral hogs. When they heard Henry had gone on the trip as well, all the "sisters" wanted the details, teasing Danielle mercilessly over every word she said about him until she threatened to hurt them all. Sometime during the conversation, Preston returned with the coffee, and he exchanged a look with his wife over the improvement that seemed to be present in Lily.

The day passed. The group took breaks to eat lunch. To everyone's delight, including her doctor, Lily took interest in the food they brought her, something she hadn't done for the past two days. No one mentioned it, but everyone was spending time when they said they were going to the restroom or the cafeteria to stop by the small, cozy chapel to pray for Lily. Mia and Avery went home for the first time in two days as Jeff and Danielle took over spending the night with Lily.

As she slept, they attended their classes via internet, asking and answering questions and preparing their homework. Their teachers were very understanding, especially when they understood that the twins were at the hospital with their "sister" and attending class as she slept. Sometimes they had to log off as BRB (Be Right Back) when she woke up and wanted to talk. Class was during the evening hours from 6:00pm on, so sometimes they could monitor a class, sometimes they couldn't. They worked on homework from midnight on, but if Lily was awake, they visited with her.

Lily asked about what had happened to them when they were in the hospital after the McAdams shot them, and they explained what they could. It seemed obvious that she was getting stronger by the hour, and they prayed it was the new medicines and not a final rally. By Wednesday morning, it was obvious the new medicines were working, and she was getting better.

Wednesday was also the day there was light knock on her hospital door early in the afternoon. A nurse opened the door softly, and when he saw that everyone in the room was awake and chatting with each other, he gestured at Jeff to come into the hall. When they were standing outside the door, he said, "There are some families that heard you were here and would like to get nicknames for their children if it's possible. I didn't want to bother you, but since Lily is responding so well to treatment, I thought you might not mind." He said this with a questioning uplift of his eyebrows.

With a smile, Jeff said, "Sure. Where are they?" The nurse answered, "In the waiting area down the hall," gesturing with a wave of his hand. Jeff nodded and stuck his head back in the door. "There are some kids who want nicknames." Lily said from her bed, "Oh, cool! I want their patches!" Danielle grabbed Jeff's backpack with his laptop and her messenger bag with her art supplies. Cindy said, "Elizabeth and I will stay here and keep

Lily company. See you in a bit." Jeff nodded, and he and Danielle followed the nurse down the hall to the waiting area where an anxious and excited group of three families waited, anxious that the twins might not come, excited that they might.

For the next while, Danielle sketched while Jeff explained, and at the end, a happy group of families left the hospital. The twins did not immediately return to the room, but visited the chapel where they thanked God and praised Him for Lily's recovery and asked Him to watch over the families they had just met. And they asked for peace in this fallen world where death and pain and sadness were such a dominant part.

On Friday, Lily was released from the hospital, again in remission, and her doctor was confident that she would remain so based on her rapid response to the new treatment.

Jeff and Danielle had been in daily contact with their parents and the Armstrong family, and they made arrangements to fly back to Australia on Saturday. They would again be flying by way of a short layover in LA and planned to catch up on their sleep, if possible, on the way back. Between watching over and talking to Lily and the others and keeping up with their schoolwork, they had had little time to sleep over the past few days, and it was beginning to tell. The time change wasn't helping. They were a little groggy.

There had also been more families desiring nicknames on Thursday and Friday. Jeff and Danielle graciously and happily provided them. Friday evening was a time of celebration at the Avery house. Lily was ensconced on the sofa, and the others spoke to her and around her, overjoyed to see the return of healthy color and appetite, but careful not to overexcite her as well. When she dropped off to sleep, they covered her up and left her snoozing as they spoke softly while she slept. Finally, about midnight, Danielle carried her gently to her bedroom.

The next morning over breakfast, everyone discussed their plans for the coming year. Elizabeth was still in the Shepherd homeschool but also taking some classes at the community college. Cindy was building her own interior decorating business using the apartments she prepared for the foundation as a base. Lily would continue with her homeschooling. Jeff and Danielle would return to Australia to school and their movie.

There was much discussion about the movie. Lily was sad that the scope of the movie did not include her. Cindy and Elizabeth were happy to use this face to face time to express their concerns that their characters portray them properly. They had at least approved of the actresses who would be playing them and made the twins promise that they would tell these actresses that they were being prayed for daily, which Jeff and Danielle promised to do. Lily said, "I can't wait! Is it really going to take all year to finish?" Jeff said, "Probably. The action scenes are tough. None of them can do what we can, so it takes a lot of slow motion and special effects." Elizabeth rolled her eyes. "You two are so special." Then she giggled as Danielle put a hand on her neck and said, "We're going to replace you with a wallaby. Cute, and silent."

The light-hearted conversation continued until it was time for all the travelers to leave for the airport. Preston said a prayer, asking for travel safety and health for everyone, and then, after hugs and cheerful goodbyes, drove them to the airport, and dropped the two groups, Jeff and Danielle, Cindy and Elizabeth, off near their gates.

# Chapter 10

Jeff and Danielle stayed awake en route to LA, but once the plane was in the air headed for Australia, they fell asleep and didn't wake up until the captain announced their final approach and the flight attendants asked them to return their seats to the upright position. As far as the crew was concerned, they had been model passengers, asking for nothing and sleeping through all the mid-flight turbulence that had disturbed some of the other passengers.

They arrived early Monday morning, in time for Jake to pick them up at the airport and rush them home to clean up, eat some breakfast, and walk to school. As soon as they walked in the front doors of the school, they received a message to report to the principal's office. Zoe and their other friends rolled their eyes, but Jeff and Danielle just shrugged and marched toward his office.

Once inside, and seated in their usual chairs, he watched them, sheets of paper in his hands. "This paperwork says a close family member was very sick." They nodded. He continued. "However, she wasn't related to you by blood." They nodded again. "Please explain why I should excuse this absence." Jeff gave the man an explanation of the unique relationship they had with their "sisters" and "brothers".

He sat back in his seat, appearing to ponder this information for a few minutes. Then he said, "I trust something like this will not be happening in the near future. Your teachers report that you attended many of your classes on the internet while you were gone and kept up with your homework for the most part." He again stared at his steepled hands for a while as they sat, relaxed and unconcerned in their seats. If he had hoped to intimidate them, he was failing miserably. He just didn't rate in the same category as raiders trying to kill them. Or Lily almost dying.

Finally, realizing his intimidation tactics were going nowhere, he said, "In the future, please try to give us more notice before you go flying off." Jeff and Danielle assured him that they would and left his office, immediately running into Zoe, Sean, and their other friends in the hall outside the door. Danielle explained how the principal had not approved of their sudden departure. "He told us the school and DE International require four weeks' notice." Zoe rolled her eyes. "Since when do illnesses give notice?"

The following Tuesday was Lucy's sixth birthday, and that evening the house was crowded with her friends from Sunday School and elsewhere. Jeff and Danielle were going to bring a petting zoo to the house, but they couldn't find one with more than barnyard animals. They wanted kangaroos and koala bears and lizards. Without those, they just said no. It wasn't as though there was nothing for the kids to do. They had egg races (with hardboiled eggs, not raw), toss the thong (flipflop for the Americans), frisbee tag, and other games.

Part of the time was spent in the lounge room where two keyboards and an electric guitar had been set up. Jeff, Zoe, and Danielle played songs for everyone to sing along with, there were karaoke contests, and even keyboard and guitar lessons. Finally, it was time for food and gifts. Jeff and Danielle, with Sophie's okay since she usually just bought a cake at the grocery, baked a cake for the birthday girl, just as they had for Sean and Zoe's birthday. This one used a koala bear mold, and, at Lucy's request, was chocolate from top to bottom. They used the icing to make a t-shirt for the animal with the caption 'Happy Birthday Lucy' in multi-colored letters. The hand that wasn't grasping the tree held a little sparkler, and they added a birthday cap, shorts, and thongs on the little feet. When they brought it out and set it on the table in front of all the children, everyone, including the adults present, clapped and cheered with delight.

At present opening time, Lucy showed amazing maturity, expressing delight over each gift and waiting until the very last to open those from her own family. With the twin's help, Zoe gave her a t-shirt that matched her cake, down to the smallest detail. This earned her a big hug. Danielle gave her a sketch of the girl wearing the shirt. Jeff presented her with her very own Stetson. He and Danielle had discussed it, and decided 'why not?'

Jake and Sophie presented her with her very first young person's Bible, one that was not mostly pictures. Since Jeff, and then Zoe, had begun working with her, Lucy's reading ability, comprehension, and vocabulary had grown by leaps and bounds. She was very excited to be in possession of, as she called it, a grown-up Bible.

When the last guest had gone home and the house was cleaned back to its pre-party condition, Lucy walked over and stood in front Jeff. "Well?" Jeff knelt in front of her. "Well, what?" "Where's my birthday song, mate?" He said, "Oh, you think you get a birthday song, do you?" She nodded solemnly and waited expectantly. Jeff said, "Well, it just so happens, we may have written one for you. Do you want to hear it?" With barely suppressed excitement, she nodded once again, and the family made their way to the lounge room.

Jeff and Zoe seated themselves behind the keyboards, and Danielle slung the electric guitar around her neck. The rest of the family took seats, but Lucy plopped on the floor in front of the three musicians. At a nod from Jeff, they began playing, and the room was soon immersed in a song about Lucy as a firework exploding across the sky, one sure to capture the little girl's attention. When it ended, she jumped to her feet and rushed to hug Jeff, then Zoe, then Danielle, finally turning to the remaining three and shouting, "Wasn't that a ripper of a song? Wasn't it?" Then she turned back to Jeff and asked, "Will that be on Terry's new album?"

Since Jeff and Danielle had written Zoe and Sean's birthday songs, Lucy had become familiar with Terry and his band, especially as Sean had given permission for his song to be included on the latest album. Lucy was not shy about playing it for people and declaring that Jeff had written the song for Sean for his birthday. Sometimes, she even remembered to include that Danielle had written it, too. Jeff answered, "If you want it to be, and if your mom is okay with it, too."

Lucy immediately turned to Zoe and, jumping up and down in time with her chants, yelled, "Can it? Can it? Can it?" Zoe smiled at her and said, "I suppose so." This was immediately followed by the small girl running around the room, arms out, pretending to be a firework. Zoe turned to Jeff and Danielle and mouthed, "Thank you." Both nodded.

Later, as Jeff and Zoe were tucking the still excited and over-sugared little girl in bed, Jeff handed her a small box. Danielle had joined them and was leaning against the wall as Jeff said, "Danielle and I have one more present for you." Zoe gave him a look as the puzzled girl ripped off the paper and opened the box. Inside were two charms of white baby seals, one with blue eyes and one green, on a gold necklace.

Lucy ooh'd and ahh'd as she examined them. Noticing the numbers etched on them, she pointed and asked, "What does this number mean?" Jeff explained that the number was how many of them there were, and that they knew who had each one. Lucy handed the necklace to Zoe to inspect, and as she did, she said, "These are so cool. What are the eyes made from?" Danielle said, "Emerald chips for mine, sapphire chips for Jeff's." Zoe gasped and Jeff was quick to explain, "They're just chips. They aren't valuable."

Lucy asked, "Who has all the others?" Danielle said, "The

brothers. The sisters. Jeff's mom. Robert and Michelle. Some others." Zoe asked, puzzled, "How do you decide who gets them?" Jeff smiled and said, "We just know who gets them and when." She asked, "Has anyone ever lost one?" Danielle answered, "Someone had theirs stolen once. It was returned before we had a chance to deal with the thief." Lucy placed the box on her bedside table and hugged Jeff. "Thank you! It's the neatest present ever! Besides the song." She waved for Danielle to come over and gave her a hug and a thank you, too." The three left Lucy to dream about her birthday, turning off the light and closing the door.

In the hall, Zoe said, "Those aren't just pretty charms, are they? They mean something. Are you sure Lucy should have one? She's only six." Jeff asked, "What do you mean?" Zoe frowned at him. There are a limited number of them, but more than one. You don't give them to just anyone. What exactly do they mean?" Danielle tried to explain. "They mean different things for different people. For Rainbow, it meant we helped her film her eulogy. For Jeff's mom, it meant we accepted her. For Cindy, it means we have a private detective agency check out all her boyfriends."

Zoe's head was spinning. "Wait! What!" Jeff smiled and slid into his and Sean's room. Zoe followed Danielle into theirs, trying to get more of an explanation with no success. Danielle said enigmatically, "When you need to know, you'll know." Zoe shot back, "You gave them to my daughter. I think I need to know now." The other girl refused to respond to any more questions. Zoe said, "What if I make her give them back?" Danielle raised an eyebrow and said, "Okay."

Zoe dropped onto her bed and put her head in her hands. "As if I could get them back. I'd have to pry it out of her fingers, and she'd be heartbroken. Sometimes I don't like the two of you very much." Danielle shrugged. "We get that a lot."

# Chapter 11

The following Friday, everyone flew to Brisbane to visit a children's hospital there. This would be the fourth hospital since the twins had arrived in the country. They were flying with Jeff and Danielle's jump pilot. When they met him at the door, Jeff asked, "Got your EpiPen?" He smiled sheepishly and patted the right pocket of his cargo pants. Jeff and Danielle also each had one in their cargo pant's pockets. There would be no chance of a mistake this time. Danielle joked seriously, "If you show any sign of an allergic reaction, we will jab you immediately with an EpiPen. If it turns out you were joking around, the next jab won't be an EpiPen." Having seen the videos of their jumps in the US, including the simulated combat jumps, he gulped and said, "There will be no joking, mates. If I look like I need it, I really do need it. But seriously, it almost never happens on the land, much less in the air. I don't even know what happened on the return from Victoria. The doctors said it was a bee sting, but you didn't see one, and I didn't see one."

The Armstrong family would have been more concerned about using the private plane and this particular pilot, but Jake had watched Jeff and Danielle in action, and he had few concerns. The rest of the family took their cue from him, and Lucy was delighted to be able to have such a closeup view of the flight controls.

With the luggage stowed and the family buckled into their seats, the plane lifted into the air for the three-hour flight.

Everyone had a chance to sit in the co-pilot's seat. Lucy had to almost be dragged out. Danielle acted as co-pilot for the flight up; Jeff would take the role for the return flight. The journey was smooth; the sun set before they reached their destination, and the lights of the city spread out below them like jewels on a dark piece of velvet. Their pilot made a smooth, no-bounce landing, and soon they were taxiing to a hanger where a rental minivan waited. Their pilot would be spending the night with a friend who was sitting on the hood of his car as the plane taxied up. On Saturday, the pilot would be ferrying sky divers as he sometimes did when business was slow at his home base.

The Armstrong group did not leave the airport immediately as their pilot's friend was interested in meeting the two young people who had landed the plane and been on the telly. Jeff and Danielle took a picture with him, shrugging off his compliments, pointing out that lots of seventeen-year-olds obtained their pilot certificates, and it was only the situation that made landing the plane anything special. The man laughed as he added, "That and the other times you've been on the telly lately for rescuing people, mate. It seems to be a right business with the two of you."

Eventually, the family was able to drive away, and they spent the drive to their hotel checking out the many restaurants and places of interest to investigate when they finished at the hospital. One restaurant that had caught their eye before leaving home featured excellent food and a live band of local artists making their debut on the music scene. This would be their choice for the following evening. For tonight, they stopped at a seafood restaurant with a decent rating before continuing on to the hotel where they spent a restful night.

The hospital visit the next day went as smoothly as most of them did, with more sketches and more children added to the website. That evening, back at the hotel, Jeff and Danielle scanned the pictures and emailed them to Abeba in Florida. But, before then, the next adventure, as Zoe had come to label them, occurred.

The group left the hospital about 3:00pm and began their tour of Brisbane, visiting one historical site after another on private tours Jake had set up before they ever left home. It was amazing what you could do outside usual hours of operation if you were willing to throw enough money at it. Jeff and Danielle had given him a budget, so it wasn't as though he was giving an extra thousand dollars for each tour, but some very nice tips were involved.

After finishing the last tour, the group arrived at their restaurant of choice at 7:00pm, just as the band for the evening was setting up. Jeff and Danielle were recognized by the entire group of six musicians as soon as the Armstrong party was seated at their table near the small stage. The twins noticed the band members staring at them and were not surprised when one of them approached their table. He was in his early twenties and was dressed like the college students they had spotted on their tour, crossing the street from the various campuses to shops. He stood there awkwardly, introduced himself, confirmed that they were indeed Jeff and Danielle, and told them the band's story.

The band, three men and three women, had met at the university totally by chance. All had discovered the twins' music within the past year, and had stumbled across each other individually as they overheard the music on a phone or tablet as they were walking by, made even more rare by the fact that most people listened to their music with earbuds. Then there was the fact that not only did they all like Jeff and Danielle's music, but each one wanted to be in a band, and they all played different instruments. This was a lot of coincidences to string together, so they felt that their band was pre-ordained. To top everything off, here were Jeff and Danielle at their very first live performance.

"We listened to all your early work. None of us realized how young you must have been when you started. Then the music changed to CCM, and we haven't learned many of your new songs. Some are okay, but most are too religious for us." Lucy asked, "Why don't you like Jesus?" The young man looked embarrassed by the question and said, "We just don't believe any of it. Science has disproved the Bible." He was staring mainly at his feet and didn't notice all the eyes at the table light up when he said this.

Danielle said, "That seems like the opposite of the facts. When was the last time you looked into the truth of that statement?" The young man focused on her thoughtfully. "I don't know. It's what I've been told for forever in school. None of us have ever really questioned it." Then he asked the question the band had hurriedly discussed when they recognized Jeff and Danielle, "Would you maybe want to play a song with us?" Jeff and Danielle shared a look. Jeff said, "We'll discuss it and let you know in a few minutes." With a disappointed but hopeful look, he returned to the stage, whispering to the other band members as they continued setting up.

Jeff asked the table at large, "Well, what do you think?" Sophie immediately said, "Do you really want to give them a boost if they aren't Christians and don't want to play any of your Christian music? And what were your early songs anyway?" Jeff explained how his first songs were mainly funny songs he'd written before he was six and became a Christian, then Christian songs for a year, then songs he and Danielle had written about their lives for five years, then Christian songs again from age twelve to the present. "They must have learned those early and in-between songs and maybe some of the others that don't have churchy words in them, especially from the Exile album. Maybe some from the cruise."

Danielle continued, "We might play a couple with the condition that they talk to us after they finish playing for the evening. This restaurant closes at 9:30pm. They could follow us back to the hotel, and we could talk for a while in the hotel room. Maybe we could even get them to visit church with us in the morning." After a final look around at everyone at the table, Jeff waved at the band, and the young man hurried over. "Jeff said, "Danielle and I will play a couple of songs with you if the band comes over to our hotel afterwards for a chat." His eyes lit up with the thought of the invitation and the chance to talk with the twins, and he immediately exclaimed, "Yes!" He named two songs that the band had quickly chosen while they were waiting for the verdict, one from the in-between years and one from the Exile album, the one Jeff and Danielle had written in New York City; they agreed to the song choice. They also agreed to play later in the evening after the family had a chance to enjoy dinner and Jeff and Danielle listened to the band to get a feel for their style and musical ability.

As he hurried back to the stage for the second time, Zoe said, "I'm not sure this will help you keep a low profile." Danielle answered, "God will work it out. I feel good about this." Their food arrived and was consumed with accompanying animated conversation regarding the hospital visit and all the things they had seen on the walking tours. Their waitress, overhearing part of the discussion, was curious about how they had managed to tour one of the attractions so late in the afternoon. "They only advertise one tour a day that starts before lunch and ends at 12:30. How were you able to see it so late?" Jake answered simply that they had paid for a private tour. The girl was impressed and thought to herself, "Must be nice to have that kind of money," although they didn't look particularly wealthy; no expensive clothes or watches or jewelry.

The band had begun playing while the family ate, and Jeff and Danielle studied their style and ability. The six musicians were not as talented as Terry's band, but they weren't bad. Their music was edgier with more of a garage band sound. As everyone finished eating, the first set ended, and the band spokesman left the stage and approached the table again, questioning look in his eyes. Jeff and Danielle shared a quick look, then nodded in agreement, rising to follow him back to the stage.

Once there, Jeff slid behind one of the keyboards while Danielle picked up an electric guitar. They visited with some of the band members while others took a break and headed for the loo. When everyone was back and ready, the band leader spoke into a microphone. "We've been playing the music of two of our favorite song writers, J and D, and by coincidence, they are here tonight eating dinner and have agreed to play a couple of songs with us. Please welcome Jeff and Danielle." There was enthusiastic applause from the audience, but none as passionate as that from the Armstrong table. Most of the diners were younger, fans of the band or friends of the fans who had been convinced or cajoled into attending the band's first performance. Others had come for the food and were discovering they were glad to be there as they enjoyed the music very much.

Jeff nodded to the band, and after a keyboard intro, they played the song about their first long underwater dive, a ballad really, exciting and funny. The crowd loved it, and there was more enthusiastic applause. Next, they played the song the twins had written in New York City during their exile after the first trip to Africa. As Zoe listened to this song, chills ran up her spine. This song was nothing like the others she had heard, and certainly not like the first song. It was dark and forlorn, but with a hint of hope running through it; someone looking for something they hadn't found yet but with the promise it might still be discovered. Toward the end, there was a guitar solo played by Danielle that was amazing, leaving the audience open mouthed. Several people were shooting video with their phones and posting it to their Facebook pages or YouTube, and Cindy, ever alert, found them almost immediately, and notified her followers and sent the links on to the Baby SEAL website.

As often happened, when the song ended there was silence for a moment before the room erupted in applause. Jeff and Danielle returned to their table where Jake, just in case they needed to make a run for it, had paid their check, including a nice tip to their waitress, who was surprised but appreciative, tipping still being a rather new concept in Australia, and only in some of the newer tourist areas. The family worked their way to the door, through the tables of admirers, and down the street to their car. Soon afterwards, they were back at the hotel, and while most of the family went ahead to their suite, Jeff and Danielle, Zoe and Lucy waited in the lobby for the band to appear. Zoe was skeptical, but Jeff and Danielle just said, "We'll see."

At 10:15, the six band members walked through the lobby doors, spotted the waiting group, and headed over. Introductions were made, and Jeff led the way upstairs where Jake and Sophie had prepared some late-night snacks. More introductions were made, and the band started right in with their questions. Some were personal, such as "Why did you switch to Christian music," and some were more general, the now usual, "How do you know the Bible is true?[3]" and "Where did the Bible come from?[4]" and "How do you know there is a God?[5]"

The six band members were all intelligent, inquisitive, and open to new ideas, and the discussion went on long after Lucy fell asleep, her head on Jeff's lap. From God and the Bible in general, the discussion progressed to Jesus and Christianity in particular. Fifty years earlier, everyone would have known who was meant when someone said God, and they would have had at least a rough idea about sin, if not the particulars. In less than two generations, Christianity had been so removed from the public square that the current generation had no idea about truths earlier generations would have taken for granted.

The questions became, "What is sin?[6]" and "Why am I a sinner?" and "What am I supposed to do about it?" The group left about 3:00am, not Christians, but at least searching in the right direction, with resources to help them along. And one had agreed to go with them to a church they were visiting the next morning. After they were gone, Sophie shook her head at Jeff and Danielle. "I never know what's going to happen with the two of you. That was very intense." Zoe said, "I want to know about that second song you played. I had chills running up and down my spine." Sophie nodded. "Me, too."

Jeff and Danielle spent another hour describing again their first trip to Africa, what had happened there, and the drive across the US that followed. Danielle went on to describe in more detail their time in New York where the song in question was written. "We had been traveling for a while, and it was starting to look like we wouldn't find an answer anytime soon. It was discouraging. The song reflects that." The others nodded. Jake shook his head. "It certainly does. You shouldn't have been on your own at a time like that." Everyone took that as the notice that it was bedtime, and headed to their rooms, Danielle lifting Lucy off Jeff's lap and carrying her on the way to the room she shared with Zoe and the little girl. As she passed Jeff, Zoe paused long enough to give him a fierce hug, then followed Danielle.

The next morning, the group drove to the church about forty minutes north of their hotel, meeting the band member in the parking lot as they climbed out. The family was surprised to see him, thinking the late night/early morning discussion would have worn off, and he would have chosen to sleep in rather than attend church for the first time in his life. He greeted them enthusiastically; apparently, the discussion had led to some serious thinking on his part. He had even brought his girlfriend with him, although she was more patiently accommodating than interested. Apparently, the two had been deep in discussion on the drive up, though, and her eyes showed at least a gleam of interest as opposed to disinterest, boredom, or hostility.

Introductions were made, and the group trooped inside, finding seats near the middle of the room. The sermon that morning was perfect for the first-time church goers, a deep-rooted refresher course for everyone, but a basic primer for the newbies, reinforcing ideas put forth the night before and developing them even further, giving even the long-time Christians more knowledge for their conversations with the non-Christian public with whom they interacted on a daily basis. When the service ended, the two non-believing visitors sat in their seats, stunned. The girl said, "Wow! Why have we never heard any of this before?" Jeff said, "I'm sorry that in all your life, you never have. That is the fault of the Christians around you. But now that you have, you have a decision to make. I hope you don't take too long to do it."

The Armstrong family wouldn't know for a while what that chance meeting at the restaurant had begun or the lives that would be touched because of it. They did agree to stay in touch, though, and parted ways, returning to the airport and the flight home. That evening, they were telling their friends at church about the trip, and the band was added to many prayers.

# Chapter 12

The next morning, the young people returned to school, and Jake set about buying property for the new children's ranch. He and the twins had been negotiating with the owners for a few weeks, and everything had finally come together for the purchase. By Wednesday, the land belonged to the foundation, and Jake began making a list of names and companies for the various roles. On Thursday, Jeff and Danielle were in the news again.

The twins were riding their motorcycles to the dive shop after school. They had taken them to school as they often did these days due to the movie production, although this time with the planned trip to shop for a new face mask for Danielle. The sky was clear with a few wispy clouds, and by unspoken agreement, the two decided to make a side trip along the harbor, not too much out of the way.

Traffic was light, and they stopped on the verge, just before the road made a right angle turn back toward the heart of the city and their destination, to stare out at the calm water, talking quietly about their time so far in Australia, church, school, the Armstrong family, the movie, and the other myriad things that filled their lives. They watched with indifference as a small SUV made its way down the road they would soon be turning onto when they left their reverie and continued on their way. A white-haired man was driving while three children sat, one in the front, two in the back, pointing and waving toward the water.

Suddenly, as they watched with sudden alertness, the man clutched both hands to his chest, and the SUV accelerated down the slope, shot across the seawall, and plunged into the water. With all four windows down, the vehicle rapidly filled with water and sank. In the seconds before it slipped under the water, Jeff and Danielle had thrown off their armored motorcycle jackets, and as a few nearby sightseers rushed toward the site, dove into the water and followed the trail of bubbles down to the sunken SUV.

Inside the vehicle, they found the three panicked children struggling weakly to unfasten their seatbelts. All of them had been stunned when the airbags deployed as the SUV struck the water, and the eight-year-old girl in the front passenger seat had a bloody nose from the airbag impact. This was definitely not a good thing since the harbor was known for its shark population and occasional shark attack. Danielle pulled (ripped was too strong a word for the underwater maneuver) her door open, released the catch on her seatbelt, dragged the girl through the opening, and headed for the surface.

From the side, she spotted the first predator, a small four-foot shark attracted by the scent of blood and the turbulence caused by the crash. Breaking the surface with the gasping girl, she stroked strongly toward the wall, the top three feet over her head. A twenty-something man plopped down on his stomach, reaching down. In the girl's ear, Danielle told her to reach up, and when she did, Danielle shoved her up, kicking with her feet. The man grasped an arm and lifted the girl onto the wall. Danielle immediately flipped over to return to the SUV, hearing just as her head went under someone yell, "Sharks!"

Jeff passed her as she headed back down, a young person in each hand. He reached the surface, and as the older boy floated, sputtering and coughing, Jeff lifted the six-year-old up, to be grasped by the hand and pulled up like his sister, followed immediately by his ten-year-old brother. The man on the wall yelled, "Look out, mate!" and Jeff turned just in time to kick an approaching shark in the nose before flipping over and swimming down to join Danielle. He met her halfway as she swam upwards with the white-haired man clutched close, spinning in the water to keep her face toward the circling sharks who fortunately seemed to be focusing mainly on the still bubbling SUV.

They broke the surface and used the momentum to thrust the man upwards, where two men were able to grasp him by the arms before the twins dropped back down. They then sank down a few feet before shooting to the surface again. Jeff shoved Danielle upwards where the two men grabbed her arms and pulled her the rest of the way. Jeff grabbed the rough stone of the wall and pulled himself high enough that Danielle, who had immediately rolled over and stuck her arm down, could reach him. They grasped wrists, and she raised him enough that he could dig his fingers into the top of the wall and jerk himself the rest of the way up, hearing a loud snap behind him and feeling a blow to one foot as his feet left the water.

Rolling over, the twins watched as a man and woman performed CPR on the older man while the three children stood around him, shivering in the cooling air. A police car and ambulance were just pulling up as other bystanders wrapped the children in jackets and sweaters. As the onlookers took pictures with their phones, Jeff and Danielle walked to their jackets lying on the ground and pulled them on. Danielle said, "Well, this is going to make riding the motorcycles chilly." Jeff smiled and nodded, watching one of the policemen walking toward them.

They spent another half hour explaining what had happened, and as soon as the police released them, mounted their motorcycles and rode toward home, escaping the news crew that was hoping to get an interview. Shopping at the dive shop would have to wait for another day. As they stopped at an intersection, Jeff lifted up his left boot to stare at the heel. A jagged chunk was missing. He showed it to Danielle. She nodded and said, "I meant to tell you, a shark almost bit your foot off." Laughing, he said, "Thanks for not pulling slower." She shrugged. "It was a bit of a temptation, but I knew Lucy would not take it kindly if I let anything happen to you."

When they arrived home, Jeff changed back into his school shoes and left the boots in the garage by the motorcycle. Now they had an additional item to add to their shopping list. Squelching their way to the back door, they slipped into the house and had changed into dry clothes before anyone noticed. Entering the kitchen, they joined the others who were preparing to set dinner on the table. Zoe looked up from the bowl she was carrying to smile at Jeff and greet Danielle, but immediately took a second look and asked, "What happened?"

Jeff sighed. It was getting harder to hide anything from Zoe. He said, "We may be on the news again." Sophie gasped. "What did you do this time?" Danielle explained about the SUV plunging into the harbor and the rescue. Over dinner, they told the story in detail, and after the dishes were cleaned and put away, everyone trooped into the lounge room to see if the evening news reported the story. It did. There was a lot of video from various camera phones, and unfortunately, along with the shots of the various fins gliding through the water, there was a clear view of the shark who had taken the chunk out of Jeff's boot as Danielle jerked him clear of the water.

Lucy, who had been cheering for them, put her hands over her face and started crying. The rest of the family, especially Zoe, did not look much better. Jake said, "You have to stop this." Jeff and Danielle stared at him helplessly. Jeff asked, "How? We were the first ones there. Should we have left them to drown?" Sean asked, "Why were there so many sharks around? I know there are some in the harbor, but I wouldn't expect to see them congregate like that in the afternoon." Danielle explained how two of the children had received minor injuries from the crash;

not life threatening at all, but they had been bleeding, and the blood and the turbulence from the crash had attracted the sharks. Fortunately, the injured children had been removed from the water quickly, but the damage, so to speak, had already been done.

Zoe said, "You could have been killed." Jeff said, "We've kinda been living on borrowed time since we were seven." Zoe stood up and left the room. Danielle glared at Jeff. "That was not the best thing you could have said." He looked down, chagrined. Jake said, "I think the best thing we could do now is just lock the two of you in the basement until it's time for you to go home. If we had a basement. And if you promised not to escape."

This lightened the mood a little. Lucy stalked over, stood in front of Jeff, and said severely, "Promise you will not get hurt, mate." He grabbed her and hugged her fiercely. "I promise to try very hard." She hugged him back. Everyone left the room to attend to various items, and, at a look from Danielle, Jeff joined her in the back yard.

She said, "I've been thinking. You know how we've always said that trouble doesn't happen because we're there, but that it was going to happen anyway, and we're put there to deal with it?" He nodded. She continued. "I don't think that's right anymore. Now I think these things are direct attacks on us, to kill us and remove us from the board." Jeff stared at her thoughtfully. "Why? Why bother with us?" She continued. "Have you ever counted how many people have come to Christ because of things we've done? And then led other people to Christ, and then those people have led other people to Christ? It's not like a Billy Graham crusade or anything, but it's more than a few. I think satan keeps trying to put a stop to it, and God won't let him. We've been lucky because the attacks have all been directed at us and not at people we care about. That could change."

Jeff was skeptical. "No one is trying to kill Pastor Shane. Or Pastor John. Or Pastor James. Why us? We're not doing that much." Danielle was not convinced. "How many times have we almost been killed since we were seven. And it isn't as though we're soldiers, or police, or firefighters, or something. We don't go looking for trouble. Why do we keep running into it?" Jeff answered, "It's like we've always said. What was going to happen was going to happen whether we were there or not. Do you think that car wouldn't have gone into the bay if we'd gone home after school?"

Danielle sat in thought for a while. Then she said, "What will Lucy do if something happens to you?" Jeff said, "The same thing that happens to people every day when they lose someone close to them. They get through it, and they go on. Not taking us as an example, of course." Danielle asked, "Should we get close to people? Is it fair?" Jeff said, "The only way we would not get close to people is if we lived in the outback hundreds of miles from civilization and never saw anyone. I'm not doing that." Danielle sighed, and they moved back inside.

When Danielle entered the bedroom she shared with Zoe and sat at her desk to prepare her homework for the next day, the other girl asked, "Did the two of you work it out?" Without turning around, Danielle said, "Jeff said we couldn't move to the outback away from everyone." Startled, Zoe said, "Wait! What?" Danielle turned around in her chair. "I asked Jeff if it was fair for us to get close to people when circumstances keep trying to kill us. He said he wasn't moving to the outback hundreds of miles from anyone." Zoe said, "Well, it's a good thing. Lucy would track him down wherever he went." The two girls chuckled at the idea, then turned back to their homework.

The next day at school, Jeff and Danielle strode into the principal's office first thing, before the bell rang. The secretary looked up and said, "Oh! I was just about to send for you." The twins shared a look, then smiled at her, and at a wave, walked into the man's office and sat in two of the chairs across from his desk.

He said expansively, "Sit down. Sit down. I caught the two of you on the news last night. Well done with the rescue."

This was said as though they had saved the family just to please him. "Your school uniforms were clearly visible, although they were somewhat wet and rumpled." This was put forth a bit critically. Jeff said mildly, "They were in the harbor, sir." He said, "That's true. That's true. I suppose I shouldn't be too hard on you although we do request that our students keep themselves neat and tidy when wearing their school uniforms. You are representing the school, you know. And the school did receive some good publicity. The mayor called to congratulate me. And a reporter stopped by my house for an interview. Luckily, I had seen the news on the telly and knew what they were talking about. It would perhaps be good if you could give me a heads up when you perform an action such as the one yesterday." Danielle said, "Yes, sir," thinking, "Sure, like that's the first thing that's going to go through my mind after a day like yesterday."

Following a few more minutes of the same, he released them to their first period classes. The secretary gave them a hall pass as the final bell had already sounded. Their first period teachers made no comment when they arrived, simply glancing at the passes and continuing with the day's lesson. Two days later, filming began on the movie.

# Chapter 13

J eff, Danielle, and the Armstrong family stood at the edge of the street where the action was to take place. The decision had been made and signed off on by the twins to shoot the movie using digital cameras. After spending hours with the team writing the screenplay and the team of directors, it was also decided to video the entire script. A verdict would be reached at the end of recording whether to edit out scenes or entire sections to shorten the movie or turn the results into two or even three movies.

All the remaining actors had been hired. There were many, although some, such as the twins' first grade teacher, had minor roles. Everyone who had a need had been given access to the gym Jeff and Danielle had created, and they were working with the cast, developing their skills. Coaches had also been hired to build on the direction Jeff and Danielle gave, although they shook their heads when Jeff and Danielle gave a demonstration of their usual routines. When there were stares of disbelief, Jeff said encouragingly, "We'll use special effects and stunt doubles where needed." This brought a sigh of relief. Harry and Henry stopped by when they could get a weekend away to assist Mike and his team's characters with their roles.

There were four directors, an almost unheard-of situation, and each one was videoing with a different set of the twins at the different stages in their lives. The cast playing the older characters such as Steve and Amy were moving from set to set as needed. It was controlled chaos with scenes videoed completely out of order. The editing team would be responsible for continuity, making sure everything blended smoothly together.

Jeff and Danielle had introduced another new feature into the movie. Instead of a scrolling line of credits at the end that no one stayed around for, they wanted everyone on the crew in the movie, from the directors to the food service. If their name would be on the screen, they would have a cameo appearance in the movie, sitting in a restaurant, window shopping on the street, the 4^(th) of July concert, and so on. The crew were all excited to learn about this. While the shot would be very brief, it would still be a giant step up from a name scrolling past an uncaring audience.

Jeff and Danielle's names were not going to be anywhere in the credits. Or in the movie itself. All the names involved had been changed. Anyone who wanted to could tell people that a certain character was them, but the twins seriously doubted anyone would. Word was still sure to leak out as friends talked about the movie, but hopefully the impact would be lessened. Of even more concern to them was making sure no one was charged with child abuse or child endangerment because of their early lives. Even the jobs Steve and his friends had paid them for could be construed as child labor by someone with an axe to grind. Their lawyer in the US had already been alerted. Many things had been left out of the movie just in case, for example, their training with explosives.

This day was the videoing of the moment Jeff and Danielle met. The house had been chosen on a quiet street for the exterior shots. A large pecan tree stood in the center of the grassy lawn, and Alexander and Bobbie, acting the parts of six-year-old Jeff and Danielle, were crawling around on the grass, picking up the pecans the production crew had scattered liberally around from a bag of nuts purchased at a local food store. There was even an animal wrangler with a trained squirrel for Bobbie to feed. This scene required three takes because the camera crew, professional though they were, was laughing so hard. Someone would say, "Squirrel wrangler," and set them off again. When Jeff threatened to kill the squirrel and eat it, everyone calmed down.

The crew would have created a house on the lot, but they would have also had to create a pecan tree and a lawn for the children to crawl around in. However, a duplicate of the front of the house had been built on the movie lot for all of the other scenes. Other homes on the street had been selected for the various odd jobs the children had performed, and these scenes were all shot in two days, with the characters changing clothes as necessary in an RV parked out of the way. Before word could get out and a crowd appear, they had moved on.

In addition to Steve and Amy's house, the two that would be needed for Danielle's and Alice's were also ready, right down to Alice's beautiful garden. The facades were built on the movie lot near the Steve and Amy "house". A rapport had also developed among all of the Danielle and Jeff characters and the woman who would be playing Alice, which, while not necessary between professional actors, was a nice addition.

The apartment building had been chosen: a two-story complex with multiple buildings and a swimming pool, although pool scenes would be shot at a private home. It didn't really resemble the Viewpoint Apartments where Jeff had grown up, but it met some key criteria such as being two-story with more than one building, and having a swimming pool, and a security fence all the way around, although the director and crew could have worked around some of those. All the work was completed in one day with multiple clothing changes and shots of Jeff and Danielle running from an apartment door to the pool, up and down the stairs, knocking on various doors. Many of the apartment's residents were at school or work, and the complete day of shooting was accomplished with no interference. The few people who were around stood at their apartment doors or at the railing overlooking the pool and had quite a story to tell their friends about the movie being produced.

Interior work would be videoed on a stage at the studio itself. A door was created, nicknamed "The Door", which represented the various doors at the apartment complex. The number was velcro'd on and changed as necessary, an activity carefully monitored by one person to insure the actors didn't inadvertently enter the "wrong" apartment door for a scene, an error sure to be posted on the internet by people who watched for those sorts of mistakes. The insides of the various houses were also ready.

Danielle found it difficult to work with the actors who played her mother and step-father. Even though she knew it wasn't them and that the traumatic day had happened years earlier, her mind still moved between fear and rage when she watched them in the manufactured set of her old living room. Sebastian, clever man that he was, worked her through it by having her sit with the two actors during their time in makeup, talking about their families and everyday events so that she saw them clearly as who they were and not who they would be portraying in the movie.

She still had difficulty with the home scenes from her young life, and for the most part waited until the end of the day, reviewed the video with Jeff, and approved it or made suggestions. As the actors performed the scenes, the camera crew filmed it, and the director oversaw it all, they understood why. There was rage on the set the day they filmed her discovery of the bear with the camera inside. More rage on the day her mother threw her new Bible in the trash. In fact, there were so many reasons for righteous anger that a special "calming down" room was set up for use after one of these days. It wouldn't have mattered so much if it had just been a story that someone had written, but they knew this story was true.

# Chapter 14

This was also the week the actors began parachute training. Technically, the four youngest children didn't need it since Jeff and Danielle hadn't made their first jump until they were ten. However, they begged to be included, and the twins laughingly added it on as a perk. A day was spent shopping for jumpsuits and helmets. If the twins thought the choices would all be camouflage, they were sadly mistaken. Both were in all the colors of the rainbow. The first time Jeff saw them, he theatrically pulled on his sunglasses and said, "My eyes hurt." Danielle just said, "Teach us to assume. They won't be wearing those during the videoing of the movie." At least their boots were standard combat boots, which everyone in the group was quite happy with. Outside of their lack of trendy style, they were really very comfortable.

On Wednesday, the young people and the actor portraying Mike drove to the indoor skydiving establishment. The excited group listened carefully through the beginner training class, then entered the chamber one by one for their first experience. Their instructor did a doubletake when he first spotted the suits and helmets, but they were actually better than what the site offered, so he let it pass, merely nodding his head at the level of commitment the group was displaying which would translate into income for the business and himself.

On day one, they learned the basics in the wind tunnel: body position, how to float steadily without rocking, turning in one direction or the other, rising slowly, returning to earth slowly. The next day, they advanced a bit more and just spent time getting comfortable. By the time Friday arrived, they could rise comfortably to the top of the tunnel, recover from a spin in any direction, and were hooked.

On Saturday, after three days of indoor training, the van containing the actors followed Jeff and Danielle on their motorcycles to the drop zone to perform a tandem parachute jump with an instructor to get the feel of a real parachute jump; most of them anyway. Two of the kids and the actor portraying Mike had no interest in jumping out of an airplane. The indoor parachuting had been fun for everyone, but it was indoors. The plane thing was totally different. This was fine with the twins. Everyone now knew the feel and excitement of freefall. Good enough. Gliding down under a canopy could be faked.

It was a perfect day for parachuting, and the drop zone was crowded with jumpers; crowded being a relative term. It wasn't like a mall on Boxing Day or anything. Still, the early fall day was a comfortable 70 degrees F on the ground with a few scattered clouds and a light breeze. Jeff and Danielle were the last out of the plane each time, and while they kept half an eye on the actors, they kept half an eye on the enjoyment of falling or gliding through the air. At their request, the three instructors had taken the actors through the paces on the free fall jumps, twisting and spinning in the air, spending some time going through all the permutations the actors had experienced at the indoor site.

They went up in two groups, and the twins accompanied all the flights. First would be a HAHO jump, high altitude, high opening, with maximum time spent drifting slowly down under the parachute, followed by a HALO jump, high altitude, low opening one with maximum time spent in freefall. Jeff and Danielle would be able to make four jumps; not a bad day's enjoyment. The only delay would be the time spent repacking the parachutes.

By the time the day was over, the group had divided into three parts. First were those who had been terrified in the end and had only persevered because they considered themselves professionals and wanted the experience. Second were those who were glad they had done it this time but had no particular desire to do it again. Third were the ones, who, like Jeff and Danielle, loved it and planned to earn their jump certifications and continue with parachuting. The first two groups still loved the indoor site. For the third group, it was no longer enough. They wanted the real thing.

Now Jeff and Danielle began working with the studio to prepare for simulated jumps for filming. Green screens would take care of the background, but they needed structures to hold a deployed parachute and release it to record the "twins" landing. Asa and Abigail had already learned the happy dance after watching the video of the real Jeff and Danielle after their first landing, playing it over and over until it was exactly right. Jeff asked Danielle, "Did we really look like that?" She laughed and said, "We were pretty happy that day. And video does not lie."

That evening at the Armstrong home, Jeff and Danielle described the day. Sophie said, "I'm surprised that they split into three groups. I would have thought they'd either like it or hate it." Jeff shook his head. "It might have been like that if they hadn't experienced the indoor site first. After that, they knew what to expect and what was going on." Danielle added, "I think the biggest shock was between the tunnel and being fifteen thousand feet above the ground. That is a huge difference." Lucy chimed in, "I want to try the indoor thing. And I want to make a real parachute jump. Bobbie is my age, and she has done both." This had become her new arguing point: if Bobbie could do it, so could she. Jeff glanced at Zoe. She mouthed, "You have created a monster." He shrugged.

That evening, when Jeff and Zoe put Lucy to bed, she began wheedling, "Can I at least go to the indoor parachute place? Please?" Jeff shared a look with Zoe. He was in favor of it, but this was Zoe's call. She was, after all, Lucy's mother. Zoe said, "I don't see any reason why you can't do the indoor thing. We'll have to talk about the jumping out of a plane, thing, though." This made Lucy almost too excited to sleep, but by the time she had said her prayers and listened to a bedtime story made up on the spot by Jeff and Zoe, who were getting quite good at it, her eyes were closed, and she was asleep. Jeff reached over and turned out the bedside light, and, joining Zoe, silently slid out of the room.

Sophie, who had been leaning against the door jamb watching the proceedings, shook her head to herself. Jeff and Zoe had taken such care not to touch each other, not to bump shoulders or brush hands or any other totally innocent contact. She wondered to herself how they were ever going to manage another nine months living under the same roof.

# Chapter 15

The Armstrong group stood in the entrance to the building next door to the church, now called The Manse, even though half of it was Sunday School classrooms. Jeff and Danielle had been heavily involved in the changes on top of all their other projects, although this one had given them a chance to study the work and character of the man Jake had recommended to be the general contractor for the children's ranch. They liked him a lot. He was different than Mike, less intense, although just as meticulous in his work. He was perhaps even better at finding less expensive ways to get the job done; not cutting corners or using materials just because they were cheap, but not putting in ¾ inch plywood when ½ inch met and exceeded the specifications.

Steven Colling was a single dad with an eight-year-old son well on his way to becoming a general contractor himself. He could name every implement in the tool section at the local hardware store, its function, and could use the tool for that function, at least to the degree you would expect from someone so young, and better than an adult who had no clue what the tool was for. He didn't have the strength required for the best usage of some of them, but with others, skill and patience made up for the lack of strength. Jeff and Danielle were also impressed that, on the few occasions that they had been with him when he hit his finger with a hammer, his only comment had been, "Mates, that hurt!" as opposed to what some of the other helpers said, Christian or not.

All the Armstrong family members had worked on the building as well, including Lucy, who wore a special pair of overalls for the projects, complete with tool belt, hardhat, and safety goggles. Her main function was to hand Jeff and Danielle tools from the belt when called for, to move the end of the tape measure to the required position, carry pieces of wood to the discard pile, and sweep up sawdust to keep it from being tracked around, and she took each of these tasks seriously. Volunteers who were careless in their habits soon learned otherwise when Lucy was around, and where they might have taken umbrage at someone else remonstrating with them to keep their work area clean, the situation was funny when Lucy, standing there in her "work outfit", encouraged them to "Toss those pieces of wood in the discard pile, mate," or "Sweep up that sawdust, mate. We don't want it to attract rats, now do we?" They might roll their eyes at their friends, but they complied.

Sheila, Pastor Shane's wife, picked out the paint colors, wall paper, and fixtures for their living quarters. All the expenses were being picked up by anonymous donors, and while some may have suspected it had something to do with the Armstrong family or their American guests, no one knew for sure except Shane and the church treasurer, and they weren't talking. None of the choices were extravagant; just tasteful and well made.

The family part of the building was completely walled off from the other half. There was a metal door on both floors between the two sections, but these were for convenience, not necessity, and were kept locked. The classes part of the building had been divided into large sections with sliding panels that could divide them into individual rooms as needed, just like the classroom section of the main building. And, the entire building had central heating and air conditioning. It was quite a nice building, and undoubtedly wouldn't support in rent what it had cost to purchase and renovate, but Jeff and Danielle had paid for it, and the foundation managed it, charging a rent that the church could afford. Both parties were happy, so life was good.

Shane's family was ecstatic. The new manse was much bigger than the apartment the church had been renting for them. Each of their two boys would have his own room, and Shane could move his study to the room that had been specially prepared for him, freeing up the small office in the church for use as a storage closet. The church and manse both were in a nicer and safer part of the city, relieving Shane and Sheila both of some worry, and the grocery store was a short, pleasant walk away. This was on top of the church itself being right next door. Central air was just icing on the cake.

There might have been some dissatisfaction from some church members because the new space was so nice; better than where some of them lived, but everyone was happy for the family. They had been a little ashamed that the church couldn't afford to do better for their beloved pastor and his family. In addition, the volunteers had spoken among themselves and made agreements and deals to help each other with small home projects such as painting interior walls. Steven had even offered to provide instructions and help if they got in a bind on bigger projects like changing out a toilet or adding a wall. There might be some disagreement later over what constituted helping and what was doing the work for someone else, but for the time being, everyone was in accord.

It only took part of one day to move the family to their new home and transport some classes over to the new building. All the families had been inviting their neighbors, co-workers, and classmates to visit the church, and while they received many friendly, and some not so friendly, no thank you's, there had been some acceptances as well, and with all of the classes growing a little, some expansion was needed. The classes with students from grade 6-12, college, and singles all moved to the new building, and the others expanded as needed. Church attendance had not quite reached the point where two services were required, but that day was rapidly approaching.

Some of the church members were excited about the change, some not so much, and others indifferent. There were at least a couple in each age group who did not respond well to change, and they were all, "Why do we have to be the ones to move?" and some anxiety about leaving the familiar behind. Their friends were encouraging while some of the others rolled their eyes. Seriously. They were only moving next door. To a different room. In a different building. It wasn't as if the move was to a different city or state, or heaven forbid, country! It had been the same when they had graduated to the older kids' classrooms, although not as much because that at least had only been the rooms next to theirs, and they were familiar with it. And, just like the last move, after a couple of Sundays, it was normal.

Jeff and Danielle were perhaps not as supportive as they might have been. Two more weeks of school, and they would be flying to Africa. Sophie would be traveling with them, and they would be meeting their friends and family from home there. Once again, they were paying for Abeba and her family to travel; the family would meet them at the African airport. Also joining them would be Dr. Flowers, making it possible for Dr. Juliana and her husband to travel to his village for a visit. And, on this trip, they would be joined by a dentist.

Dental care had been one of their concerns for a while, and they had requested the foundation find the perfect dentist, just as the twins had a doctor. It was rare for someone in the village to reach old age with many of their teeth. Improper dental hygiene and total lack of a dentist took its toll. Using the same technique as had been employed to find a doctor, a dentist would be arriving along with all the equipment needed for typical dental work. Ejigu, the village headman, had overseen the expansion of the clinic, adding the extra space necessary. The medical and dental sections of the clinic would share the same waiting area, although most of the patients sat around outside chatting, weather permitting.

Sophie was excited to be traveling with them, a decision she had made as soon as she learned the twins would be traveling there when school let out in April for the three-week break. Her immunizations were complete, the clothes she wanted to take were picked out, and she was leaving a complete list of instructions for the maintenance of the home while she was gone. The instructions had led to much joking and eye-rolling, but the family members staying in Australia appreciated her effort and concern. Except one young girl.

Sophie was leaving behind a very unhappy Lucy. The girl wanted to go with Jeff. She wanted to see elephants and giraffes that weren't in a zoo. Jeff soothed her bruised feelings a little by explaining that they didn't want to risk exposing someone as young as she was to the diseases present there. She pointed out that children her age lived there. He pointed out that many of them didn't survive childhood. She pointed out that he was going. So was Danielle. So was her grandmother. He pointed out that they were older and tougher, adding that they would only be gone a couple of weeks and would be able to talk to her every day once they arrived in the village. She was not satisfied, but she was resigned. School ended, the next day arrived, Jake and the children drove them to the airport, and the next African visit began.

# Chapter 16

The two SUV's and the two-and-a-half-ton truck rolled into Izersteling late in the afternoon on the all-season road that now ran from the city to the villages and ended a couple of hundred yards past Izersteling after passing through Tsege Mariam. For the last half mile, movement had been slow as the village young people ran alongside, waving and calling greetings. The vehicles pulled to a stop in front of the clinic where groups of people sat on benches under the veranda, new since Jeff and Danielle's last visit. Fans in the veranda ceiling, run on the clinic generator, moved the air; those and the shade made the area a comfortable place to wait for treatment.

Jeff and Danielle had taken turns riding in the truck with Pvt. Rada, hearing of the changes that had taken place in his life over the past year. Mike rode in the front of the Land Rover driven by Sgt. Etefu, and the two men discussed training methods and life in Africa compared to the less populated areas in America. Dr. Munoz and Dr. Flowers rode together as the GP continued to explain to the dentist what he could expect. They also exchanged tales of their lives before Africa. Dr. Flowers only experience with gangs had been the gang members who showed up in the ER. Michelle, when she wasn't talking to Sophie about the twins and their life in Australia, causing Danielle to throw in the occasional, "Sitting right here!" spoke with the two doctors about her experiences in the ER before she moved to the pediatric intensive care unit.

Doctor Flowers swung out of the SUV he was riding in and was immediately swamped by the villagers he had treated, overjoyed to see him again. There were women with the babies he had delivered, now one or two years old and still in good health, as were their mothers. A man whose arm he had saved from an accident with an axe waved at him, showing the limb was almost as good as new. Everywhere he looked were villagers he had treated for everything from ear aches to appendicitis, even a man who had been careless enough to stand in the way of a falling tree he had cut down. The good doctor was pretty sure alcohol had been involved in that accident, and the man had been lucky to survive with only a concussion and not his entire body crushed beyond repair.

The crowd in front of the clinic parted, and Dr. Juliana emerged, followed by Dinha and the nurses in training, and, bringing up the rear, still moving spryly with the aid of her cane, Haimanot. Jeff and Danielle greeted everyone, but made their way as quickly as possible to the older woman, hugging her gently. She seemed as full of energy as ever, but her body seemed frailer. It struck them that on one of these visits, she wouldn't be there to greet them, but also that, if so, she would be at Jesus' side, along with her friends and relatives, Village Sunshine, and Rainbow.

She looked up at them and again made fun of their height. They were only an inch taller than the previous year, but she was perhaps an inch shorter, making the difference more pronounced. Behind her was Hanna, her young apprentice who was learning to judge the value of the service the doctor provided against the ability of her patients to pay. At the moment the teenage girl was telling an unhappy man that his bill was two hundred hours of pedaling on foot powered generators around the village. The man was outraged and was arguing quietly with flailing hand gestures and foot stomps. The girl listened to him patiently until the tirade paused and then said, "That's fine. If the cost is too high, we will simply remove the treatment, and you can have your disease back." He immediately backed away, hands out, stammering that he would be happy to pedal the generators.

Danielle raised a questioning eyebrow at the girl, and she stepped over to whisper, "He has a disease he doesn't want coming back, and he doesn't know we can't remove the treatment." She sniffed. "Besides, he needs to lose some weight. The exercise will do him good." Danielle smiled and shook her head. She liked Hanna, who must be what Grandmother was like when she was young. Assuming Grandmother was ever young. She may have been born just like she was today.

Dr. Carlos Munoz, the new dentist, was brought forward and introduced. The thirty-year-old man had a colorful history which was one of the reasons he was here, several thousand miles from where he grew up. His single mom had raised him in a poor part of town, and he had joined a gang when he was ten. Many of his peers were either dead or in prison. When he was eighteen, his life was headed in the same direction. Then a street preacher had spoken to him and somehow broken through the tough exterior and brought him to a life changing experience with Christ. Carlos had turned his whole world around, earned a scholarship through college, then dental school, and had been employed in a practice with two other dentists, spending much of his time outside of work serving at a free clinic.

In the past several months, his gang history caught up with him, and men he hadn't seen in years stopped him outside the free clinic, explaining that they expected him to write prescriptions for pain killers, opioids, that they could then sell on the street. He refused. First, he was beaten and left near the emergency room entrance to a hospital. The gang didn't have a lot of leverage. His mother had died in a car accident the year he graduated college. He wasn't married and had no other family. The options were to make him give in or kill him. After several refusals, the option to kill him was chosen.

Then he had heard through the grapevine about the need for someone to set up a dentistry in an African clinic and applied to the foundation for the job. Steve turned the private investigators loose on him, and they confirmed his story, from the gang membership to the dental work at the free clinic. The foundation board voted unanimously to accept him after Jeff and Danielle interviewed him via video chat; he was thereafter escorted daily from his job to a safe house. From there, he planned and ordered equipment for the dental addition to the clinic. The dental chair, dental x-ray, and other equipment had been transported, along with additional supplies, to the village from the warehouse.

Now, after the introductions were made, unloading of the truck began, and the dental room in the clinic began its transformation from an empty space to a modern dental examination and treatment room. Dr. Juliana had already lined up assistant candidates for him, and Hanna was prepared to take over billing. Most of his salary would go to a bank account in the states since his pay here would mostly be in service of some type or livestock. The plan was for him to stay here until the heat was off at home, maybe a year or two. He would probably need to change his name and city, if not state, to return home, though.

As the truck was unloaded and setup of the clinic addition began, the visitors took a tour of the village. The Freedman family, along with Cindy and Sophie, stared around them. Sophie had never seen the village before, but it didn't meet her expectations of a few mud huts with thatched roofs and animals and children running around on bare dirt. That impression wasn't too far from the way the American visitors had found it on their first well-drilling trip, when the village had its collection of mud huts, with a few made of stone, and daily trips to the distant water source for dirty water.

The village no longer resembled those early days, beginning

with the all-weather road they had driven on to reach their destination. Now, above each of the three water wells stood a water tower; not a huge one like those found in American or Australian towns and cities, but a much smaller version. These towers allowed for the next improvement: some of the stone huts, beginning with the headman's, had a water source inside their hut. Trenches had been dug and pipe laid to the huts nearest the wells. Dr. Juliana and her pastor husband had reported the wished-for improvements, and Jeff and Danielle had arranged for a civil engineer to design the layout before a complete jerry-rigged nightmare was in place. At present, it was only a convenience for those who could afford it, but even the farthest hut was only a quarter mile from a water well, an unheard-of luxury for most of the villages in the country. In addition, part of the planned improvements was a water line and faucet placed every hundred yards. Soon, even those at the edges of the village would have a nearby water source.

Ejigu proudly led them to improvement after improvement. Each hut occupied enough land to have its own garden, and most had chickens, the birds and their eggs forming a portion of their daily protein. Pigs were raised in an enclosed area on the usually downwind side of the village, each one tagged to show its owner, and fed whatever was available. Younger members of the village herded the cattle, sheep, and goats on the land used as pasture. Which led to the farmland and the newest additions: two tractors. With the addition of the tractors, the farmland had doubled, leading to not only more surplus to be sold in the city and villages on the way to the city, but even more cottage industries, such as the cotton gin and power loom.

The village had been buying their t-shirts from the growing industry in the city, but with the additional land under plow due to the addition of the two tractors, they could grow enough cotton to fill their needs; once it was turned into t-shirts, of course. This required a cotton gin, which unlike the huge factory-like buildings the Americans were accustomed to, was a small, hand-cranked affair which was entirely adequate for their current needs. The output of this small gin was fed into another hut where the cotton was turned into thread, then into a hut where the thread was turned into cloth. Various homes had set aside space to turn the cloth into the t-shirts which fed the already existing hut where Abeba's artwork was added.

Each of these tasks was filled by a villager who was then able to help support their family and improve the village. And each step brought them closer to being totally self-sufficient, no longer dependent on the generosity of their American friends to improve their lives. They had already passed the stage where they needed the support to survive. The water wells had made that possible. Someday, they would even be able to support the clinic without help.

The village also learned about taxes. At first, they resented the taxes, feeling that if anyone should be paid, it was the church in America that had helped them. However, as their lives improved, so did the government presence, which took over maintenance of the road to the village. The police sent weekly patrols through the area. Civil engineers from the capital were working with the village to set up a water treatment plant suitable for their current size and scalable for future growth. Their new pastor was showing them the appropriate Bible verses concerning "rendering unto Caesar." There was still some grumbling, but as there was no obvious corruption, it remained good natured.

Video chats went back and forth daily with the Armstrong family. Lucy was not happy to be missing everything but was waiting semi-patiently for the two weeks to end and everyone to return home. It helped when Jeff took her on a visual tour of the village within the range of the clinic router's Wi-Fi, introducing her to Grandmother, Dr. Juliana, Pastor Ezera, Dinha, and the others. The children in the village called her Little Music Maker when Jeff showed everyone a video of her playing the guitar for Sean's birthday song. They made him promise to bring her whenever possible, and he assured them he would.

The group visited Village Sunshine's grave. This time Elizabeth did the talking, telling Sophie how the young girl would have loved the changes that were taking place; there were so many new opportunities for pranks. And with the clinic internet connection, they would have been able to communicate all they wanted to, including telling Jeff and Danielle that Sebhat was doing an excellent job of keeping the villagers on their toes. Jeff, and especially Danielle, felt the pressure rising within them from the young girl's loss, and Michelle watched them with some concern. Then, she saw the moment when they released the sorrow and guilt. It was almost as though they could see the girl, along with Rainbow and Marilyn, watching them from heaven and knew they were all okay.

One of the villagers who worked with stone had carved a headstone for her, adding her name, her nickname, and the years of her birth and death. It was sad to see how few the years were, but hers was certainly not the only one like that, and many had even fewer years than that on their headstones. Her grave was covered in flowering native roses, and honey bees from the beekeeping operation one industrious village family had started flew busily around the blooms.

On the walk back from the gravesite, the group passed other native industries. One building was a canning factory, if the term could be stretched to mean a large stone hut where food could be sealed into glass Mason jars[7]. A number of pressure cookers were heated over gas stoves. This was a relatively inexpensive process since after the initial purchase of the jars and lids, all that was needed to reuse them was new seals. The owners of the hut were paid with a portion of the product they canned, and they sold what they didn't need to the village store or sent them on to the city.

Discounts were offered if the families provided their own

jars, metal rings, and seals, which most did after the first round of canning. The villagers could can their own food in their own huts of course, but with their own garden plots, it was easier to just plant a few more seeds and harvest a few more plants to offset the cost of the extra jars and the fire to heat them than to do their own canning. Only the most frugal of the villagers did their own.

A little surplus to sell was only a secondary benefit. Since the operation had begun, no family had gone hungry during the dry season. Before, they had not planted gardens and their farmland for maximum yield, nor harvest crops they could not use immediately, allowing the crops to rot in the fields. As for crops that were harvested, bacteria, fungi, rodents, and insects damaged these foods. Worse than that, crops that ripened at the same time could not be profitably sold in the city because of the overabundance of crops already flooding the marketplace. This all changed with canning, one success feeding another in a positive feedback loop; hunger had become a thing of the past.

Some families did their own canning because their secret family combination of spices made their food very popular, and a jar of their fruit or vegetables was welcomed at special occasions and celebrations. It wasn't uncommon to hear lively bargaining take place as families bartered for some item to be consumed at an upcoming event. Some of the jars were purchased by a group of women who would gather around a secret spot and work to guess the recipes. So far, no one had been successful, with the guessing or the sly questions asked to try to coax the recipe out of the family. The entire situation was quite the village joke.

Further along was the hut where various meats were smoked to preserve them. This hut was placed where the fragrant odor would occasionally waft into the village. Meat was becoming more plentiful as villagers raised cattle, sheep, and goats, but the pulse family of vegetables, including beans, lentils, and peanuts, was still the main source of protein in the village; and, they stored well.

The family that ground grains for the village had added another grinder and were hard at work. Few families ground their own grain anymore unless it was a very small amount. Why spent hours with a mortar and pestle when machines could do it in minutes. Even the small grinding machines a few of the families owned were no match for the larger ones if the family needed to process much volume. The village as a whole was growing prosperous enough that paying a percentage of the grain being ground was not a hardship.

The beekeeper's hives stood to one side of the fields. The family fiercely guarded them as the bees were their main source of income, and the tasty treat was tempting, especially to the children. It wasn't that difficult to stroll past a hive, pull out a frame, and keep on walking. People who wouldn't consider breaking into the family's home and making off with a jar of honey thought nothing of taking it from the hive, considering it more like scavenging in the wild. Notwithstanding the lost income from the stolen honey, the missing frame gave the bees an opportunity to create rogue combs in the open space.

Pastor Ezera preached a series on the ten commandments and used the honey prominently for the eighth commandment, "Thou shalt not steal." After that, the honey pilfering dropped off, at least among the Christian inhabitants of the village. For the rest, a few days in a work gang, removing rocks from the fields and being fed the equivalent of bread and water while their fellow workers availed themselves of glorious smelling foods as they made fun of the prisoners, proved to be a strong deterrent.

# Chapter 17

Back at the clinic, they helped with the setup of the new dental room. Jeff and Danielle installed the water purifier that would feed the water syringe and the rinse cup. This water had to be germ free. As they worked, they chatted with Dr. Munoz, who learned a bit about their history as they became more acquainted with his. After half an hour of discussion, he admitted that he might need to stay at the clinic for longer than a year until things had a chance to cool off back home. In fact, he might need to return to another country entirely. He didn't think he wanted to stay here for the rest of his life; maybe he would go somewhere like The Netherlands. It was unlikely his old gang would think to look for him there.

Danielle said, "You should put it in God's hands, and let Him guide you to where you need to go. Maybe He won't even want you to be a dentist anymore." The doctor snorted. "Why would God care about something like that?" Jeff said, "God cares about every decision in your life, from the smallest to the largest. Have you ever tried asking Him for help?" Carlos shook his head. "Me and God don't talk to each other much." Danielle asked, "Why not?" He shrugged. "Where was he when I was growing up in the hood? Or when my mom died?" Jeff said, "You made it out, right?" He nodded. "And received your education on scholarships?" Another nod. "Did you work really hard to get those scholarships, applied everywhere, performed a lot of community service to get your name out there?" He laughed. "No, they kind of fell in my lap." Danielle said, "And maybe God did all that to get you here to this place today to help these people." Carlos looked skeptical.

Jeff continued. "You know, God has a plan for your life, but you don't have to accept it. You can turn your back on Him, and He'll leave you alone. But if you want His assistance and His blessing, it would help if you met Him half way." Carlos said, "What do you mean?" Danielle asked, "Are you a Christian?" The man shrugged. "My mom took me to church some when I was little." Jeff continued patiently, "Did you become a dentist because you visited the dental school?" He laughed at that thought. "No, I worked harder than I ever did before in my life." Danielle nodded. "Well, you don't become a Christian by attending church either. The good news is, it's a free gift. You just have to accept it." He snorted. Accept it how?" Jeff said, "You just pray, 'Thank you, heavenly Father, for sending your own Son, Jesus Christ, to die on the cross and pay the penalty for my sin. I believe in Him and accept Him as my Lord. Thank you that I am saved in Him.'"

Carlos looked away and said, "I'll think about it." Danielle said, "Don't take too long. No one knows how many days they have." He smiled weakly and said, "You know, that's really annoying." She stared at him in surprise. "What's annoying?" "The way the two of you take turns talking." Jeff said, "We do that?" Carlos laughed again, and they continued with the dental chair assembly.

Carlos did not become a Christian before the visitors returned home, but the seed had been planted. The villagers watered the seed with their friendly challenges, and two months later, Pastor Ezera harvested the crop when their dentist professed his saving belief in Jesus and was baptized before the entire village, which spent the rest of the day in joyous celebration. He emailed the twins the news, and they held their own celebration at the Armstrong dinner table as they shared the news.

The villagers weren't as excited about having a dentist in the village as they had been about the doctor, or their new pastor for that matter. Injuries and illness were things that could kill you or keep you from providing for yourself or your family, but bad teeth were just a part of life. Very few people reached old age with many of their teeth, but they still lived full lives unless the dental problem was something like destructive periodontal disease or oral cancer, the first caused by poor oral hygiene or poverty. The poverty was being taken care of in the two villages. Now they could also start on dental care. Dr. Munoz was step two.

Soon the dental clinic was fully operational, and Carlos was treating his first patients. It would be a while before the villagers could be convinced to pay for routine exams and cleaning, so his first patients were toothaches and bad teeth, mixed with bad gums. He sighed as he treated problems that could have been prevented by regular exams and cleaning and explained patiently over and over to each patient that they didn't need to lose their teeth in old age.

Before a week had passed, he made sure everyone in the village had a toothbrush and toothpaste. He promised that a replacement toothbrush would be provided each time they visited for a routine exam, along with dental floss and toothpaste. The dismay almost gave him a heart attack when he discovered some of the villagers using their toothbrushes to clean the hard-to-reach places on their griddles. After everyone had their chuckles at his expense, one kind soul pointed out that the villagers were not only waiting until he appeared to perform their cleaning, but the toothbrushes were old ones, not the new ones he was handing out. He got his revenge by pointing out to some of his patients that while his treatment would cure their problem, it would make certain of their body parts fall off. This was funny until villagers stopped coming, and he had to explain that he was kidding. Then it turned out that they knew he was kidding, and were getting him back. The villagers and their dentist developed a strange relationship.

# Chapter 18

Two days before the visitors were scheduled to leave, a message was delivered to Girma as he made his rounds of the village. The truck, with its load of empty gas cylinders, t-shirts, honey, and other goods destined for the city did not arrive as scheduled. The owner of the market where the honey was sold was particularly upset because his customers preferred the Izersteling honey, and it sold quickly. He had told everyone it would be there that day. Where was it?

Pvt. Rada had been with the truck and possessed a satellite phone which he could have used to call Sgt. Etefu if the truck had broken down or there had been some other delay. This did not bode well, and tension spread through the village as word spread of the missing truck. Girma selected three of his men. Sgt. Etefu chose three of his men. Izersteling and Tsege Mariam both went on alert. Jeff and Danielle had a brief argument with Robert, Michelle, and Sophie. The result was that they were reluctantly allowed to accompany the two vehicles that roared out of Izersteling, passed through Tsege Mariam, and continued on toward the city. Mike traveled with them as well.

At a distance outside the second village, Girma's men deployed drones, one to each side of the vehicles, searching the area on either side of the road. As the charge ran low on each drone, it was recovered for a battery change while another took its place. Twenty miles from the villages, they found where the truck had been ambushed. An attempt had been made to clean the area, but there were still traces of broken glass and bits of debris. Even more telling was the circle of birds hovering over a copse of trees to the north less than a mile from the road.

A drone sent in that direction spotted the truck on the far side of the trees parked next to an old sedan. Four men were seated on the ground near the two vehicles, spooning honey from jars into their mouths as they laughed and joked. Two bodies lay in a shallow ravine nearby. While one man remained with each vehicle, the police, soldiers, Jeff, Danielle, and Mike spread out and made their way silently toward the trees. The twins each carried a borrowed sniper rifle; Mike an AK-47, the same as the other men. Once at the tree line, they converged on the two vehicles.

Jeff and Danielle ghosted ahead of the others. It was a good thing they did. There was a fifth man, obviously not as complacent as the other four, who was keeping a lookout toward the south and the road. He was uneasy enough to keep watch, but not smart enough to move far enough away to be able to see the road. He had no opportunity to grow any wiser as the twins found him and disabled him silently, tie-wrapping him where he lay and signaling the others that the way was clear. Then, following a brief but silent conversation between Mike and Sgt. Etefu, they were instructed to take out two of the four remaining.

Short seconds later, their rifles fired, and two of the men fell over. Before the remaining two could even move, the soldiers, police, Mike, and the twins rushed them, and it was all over. The story was not difficult to extract. After weeks of the truck making its frequent trips to the city to deliver goods for sale and pick up items for the village, the men had decided to steal the truck and whatever was in it and sell the truck and its contents themselves. They were smart enough to plan the ambush, but not smart enough to realize what would the result would be if they followed through with their plan. That would change as word of what happened to them made its way around, and the village beefed up security on the truck to make it not worth someone's effort to steal it. The contents of the truck were nice, but just not that valuable in a single delivery.

Meanwhile, everyone stared at the two bodies in the shallow ravine. Pvt. Rada would not be flirting with any more of the women in the villages. If this had happened the previous year, Jeff and Danielle would have barely been able to keep their rage in check. Now, they were just sad. One thing that helped with their sorrow was the story the private had told them of his conversion to Christianity and the change it had made in his life. His flirting had changed to more serious courting, and he would have made one of the women a fine husband.

They hadn't known the other man. He was new to the village, a quiet and competent worker who labored in the fields and could repair anything mechanical, including the truck, tractors, and Pastor Ezera's motorcycle. He was a church member, but a loner, and had no family that anyone knew about. There was probably some history there, but no one knew what it was.

The three prisoners were loaded in the back of the truck with two soldiers as guards, and it continued on the road to the city with another soldier driving the car, which would be sold with the proceeds going to the two villages. Pvt. Rada and the other villager were loaded carefully in the two vehicles that would be returning to Izersteling. The two thieves who had been killed were also loaded in the truck to be turned over to the police in the city along with the prisoners. It was a sad and angry group that returned to the village.

When the two vehicles reached the village, there followed a time of mourning and grief followed by anger and outrage and then some fear. Really, it had only been a matter of time until something like this happened, with the truck making regular runs in both directions loaded with goods to sell in the city or goods for the people in the villages. Long stretches of the road were desolate, between villages and far from any patrol by authorities. Girma sat down with Sgt. Etefu to plan the security of future trips. The participants would be much more alert. And there would be more of them; at least four. There would be regular communication between the truck and the village so a disruption wouldn't take so long to discover. And life moved on.

The funeral for the two men was held the next day. Pastor Ezera led a beautiful service under the partly cloudy sky, with the entire village present along with many from Tsege Mariam. The visitors were there as well. Grandmother stood beside her son, the headman, with Jeff and Danielle on her other side. When the service ended, she said, "It is well with their souls," turned, and made her way slowly back to the clinic where the people seeking treatment waited patiently on the shaded veranda. Some of Girma's men had patrolled the village during the service, but the town was quiet. Anyone who might have taken advantage of the empty village to do mischief thought better of it, considering the present mood of the villagers.

The following day, all the visitors, American and Australian, loaded their luggage into the two SUV's and, following the truck with its driver and three soldiers and their own driver/escorts, wound their way to the city and the airport for the flights home. As they stood by the vehicles saying goodbye, Danielle sighed, "I'll miss Pvt. Rada. He was a mess, but he was fun to be around." Sgt. Etefu nodded. "There is a hole, but it will be filled by someone. Just like Sebhat took the place of Village Sunshine. As always, the sergeant left them with a local proverb: "Don't blame God for creating the tiger -- instead, thank him for not giving it wings." The twins both shook their heads at him, shouldered their bags, and headed into the terminal. The others gave him their own goodbyes and followed.

# Chapter 19

Twenty and a half hours later, Jeff, Danielle, and Sophie were clearing customs, and an hour after that, they were sitting in the Armstrong kitchen, munching on Chinese takeout, lunch for the travelers while those who had stayed in Australia enjoyed a late dinner and listened to the stories and descriptions of all they had seen and done. Lucy tried to make them promise to take her the next trip, but Jeff said, "Maybe when you're ten", and she sat there in a huff for a while. She couldn't keep it up for long, though; she was too happy to have the three, especially Jeff, home again.

It wasn't until she was tucked safely in bed, after two bedtime stories from Jeff because he had missed so many, that the story of the hijacked truck was told. Sophie had not been told the whole story, and Jeff and Danielle didn't tell it now; only that the truck had been recovered with two of the thieves killed and the others captured, but too late to save Pvt. Rada and the other villager. Later, as Jake and Sophie prepared for bed, he said, "Jeff and Danielle aren't saying much about the recovery of the truck. Why did you let them go?" She answered, "You know what they're like. They've trained for these sorts of things their entire lives, and it just seems natural to let them do it. Robert and Michelle weren't happy about it, but they were okay with letting them go." As an afterthought, she added, "At least Mike went with them."

At church the next morning, Jeff and Danielle were asked to

tell about the trip. Anticipating the request, they had prepared a short video presentation which showed the two villages before the first well was dug and then the changes over the following visits. They did not include anything about the raid their first visit or the ambush of the truck this time. Pastor Shane asked, on behalf of the entire congregation, if the change between the first visit and the last was all just because of a water well. Jeff said, "No. Our church at home was much more involved, sending gifts and making microloans available." Danielle added, "Once they had the chance, though, they took the opportunities and ran with them. These two villages may have more breaks than some others, but just having water available without spending most of every day hauling it, and clean water at that, makes a world of difference. The next big difference is not having to find something to burn for cooking and other uses."

The church buzzed, and after the morning service ended, Jeff and Danielle were swamped with members who wanted to know the cost of a well and what, if anything, they had done about fuel for heating. When they heard how little it cost to dig a well, many members thought it was something the church, if not individual classes could take on. Jake, Sophie, and the other members of the Armstrong family finally surrounded the twins and escorted them out of the building, leaving behind a buzz of conversation. Zoe commented, "Well, you have things stirred up. Again. Although it would be really cool if our church could sponsor a well, and the village turned out anywhere near as well as those in your video."

Lucy agreed with a hearty, "Good on you, mates!" She was very proud of her Mummum, and, of course, Jeff and Danielle. She was also very proud of the hippo plush toy one of the villagers had created for her. The little girl's picture and the short videos on Jeff's phone had made her a favorite, and she would receive quite a welcome anytime she was allowed to visit. Which wouldn't be for a few years yet.

The next few days were spent returning to a normal lifestyle.

Jeff and Danielle took up their running, swimming, and gym routines. They visited the shooting range regularly, keeping to their strange method of making sure no one knew how well they could shoot. The one member who had figured out their method still amused himself, pulling their targets from the trash and laughing over them to the bemusement of his fellow club members who still thought the twins were a major disappointment to their plans to win the competition with other clubs.

Jeff and Danielle also continued their weekly visit to the various locations filming their movie. Wednesday had become their day to check on progress and review the video collected so far. Although it had only been in production for a little more than a month, the movie was coming along nicely.

The young actors and actresses were a funny group. The Steinfield and Leighton families, the children who would be portraying Jeff and Danielle, ages six through twelve, got along so well they might as well have been one large family. When eight-year-old Merit balked when the time came to cut her hair for the role, eight-year-old Ashton cut his first, in front of her, by himself, before anyone realized what he was up to. She was so impressed, she would have copied him and cut her own, but wiser heads, including her sisters, her parents, and her hair designer stopped her. As it was, the director had to wait two weeks before Ashton's hair grew long enough to trim into a proper military style haircut. He had neglected to use any type of guard on the hair trimmers and basically shaved his head; not the look the movie called for.

# Chapter 20

The weekend after their return from Africa, the family visited a hospital in Adelaide. They decided to fly by commercial air. The travel time, with the early check in to clear security both ways, would be about the same as using their jump pilot, but two hours in the air sounded better than five. On the other hand, Jeff and Danielle could have added some more flight time. On the other, other hand, what would be fun for them would be boring for the others, so commercial jet it was.

The trip went smoothly with an early Friday morning arrival that gave them time for a city tour including a boat ride and an evening spent visiting the city's nightlife for dinner. No one recognized Jeff and Danielle outside the hospital, not on the city tour, nor at dinner. There were no impromptu band accompaniments and no rescues. In fact, nothing out of the ordinary happened at all, and upon their return home Sunday morning, the trip was declared a complete success. Lucy capped it off with, "Good one, mates!"

School resumed the next day, and all the problems missed over the weekend made their appearance. Ever since their first day of school, Jeff and Danielle had had problems with cliques. These were different from anything they had experienced at their one year of high school in the US. There, the cliques were the popular kids, who might or might not also include the "mean girls"; jocks, geeks, emos, etc. The twins usually moved effortlessly between these groups, being friendly to everyone who wasn't actively against them.

Here, the groups seemed to have keyed off their activity since they had arrived, particularly the events in the grocery store. One group considered Jeff and Danielle heroes for the things they had done. This group hung on their every word, whether in the classroom or sitting outside on the grass for lunch. Another group thought they were American cowboys, not in a good way, for the same things. They made snide comments about the actions in the grocery store and the later rescue of the children from the car, saying anyone could have done them, and it didn't take Americans. It was almost as though they were jealous.

Still another group thought they were a pair of thugs, especially after the incident with the little girl who was injured. Jeff and Danielle might have almost agreed with this group. Danielle had acted impulsively, and the parents had almost lost custody of their daughter over the incident. Thanks to the twins' intervention through their lawyer, this had been averted, and on the positive side, the parents had taken several weeks of anger management classes which had been good for them and their daughter both.

There were other factors at play. Some were between the haves and the have-nots. One group was proud that their school uniforms were brand new each year. They made fun behind their backs of the students whose families bought them used from the school store. Of these, some were at least mildly ashamed that their parents couldn't afford all new school uniforms each year. There was another group, however, who were simply cost conscious and thought people were insane to put out good money each year for school uniforms they would probably only wear for one year, if that, before outgrowing them. It wasn't as though they were designer clothes that could be worn anywhere. Not that the uniforms couldn't be worn anywhere. But they weren't the sort of thing one would wear to, for example, a wedding. Sometimes the discussions he overheard made Jeff's head swim.

And while the uniforms might be all the same, the accessories weren't. There were Rolex and Cartier watches, and there were inexpensive plastic watches; diamond studs and inexpensive earrings; top of the line makeup from Ulta and inexpensive products from the corner grocery; plain phone cases and LifeProof phone cases; expensive haircuts and those from the local barber. Those with money would always find a way to let it be known. Most of it wasn't an intentional put down of those who didn't spend as much. It was just that those with money spent it.

Most of the school, thankfully, fit none of these groups, and went about their business treating the twins no different than anyone else, as far as foreign exchange students went, at least. While this group was not as vocal or demonstrative as the other groups, they were by far the majority. Even they kept an eye open for what might happen next. You never knew with the two Americans. Any day could be an exciting one.

The principal seemed in danger of a stroke or heart attack. It was a rare week when Jeff and Danielle were not called into his office, either for congratulations, as in for the rescue of the family from the car, or a dressing down, as in for their disagreement with the biology teacher over the supposed facts of evolution. Really, it was hardly their fault that outside of the different interpretations possible over historical science vs observational science[8], it was amazing that some of the information was still in the textbook since it was even condemned by leading evolutionists as false and misleading[9].

The class listened to these exchanges with interest, and the instructor was on one hand happy because the students no longer stared at him or at their desks with glazed over eyes. On the other hand, his day of lecturing, with the students taking notes, was disrupted. He had many after class discussions with the twins, and although neither convinced the other, they were enlightening. And, evolution was not a large section of the biology textbook anyway.

The principal was also not happy when he found out about their tattoos. Someone had spotted them one early morning at the swim center. Danielle's swimsuit and Jeff's sleeveless shirt both left their tattoos clearly visible, and this someone had taken photos with their phone and posted them to the school website. The pictures may or may not have been meant to cause them problems as a video of their swim style was also posted, and it was impressive. The teacher monitoring the postings saw no reason to delete them and only later, after a lecture from the principal, had an 'Uh oh' moment about the pictures with the tattoos. The pictures were subsequently taken down, but by then, copies were everywhere.

Jeff and Danielle were never sure after their meeting with the principal if he didn't like the fact that they had tattoos, or that the tattoos were of crosses. He never came right out and said that, but they were familiar enough with his dislikes to make the connection. It wasn't as though they were in their school uniforms, but they had been on the news often enough that when the pictures showed up on students' social media, many people recognized them. They received some comments at school, but as with everything else, if the comments were kind, they thanked the giver, and if they were unkind, they ignored them. Their friends were more upset over the comments than they were.

Jeff and Danielle were not particularly good at chemistry, biology, or physics except in specific areas. In chemistry, they could make explosives and other weapons out of many common household items, but only their excellent memories brought them safely through the shoals of the various chemistry tests. In physics, they could calculate the trajectory of a .50 bullet using different gun powders with different burn rates and varying wind conditions, or calculate the impact point of an artillery or mortar shell, but again, only their ability to memorize large amounts of information secured passing grades. Ditto for biology.

They were excellent at math and languages and enjoyed

history. Thanks to Tina, the foundation's IT expert and head of their website and IT security team, both Jeff and Danielle were above average in their computer skills. These all brought them approval from some cliques, disparaging remarks from others. They thanked the one and ignored the other. One thing all the cliques had learned, though, was not to touch the twins aggressively, especially Danielle. After two boys had gone home "not feeling well" after an instantaneous elbow or finger jab for something as simple as flinging an arm around her shoulders, she acquired a clear zone around her person. It was interesting to watch the twin's progress through the hallways as space magically opened in front of them and closed behind them.

Jeff and Zoe tried to avoid any apparent interest in each other, and although no one observed anything obvious such as sitting together or holding hands, it was clear to their friends that there was a tension between the two, if only from the way they avoided contact or the way they spoke so formally to each other. When one of their friends asked Danielle how the two acted at home, she shrugged and replied, "The same as they do here."

She didn't mention that even when the two told Lucy a story at bedtime, a made up one since she could read her own stories now, they sat on opposite sides of her bed, seamlessly melding the story together. Lucy just thought the story was cool, but Danielle, sometimes leaning against the doorframe to watch, noticed the interaction. And hoped that she and Henry would possibly have the ability to interact so well. It didn't seem likely. Jeff saw Zoe every day; Danielle only saw Henry sporadically. The school year continued to rush by.

# Chapter 21

Lucy sat at the kitchen table cracking eggs and separating the whites for chocolate souffles. She wasn't performing too badly. There might be a few pieces of egg shell in the mix, and possibly a little egg yolk was ending up in the whites, but Jeff declared himself satisfied with the result although he did remove the pieces of shell. (And all of the egg yolk since the whites would not beat up properly if even a tiny bit of yolk was present. Really!) He started the little girl to work with the electric mixer, adding the other ingredients and beating the egg whites into a shaving cream lather while he melted the chocolate and prepared the egg yolks and other recipe components.

The entire family was in the kitchen, watching with interest. It happened that dessert souffles were a rarely enjoyed favorite of the entire family. Few restaurants made them, and Sophie had never tried. When Zoe and Sean became aware, pretty much by accident, over a casual lunch conversation one day at school with their friends, that not only did Jeff and Danielle know how to make souffles but didn't consider it particularly difficult, they immediately clamored for them to make the treat, that evening if possible. Aware of the items that were and were not available in the Armstrong kitchen, the twins agreed with the caveat that a trip to the shops would be necessary.

After school, the four walked the few extra blocks past their home to the store. Since their somewhat rocky beginning the previous year, there had been no further incidents; no girls to rescue, no criminals to apprehend. Jeff and Danielle were sure that the employees kept a wary, possibly hopeful eye on them each time they visited. Management undoubtedly wished that nothing would happen, but the twins thought the younger employees might be hoping that something exciting would. No matter. They bought the additional eggs, chocolate, and raspberries needed for the dessert and finished the walk home with nothing unusual to mark the trip.

Upon entering the house, it was immediately apparent that Lucy had been told about the upcoming treat as she ran screaming to greet them with, "Yaaay! Soufals! Yaaay! Soufals!" This was followed by, "May I help make them? Is it hard? Mummum says it's hard. She says we have to be really quiet while they cook. How quiet is really quiet? Do I have to take off my shoes and tiptoe?" Her shoes already absent, not uncommon as they seemed to disappear from her feet the instant she was in the house, she performed exaggerated tiptoe steps down the hall toward the kitchen as the others followed to put away the groceries before dropping off their school backpacks and changing into casual clothes.

Zoe and Danielle were responsible for dinner that evening, and they sat at the kitchen table discussing the menu and timing with Jeff. Since the souffles needed to be served right out of the oven, timing was important. As soon as dinner was on the table and ready to eat, the tasty dessert could begin to cook, and if there wasn't too much delay over eating, the timer should go off just about the time they finished. Lingering conversations could take place as they enjoyed the souffles, assuming anyone was interested in talking. Timing settled, Zoe and Danielle began food preparations, and Jeff and Lucy started on the souffles.

Lucy took a second when Jeff's back was turned, reached over, grabbed one of the pieces of 72 percent cacao, and popped it in her mouth. This was immediately followed by a face, which Jeff spotted as soon as he turned back around. With an idea in mind as to what had happened, he asked, "What did you do?" She squeaked, "I ate a piece of chocolate." Jeff shook his head. "That isn't chocolate candy, sweetie. It's baking chocolate. It doesn't have any sugar in it." She said accusingly, "You could have told me before I ate it, mate. I don't think I want one of the soufals." He asked innocently, "How was I supposed to know you would try to eat it? They will taste fine, especially with the chocolate raspberry sauce we'll be making next. And it's souffle, not soufal."

He let her stir the egg yolks into the chocolate mixture while he made the chocolate raspberry sauce, then taught her to fold the egg whites into the mixture. When that was ready, he checked with Danielle and Zoe to see where the rest of dinner stood, and, seeing they were placing the last of the food on the table, poured the souffle mixture into the buttered and sugared ramakins and popped them in the oven.

Soon the family was seated at the table, helping their plates or passing food around the table, with one ear toward the kitchen waiting for the ding of the timer. Quickly enough, though, they were immersed in the discussion of everyone's day, and it came as a surprise when the awaited sound rang out. Lucy was immediately out of her seat and racing into the kitchen, Jeff close on her heels to ensure she didn't grab something hot.

Nudging her away from the oven with his hip, he removed the cookie sheet holding the ramakins and set it on the stove. One by one, he placed each of them on a dessert plate with a spoon and finished them off with a sprinkling of powdered sugar because, well, a thousand calories for the dessert just wasn't quite enough. Danielle and Sophie joined him in the kitchen as Lucy rushed back to her seat and climbed in, ready to pounce. They brought in six of the plates and arranged them in front of everyone except Lucy and Jeff, but before the shocked girl could complain, Jeff returned with the last two as Danielle brought a gravy bowl containing the sauce.

One by one, she glided from plate to plate, using the spoon to punch a hole in the center of each souffle and pouring in a portion of the mixture, scooping the last bit into Jeff's. Soon there was no sound except for contented sighs and Lucy's exuberant, "Yum!" In no time, the dishes were clean. Sophie commented, "That wasn't as difficult as I thought it would be." Jeff smiled. "They're really pretty easy. And they make good main dishes, too: ham and cheese or chicken and almond. Takes a lot of eggs, though." Leaning back serenely in her seat, hands clasped over her stomach, Lucy said, "I like eggs. We should raise some chickens." The meal was declared a success, but the left-over raspberries led to the great refrigerator cleanup.

# Chapter 22

That Saturday, Jeff and Zoe cleaned the refrigerator. It hadn't been the original plan, but outside, the day was gray and dismal, alternating between rain and drizzle. Jeff and Danielle began their morning with a twelve-mile run, returning drenched and muddier than someone would expect from a trek through a city. Runnels of dirt washed off bare patches by the rain flowed onto the sidewalks and into the street, and the twins splashed it on themselves and each other as they swept through. Long-sleeved shirts, cargo pants, and boonie hats were liberally sprayed with Scotchgard, but it wasn't enough to keep the twins dry for the duration of the run, and eventually cold rainwater wormed its way through clothes and hats and dripped down their necks. Stoically, they continued on the morning's trail.

Officer Cameron and his partner watched from the comfort of their police car as the twins ghosted silently past, lifting hands in a wave. At the time, the two officers were parked near a coffee shop, taking a short break between calls, and the officers lifted cups of steaming coffee in response. The partner commented, "Those two are a bit insane, out in this weather. Don't they ever take a day off?" Officer Cameron laughed. "They don't train on Sunday. I think they call this 'interesting training conditions'. I guess they thought it was too wet today for the swimming pool." Both officers chuckled at the joke, finished their drinks, and continued their patrol.

Jeff and Danielle returned by a different route, crept through the rear gate, splashed across the soggy back yard, and entered the hallway, trying to bring as little weather in with them as possible. Standing in two dripping puddles, they removed their muddy combat boots and left them by the back door with their soggy socks draped over them. Lucy ran down the hall from the laundry room with two towels over her arms, Zoe following behind. "How was the run, mates? You're dripping wet!" Zoe added, "I can't believe you went out in this weather. You might as well have gone to the swimming pool. You wouldn't be any wetter."

Jeff and Danielle accepted the towels from Lucy and scrubbed their heads and faces after dropping their boonie hats on top of the boots. He said, "It was a great run. We passed Officer Cameron. He and his partner waved their coffees at us." Lucy sniffed. "They should have given their coffees to you." Danielle ruffled her hair. "It would have been tough to drink it while we were running, sweetie. And I'm sure they needed it more than we did. There probably isn't much going on in this weather." Hair mostly dry, Jeff's anyway, they dried their feet, and headed for their bedrooms to shower before breakfast.

Clean, dry, and dressed in dry clothes, they stopped by the laundry room long enough to drop their wet things in the wash before popping into the kitchen to help cook breakfast. As Sophie opened the refrigerator to remove eggs, butter, milk, and oranges, she made the discovery that resulted in the cleaning: someone had shoved leftovers on the shelf under the meat drawer after dinner, and the new items had tipped up the leftover raspberries from earlier in the week, resulting in sticky red juice spilling down the back of the refrigerator, past the bottom shelf, and under the crisper drawer. Sophie gasped, "What in the world?" as the pulled-out drawer brought the red smear into view, and kneeling to peer inside, she gaped at the full extent of the mess. Fully half of the refrigerator would need the drawers and shelves removed to make the gunk accessible.

Glancing over to determine the cause of the gasp, Danielle immediately located the problem and said, "Jeff and I can clean that up after brekkie." Lucy immediately spoke up. "Nu-uh! You promised to give me a guitar lesson after brekkie, mate!" Sean said, "I'd be glad to help, but I promised to help at school setting up the new shelves in the library." Jake added, "I promised to drive him over." Sophie glared at them all, and Zoe said, I'll help Jeff. It won't take long." Everyone except Lucy shared a look. Then, Sophie said, "Fine. I'll continue with the laundry." Preparation of breakfast continued, and soon the family was sitting down to their new, typical, Saturday morning meal of scrambled eggs, bacon, and waffles.

The meal finished and the dishes washed and put away or rinsed and in the dishwasher, the others scattered to their various tasks, and Jeff and Zoe set to work on the cleanup. As they removed items from each shelf or drawer and set them on the table or a counter, Jeff would remove the shelf or drawer and wash it in the sink while Zoe scrubbed the congealed raspberry juice from the back wall using a bucket of warm water and a sponge. As they worked, they carried on a self-conscious conversation about school, church, and their friends; anything to keep their minds off the fact that they were alone together in a room.

Occasionally, as they removed food from the refrigerator or returned it, their arms or hands would brush together, and each time it was as though a spark jumped between them. Sophie, passing the kitchen from time to time as she gathered clothes or towels to be washed or returned them to their proper place, glanced in and had to shake her head as she watched the two young people trying so hard to act as if they were not affected by the other's presence, striving to avoid contact. She was proud of them, and also sad and concerned, knowing that in all too few months, Jeff and Danielle would be returning home.

When the job was finished, the bucket and sponge cleaned and returned to the laundry room along with the cloths the two had used, Zoe turned to face Jeff and said, "I'm really glad you and Danielle came to Australia this year, and that you're staying with us." Jeff, thrilled to his core, responded, "I'm glad we came, too." Danielle, passing by at that moment, continued on to the room she shared with Zoe, thinking to herself, "We're going to have to come up with a solution to this." When Zoe entered the room a short while later, she sat on her bed with her face in her hands and said in despair, "What am I going to do? What is Lucy going to do?" Danielle gave her a serious look but said serenely, "When the time is right, there will be a solution."

# Chapter 23

The schedule called for it, and Sebastian and his team were hard at work preparing for the movie's concert scene. Jeff and Danielle made inquiries back home and collected quite a bit of video from the actual concert that could be used for background to show the size of the concert. This would be the event where many of the crew members would be added to the closeup scenes which would be shown during the credits. The director wanted to shoot this while the weather outside still resembled summer since the concert had taken place over the 4th of July holiday in the US. He could have made it work in the dead of an Australian winter, but it would have been harder for the actors to appear hot and sweaty and enjoying the cooling mist stations in milder weather.

Jeff, and especially Danielle, spent time with Alexander and Bobbie, preparing them for their roles on the stage. The first, smaller concert at the street fair, had been videoed with bits of several songs and lots of shots of the band and the audience. For the concert, though, outside of the shots of them moving around the concert grounds, the main focus would be on the last song, and Danielle wanted Bobbie's guitar playing to be as realistic as it could be with her not actually being Danielle.

Fortunately, among all the actual footage they had collected of the concert, there were a couple of closeups of Danielle's hands as she played, and the person whose role it was to keep up with such things took copious notes to make sure Bobbie's hands and arms appeared as close to Danielle's as possible: no different fingernail polish colors, no different scars or other distinguishing marks, etc. Bobbie liked the guitar, a plus, but her fingers could not move over the frets like spiders the way Danielle's could, a minus. Still, in the weeks since Danielle had been working with her, the young girl had improved immensely, a combination of natural talent and patient tutelage.

The voices would be young Jeff and Danielle, dubbed into the soundtrack. Alexander and Bobbie spent additional time practicing lip-syncing to the songs, singing them over and over while they waited for their part in a scene or studied or exercised. An additional bonus was that the faith and encouragement filled songs settled firmly in their hearts and minds, providing a firm foundation for their young convictions.

The four girls were also developing a soft New Orleans accent, just like Danielle's, while the four boys now spoke in Jeff's light Texas drawl. By the time the movie was complete, they might have to spend some serious time recovering their Australian accents. The crew, however, were often amused at the typical words such as brekkie or mates breaking out in the new accents. In fact, the biggest problem for the children was not the accents but throwing in the odd Australian word or phrase, causing a reshoot of the scene. Rarely more than once, however. Many times, they did not even realize they had made the error until the recording was halted and the error pointed out, resulting in a rueful laugh and a promise not to do it again. In that particular scene.

The day arrived, clear and sunny. The temperature was warm but not over 100. Heat lamps were used to add authentic looking sweat. Cameras recorded the bus arriving and the actors playing the members from 2nd Street Bible Church exiting. Some of these were crew members who would be filmed for their addition to the credits. Only a few voices were carefully recorded. In general, there were far too many references to eskys, sunnies, and thongs. Alexander and Bobbie were videoed walking through one of the misting stations but then had to be dried up and warmed back up with blankets. In the moderate temperatures, the chilling air was more like being stuck in a freezer.

They spent some time in the booth with the actors playing the group from 2nd Street Bible Church selling CD's as the cameras recorded it. Finally, on the stage, the "band" pretended to play their final song. This would be mixed with actual concert crowd footage as well as the cheering crew acting as concert goers. Then everyone took a break to eat dinner and wait for dark to video the final scenes of the fireworks show and the bus and cars leaving for home. When Jeff and Danielle reviewed this later in the day, they were completely satisfied with the results, and unless someone spotted something that shouldn't be there, the concert scene was a wrap.

# Chapter 24

The weekend after the videoing of the concert, the Armstrong family flew to the Gold Coast to visit a hospital there. Even though they had flown in the jump plane to Brisbane, which was farther, they weighed the time involved and decided to travel by commercial air. Jeff and Danielle would have enjoyed getting in some more flight time, but it didn't seem fair to double the flight time for the others. It was just as well. The pilot was tied up all weekend with new students on their first jumps anyway. The flight departed late Friday evening after school, dinner, and homework, leaving everyone with a completely free weekend.

A cab drove them to their hotel which was located an easy ten-minute walk from the hospital. As they checked in, the night manager recognized Jeff and Danielle immediately, as did her twelve-year-old daughter who was reading quietly in the lobby when they entered. The tall, pale girl with bright blue eyes stood as the group entered and approached them slowly as her mother watched from behind the check-in counter. Jeff and Danielle knelt and hugged the girl as the others moved on, Zoe dragging Lucy by the hand, as she wanted to stay by Jeff.

The girl introduced herself as Katie, and sobbed happily on Danielle's shoulder, telling the two of them that she had missed them in Brisbane, and was so happy they had traveled to the Gold Coast as well. When the rest of the group took their room cards and headed for the elevators with the luggage, Katie's mom told Sophie she would let the twins know the room numbers. Soon, Katie was in possession of her nickname and had approved of her sketch. In addition, she convinced Jeff, Danielle, and her mom to let the twins take her with them to the hospital the next day so she could exchange information with the other patients and begin her own patch collection. When Jeff and Danielle left to find their rooms, they left behind a very happy mother and daughter.

Upstairs, Jeff and Danielle found everyone in Jake and Sophie's room. Their room was on the end with large windows on two sides as well as a breakfast nook, microwave, full size refrigerator/freezer, kitchen sink, and large counter space, most of which was unneeded. Lucy was standing in front of the windows pointing out the city lights to Sophie and Zoe, while Jake and Sean sat on the sofa in front of the large screen television commenting on a rugby match that was underway somewhere, or possibly recorded; they weren't certain. It was rugby. That was enough.

Mindful of the busy day ahead, Jeff and Sean said goodnight and headed for their room across the hall. Danielle, Zoe, and Lucy did the same and were soon asleep in the room next door. The night passed quietly and uneventfully, and after breakfast the next morning, the family, accompanied by Katie, walked to the nearby hospital for the usual round of sketches, nicknames, and website access. After the last goodbyes to the hospital staff, the group returned to the hotel to drop off Katie before boarding a shuttle for their private city tour.

It was on the shuttle that Zoe, sitting across the aisle from Jeff, reached across and ran her hand through his short haircut. Danielle stared in surprise, as did Jake and Sophie, who were sitting behind them. The two had been so careful to avoid touching each other, even bumping into one another when passing in the hall. Zoe said, "You should let your hair grow out some." Lucy, sitting beside Jeff and staring out the window at the passing city, immediately agreed. "Yeah, mate! You should at least let it grow as long as Poppop's." Jeff raised an eyebrow. "It's been this short since I was seven." Danielle added, "My hair was that short until I was thirteen. Then I started letting it grow." Zoe turned back to Jeff. "Why didn't you start letting yours grow, too?" He shrugged. "I was used to it by then." She smiled. "So, it's this short because it has always been this short?" Jeff answered with a questioning, "Yes?"

Lucy began chanting softly, "Grow your hair! Grow your hair!" Zoe joined, then Danielle, then Sophie. Jake and Sean shared a, "I'm not getting involved in this" look, and returned to watching the city pass by, keeping one eye on Jeff for further developments. Jeff said, "How about if I say I'll let it start growing, but the first time someone grabs it in a fight, I'm cutting it back off?" Lucy and Zoe started to object, but Danielle leaned around Zoe to interject, "That's what I said. I've never had to cut mine." Jeff rolled his eyes, but said, "Okay. I'll let it grow some. Not as long as Danielle's, though." Lucy asked, "As long as Uncle Sean's?" Sean's hair was surfer long, and the bangs fell over his eyes, requiring the occasional casual flip to move them away. Danielle laughed, and Jeff gave a solemn, "No." Zoe asked, "How about as long as Dad's?"

Jake's hair was cut in a conservative style, perhaps a couple of inches long. Jeff gave the man a casual onceover and received a sympathetic smile in return. "Okay. We can try that." Danielle joined the other females in applause, adding, "Maybe I'll just take your hair clippers to remove the temptation." He gave her a look and murmured, "Uhuh." The point won, everyone returned to the tour. Their bus driver and guide had listened with humor to the discussion behind him and added to the fun by pointing out every hair salon they passed for the next several blocks until Jeff said, "I'll give you twenty dollars if you don't point out any more hair salons," and surprised the driver even more when he gave it to him on top of the generous tip Jake had supplied at the end of the tour. The driver laughed and objected, but Jeff insisted, and he gratefully took it, looking forward to the take out he and his girlfriend would enjoy at Jeff's expense and the fun of sharing the story. He would, however, have no answer to her question as to why Jeff's hair was so short or why Danielle's had been the same at one time.

Their driver dropped them off at the entrance to Dreamworld, and they entered to sympathetic looks from the attendants since they would only have a couple of hours at the park. The group strode briskly around, Lucy on Jeff's shoulders, and, due to the light crowd, were able to enjoy many of the rides, although they skipped all of the shows. And the food. Two hours later, they were among the last to leave, climbing aboard their shuttle just as the sun was setting. From there they rode here and there, looking at places from the outside, agreeing that, like Brisbane, they had to come back when they could spend a weekend during the day, maybe in a few weeks.

Their driver left them in front of an Italian restaurant and took his leave, happy with his day and the story he had to tell his girlfriend. In the restaurant, everyone noticed that Zoe and Jeff sat together, not totally unusual as it had occasionally happened before, and the two didn't make a big deal out of it. But it had happened a lot today, on the bus, now, and at Dreamworld where it had been the two of them who took Lucy on all the children's rides. Something had happened since the cleaning of the refrigerator.

Dinner finished, they walked around for a while in the area near the beach before calling for a ride to take them back to their hotel. A well-earned night's sleep later, they were on the plane for home and back in church Sunday evening, telling their friends about the trip. Lucy seemed excited to tell people that Jeff was going to start growing his hair. After the third comment, he muttered to Danielle, "Seriously? You didn't get this when you grew yours back." Her only response was a knowing smile.

# Chapter 25

The next Wednesday, Jeff and Danielle were working with all four sets of actors at the gym. The young people were all good natured about the exercises they were being put through, considering it free training for their various sports. Some were more interested in certain regimens that others, such as inline skating or gymnastics or kendo. Everyone loved the hand to hand combat. No one liked lifting weights.

At the moment, as the Armstrong family, coaches, some crew and other cast members looked on, Jeff and Danielle were running the group through a kendo kata, first in slow motion, then faster and faster. For the movie, they only needed to be good enough for the videoing. No actual fighting took place until they were twelve. It was during the sword training that they realized Bobbie had no depth perception. No one expected great things in sports from a six-year-old, so her missteps were not out of the ordinary. Her eyesight was 20/20 in both eyes, but no one had ever tested to see if she used them both together, a necessity for depth perception.

After she missed badly on two practice lunges at him, Jeff stopped her and began asking some simple questions such as, "Which hand is farther away," as he held his hands in front of him from a distance of ten feet. She couldn't tell. Her sisters stared at her. None of them had ever noticed. Neither had her parents. She had already unconsciously developed several coping skills that helped her catch a thrown ball or frisbee, but it was not uncommon for her to reach for something and close her hand too soon, resulting in overturned glasses. Her family blamed this on six-year-old clumsiness. Now they knew better. An appointment was made with a specialist who worked with this sort of problem, and by the time the movie was completed, her eyes were normal. One of Jeff's greatest rewards from the movie was Bobbie's tearful hug and thankyou when she was declared cured.

None of the young people were allowed to try the complete obstacle course that Jeff and Danielle worked through almost every time they visited the gym. They could attempt pieces of it with spotters and supervision, but no one wanted to risk an injury unnecessarily that would slow down production of the movie. Jeff and Danielle were superb encouragers for the other training, though; even the unpopular weight training. Bobbie and Alexander were only allowed light weights for now for some toning and as a precursor for the more serious stuff; their serious work wouldn't begin until after the hospital scene. The other six were well on their way with the body sculpting, and were showing amazing results, which they were quite proud of, both boys and girls. The changes were obvious enough that people they knew but didn't see that often due to the movie schedule exclaimed when they ran into them unexpectedly.

Danielle wanted to teach them her favorite fighting move, the single-handed handstand and snap kick combination as well as her second favorite, the swarm up the opponent like a spider monkey and throw them move. These would require more strength and gymnastics training first, but it gave them a goal to pursue. They learned the more conventional unarmed combat moves Jeff and Daniele could teach them. The twins weren't that concerned that the young people become proficient; they just didn't want them doing the obvious such as winding up before throwing a punch or setting their legs before delivering a kick. The punch or kick didn't need to be delivered with that much power; special effects could handle the results. They just needed to look good during the delivery.

Another move they wanted the young actors to learn was spinning in midair; their waists would stay in place, but their feet would spin over their heads and return to the ground. The older children who were budding gymnasts could already perform the move, and the others were learning. Using cords strung from the ceiling was acceptable; again, special effects could straighten out the results, but they needed to be able to perform the move so it looked realistic. At least the six oldest. The youngest pair could start the process.

The gym became the place to hang out, to practice skills, run lines, exercise, receive their tutoring, do homework, and eat. Food crafts set up an area in one corner near an exhaust fan and were ready to prepare meals at any time of the day or night. No matter what time the training for a scene took place, meals or snacks could be requested. The Armstrong family had begun eating there on Wednesday's, exercising in the gym and wandering around to see what was taking place, working on their own homework, listening to the various discussions taking place about the movie.

Officer Cameron was often present as well, sometimes with Acacia, sometimes not. A police presence had become necessary as the traffic entering and leaving the gym had increased, drawing some notice. Everyone associated with the movie possessed a photo ID on a lanyard which would also unlock the front door. Everyone was required to badge in, everyone was required to badge out, for safety as well as security. No one but the twins and Jake knew that security was also monitored by Tina and her crew back in the US. The police officer and some of his off-duty friends were a constant presence when the gym was in use and became part of the cost of production. Their appearance when someone tried to tailgate their way in or knocked on the door for admittance worked wonders. And the regulars were allowed to use the gym as well so long as they didn't interfere with preparation for the movie or the twins' workouts. Or Lucy's rollerblading.

With so many people using the gym, Jeff and Danielle hired a cleaning crew to come in every evening. They wiped down all the equipment, swept, vacuumed, and mopped. The young husband and wife team were students at the university using the job to save money for a house. From all appearances, they were conscientious and quick workers. Tina confirmed this from the video feeds when the twins asked.

Today, gazing around at all the activity, Jeff and Danielle shared a smile. The gym had been an excellent investment, surpassing their wildest dreams. Their primary goal had been a place for themselves with hopes that the Armstrong family would join them. Now, with the actors and crew, Officer Cameron and the other off-duty police officers, and Harry and a few of the members from his team occasionally, the gym was a very busy place. It was hard to believe they had almost left it behind when they had decided to return to the US after that incident the previous year.

# Chapter 26

A few days later, on a mild Saturday, the Armstrong family climbed out of Jake's vehicle at a church several miles to the north of their home. The eldest daughter of the Moncrieffs, good family friends, was getting married this evening, so not only were the Armstrongs attending, along with Jeff and Danielle, but Lucy was to be a flower girl; a very excited flower girl. She had spent hours preparing for her role, being fitted for her dress, and attending the wedding rehearsal. Now was her time to shine, although it was emphasized more than once that this was the bride's day, not hers. She said she understood. The others doubted it.

Inside, they met the nervous father of the bride, faced with the marriage of the first of his children. He explained the obvious, that his wife and daughter were in the bride's room preparing for the wedding. His youngest daughter led Lucy away. Jeff gave her the 'I'm watching you look', two fingers to his eyes and then pointing at her, causing her to giggle, and the young girl with her to raise her eyes in alarm, followed by a frown at Jeff. Zoe and Danielle both gave him a look, and he said, "What? I was just telling her to not upstage the bride." They didn't believe him.

Ushers led them to their seats, where Sophie and Zoe discussed the wedding arrangements inside the church, while the males and Danielle debated the chances that the NSW Blues could win the upcoming State of Origin series. The rows slowly filled, and the moment arrived when music played and Lucy strolled solemnly down the aisle, tossing flowers gracefully left and right. Jeff overheard Zoe, who was sitting beside him, muttering to herself, "Please don't do a kata. Please don't do a kata."

Nothing unusual occurred, and the wedding proceeded smoothly, through the vows, the exchange of rings, the introduction of the newlywed couple, and their departure amidst cheers and applause. This was followed by a wait as the wedding party was photographed by their professional photographer. Friends clustered in groups to comment on the wedding, the bride's dress, the bridesmaids' dresses, Lucy, and so on. Others discussed the upcoming rugby match. Jeff, Danielle, and Zoe were part of a group of young people who discussed the future for the bride and groom and the massive change that was about to take place in their lives. And this was when Zoe discovered that Jeff's first kiss would be on his wedding day.

It came about when one teenager made a comment about the kiss after the minister said "You may now kiss the bride." She said, perhaps a bit cattily, "It certainly wasn't their first kiss," which brought a chuckle from most of the group. "Jeff remarked, "That's too bad," and the girl responded sarcastically, "Is that when you're going to get your first kiss?" When Jeff said, "Yes," the group went silent. The girl asked in disbelief, "You've never kissed a anyone?" Jeff shook his head no. She turned to Danielle for confirmation. "For real?" Danielle shook her head no as well. "We both decided that our first kiss will be on our wedding day when the minister says, "You may now kiss the bride.""

This led to a heated discussion into why, and how it was totally impractical, and no one could follow through on that decision unless they had absolutely no hope of dating anyone. The group turned to the twins questioningly. Danielle smiled and said, "Jeff broke up with his second girlfriend just before we left for Australia. He dated her for over a year and his first one for over two years. "And he never kissed either of them?" "No." "Are you sure?" "Yes."

The bridal party returned then, and the discussion ended as everyone welcomed the bride and groom, and the reception officially began. The cakes were cut, toasts were made, and the father of the bride led her out on the floor for the father/daughter dance. While all this was going on, Zoe's mind raced with this latest information about Jeff. She was already halfway in love with him, because of the way her treated her, the way he treated Lucy, and just the person he was.

Now, as everyone joined the newly married couple on the dance floor, Lucy ran up to Jeff demanding he dance with her and tugging on his hand. As she pulled him away, he reached back and took Zoe's hand, pulling her along as well. She laughed and joined him, quickly followed by Sean and Danielle, and the group moved gracefully and/or energetically around the edges.

Different styles of music played, some fast, some slow, and Jeff danced many of them with Zoe. Her parents observed this with some concern, noticing the glow on her face, but also the serene appearance of Jeff's, and they shared a look of apprehension at the still distant departure of the twins.

Moments later, Jeff's danger sense prickled. He glanced up at Danielle and noticed she had felt it as well. As they moved, they casually observed everyone in the room, but didn't spot anyone or anything out of the ordinary. The young man who had set off the alarm in their heads was turned away from them, laughing with some others in his group. His thoughts, though, were on Zoe, and they were not good thoughts. Having discovered that Lucy was Zoe's daughter, he was making assumptions about her character.

Later in the evening, the Armstrong family stood around the refreshment table, drinking punch and chatting. Lucy was waiting for Jeff to dance with her again. Zoe excused herself to visit the loo. Danielle said, "I'll go with you," and the two girls left. The loos were located down a hall that ran perpendicular to the one leading into the large room where the reception was being held. The loo was fairly large, built to accommodate more than one person at a time, and Zoe finished first, washed her hands, and stepped out the loo door several seconds ahead of Danielle, and straight into the arms of the young man who had followed them from the reception.

Before she could react, he had pushed her across the hallway and was trying to kiss her while his hands tried to roam. She was paralyzed, in spite of the training Jeff and Danielle had given her, trying to dodge his mouth and hold his hands away. Suddenly, his hands froze, his eyes opened wide, and he moved slowly away from her. Opening her eyes, Zoe saw Danielle behind him, one hand clutching the nerve in his right shoulder. Staring into her eyes, Zoe saw nothing but cold fury, and she squeaked, "Don't kill him!"

Danielle shook her head, and reached up to grab the nerve in his other shoulder with her left hand. He dropped to his knees, tears of pain rolling down his cheeks. She said, "The police can handle this." Zoe shook her head. "Please! No! I can't be the one to ruin their wedding! Please!" Danielle gazed at her for a moment, then, after one noticeably harder squeeze, released the boy, pushing him forward. His arms paralyzed from the shoulder down, he was unable to slow his fall as he slumped forward onto his face. Danielle picked him up by the back of his jacket, opened the door to the men's loo across the hall, and tossed him inside. She returned to Zoe and guided the girl slowly back to the reception, arguing with her the entire way.

"We should call the police. He'll try this with someone else, and I won't be there. It's not like you don't have a witness." Zoe shook her head. "No. He didn't do anything. It will all just be a horrible mess. I can't do that to Lucy. How would I ever explain it to her. You did something to him. He won't forget today." Danielle sighed. "We're going to regret this." Prophetic words.

They returned to the reception where Zoe put on a brave face.

Jeff immediately knew something was wrong, and he searched Danielle's face for the answer. She shrugged and signed, "Later." Soon after, the bride and groom made their escape, and the guests departed for their homes. Jake and Sophie were silent on the drive home, thinking about Jeff and Zoe. Zoe was silent, as were Jeff and Danielle. Lucy chattered enough for everyone, and Sean laughed with her, oblivious to the tension around him.

As soon as they arrived home, everyone headed for their rooms to change clothes from the wedding. Jeff and Danielle were into their usual clothes and in the back yard before the others had seriously begun to change. He glanced at her, and she explained what had happened, showing him the video from her bodycam. His eyes glowed with anger. He didn't say anything, but Danielle knew he was wondering why she hadn't at least ruptured the boy's kidneys, knowing also he would think it through and calm down in a bit, which he did. He said, "This won't be the end of it." Danielle nodded.

They returned to the house, and Danielle entered her and Zoe's room. The other girl was still standing in front of her dresser, still in her dress from the wedding, tears running down her face. She asked, "Jeff isn't going to track him down and kill him or anything, is he?" Danielle came up behind her and engulfed her in a hug. "No. Not unless he talks to you again. Or tries to touch you. Or looks at you. Or says anything about you. Even then, Jeff wouldn't kill him." Zoe gave her a look. "What would he do?" Danielle shrugged. "He doesn't really need both his arms. Or legs. Or other body parts." Zoe had to laugh at that, and some of her anxiety faded away. She said, "I really do like Jeff." Danielle said, "I know." Soon after, Lucy had her bedtime story, and the house was quiet.

135

# Chapter 27

On Monday, Jeff and Danielle made an appointment with their lawyer to discuss the incident at the wedding. They stopped by his office on the walk home from school. Zoe was not happy. Sean thought they were just stopping by for one of their occasional visits, but Zoe knew it was about the weekend. As she walked behind the two boys with Danielle, she hissed, "You can't tell him what happened!" The other girl explained, "This isn't about what he did to you. This is about what I did to him. Oliver needs a heads up in case he ends up defending me. I don't think the guy will say anything, but you never know. It's up to you if you want to pursue anything." Zoe wasn't happy, but she reluctantly agreed.

When Jeff and Danielle appeared in the lobby, the receptionist, now quite familiar with the pair, greeted them warmly and called Oliver to announce them. He appeared shortly, minus his jacket, shirt sleeves rolled up, slightly frazzled look on his face. Leading them back to his office, he said, "I've just come from court. There were some dodgy surprises from a new client. Once this case is settled, our firm won't be representing him again." Waving them to a couple of chairs, he sat at his usually uncluttered desk which was currently strewn with stacks of paper. The receptionist brought in a tray containing a pot of tea, cream, sugar, and biscuits, searched for a place to set it on Oliver's desk, gave up, and placed it on the shortest and most solid appearing stack of paper, raising an eyebrow at Oliver before leaving, closing the door behind her.

Oliver tilted his head back, rolled his neck, then poured tea into three cups, loaded his with sugar and cream, stirred, picked up one of the biscuits, leaned back in his chair, and asked, "What have you done now?" They each took a cup, and Danielle explained what had happened to Zoe at the wedding. Oliver listened without interrupting until she finished, then asked, "Do you have video?" Danielle handed him a flash drive which he inserted into a USB port on his computer, opening and playing the attached file. When it finished, he looked up and asked Jeff seriously, "Is he still alive." Jeff answered just as seriously, "Yes. So far."

Oliver sighed. "I assume Zoe doesn't want to press charges?" Danielle said, "Not at this time, no. She is adamant that Lucy not find out about it." Oliver frowned. "She isn't blaming herself at all, I trust?" Danielle said, "I don't think so. But Lucy doesn't know about her origins, and Zoe doesn't want her to find out this way." Oliver pivoted his chair sideways and stared at one of his bookcases. "That young man will probably try this with someone else. He may have already done so." Danielle nodded. "I know. I told her so. It didn't change her mind." He swung back to face them. "All right. Thank you for the heads up. I assume should he be foolish enough to press charges, this video will be available, and Zoe will press charges?" Danielle said, "The video will be available. I don't know if she'll press charges, but after anyone views the video, she would about have to, wouldn't she? I like her, but I won't put her ahead of Jeff, whether he wants me to or not." Jeff gave her a look. She gave him one back. "I won't. Sorry." He nodded.

Oliver walked them out, and they slowly made their way to the Armstrong home, discussing the situation. Danielle said, "You know, the easiest solution would be for him to make a try for Zoe in public, and we could deal with him publicly. No muss,

137

no fuss. The incident at the wedding would never have to come up." Jeff answered, "Like that will happen." Little did they know that events were in motion that would lead to the solution they envisioned, just not the way they thought.

When they arrived home, dinner was almost ready, and Lucy met them at the door, hands on hips, inquiring in her most grown-up voice, "What have you two been up to now?" Danielle scooped her up under one arm and carried her toward the kitchen from which some really good smells were emanating. Jeff said, "Nothing, sweetie. We just needed to check-in with Oliver." Zoe, who had stuck her head into the hall in time to hear this pronouncement, gave Jeff a glare. She said, "And?" and he answered, "Everything is up to date. No other action required at this time." She nodded, and returned to help Sophie with dishing out the vegetables.

Over dinner, Jake also asked, "How did the meeting with Oliver go? Meaning, of course, "Why were you meeting with Oliver? What have you done that we don't know about?" Jeff replied blandly, "Just checking in with him. We haven't been in any trouble in a while." Jake had to laugh at that reply even though he suspected there was more to the visit than Jeff was saying. Lucy interrupted then to tell about her day and begin asking the latest in her store of questions, and the subject dropped.

# Chapter 28

The week of the visit to Oliver was also the week the film crew shot the video of "The day". Action took place in many little snippets over a few days. Morning scenes took three days. First, one ambulance was videoed leaving the hospital emergency room to return to their station; then, the second one being picked up at the service center and driving down the street on the way to their station. Next, Robert in the police station placing the hoof trimmers his friend Chris had returned in his briefcase and tossing it into the trunk of his police car. There was already video of Robert on his ranch, working with his horse, Chester, talking to the horse about Chris and how he didn't want to board his daughter's horse there because of the lessons she received at her stable as well as trailering to horse shows, chuckling to himself about how that would change when that daughter needed braces or there was some other expense that boarding the horse at the expensive stable would cover.

Following was video of Robert pulling over the driver who ran a red light in front of him. Then the radio call and the rush to Danielle's house. There was the video of Alice listening to the strange sounds coming from next door, then her on the front porch of her home, dropping her coffee cup when she heard the screaming from next door and calling the police. Jeff crossing the street from the apartment complex to walk with Danielle to church, then breaking into a run when he heard the screams, Alice yelling at him to stop, Jeff stooping to pick up two pieces of brick from the flowerbed, then rushing through the unlocked front door; Robert charging through the open front door; the second police car arriving and the officer rushing inside, followed by the arrival of the two ambulances and their two crews running inside; Robert dashing to his trunk to retrieve the hoof trimmers; and finally, the two ambulance gurneys pushed to the two vehicles, loaded inside, and both roaring away, sirens blaring, lights flashing.

The movie almost crashed to a halt, however, not on the action around Danielle's house, but on the first hospital scene when the young actors were bandaged. That was the first time they, or any of the others really, realized the extent of the injuries Jeff and Danielle had received that fateful morning. The older "twins" had not shot any scenes requiring scars be added. The most they had needed so far was gloves. Everyone had read the lines, but the bandages truly brought it home. The actress playing Alice sat in a chair near the hospital stage and cried when she saw the young "twins". Everyone was shaken. The mood didn't improve when they shot the scene of Danielle screaming at Sarah Patton when she visited her room. Finally, Jeff and Danielle had to personally intervene, making light of it, reiterating how long ago it had been.

Still, the mood of the hospital scenes didn't really improve until the Elizabeth character was introduced. She made such an excellent Lizzie that the scene had to be shot three times due to the laughter her enthusiastic chatter called forth. Even so, she was hard pressed to offset the negative feelings that the Marilyn character aroused. The rest of the cast didn't understand why she didn't raise the negative feelings with Jeff and Danielle that the girl's mother and step-father did. They promised to explain when the movie was finished. It was with welcome relief that Jeff and Danielle declared themselves satisfied with all the difficult emotional scenes of that day and its aftermath. And the year marched on.

# Chapter 29

Jeff, Danielle, and their group of friends sat on the school lawn with their backs against a wall, eating lunch. One difference they found odd about schools in Australia was their lack of a school cafeteria where the students sat at tables and ate mostly what they purchased in the cafeteria, only a few bringing their own lunch from home. Here, practically everyone brought their lunch from home, mostly sandwiches. Except Jeff and Danielle. They brought everything: Caesar salads with homemade dressing, hot homemade soup in a thermos, lasagna packed in an insulated carrier to keep it warm, Mexican food, and so on.

Sean and Zoe were beneficiaries of this largess, and very happy about it. Except on the days Jeff and Danielle decided to bring MRE's, which Sean and Zoe considered a big letdown to the usual fare. On those days, the Australian twins usually brought sandwiches or bought something in the school canteen. Today was stroganoff day, and their friends clustered happily around, prepared to share in the bounty. The group included eleven-year-old Gerald, a child prodigy who was a senior like the rest. Jeff couldn't imagine what the parents were thinking to put the young boy in with kids so much older. There was really no chance for social or physical development, and being smarter than his peers did not help, especially with his attitude. With no social skills, the only thing he could think of in self-defense was to prove how much smarter he was, which only made things worse.

Jeff and Danielle had taken him under their wing the second week of school when Jeff found him crying in the boy's loo. Word quickly spread that the other kids could ignore him if they wanted to, but if they picked on him physically, things would go badly for them. Then they began teaching him social skills; trying to rather. Although he had eidetic memory among his other skills, he could not grasp the subjective nature of many social rules; his desire was for tried and true, firm, black and white rules. He wasn't alone in that desire. All of their friends would love to have had some social rules that didn't change depending on the situation.

Jeff and Danielle did their best. Rule 1: it's always safe to be nice rather than cruel (or love your neighbor as yourself). There was some disagreement over that one. Someone brought up bullies. Danielle asked, "Do you think things would be worse for saying something kind instead of something mean?" The guy who had brought it up answered, "Well, yes, mate. They'll think you're scared of them or you're backing down, and they'll just be worse." Danielle came back with, "So, if I say, 'I'm sorry we can't get along,' instead of 'You look like a pig,' it will make things worse?" He said, "Well, if you put it like that." Rule 2: Don't lie. That one brought instant disagreement. "What if a girl asks you if her clothes make her look fat?" That was asked with the high expectation that the twins would be stumped. Jeff asked, "What is fat?" Puzzlement. "What do you mean, 'What is fat?' Fat is fat." Danielle asked, "Is it? Whose standard are you using?"

That discussion (argument) went around and around and was of no use to Gerald at all, especially when someone pointed out that the person might be asking what most of the people who saw them in the clothes would think, not just the person being asked. This led to a discussion regarding the purpose of questions: asking for information or fishing for a compliment, and how to tell the difference. Jeff turned to Gerald and said, "If anyone asks you that question, the answer is always no. He asked, "What if the next person they ask says the clothes make them look fat?" Jeff said, "That is their problem, not yours." He asked, "Am I lying?" Danielle said, "No." Gerald asked, "What if they're wearing one of those sumo wrestler suits?" He had a twinkle in his eye when he said this, and Zoe exclaimed, "Gerald! You made a joke! I am so proud of you!" Gerald blushed.

The boy was eating a helping of the stroganoff from a paper plate, his own lunch sitting ignored in its carrier. For some reason, his parents sent him off to school most days with decent food, if it was hot, but pretty unappetizing when cold. They couldn't seem to grasp the concept that he had no way to heat the food. He reported that his mother had told him to just ask the cooks in the canteen to heat it for him. He commented once that it would be way better than the MRE's if it were heated; MRE's were not his favorite, especially after tasting the other meals the twins brought to school. Jeff had explained that they were an acquired taste, were better than nothing, and that they tasted almost good if you used the included pouch of Tabasco sauce, which Gerald so far wouldn't try.

Gerald was also not very athletic; he tended to think too much, trying to tell his body what to do every step of the way. Jeff and Danielle had been spending a little time with him each day at lunch teaching him a simple kata. As he learned a piece, they would add to it. The group of friends encouraged him, and as he improved, his attitude improved as well. Over time, the other students were beginning to shift their treatment of him from annoying person to more of the school mascot. They would greet him when they spotted him about town instead of avoiding him or pointing him out and snickering to their friends. It helped that he was happy to assist with homework problems, although Jeff and Danielle had to set up rules to define the difference between helping and doing it for them. Zoe summed it all up one day as they left school by saying, "I think the kid is going to make it after all."

# Chapter 30

Jeff, Danielle, and the entire Armstrong family stood at the northern edge of the property that would eventually become the Australian Children's Ranch. All of the land now belonged to the Australian branch of the foundation, thanks to Jake's efforts. Survey stakes sprouted like flowers everywhere, their red flags waving in the breeze like long, thin flowers. Stakes and twine marked the edges of the property where soon a fencing company would install fence along the borders of the property. The dimensions of the first three buildings were clearly marked, as were the roads and locations of utility lines for water, sewage, electricity, and phone/internet.

Soon the training buildings would be marked as well, as would the swimming pool. The land was located next door to an equestrian center, and agreements were already in place for riding lessons for the students. Part of the agreement included training in managing a stable, from mucking out the stalls to maintenance and repair, proper disposal of the muck from the stalls, ordering feed and supplements, and more. This meant a stable, arena, and riding paths on the property would not be necessary. Jeff and Danielle thought they would try this for a while, especially with input from Robert, and if they weren't happy with the results, they would add the necessary buildings and support structure.

Sean was perhaps the least imaginative of the group. While Lucy ran from area to area calling, "This is where the girls will live," and "This is where the boys will live!" Sean stared and said, "This is just dirt and weeds." While he was happy that the project was underway, he couldn't visualize the structures to come the way the others saw them in their minds' eye. No matter how much the excited Lucy described the buildings that would appear, he couldn't picture them. "I'll admire them when they're finished, mates." That was as far as he was willing to go. Danielle told him, "We'll be flying to the states in a little over a month. Then you can get an idea of what this place will look like since we're basically using the same plan.

The next school holiday was coming up the end of June, and plane reservations had already been made and tickets secured. The family would be staying with Robert, Michelle, and Elizabeth at the ranch. Meanwhile, the seven people walked around the site. It was located on the north side of the highway to the parachute drop zone. The property was deep enough that all of the buildings would be well away from the highway, for safety and for the noise factor. The main building would be located far enough south to allow a great deal of expansion to the north, giving more privacy. Jeff and Danielle would have considered it perfect if it were close enough to fly over in the wingsuits, but they would have to jump from so high to make that work that it would be useless. They would just have to stop by on their way out or the return trip.

As they moved about the property, Jeff and Danielle kept a careful lookout for poisonous snakes or spiders. It didn't seem to be the type of land for either, but that could change with the construction. The mice that snakes could feed on would more likely be next door with the horses and their oats than here. Still, the small onsite clinic would be stocked with anti-venom. They would also be building a helicopter landing pad for emergency transport.

Stepping out of the car, both had strapped on tool belts. They only contained four items: a hammer, two chisels, and a can of bug spray. The twins had not been happy ever since arriving in Australia because of the knife laws and had been searching for a substitute they could legally carry. Searching through the tool section at the local hardware store they had considered screwdrivers, which would work, but they wanted something with more weight. Then they had reached the chisel section, and their eyes lit up. By sharpening the edge just a bit, a throwing weapon could be added to their arsenal. While it would undoubtedly raise some alarms if found in their backpacks at school, a couple of chisels in the car should raise no concerns, and would certainly raise no eyebrows in a toolbelt with a hammer, which itself made a nice weapon.

Jeff proved what a great weapon the chisel was when, as they walked about the staked areas, pointing here and there, Lucy startled a red-bellied black snake, that, instead of retreating as they would have expected, flattened its body and began hissing loudly. The noise cut off abruptly when the chisel Jeff threw severed the head, and the large body thrashed around as Lucy climbed Zoe's body like a monkey and looked on from her perch in her mom's arms. When Zoe set her back on the ground, the girl stayed between Jeff and Danielle instead of running here and there as she had been.

Jeff pointed. "Swimming pool here. Tennis courts over there. Beach volleyball courts just past them. Welding, carpentry, and so on in the other direction. The main building will have classrooms for computer training and everything else. The kitchen will be large enough for cooking classes." The others smiled at him and Danielle as they told about everything that was planned. It was easy to see they were really excited about the project. And the family was proud of Jake for making it happen. After another hour spent walking around and imagining, they returned to the car and headed for home.

# Chapter 31

On Wednesday, Jeff, Danielle, and the other instructors began teaching the actors about the guns they would be using in the movie. Just as Mike had taught them, it all began with taking them apart and putting them together again until they could perform the task smoothly if not quickly. Speed could be taken care of in the filming; trying to slot a part in the wrong place or dropping it couldn't. None of them had ever handled a gun before, and after the tenth time picking up the wrong piece, ten-year-old Abigail said, "How old did you say you were when you learned this?" When Danielle answered, "Seven," she sighed and went back to work. Alec asked hopefully, "Will we get to shoot any of these for real?" Jeff said, "Yes. We have range time set up in a few weeks." All of the children looked excited at this prospect, as did the actor playing Mike.

The biggest burden was on the youngest pair. Jeff and Danielle had learned to disassemble, clean, and reassemble weapons soon after they left the hospital when they were seven, so the older ones didn't really need to learn that part. All of them wanted to, though, perhaps even more than the youngest ones because they were under no pressure to learn. The actor playing Mike was excited to have picked up a new hobby, and along with Bobbie and Alexander, was learning to reload as well.

Jeff and Danielle left them with the instructors and began reviewing the video taken over the past week. After checking it all, they had no criticism or suggestions to make. The movie was progressing better than they had hoped or expected, was on time and on budget. Sebastian had performed an excellent job of hiring everyone involved. The cast and crew were working together like a huge family, something Sebastian said seldom if ever happened, and Jeff and Danielle gave all the credit to the prayer that bathed the project every single day.

# Chapter 32

In early June, the State of Origin rugby matches reached the city. Preparation had been underway for days in the Armstrong household with the purchase of new NSW Blues jerseys and caps and friendly insults with friends who had grown up in Queensland and were supporting the Maroons. Jeff and Danielle explained that these insults were called "trash talk". Lucy was delighted with this and had to be calmed down more than once as limits were placed on her exuberance.

On the day of the first game, the family drove to catch a bus to the stadium. Jeff and Danielle had been feeling uneasy all day for reasons they couldn't explain, and had almost added the armor to their motorcycle jackets, which they had decided to wear in spite of the mild weather. Only the possibility of problems with security at the stadium prevented them from loading the armor plates into their clothes.

Jake and Sophie gave them curious looks since they were wearing Blues jerseys and windbreakers, and Zoe even asked Jeff, "Why those jackets?" He didn't have an answer, so he just shrugged. She noted the concerned looks in his and Danielle's eyes and asked, "What's wrong?" He said, "I don't know. Just a feeling." Then the family was caught up in the excitement of attending the game, and the concern faded into the background.

At the stadium, they made their way to their seats. Unnoticed, the young man who had assaulted Zoe at the wedding dropped into his own seat ten rows behind them. He had arrived with his friends, parking in the close in parking that the pass his parents had given him allowed. The group of three guys and two girls was pumped and cheered for the Queensland Maroons all the way from the car to their seats since all five were huge fans. They stopped at a concession stand to purchase beers on the way to the seats, and the rest of the group marveled at the excellent seats. The boy's father had purchased the tickets for the family but had then been unable to attend and had given all five tickets and the parking pass to their son, who invited the others to join him.

Only Zoe and Danielle knew the boy by sight, although Jeff had seen his image on the video from Danielle's bodycam. The young man remained unseen throughout the game, staring at the two girls and helping himself to beer after beer, cheering for the Maroons, and fueling his anger over what had happened to him at the wedding. The game did not help his mood as his team fell behind and never caught up.

The Blues won the game, and the boy left in angry disgust, leaving behind the joyful Armstrong group who were now discussing a late-night snack to celebrate. His friends were much more matter of fact, trading friendly insults with the Blues fans they passed on their way out; they didn't understand their friend's anger. If history was any indication, the Maroons would win the next game and the championship as well. Let the Blues' fans enjoy their little victory. It would be short lived. Danielle and Zoe could not see the boy or his friends through the intervening crowd and never spotted him. Still, Jeff and Danielle's feeling of doom did not lessen.

After a wait in the parking lot, the family finally boarded a bus for the return ride to their car. Once there, they drove out of the parking spot with Danielle at the wheel. Sophie was with her in the front passenger seat. Jeff sat behind Sophie with Lucy in her car seat beside him and Zoe on her other side behind Danielle. Jake and Sean were in the back.

As Danielle made a right turn through an intersection, the unthinkable happened. Witnesses, who told their story to police later, couldn't believe it. As Danielle drove through the intersection, a car stopped on the other side suddenly accelerated straight at her, apparently intent on ramming the Armstrong vehicle. Danielle couldn't drive out of its way, but she was able to skid the car into a pivot so the other car hit them a glancing blow down the passenger side instead of plowing solidly into the side of the vehicle.

The blow set off most of the airbags in the car, stunning those who were not in shock from the accident. Danielle glanced around the vehicle, evaluating injuries, beginning with Sophie. Jeff was doing the same in the back, talking calmly to Lucy and Zoe. Lucy was fine, secure in her car seat. Zoe had been struck by the side airbag and was complaining that she couldn't feel her arm.

Danielle noticed movement in the passenger side rearview mirror and saw the driver of the other car stumbling around the rear of his car with a jack handle in his hand. She immediately shoved her door open, which fortunately wasn't jammed by the collision, slid across the hood of her vehicle, and moved to meet him. The young man from the wedding watched her approach, first with anger and anticipation, then with fear.

At first, when he recognized her driving the car across the intersection, it was with the idea of bringing her down after his humiliation. Then, it changed to watching the monster from *The Ring,* who was suddenly closer each time he blinked his eyes. Suddenly, she was right in front of him, and he swung the jack handle. Later, eye-witness reports said that she grabbed the tool with her left hand, struck him once with her forearm and kicked him once. He fell to the street and didn't move. She returned to her vehicle and, finding the rear passenger door jammed by the collision, ripped it off.

His friends, who had been watching him with curiosity and some concern, hadn't been able to believe their eyes when he accelerated across the intersection straight at the car making a turn. Their yells and screams of warning became ones of horror as they realized what he was doing, and they watched helplessly as he rammed the car, then climbed out, reached under his seat, brought out the jack handle, and stumbled toward the other car. From inside the car, they saw him swing the jack handle at the girl, watched him fall, and then sat stunned and paralyzed by the flow of events.

While the news later that evening described the brief fight, it didn't show video. It did show Danielle removing the vehicle door, but it didn't show the assistance Jeff gave by ramming the door from the inside with his shoulder as Danielle pulled. To her dismay, he was careful to play down his assistance, and her reputation grew proportionally, much to his amusement. At one point, after hearing comments from people, she muttered to him in elvish, "I hate you so much," causing him to chuckle.

With the door removed, and with the first aid kit from the glove box, she and Jeff treated the other passengers for injuries caused by the collision; mainly these were minor cuts and bruises produced by the airbags. They assured Zoe that feeling would totally return to her arm soon, although she would have a colorful bruise, and as time passed, the feeling did indeed return, as predicted. Sean and his father had injuries that needed gauze and tape from bumping heads. Sophie joked about their hard heads protecting them. Thanks to Danielle's quick thinking and driving, what could have been a very bad accident was reduced to a minor event. Except for their totaled vehicle, of course. The rear wheel was bent beyond repair, and the insurance company, upon later inspection, totaled the car.

Onlookers had called emergency services, and police and an ambulance arrived. Officer Cameron was the first officer on the scene, and outside of his professional attitude, his first thought when he spotted the twins was "Now what?" and "Where's their lawyer?" In fact, Danielle had phoned Oliver as she walked away from the young man on the ground, and he arrived shortly after the police and ambulance, having been watching the game at a nearby sports bar. No one in the Armstrong vehicle had been injured enough to need the ambulance, but the young man on the ground received their attention, and soon he was loaded on a gurney and on his way to a hospital.

The police spoke with the witnesses who were standing around, eager to tell what they had seen, describing how the car had been stopped at a red light and ran the light to seemingly ram the Armstrong vehicle intentionally. This was supported by seeing the driver climb out of his car with a jack handle and approach the other vehicle. They excitedly described how the driver of the other vehicle had met him, caught the jack handle as he swung at her, hit him twice, well, hit him once and kick him once, and left him lying in the street to return to rip the door off her vehicle.

Meanwhile, Jeff had shown Oliver the video from Danielle's bodycam. He asked, "Do you know this bloke?" When Danielle told the lawyer it was the guy from the wedding, his eyebrows went up. "Seriously? That's going to either complicate things or make them simpler." He called Officer Cameron over to show him the video. Naturally, the officer asked if any of the Armstrong group knew the young man which led to the longer explanation of how Danielle and Zoe knew him, which even Zoe's parents didn't know. Jeff and Danielle shared a look. Their theory that things happened because of them seemed more and more to be true.

Eventually, everything was sorted out. The Armstrong vehicle was not drivable. A tow truck loaded their vehicle for transport to a garage, a taxi van took them home, and their celebration snacks around the table included thanks that no one had been seriously injured by the accident. Finally, they all went to bed, anticipating days of paperwork and even a trial ahead if the young man was charged with vehicular assault. Lucy thought the entire event had been awesome, especially when she realized what Danielle had done. She loved telling her classmates in Sunday School about the crash. The next week, things were not so cut and dried.

# Chapter 33

The remainder of the week after the wreck flew by, helped along by YouTube videos of the fight. While the news stations hadn't shown it, several people had posted their videos to the site, and the kids at school were treating Danielle to exaggerated fear, followed by laughter since they knew she wouldn't attack them just for being annoying. She and Jeff were called into the principal's office again so he could reiterate the school's non-violence policy, which they could both state from memory. They avoided rolling their eyes at his speech, difficult though it was.

On Monday, things changed. The young man was now saying that he had accidentally hit the gas pedal and was coming to aid the Armstrong vehicle with his jack handle, thinking doors might be jammed or windows might need to be broken. He had only tried to defend himself with the tool when Danielle seemed intent on attacking him.

Officer Cameron brought them this news, and they returned with him to the police station along with Oliver, who added sexual assault to the previous charges against the young man. The prosecution, who on the face of the boy's statement, were unsure about the assault charges, became suddenly re-energized by the new charges and the video supplied from Danielle's bodycam. They already had a solid case for driving while intoxicated.

Zoe and Danielle weren't faring so well at the Armstrong

home. Jake and Sophie both were angry and disappointed that neither girl had told them what had happened at the wedding. This was tempered a little by the video of Danielle's intervention, as well as the knowledge of what Jeff had refrained from doing, knowing it was a major show of restraint on his part since they suspected his true feelings toward Zoe.

Jeff and Danielle were more worried about something else, namely, what Owen might do about this. They were certain that the American crime boss was keeping tabs on them and, judging from what they suspected he had done just because someone pirated their t-shirt design, there was no telling what he would do to someone who rammed their car with his. If he suspected just how much Jeff cared for Zoe, which he might, whatever his sources, the young man was unlikely to survive. His demise might also be long and painful. The twins hoped to nip this in the bud.

To forestall any action by the man, they had Sean purchase a burner phone at a local discount store. Mid-morning back home, they made a call to Owen's bodyguard. He answered with a laconic, "Yeah?" Jeff said briefly, "Ask Mr. Morris to leave this alone. We'll take care of it." Then he hung up. He didn't say who was calling or what "this" was, assuming that Owen would figure it out. Which he did when his bodyguard told him about the phone call. He thought it was hilarious, and he was still laughing when he made a phone call of his own to ask his friends in Australia to put their plans on hold for the time being. This call was just in time because by the end of the day, the young man would have disappeared, never to be seen again.

Not knowing how close he had come to disaster, the young man, aided by his wealthy and influential parents, pursued his description of events, passing off the scene at the wedding as an overly aggressive but not ill-intentioned advance. At Jeff's request, Oliver hired a private investigations firm they occasionally used to find the answers to some questions, such as, was the young man at the game; where did he park; where did he sit; did those around him notice anything unusual about him; who were his friends; did he say anything to them about the wedding; had he expressed any animosity toward Danielle; and so on. Also, was Zoe the first girl he had attacked, and had there been more since.

As the days went by, the answers trickled in. Jeff and Danielle were not surprised that he had been sitting so close to them at the game, but they were surprised they had never noticed him, especially the way their danger senses kept them tense the entire day. His friends were recorded discussing how he hated Danielle and wanted to get even. More than one of the fans sitting near him at the game commented on how angry he seemed, which wasn't unexpected since his team was losing, but he seemed to be glaring specifically at the Armstrong family, although there were NSW fans all around him, and the little girl in that group was so cute.

There were also stories about other girls he had attacked, none of whom had pressed charges. Yet. When they found out how many others there were, several were ready to step forward. All this information was filtered to the prosecution, who steadily built their case. Charging Danielle with assault was on hold pending the outcome of the first trial. If the young man was convicted of assault, then Danielle would not be. If he was found innocent of assault, then she would be. Maybe. Time would tell.

One result of the crash was that the twins, with Jake and Sophie's permission, installed cameras in both cars for a 360-degree view: front, rear, and both sides. The cameras fed a monitor that would split into four views and a multi-terabyte hard drive that stored data until overwritten. The chances of this data being needed again because of a wreck were thankfully slim, but there were some other advantages as well, such as someone hitting the vehicle in a parking lot and driving away without leaving a note. Both Sophie and Jake appreciated the rear-view camera when backing out of a parking spot. And, for Jeff and Danielle, it wasn't expensive.

The cameras had an additional use. Lucy, when in her car seat, could not see very well out the windows. With a tablet, she could see what everyone else was looking at, and, if the scenery was really something special, she could enlarge it, freeze it, or replay it. Sometimes, she was even called upon to share her tablet so the others could replay a view or get a closer look at it. What had at first been viewed by the older Armstrong family members with eye-rolling indulgence became a necessity, and it wasn't unusual for family members to make sure Lucy had her tablet before making sure she had a sweater; or her shoes.

# Chapter 34

On Saturday, one week before the July holiday, and a trip back to the US to visit, the robbery occurred. Occurred. Took place. Those are such calm words for the actual event that pulled in Jeff and Danielle. Sophie was furious with her brother although neither he nor the twins would discuss the event, so she wasn't even 100% certain Jeff and Danielle were involved. But in her heart, she knew.

Before lunch on that day, the six men entered the bank. They stood out because, even on a Saturday, or perhaps because it was Saturday, or perhaps it was just the hour, the bank was practically empty. One teller was behind the counter, cashing a check for an elderly gentleman. A young couple were returning from the back after depositing their wills in their safe deposit box, something her father had been on her about for ages. Next on their Saturday agenda was a cricket match, where the husband would play, and the wife would chat with her friends in the grassy area near the pitch. Two bank employees were at their desks using the quiet time to catch up on paperwork.

The six men spread around the bank, and one fired a pistol into the ceiling, immediately gaining everyone's attention. All six began yelling for everyone to get on the floor with their arms spread out to their sides. It didn't take them long to move among the few people and remove any cell phones people had in their hands. One man rushed to the single teller, handed her a cloth bag, and told her to empty her cash drawer into it. That's when their robbery went sideways.

She was new, and while she was meticulous and detail oriented and even fairly stable, she was not up to this level of stress. The man yelling at her and pointing his pistol in her face did nothing to calm her, and she dropped the key to her cash drawer on the floor, accidentally kicking it under the counter, and in her frantic efforts to retrieve it, setting off by accident the silent alarm, which she was too frightened to do on purpose.

The furious man thrust his weapon in his waistband and hopped up on the counter, jumping to the floor on the other side. Snatching the key from her upraised and trembling fingers, he unlocked the drawer and dumped its contents into the bag. Moving swiftly to the next drawer, he tried to unlock it, only to find the key wouldn't fit. He glared at the teller kneeling on the floor and screamed at her to open the other drawers. In a squeaky voice, she said, "My key will only open my drawer."

None of the robbers had ever worked in a bank, and they didn't know what they didn't know. Vicious and cunning but not clever, they assumed many erroneous things such as that the teller drawers would be full of money and easy to access. They had planned to be out of the bank in a set amount of time, thinking someone would set off an alarm. Their time was up, and the men had little to show for it.

Their backup plan was to grab hostages and drive to a house owned by one of the men. It sat in the middle of a large field with a clear view for 2000 meters on all sides. With seconds remaining on the leader's timer, the men hustled the six people out of the bank and into the panel van parked out front, piling in after them. Had they driven quietly away from the bank, there was a slight chance they would have made it unnoticed until too late, but the driver drove away with tires screeching, and they soon had a police escort.

Witnesses on the street near the bank told the police about

the hostages, and the van was allowed to proceed unhindered. In an hour, they were parked beside the two-story farmhouse with all the hostages inside. The police originally tried to set up a perimeter a thousand meters out, but one of the men, sitting in one of the upstairs windows, was quite a good shot with a rifle, and after he had damaged all the cars within range and injured some of the officers, the perimeter was pulled back to 2000 meters. Even there, they found it necessary to stay under cover as the shooter would lob an occasional round in their direction, and the bullets had enough momentum to cause damage to vehicles and harm to the officers if they struck.

Soon after their arrival at the farmhouse, the leader was on his cell phone, giving the groups' demands: millions in cash and a helicopter to take them away. He made these demands from the front yard of the house, holding a hostage by the neck as he spoke into the phone, confident in his knowledge that no police sniper could hit him at this range without putting the hostage at risk. Just in case, though, another robber stood just inside the farm house's front door, ready to shoot the hostage. The demand that started a deadly clock ticking, however, was the promise to kill a hostage every hour until their demands were met. If they were attacked, they would kill all of the hostages. The countdown began as soon as he hung up.

The police had no sniper trained at 2000 meters. Their skill was seldom even needed at 1000 meters. The officer in charge called the military, and eventually he was put in touch with Captain Harry Webster. Harry stared at the phone. The base's long-range snipers who might be able to consistently hit a target at 2000 meters were deployed or at a competition over a thousand miles away. There was no way one could be brought to the site before several of the hostages were killed, if the maniacs in the house kept their word, and the police had no reason to doubt them.

Then, as the police officer waited on the line, a thought

entered his mind. What about Jeff and Danielle. He knew how good they were. He had seen it with his own eyes. He had the weapons in the armory they would need. He could pick them up by helicopter and have them at the site just barely in time for the first deadline, if he could reach them immediately, and if he started now. He told the officer on the phone he would call him back, and hung up.

Pulling his cell phone from his pocket, he used his contact list to call Jeff. When the young man answered, he quickly told him the situation and asked if he and Danielle would help. Jeff immediately answered yes, and Harry explained that a helicopter would pick them up at the park by their house.

Inside the Armstrong kitchen, the family had been eating lunch. Jeff and Danielle had cooked vegetable beef soup with jalapeno cornbread. The family loved the soup, but except for Lucy, they were undecided about cornbread. It was, after all, baked corn flour. The jalapenos helped, but still. Lucy declared it, "ma'velous, da'ling," because Jeff liked it, although she really did seem to enjoy it. The phone call came in the middle of the raucous discussion.

As always, Jeff checked his caller ID before sending it to voice mail, but when he saw it was Harry, he answered. "Hi, Harry. What's up?" Harry, already unhappy that Jeff had announced his name, immediately said, "This is a priority, top secret call." Dramatic, to be certain, but he didn't want Jeff to put him on speaker phone with the family. Jeff blinked, but said, "Okay," and to the family's surprise, left the kitchen and walked to his room, Danielle following him, and closed the door. The others remained in the kitchen in stunned surprise.

Harry outlined the situation and asked if they could help. Jeff explained to Danielle, and both immediately accepted. Harry said he would bring clothes and weapons. Danielle said, "And ghillie suits", the camouflage clothing designed to resemble the background environment such as foliage, snow or sand. Harry agreed and hung up. The twins returned to the kitchen where Jeff said, "We have to go out for a while. I don't know when we'll be back. Later today, I assume. Harry needs us for something. Don't say anything, okay? It's a secret." With no idea what could possibly be going on, the family laughingly agreed, and the twins left for the park.

They waited more than half an hour at the park. It had been necessary for the captain to arrange for a helicopter, draw weapons and ammunition from the armory, and borrow clothes and ghillie suits. After speaking with the police officer in charge and giving him the time constraints, a police negotiator had attempted to buy another half hour of time, to no avail. As the seconds ticked down to the end of the first hour, the leader had walked out into the front yard of the farmhouse, and as the first hour ended, executed the elderly man who had visited the bank that morning to cash a check for spending money for the upcoming week. The police stared in fury and frustration at the body lying there, helpless to interfere less the other hostages die as well.

At the park, the unmarked helicopter flared to a halt, and as a few visitors to the park gawked in surprise, Jeff and Danielle ran to the helicopter and threw themselves on board. The aircraft immediately rose into the air and headed toward the farmhouse. The twins had dressed in plain gray sweat clothes, and with caps pulled low over their foreheads and wearing sunglasses, they were unrecognizable by anyone who didn't know them well. Videos of the departure ended up on YouTube but not the evening news due to coverage of the standoff at the farmhouse. Had it been a slow or even moderate news day, it would have, but the drama at the farmhouse took up all of the news bandwidth. The Armstrongs heard the helicopter, but they did pass by occasionally, and the family paid it no particular mind.

Inside the helicopter, Harry handed the twins two sets of camouflage clothing, which they pulled on. Then they opened the two cases containing the M107 .50 sniper rifles. They were fitted with noise suppressors and scopes but could be fired using the calibrated iron sights instead which the captain assumed Jeff and Danielle would prefer. There were magazines in the case as well. They inserted a magazine in each weapon and two additional ones in the button-down pockets of the pants. Next, Harry handed them transceivers which they inserted in their ears, around their throats, and clipped to the backs of their belts.

The two ghillie suits were lying in rolled bundles on the floor. As the helicopter approached the site of the standoff, the twins shook them out and put them on. Finally, Harry handed them each a balaclava, which they slid over their heads. He produced a hand-drawn layout of the farmhouse, the police lines, and the land surrounding the house. The helicopter would drop them just in front of the police lines, on the forward slope of a hill facing the front of the house. It would hover while they dropped off and went to ground.

He didn't tell them that an incredible amount was riding on them besides the lives of the remaining hostages, including his career and possibly a court martial. And his sister's anger. And that of their parents. He did, however, pray with them as the helicopter approached the landing zone. Then the twins perched in the doorway facing away from the house, and as the helicopter settled to the ground, they dropped out and immediately disappeared into scrubby ground.

# Chapter 35

As soon as the twins were out of sight, the helicopter lifted again, moved a hundred yards behind the police lines, and landed behind a stand of trees. To the men in the house, it might appear it had landed in the wrong position, realized its mistake, and moved out of harm's way. The marksman in the house had taken the opportunity to fire several rounds at the machine, two of which hit it, leaving small holes in the side but hitting nothing of any importance, including the occupants. The leader ran screaming up the stairs to stop him, thinking it was their transportation arriving to take them out of there.

Jeff and Danielle settled into position and began studying the house, by sight and by feel. Time ticked by and they were silent outside of a brief broadcast soon after the helicopter had moved to say them were in position. Captain Webster met with the police commander who asked him what the plan was, and if the two snipers could indeed hit their targets at this range. Harry assured him they could and stood with the man pouring over the layout as they reviewed options.

On the slope, Jeff and Danielle were discussing what they saw and felt. Silently, they prayed for guidance and direction, and slowly, miraculously, details of the scene were revealed, including the interior of the house. As the second deadline approached, Jeff keyed his radio. "There are six hostiles in the house. Two are in the front, one is on each side and the rear, one is on the second floor at the front window. There are five hostages, all sitting with their backs to the front wall of the house."

The police commander asked Harry incredulously, "How could they possibly know that?" The captain shrugged and said, "That's what they do." Next, Jeff asked, "Are weapons free?" The police commander and Harry shared a look. Harry asked, "What's the plan?" Jeff replied, "If events move like the last time, when a hostile brings a hostage outside, we will neutralize him. Then the one in the doorway. Then the sniper on the second floor. When we fire, attack the front of the house. We will keep the hostiles away from the hostages, eliminating them if possible."

The police commander stared at Harry. "That's the plan? What if they're wrong?" Harry answered, "We're going to lose the hostages one at a time. This gives us a chance. I think you'll find that what they said is what will happen." They were out of time, and the police commander accepted the plan, ordering two armored police vehicles readied. Police climbed aboard and the doors closed just as a robber shoved a hostage out the door in front of him, this time one of the bank employees.

The police commander's phone rang. He answered. From the speaker came a cold voice, "Where's my money and my helicopter? I need it over here, not over there." Under their ghillie suits, Jeff and Danielle both held their breath, waited between heartbeats, and squeezed the triggers. A loud whuff was followed by a supersonic crack as the bullets broke the sound barrier. The robber in the front yard was flung away from the hostage, and the second one standing in the doorway disappeared. As the two armored police vehicles roared toward the house, a third robber grabbed the young wife and dragged her out the side door toward the parked van.

The twins fired again, and the second-floor sniper spun away from the window. In the side yard, the young wife fell to the ground and rolled away as the robber suddenly released her. Inside the house, the remaining two robbers stared at each other, undecided. The six men had discussed what to do if the police launched an attack, and having determined they would die anyway, decided to take the hostages with them as revenge. They didn't know if they were the only ones still alive, but it seemed so. There was no sound of firing from the second floor, and their friend had not appeared on the stairs. No living robbers were visible.

They hovered between surrendering or carrying out the plan. Then the two police vehicles slid to a halt in the front yard, and their minds were made up. Pointing their pistols at the hostages, they prepared to fire. On the slope, Jeff and Danielle made their final two shots, through the front wall of the house. When the police crashed through the front door seconds later, they found no one living except the hostages. In the side yard, two officers hustled the young wife to one of the police vehicles, protecting her with their bodies in case any fire came from the house. However, no one was left to shoot at them.

At the command center, the report came in: hostiles down, hostages secured. Harry relayed this to Jeff and Danielle, and they appeared as if by magic, trudging up the slope to join him, heavy rifles over their shoulders. They had fired three rounds each. The police commander shook their hands briefly before Harry hustled them back to the helicopter, which lifted off and returned to the base. As they flew, the twins returned the rifles to their cases along with the unused ammunition and spent brass.

Harry asked, "Are you two all right?" They shrugged. Danielle said, "Yes. It turned out okay, didn't it?" Harry said seriously, "We had absolutely no reason to think it would end as well as it did, with no one injured but the robbers. No police, no hostages except the first one. Everyone owes you a great deal, and I hope no one ever finds out it was you." Jeff nodded. "That makes two of us."

The helicopter landed at the base, and a G Wagon[10] drove them to the armory, where, under the watchful eyes of a sergeant, they cleaned the two rifles before Harry checked them back in along with the unused ammunition and brass. The three were then driven to a building where a number of personnel were constantly on the move. They passed through only long enough to remove the balaclavas unobserved, then climbed back in the empty vehicle where it had been parked in the full parking lot. After another brief stop to transfer to Harry's car, all three were on their way back to the Armstrong home, the twins changing back into their sweats as Harry drove.

The older man dropped them off a block from home, and after a final wave, accelerated back toward the base. Jeff and Danielle swiftly covered the short distance to the front door and entered silently to find the entire family in the kitchen, baking cookies. Lucy was the first to notice them, and came bouncing over, cookie in hand. "Where have you been, mates? We're baking cookies, and they're most excellent!" She offered the twins a bite, and after taking a small bite each, they agreed with her.

Sophie added her question to Lucy's. "Where HAVE you been?" Jeff shrugged. We had to help Harry out with a problem. We can't talk about it." Jake asked, "Do we need to call the lawyer?" Danielle shook her head no. "We should be good this time." No one but Lucy was happy with their answer, and after watching the news and hearing about the two snipers that had been brought in, Jake, Sophie, and Zoe were pretty sure where the American students had spent the day. Sean was a bright and personable young man, but he could be oblivious to the goings on around him, and all he said after viewing the newscast was, "I'm glad they were able to save the rest of the hostages."

Later that evening, after Lucy was in bed, Jeff and Danielle had run to the gym for a quick workout, and Sean was absent at a birthday party for one of his chums, Zoe entered her parents' bedroom and sat on the foot of the bed. She was quietly furious. "You know those two were Jeff and Danielle. I can't believe Uncle Harry would use them like that and put their lives in such danger.

It's even more disturbing that it doesn't seem to have bothered them at all." Sophie said, "Your uncle isn't answering my calls. I know he won't admit it was them. It will be 'You don't need to know', but I will yell at him regardless, the drongo. Those poor children."

Jake broke in. "In Harry's defense, that is what they've trained for all their lives. And you know how tough they are. Plus, Harry might not have had anyone else. A lot of the shooters are at that competition. Henry is. That house was 2000 meters from the police lines. Not many snipers could make those shots." Sophie and Zoe were not convinced. In their heads, they could understand the reasoning. In their hearts, though, Jeff and Danielle came first. They loved those kids.

That evening as they prepared for bed, Zoe said, "So, what did you do for Uncle Harry today?" Danielle said, "We can't talk about it." Zoe snorted. "Mom is fair furious with him. I'm not sure why." This last was more of a question than a statement, but Danielle shrugged again. "She'll get over it. Or not. She shouldn't be mad at him, though."

Harry was at that moment speaking with his superior officer about the affair at the farmhouse. The man was asking, "Who did you use? I was under the impression that all our best shooters were out of country or at the competition." Harry said, "I'd rather not say, sir. I brought in two civilians who could do the job." The man said, "They were fair amazing. I'd like to meet them one day. I'd give them a medal if I could. Off the record, of course." Harry nodded. "Yes, sir, but I think this is a case where the less known, the better."

Unfortunately for Harry, informants in the police department had told their news contacts that the snipers were military and not police department, and this information had made it into the news cycle. Harry stayed on the base where reporters could not reach him, but it didn't save him from his sister's phone calls, which he didn't answer. He knew he would pay for that at some future date.

The points against him were piling up, too. Sophie had called Robert and Michelle and told them what she thought had happened. They immediately called Jeff and Danielle, and were unsurprised that they wouldn't talk about it. Their main concern was that the twins were okay, and after speaking with them, were assured that they were. They didn't understand this part of the twins. Normal people wouldn't be. Had they worked for the police department, a psychological evaluation would have been mandatory. And, they could go suicidal over Rainbow's death and murderous over Village Sunshine's, but remain calm and normal over something like today. Sometimes it was like they were from another time.

Since Robert and Michelle weren't supposed to know about the twin's involvement, they didn't call Harry, but his problems didn't end with Sophie. Henry and the others heard about the event and had quite the discussion, wondering who the snipers were. They knew it wasn't them, and they knew the police didn't have anyone trained for that range, or the weapons for it. Henry didn't say anything then, but upon his return to the base, and after a discussion with the other members of his team who had seen the twins shoot, he confronted Harry. If he hadn't had feelings for Danielle, he would have been one of the first to congratulate the captain for his choice. But he did have feelings, and he came very close to striking a superior officer.

Harry, pretty sure what Henry's attitude would be, met the sniper in the company of his second in command and Angus, the lead scout, both of whom knew about the twins. Harry, facing three to one, two of them superior officers, was only vocally insubordinate, and not physical. "You had no right to drag them into that situation! You put their lives at risk, and they had to kill six people! They're only seventeen!" He said, well yelled, all this while leaning on the front of the captain's desk.

Harry said, "They're all I had. You'll see Danielle soon enough. Why don't you ask her what she thinks about it? And if she's seventeen, what are you doing hanging about her anyway?" Henry was somewhat set back by that argument. He couldn't very well use the argument that she was only seventeen if he wanted to keep seeing her. Before he could say anything else, Harry continued, "They were in a village in Africa that was attacked by over a hundred raiders. They stopped them with two old Enfields. Only twenty of those made it to within five hundred yards of the village. They aren't normal young people. You already know that. So, support me and them instead of acting all indignant." A somewhat quieter Henry said, "Yes, sir." Harry waved. "Dismissed," and Henry left the room. After he was gone, the other two turned to face the captain. Lachlan said, "Harry, what were you thinking?"

# Chapter 36

The following weekend, the family drove to Canberra to visit a hospital there. It was only a three-hour drive, and they had daylight for about two-thirds of it, through small towns and past farms and wineries, arriving in the dark at their hotel. As Australia's capital city, it was mostly known for being the country's political hub and had a proliferation of museums, galleries and one of the world's leading research facilities. Some of the sights were open 24 hours and others were available by appointment, so they had a chance to walk about and mainly get Jeff and Danielle out of town for a few days, the main goal of the trip after the hospital.

The hospital visit went by normally with no surprises, and they finished in the early afternoon, heading straight to one of their tour appointments followed by walking to a couple of the 24-hour ones, then dinner and more walking. On Sunday morning, they visited a nearby Bible Church, visited more 24-hour sites, ate lunch, and drove home. The bank robbery was still being mentioned but had been pushed off first place by a large fire. Everyone breathed a sigh of relief.

On Wednesday, Jeff and Danielle were in the news again. They spent their normal Wednesday at the gym, working with the actors and reviewing video. The Armstrong family returned home at six to eat dinner, work on homework, and so on, but the twins stayed until ten, grabbing dinner from the canteen. They were the last to leave, passing and greeting their cleaning crew on the way out, and strolled along on the twenty-minute walk, discussing the movie and its progress.

Halfway home and passing through a quiet, residential neighborhood they had been through many times before, they heard loud music blaring from one of the homes for a few seconds as a door opened and closed. More cars than usual were parked all up and down the street. That and the music indicated a possible party in progress. They didn't think much of it except that it was unusual for the neighborhood until they reached the house, spotted the van double-parked in the street, and the two boys helping a girl down the sidewalk from the front door to the street.

All three seemed to be young, probably university age, and the girl seemed to be barely able to walk. At first the twins thought she was drunk and the boys were helping her home, but something about the whole situation just seemed off. The two boys seemed more furtive than helpful, glancing around and back at the house as they walked and speeding up when they spotted Jeff and Danielle.

Two things happened that totally changed the situation and galvanized the twins. The girl raised her head to stare with unfocused eyes and whispered, "Help me." Then, the driver of the van stage-whispered through the open van door, "Hurry up." Jeff and Danielle sprang forward with lightning speed and stopped between the group and the van. Jeff turned sideways so he could keep the interior of the van and the group both in his vision; Danielle faced the group. She said, "Why don't you set her down on the sidewalk, and let's see how she's doing." One of the boys, a large young man with weight-lifter muscles snarled, "Why don't you mind your own business, mate," and lifted an arm to shove Danielle out of the way.

He found himself kneeling on the street as Danielle put the offending arm in a painful lock. Now the smaller boy was supporting the girl's weight by himself, and he staggered under the unexpected load, almost dropping her. The sound of a car door slamming echoed around the street, and the driver dashed around the front of the van. He was another large man with the oversized triceps of a body builder. Jeff met him, grabbed one outstretched arm, and threw him onto the street where he landed with a crash and didn't move. The third boy released the girl and sprinted down the sidewalk away from the group. Jeff caught the girl before she hit the ground and eased her the rest of the way down.

The boy Danielle was holding was cursing and grasping ineffectually at her. She nodded to Jeff that she had him under control, and he pulled out his cell phone and called emergency services, requesting police and an ambulance, briefly explaining the situation, giving the address. The operator asked him to stay on the line, but he said he had to make another call and disconnected. Dialing again, he called Oliver, whose only comment besides, "I'll be there as soon as possible," was, "It has only been two weeks since the last call." Jeff thought, "If he only knew about the robbery in between."

The ambulance arrived first, and Jeff pointed them toward the girl, saying, "I think she may have been given GHB." The guy still in Danielle's grip yelled, "It wasn't us." One of the ambulance attendants pointed to the guy on the ground and asked, "What about him?" Jeff said, "He may need some help, too, but check her out first." The police arrived then, followed shortly by Oliver. Jeff and Danielle didn't know the officers, but they knew about the twins and recognized them. They were also aware of the relationship with the lawyer. One of the officers told Danielle, "You can let him go." Danielle released the arm, and the boy clambered to his feet, rubbing the arm and saying, "I want to press charges against her for assault." The officer said to the twins, "Why don't you two save us some time and go talk to your lawyer.

One of the ambulance attendants told the police, "This girl

seems to be under the influence of GHB." Again, the boy rubbing his arm declared, "We didn't give it to her." The other attendant had been kneeling beside the boy on the ground, and he said, "We'd better get another ambulance here for this one. It looks like he has a concussion, and his back may be broken." Both officers stared at the huddle of Jeff, Danielle, and Oliver who were gazing at Jeff's smart phone. Oliver said something, and the three walked over. The lawyer said, "My clients are ready to make a statement. Instead of saying anything, Jeff handed one officer his phone and started the video.

A second ambulance pulled up as they watched the video, and the boy on the ground was loaded in. Two more police cars added their flashing lights to the vehicles on the street. This time a couple of the officers were part of the group who provided security at the gym. The first police car followed the ambulances to the hospital. Jeff's phone was passed around among the newcomers, and the video was viewed by the new arrivals. It was clear that the girl had asked for help and that the two boys had made the first aggressive moves. It was also clear that one more boy was involved. One of the officers said, "Let's move this to the station and clear the street."

The remaining protesting boy was handcuffed and put in the back of a police car. A crowd from the party and from neighboring houses had spilled into the street and surrounding yards, and Jeff and Danielle had been recognized. Whispers of "The Americans" could be heard. The police waved Jeff and Danielle into the back of the third police car, and both cars headed to the station, Oliver following behind. He had already called Jake to tell him about the situation, and he said he would meet everyone at the station. Soon, Jeff and Danielle were giving their statement, backed up by the video. The remaining boy had given up the name of the boy who had run and said he was the one who had drugged the girl, although his story was still that he and the boy who had stayed were just going to take her home. This story came apart when he admitted that he didn't know who she was or where she lived.

The policeman who interrogated him asked if he had known who Jeff and Danielle were when he attacked them. Laced with some profanity, his answer was basically, "No. Who would be stupid enough to attack them if they knew who they were?" Jeff copied the video file to a flash drive, they signed their statements, and the two were finally allowed to leave. One of the policemen shook their hands but commented, "It will be much quieter here when you leave the country." Danielle commented jokingly, "We're thinking of immigrating," and Oliver hustled her out the door, whispering, "I thought you knew when to keep your mouth shut!"

Jake drove them home where they explained to the rest of the family, except for Lucy who was in bed asleep, what had happened. Zoe and Sophie were livid, and Zoe told Jeff, "I hope you broke his back." They found out the next day that outside of the concussion, he only had a badly bruised back, and Zoe had calmed down enough by breakfast to apologize to everyone for what she had said. She had been not only angry at the event but frightened for Jeff and Danielle. When the Freedmans were told about the incident, Elizabeth told Zoe confidently, "You'll learn that Jeff and Danielle can take care of themselves. Plus, God watches out for them."

The story made the morning news. Linda had her scoop, calling as soon as the twins were up to get the details. The third boy had been arrested, and a search of his apartment found vials of GHB he hadn't disposed of, thinking he was in the clear. The girl had fully recovered after a night in the hospital and had no memory of anything after a certain point at the party. She was so frightened by the turn of events that she abandoned her flat mates, left the university, and returned home to live with her parents for a while.

Jeff and Danielle received the usual attention at school the next day after one of their "events". The principal called them to his office again to congratulate them on the positive coverage the school had received and to mention that they might be wearing their school uniforms next time. Jeff thought he was looking a bit older than when they first met him, a little more gray in the hairline that had receded a bit over the past few months. A crowd gathered around them at lunch to hear the details the news might have left out. Zoe, standing beside Jeff as they put away the lunch things and prepared to return to class said quietly, "You and Danielle are looking a little tired." Jeff smiled and said, "It has been a trying couple of weeks."

# Chapter 37

School let out that Friday for a two-week holiday, and the Armstrongs were happy to load Jeff and Danielle on a plane and get them out of town. Lucy was bouncing up and down in her seat between Zoe and Jeff, excited to be traveling to the US for the first time. She had a list of things to see, first of which was armadillos. When she had mentioned how strange she thought they looked, Jeff had raised an eyebrow and said, "Seriously? From the country that has the platypus?" Lucy had given a surprised shrug and asked, "What's wrong with the platypus, mate?" Jeff just shook his head.

Also on her list were longhorn cattle. Robert had introduced a few head on his ranch in the past year as a way to help the ranch retain its agricultural tax exemption. It was turning into a money maker, though, as restaurants began offering the lean meat to their fat-conscious customers. He dedicated five acres to the project, rotated the cattle around, irrigated the grass if necessary, and the cattle were paying for themselves and then some. He laughingly called it Elizabeth's college fund. This was a joke since Jeff and Danielle had already set up a scholarship for her to the college of her choice.

Their flight departed Friday evening and, after a two-hour layover in Los Angeles where they cleared Customs, continued on their way, arriving Saturday morning. The family had flown in first class comfort thanks to Jeff and Danielle, and Lucy, in spite of her excitement, had dropped off to sleep part way across the Pacific. She was one confused little girl when they landed in the west coast city, but dashed about with excitement in the airport terminal, causing other travelers to laugh with her excited, "Look at this, mates!" and calls of, "Let's get some brekkie!"

Finally, they arrived home and after collecting their luggage, exited the terminal to find the Freedman family waiting for them. After hugs and greetings, everyone was guided to the two vehicles Robert and Michelle had brought, the luggage was loaded, and the short drive to the Freedman ranch began. Before he pulled away, Robert handed Jeff a small packet from the console. He opened it and sighed with relief to find it contained his and Danielle's knives. Taking his four, he passed the bag back to Danielle before sliding his four into his cargo pants pockets. Danielle did the same.

Lucy watched with interest, as did Zoe sitting on the other side of the young girl's car seat, and she asked, "What are those, mate?" Jeff smiled at her and answered, "My knives." Zoe asked, "Why do you need knives, and why four?" Then she thought about the custom steak knife set and the chisels the twins had carried in the tool belts at the children's ranch site and the snake that had been killed, and said, "Oh. You have really missed being able to carry a knife, haven't you?" Jeff shrugged. "Not all the time, but there have been moments." Lucy poked him and said, "We're only here for two weeks, mate." Jeff poked her back and said, "I know. But two weeks is two weeks."

The conversation in both vehicles was lively, especially as Jake and Sophie tried to bring Robert and Michelle up to date on the latest incident. Michelle's first question was, "Are they in trouble?" Robert's was, "Did they hurt anyone?" The answer to the first was no, they appeared to be heroes of this particular incident, and the answer to the second was, "Not too bad. The boy will recover quickly from the concussion and bruising." Jake didn't mention that if Jeff had thrown the boy a little harder, he could have broken his back and paralyzed him for life.

At the ranch, the family found Cindy and Lily preparing breakfast. It was a suitable meal for everyone: actual breakfast for some, a VERY early morning meal for the group from Australia. Everyone's luggage was moved to a room. Zoe and Lucy would be in Danielle's room, while she bunked with Elizabeth. Jake and Sophie were put in Jeff's room. Lily was staying at the Jacobs with Cindy.

Jeff and Sean would be sleeping in the basement. One of the additions made to the house when Jeff and Danielle's bedrooms were built was an expansion of the storm shelter located twenty feet from the back door. A large, square hole was dug in the ground between the back door and the cellar and lined with cement. The original steps to the shelter were removed, and the new entrance was from a door in the kitchen that led down into the space. Stairs were poured at the side of the extension out in the yard as an emergency exit. The new basement held a pool table, comfortable chairs, and space for several air mattresses. There was also a small room with a chemical toilet.

As she looked around, Sophie asked, "How many times have you needed this?" Robert answered, "None. But it's better to have it and not need it than to need it and not have it." Elizabeth added, "Besides, it gave us a place to put the pool table. And to put the boys. Otherwise, they would have had to sleep in the barn with the horses."

After breakfast, the Armstrongs were given a tour of the property, and Lucy was introduced to Chester and Cinnamon. She immediately fell in love as first one, then the other of the horses nuzzled her hand gently as she petted their soft, velvety noses. That was almost as far as the tour went. The small girl would have fed them a million carrots had she been allowed, and Elizabeth promised to take her riding and give her a lesson later in the day. Jake and Sophie exchanged a look. Was the girl going to want a horse and riding lessons when they returned home? They knew Jeff would give her one in a heartbeat if asked.

At the end of the barn, a wide steel door opened into an enclosed space with a concrete ramp leading down to another wide steel door. This one opened into an underground storm shelter for the horses. There were four stalls and a kitchen/living room with a widescreen TV and battery powered emergency radio. Ventilation was provided through an electric fan which could be cranked by a foot pedal if necessary. Jeff and Danielle had paid to install the structure soon after their adoption, deeming safety for the horses as important as that of the humans. The entire space was as spotless as the house thanks to the efforts of the woman who cleaned for them, bringing her family members to help as needed.

From the tour of the ranch, everyone drove to the nearby children's ranch where the Armstrongs received an idea of what the Australia one could develop into over time. Zoe commented that this one had its own stable and arena, and Lucy gave Jeff an accusing look and said, "Yeah, mate!" Jeff smiled and said, "There's already a stable next door with everything already built. If it doesn't work out, we'll add one to the children's ranch." Lucy nodded, satisfied with the explanation.

The Armstrongs were a bit overwhelmed by the enthusiasm with which the children greeted Jeff and Danielle, clamoring to know when they'd be coming back and wanting to show them this and that, telling about tournaments they'd won and placing in horse shows and cooking and sewing. They were dragged on a tour of the various training buildings and shown displays of welding and woodwork, and they exclaimed over the car that had been rebuilt. One seventeen-year-old girl pointed out that she had painted the car, and the visitors all admired the job. Then Pastor Marcus appeared and took them away to his office.

Once there, the visitors, as so many before them had done, examined the pictures of Jeff and Danielle in the various stages of their lives. Lucy, upon seeing Danielle with her hair cut military short, exclaimed, "Wow, mate! What happened to your hair?" Zoe shook her head and admonished her, "Lucy!" The girl explained, "But, look, mom. It's as short as Jeff's." Jeff said, "Hey, my hair is growing." Zoe gave him a look. It had only grown half an inch so far; hardly a stellar amount. He said, "Well, it is."

They sat in Pastor Marcus' office for a while and talked about the children's ranch, Jeff and Danielle, the new children's ranch in Australia, Jeff and Danielle, all the travel plans for the coming two weeks, and Jeff and Danielle. Pastor Marcus had quite a few stories to tell, and finally Danielle stood and said, "Okay, we have a young lady who needs a riding lesson," and everyone else rose as well. Soon they were back at the Freedman ranch, and Lucy was sitting in front of Elizabeth on Cinnamon, riding around the arena and then the pasture.

Danielle saddled Chester and rode along with them as they toured the property, then crossed the road and tooled along the riding trails on the children's ranch that Jeff and Danielle had designed. After a couple of hours, they returned to unsaddle, cool down, and brush the two horses. Lucy performed an admirable job of brushing the horses' shoulders and front legs; all the older girls would let her near. She was also allowed to give both horses more carrots before the three trooped inside to find food.

# Chapter 38

The next day was Sunday, and everyone drove in two cars to 2nd Street Bible Church. Cloudy but not rainy, the day promised to be a pleasant one. It was warmer than the weather they had left behind, but not by a lot, even though it was now winter in Australia. The road into the city was bordered by green pastures and farmland before they reached the suburbs and then the city.

As they pulled away from the house, Jeff linked Lucy's tablet to the car's camera system. At his and Danielle's request, Robert had taken both vehicles by a car accessory shop and had the front, rear, and side cameras and backup system added. The cameras connected directly to the display mounted in the dash but could also be linked by Bluetooth to a smartphone or tablet, just like the cars in Australia. The family could see the usefulness in case of a wreck for insurance purposes, but otherwise expected them to see little use. Lucy soon showed them the error in their thinking.

Sitting in her booster seat, the six-year-old could see the sky through the side windows, but not the ground. With her tablet, she could see everything in all directions which was why she was the first to spot the car approaching rapidly from the rear. She was experienced at watching cars pass on the highways back home, and knew what an approaching car should look like. This one had changed from a spec to a bug to a car way too fast. She squeaked, "That car behind us is going too fast!" Robert, who had been chatting with Jake and pointing out the scenery gave a quick glance to the rear-view mirror, and was startled to see the car approaching at what had to be over 100 miles per hour.

In his defense, as Lucy had noticed, it had approached very quickly, between Robert's frequent glances at the mirror. Before he had time to do anything, what little he might have done, the car was past him and the vehicle ahead driven by Michelle. Jeff said, "They're not going to make the curve by the golf course if they don't slow down." His words were prophetic. Even as he dialed 9-1-1 and scrolled Lucy's tablet back to see the license plate on the car, they came up on the aforementioned curve and spotted the bright blue car sitting in a pond, or possibly a stock tank, on the opposite side of the road, steam rising from the engine and the exhaust. Tire tracks and pieces of the car ran through the median between the north and south bound lanes, down the slight incline to the service road, across another slight incline to a barbed-wire fence that was still curling and twanging with broken strands, over dirt tracks in a bit of pasture, smashed weeds and brush all the way, and ending in the pond.

Both Freedman vehicles pulled over to the far left of the southbound lanes, out of the way of traffic, and turned on their emergency flashers. Jeff snatched his backpack from the floorboard at his feet and rushed toward the car to be met by Danielle, running from the other vehicle. After a quick glance to make sure the northbound lanes were clear, they crossed the highway, service road, and pasture and made their way through the water which reached halfway up the car's doors.

Two people were slumped forward in the front seat belts, stunned or worse, collapsed airbags in front of their faces. Both appeared to be college age, a boy behind the wheel, a girl in the passenger seat. Jeff muttered to himself, "What is it with us and cars and water?" Water was already seeping into the car and was over the tops of the passengers' shoes. Trying the door handle and finding it locked, he called across the top of the car to Danielle,

"Is that door locked?" She confirmed that it was. The girl on Danielle's side looked most out of the way, so Danielle pulled out one of her knives and smashed it into the side window, hard enough to shatter it into beads, not hard enough to knock it into the car. Pulling out a second knife, she maneuvered the window until it tumbled into the pond, then reached in to check the girl who was beginning to groan and stir.

Jeff handed her a six-foot piece of wood, possibly fence post, that was lying across the hood of the car, apparently picked up sometime during the wild ride, and she used it to reach across and unlock the driver's side door. He forced the door open, and water rushed in around the passengers' feet and legs. The girl jerked upright, and the boy groaned and slowly sat up, staring groggily around, then down at himself as the water settled around his waist. He gave Jeff an angry look and snarled, "What did you do?" Jeff raised an eyebrow. "You flooded my car! I'm going to sue you!" Jeff, glancing around at the parts of the car he could see, said, "I think water in your car is the least of your problems."

Across the roof of the car, Danielle rolled her eyes. The girl unfastened her seat belt and tried to climb out. Danielle said, "You'd better wait until we're sure you haven't broken anything," but the girl pushed at her and said, "Get away from me! I have to get out of this water! It's ruining my clothes!" As the boy continued to rant, Jeff called Robert, giving him an update. Even as they spoke, a police car, ambulance, and paramedic truck rolled down the service road, and, entering through the now open fence, pulled up to the edge of the pond.

The girl was standing in the thigh high water, and, with Danielle's help, sloshed her way to dry ground. She apparently would have continued walking away, but one of the two police officers stopped her. The girl went into a tirade of, "Take your hands off me," and "Do you know who I am?" which was not as impressive as it might have been if she hadn't been such a soggy, bloody mess. The officer led her, complaining all the way, to the ambulance to be checked out.

Still in the car, the boy was announcing loudly that his neck and back hurt, and that Jeff had moved him, causing possible irreparable damage. Since he was still in his seat belt and Jeff hadn't touched him, and as every moment was on Jeff's bodycam, he was not concerned. Shaking his head, he waved to the officials that it was all theirs, and walked over to join Danielle, who was giving a statement to the second police officer.

Robert walked over with a flash drive that contained the camera views as the car overtook and passed the two cars. He had also borrowed Lucy's tablet to show them what the drive contained. The officer shook his head. "Their parents do have some clout and have managed to buy their way out of trouble before. They'll probably buy their way out of this, too. At least no one was hurt, and they'll have to fix a fence and replace a car. That's about the most we can hope for." On Monday, the lawsuit arrived against Jeff for causing bodily injury to the boy.

# Chapter 39

An hour later, the two Freedman vehicles were on their way. If there were no more delays, they would probably make it to church in time for the second service. Michelle had called to tell Amy know what was going on, and the exasperated woman had told Steve. When he told Cindy and Lily that the twins would not make it to Sunday School and the reason why, Lily exclaimed, "Everything interesting happens to them." Then, remembering that she had been kidnapped, amended, "Mostly everything."

When the two cars arrived, the twins were mobbed. The Armstrong family was stunned. Jeff and Danielle had their friends back in Australia, but it was nothing like this. The family had gotten a hint at the children's ranch, but this greeting was even crazier. People wanted to know about the connect-the-dot pictures. Danielle was sending the ones she drew to Elizabeth who made them available for the church, but none of them were of the people here, and everyone wanted to know when those would be back. Danielle had to say, "Not until we're back," which was a disappointment, but still, the pictures were all Bible based, so they were cool although not as personal as they had been before.

Everyone also wanted to know when they would be writing more music for the church. They were singing the songs Jeff and Danielle had written for Terry's band, but the church hadn't received anything new just for them since Jeff and Danielle went to live with Marilyn in the mobile home. Again, they answered, "Not until we're living back here again. Maybe next year."

Rachael appeared, hugged Jeff and Danielle, and waited to be introduced, saying, "Word is you two got in trouble on the way to church. You've been home how long? A day? And why are you dressed like that?" Jeff glanced down. The two cars had stopped by Steve and Amy's house, and the twins borrowed some of Steve's sweat pants. Danielle said, "We were standing in a pond not long ago." Rachael laughed. "This has to be a good story, but tell it later. Church is about to start."

Zoe watched Rachael curiously, but Lucy said, "You know Jeff is marrying my mom, right, mate?" Everyone stared at her, and there was more than one embarrassed, "Lucy!" Rachael just laughed. "I'm sure he will if it's supposed to happen. He and Danielle and my family are friends." She whispered, "They found my dog when she was stolen." Lucy's eyes went wide. "Really? They do things like that. They rescued a family from their car and some sharks. One almost bit Jeff." Rachael stared at her with wide eyes. "I know. Aren't they just amazing?" Jeff muttered, "Church?" and everyone headed into the sanctuary.

Elizabeth leaned over from where she was sitting behind Jeff and whispered, "How did she know Rachael was an old girlfriend? She just met her." Jeff whispered back, "I don't know. She's a very perceptive little girl." Lucy looked up from the new picture she was working on and asked, "What's perceptive?" Jeff whispered to Elizabeth before she sat back in her seat, "And has excellent hearing." Lucy just grinned to herself.

The church service commenced, and Jeff and Danielle lost themselves in memories. So much had happened with this church, and though it was different than the first time they walked through the doors when they were seven, much was still the same. Some of the members who had been young adults when they joined were now married with children of their own. Others who had been old when the twins joined had gone on to their reward. Alice and

Eunice were getting on in years and were not as spry as they had been ten years earlier. Time was moving on.

Lunch following the second church service was an affair catered by a local BBQ restaurant. No one said, but Jeff and Danielle were footing the bill. Pastor John said that a church member had donated the meal in celebration of Jeff and Danielle's visit. The twins wandered around, plates in hand, Lucy in tow along with Zoe, and visited briefly with as many people as they could, answered questions about life in Australia. Lucy was a hit, and people wondered about Zoe, knowing she was a member of the host family.

By midafternoon, the church had been put back in order for the evening service, and the Freedman group, along with the Jacobs, was on the way back to the ranch. Elizabeth, riding in the Jacobs' car, pointed out the pond from which the car had been removed. A few vehicles were parked along the edge of the service road staring at the field and the water. Nothing had been taken away yet except the car itself, and the path of destruction was clearly marked with pieces of car and beaten down weeds, brush, and grass. Elizabeth exclaimed angrily, "The guy made the ambulance take him to the hospital. He was saying he's suing because Jeff hurt him by moving him. Too bad for him Jeff's bodycam will show he's a liar. Jeff should countersue. And the guy's saying he's going to sue because Jeff opened the car door, and the pond water flooded the car. Ha! It was already leaking in before Jeff even opened the stupid door." Steve agreed. "He doesn't know who he's dealing with. Guess he'll find out soon enough."

They wouldn't even have bothered to drive to the ranch since they'd be returning for the evening church service, but Cindy and Lily wanted to see the wreck site, and it wasn't that long a drive. Plus, Lucy wanted to spend more time with the horses. As they passed the wreck site, Sophie asked, "Is it strange that what happened this morning doesn't seem that unusual anymore?" Michelle answered, "You have seen much more than we ever did." She added uncertainly, "As far as we know. I'm not sure Jeff and Danielle shared everything they've been involved in." Jake asked, "Would they keep something from you?" Robert answered, "They might if they thought us knowing it might put us in some kind of risk." Michelle added, "Sometimes I think it doesn't occur to them to share."

In the backseat, Sean was pointing out the wreck site to Cindy who was indulgently listening to him. After all, she was twenty to his eighteen, and he would be leaving in a couple of weeks anyway. For the other side of the world. She smiled to herself as he told about the car in the pond as though he had seen the whole thing, thinking to herself that at least Jeff and Danielle would have cleared him personally. Since the time they had set a private detective agency loose on her boyfriend and found he had two other girlfriends as well, she had been a bit gun shy.

Once at the ranch, Lucy ran to the fence where Chester and Cinnamon stood munching on grass in the turnout. To her delight, both horses left their grazing to amble over to her, expecting a treat. She didn't disappoint them as Elizabeth handed her a couple of horse treats from her pocket, where she always seemed to have something the horses would like. The adults went inside while the young people stood at the fence, petting the horses and chatting, talking about Australia until the horses, giving up on more treats, returned to their grazing. Then the group wandered over to the pasture where the longhorn cattle stood about.

One of them, the bull, snorted and charged halfway to the fence. Lucy squealed and climbed up Jeff to rest in his arms. He watched as the bull stopped before reaching the group, tossed his head, and returned to the herd. Zoe noticed a snick as Danielle closed a knife and returned it to her pocket although she didn't know what the sound meant. "How did you know he would try to attack us?" Jeff smiled. "He was just saying, 'These are my women.' Besides, if he had kept coming, he would have gone into the freezer." She gave him an uncertain glance, but he seemed sure of himself, and when she glanced at Danielle, she winked at her. None of the others seemed concerned, so she shrugged it off as well, thinking to herself that sometimes being around Jeff and Danielle distorted one's view of reality.

Later, as they ate dinner before returning for the evening church service, Zoe told everyone about the experience. Robert laughed. "He does try to protect the herd." Sophie asked curiously, "What if he had kept coming?" Robert said, "He would have stopped at the electric fence." "Sophie pursued her question. "What if he hadn't?" Robert gazed at her calmly and answered, "He would have ended up in the freezer, and I would have bought another bull." Sophie wasn't sure what to ask next, so she let it drop, not entirely happy with the answer.

Michelle cleared it up for her on Monday as the group prepared to leave the next day for San Antonio. As Sophie watched, she drew an X on a couple of paper plates and walked into the back yard where the young people were all gathered. She called, "Danielle," and tossed one of the paper plates. Danielle spun and two knives appeared in the X, bringing the paper plate to the ground. Michelle tossed the second plate and called, "Jeff." He had turned when Danielle threw her knives, and a second later the second plate was also transfixed through the X with two knives. Turning to Sophie, Michelle said, "If the bull had kept coming, he would have died." Sophie gulped and nodded. Zoe smiled in gratitude and satisfaction. Lucy cheered.

Sunday evening, the church service was much calmer than the morning. Jeff and Danielle were able to keep their original clothes; no crazy wrecks. People stopped by to say hi, but the Freedman group was driving home within half an hour of the service ending. Later, in the kitchen, they discussed the difference between the church services that day and the ones back in Australia. Then the talk turned to the upcoming trip to San Antonio. The next day the lawsuit arrived.

# Chapter 40

Jake and Sophie wondered about all of the Americans' lack of concern for the lawsuit. It arrived Monday afternoon, Robert updated their lawyer who had already been given the specifics and the video and had obtained a copy of the police report, and then the family promptly forgot about it as they planned for the coming week and their drive to San Antonio and the surrounding countryside. The trip did not include a drive to any Texas beaches, pretty sure the Australians would be unimpressed with the murky water of the Gulf of Mexico after the clear, beautiful water off the shores of Australia.

After five days of driving south, then east, then northwest, they had touched four of the geographic regions, toured countless historical and interesting sites, and posed for pictures in front of all of them. Now they were back in the Freedman home, unpacking from the trip, and, in the case of the young people, getting reacquainted with the two horses who were very happy to see them, or at least the carrots and other treats they had brought.

Inside the house, Robert, Michelle, Jake, and Sophie were discussing Jeff and Zoe. Robert and Michelle had become very aware over the past few days of the relationship between Jeff, Zoe, and Lucy. Sophie said, "If Lucy could have her way, Jeff and Zoe would be married already, and she would be calling Jeff Dad. Michelle commented, "It's kinda amusing to watch how Jeff and Zoe keep a proper distance between themselves at all times. They have to be very aware of each other. Jake asked, "What happens when Jeff and Danielle come home at the end of the school year?" Robert said, "I only see two possibilities: either Jeff and Danielle stay there, or Zoe and Lucy come here; at least until they work this out." Michelle and Sophie shared a look, and Michelle mused, "Or they do both."

Jake asked, "What do you mean?" Sophie said, "They both want to go to uni. I don't think either one cares about a degree, but I know Jeff wants more business classes, and Zoe would like some music classes now that Jeff has taught her to play keyboards. So, they could spend six months here and six months there, going to school. Lucy is doing fine with homeschool there, and I assume she could continue here somehow." Everyone sat in thought for a bit, then Jake said, "That could work. They need to get started on their applications if that's what they want to do, though."

The conversation was interrupted at that point by Robert's phone ringing. Glancing at the caller ID, he said, "Our lawyer," and answered. After listening for a moment, he said, "Thank you," and disconnected. "The lawsuit against us was dropped. Our lawyer convinced them that we wouldn't give in, even if it turned out to be less expensive, and they have their own problems now with the video of the car speeding and the damage it caused when it went off the road. Plus, the video shows that the car was already flooding before Jeff opened the door. It's amazing how many times their bodycams have turned something around. Although it's sad that they so often get into situations where they have to defend themselves."

So, the discussions were begun concerning Jeff, Zoe, and Lucy. None of them knew if Jeff and Zoe were thinking that far ahead. Considering how far apart they kept themselves, everyone doubted it. Michelle said she would bring up the subject with Jeff, and Sophie would do the same with Zoe. All agreed that they needed some way to continue to grow together until they were older. Michelle wanted Jeff to reach at least 21. Zoe would be 22.

They could live with that. Whether or not Lucy could wait until she was ten was another question. Sophie strongly doubted it.

Then Sunday rolled around, and Zoe met Sydney. After spending the first Sunday at 2<sup>nd</sup> Street Bible Church, Jeff and Danielle wanted the Armstrong family to meet their other church friends and at least do a drive by of the mobile home park where they had lived with Marilyn and take a tour of the tornado shelter they had built. When the group walked through the door, they were immediately swamped, primarily by the Edwards extended family. Levi and Mckenzie ran up exclaiming, "We have our own secret room! Mom and Dad had it built for us."

Jeff and Danielle already knew about the room through Sydney, but they listened as the two children described it for them, oohing and ahhing at all the right places. Then Sydney bumped them aside so she could hug the twins and be introduced to Zoe and Lucy, both of whom she had heard so much about. Lucy eyed her suspiciously, not sure what to think of this particular girl, but when Zoe hugged her, Lucy relented, at least enough to shake her hand and say, "G'day, mate!" Then she turned to Mckenzie and asked what she was talking about with the secret room.

The four children told about their secret rooms, and after understanding what they were talking about, Lucy turned to Jeff and said, "I want a secret room. With a wardrobe for the entrance." Jeff just said, "Okay. We'll have to talk to your mom and grandparents about it and see what can be done. It will take some remodeling." Sydney shared a look with him and mouthed, "Sorry," but Jeff just shrugged. "If there's room, it will be pretty simple. This one won't have to withstand a tornado."

Zoe wasn't sure what to think about Sydney. It wasn't as though she could take Jeff's arm possessively since they weren't touching each other. She caught Sydney's sympathetic look and decided she might like her, as long as she and Jeff were really just friends. Everyone made their way into the sanctuary, the crowd swirling around Jeff and Danielle while the Armstrong family watched in bemusement. Sophie remarked to Michelle, "It isn't like this back home. People like them, but it's more normal." Michelle answered, "They've had a lot more time here, and they've done some pretty spectacular things, although seriously, not as much as in Australia. Here, they didn't work so hard to stay out of the news. They're learning.

The next day, the group headed out again, this time driving north and west. By the time they returned home on Thursday, they had covered three more of the state's geographic regions and learned more about each other and especially about Jeff, Zoe, and Lucy. The adults were as certain as they could be that the three were in it for the long haul; as much as they could tell, anyway, as young as those involved were. On one of the days, the opportunities arose to bring up to Jeff and Zoe both the idea of attending uni in both countries, six months at a time. Both were receptive, and the plan had the beginning of a framework.

On Friday, the travelers returned to Australia for the next few months, not expecting to see their friends in the states again until Christmas.

# Chapter 41

School began again the day after their return to Australia with tons of homework. The movie was still progressing on schedule. But, the main topic of discussion around the Armstrong table was Lucy's secret room. Over dinner Monday, Lucy gazed at Jeff with her wishful eyes and asked, "When can you build my secret room?" Jeff smiled back at her and said, "Have you asked your mother if you can have a secret room?" The girl switched her gaze to Zoe and pleaded, "May I, mom?" Zoe grinned back at her and said, "Have you asked Grandma and Grandpa? It's their home that will be torn up to make the room." Jeff was impressed that Lucy had used may I instead of can I.

Lucy's gaze moved to Jake and Sophie, and she said, "Please, please, please! It would be so cool!" Jake asked Jeff and Danielle, "Is it possible?" The two had spent some time Sunday evening walking around the lounge room that bordered Lucy's room, eyeballing the dimensions and rearranging furniture in their minds. It would work without too much trouble. There was room for the furniture to move in a bit, and the pictures could be rehung on the new wall. Danielle said, "It wouldn't be too much trouble if you don't mind losing some space in the lounge room. We can show you what we're thinking."

Lucy could barely finish her meal, and rushed everyone through the cleanup. As soon as the leftovers were in the refrigerator or the freezer and the dishes were washed and put away, the family trooped into the lounge room as Jeff and Danielle described what they had in mind. Then they moved to Lucy's room to show where the entrance would be. The small girl squirmed with excitement, and she exclaimed, "It's perfect! When will it be finished?" Jeff and Danielle exchanged a look, and he said, "Maybe a couple of weeks? We're visiting the hospital in Darwin this coming weekend, and with everything else going on, we will have to take it in stages, but a couple of weeks should do it."

That became the plan, and an impatient Lucy watched as it unfolded. Sophie and Lucy went shopping at antique stores until they found the perfect wardrobe. Jeff and Danielle framed the new room, put up the sheetrock, taped and bedded, and painted it to match the rest of the lounge room. Actually, the rest of the lounge room was painted to match the new walls as Sophie declared it time for a change. The rest of the family worked on that while Jeff and Danielle built Lucy's secret room. Lights were added to the room as well as a single bed with drawers underneath.

Midway through the project, the family flew to Darwin for the weekend, leaving Friday evening after school and returning Sunday afternoon. By the following Friday, the room was finished, and Lucy could be found in it much of the time. In fact, it proved to be quite convenient. If anyone was looking for her, they knew where she could be found. A week later, Robert, Michelle, Elizabeth, Cindy, and Lily flew in. The family was on pins and needles wondering what this could be about, but all the Freedmans would say was that they had some majorly important news, and they would tell them about it when they arrived.

# Chapter 42

Early in August, Robert's phone had rung. The call was from the detective agency they had hired when Michelle showed him the DNA results. The next day, the couple walked anxiously into the office of the head of the agency. After the usual pleasantries and offers of coffee or cold drinks, he pointed to a round table and asked them to be seated. On the table rested a red folder marked SECRET and URGENT. Smiling at the folder, he said, "I know it seems a bit melodramatic, but we have worked with Jeff and Danielle for years, and the results have been of as much interest to us as they have been to you, although possibly for different reasons.

To begin, I will summarize with the main points. Then I will tell you a story. First, the DNA results proved that Jeff and Danielle do, indeed, share the same father. The odds against that seemed very high, but not impossible. Second, the DNA results proved that Jeff and Danielle shared the same mother. Thanks to the second DNA sample you submitted, we know that the mother was Marilyn. That seemed to come completely out of left field and had no known explanation. Third, the birth certificate Danielle has possessed all these years is a fake. Fourth, the birth certificate issued at the time of her birth is also a fake."

Robert and Michelle stared at the man as though he was speaking Klingon. When they had seen the original DNA results, the question that immediately came to mind was, if the twins had the same parents, who were they? Earlier that same week, Michelle had found in an old purse the makeup bag she had used when she was caring for Marilyn during her final days. After the funeral, she had switched to a new purse, shoved the old one on a closet shelf, and forgotten about it until she came across it by "accident?" In the makeup bag was a brush that still held strands of Marilyn's hair.

She and Robert had immediately sent a sample to the DNA company as a follow up to the original. Soon enough, the response showed up on the website: Marilyn was Jeff and Danielle's mother. Using his police contacts, Robert had submitted a DNA request to a wide variety of databases, but the father did not appear in any of them. He was still a mystery.

The man smiled at their stunned expressions. "Now, the story. A young woman became pregnant and moved away from home to a new city. During her pregnancy, she never visited a doctor or took any particular care of herself until the last week of her pregnancy when, apparently by accident, she was introduced to a midwife whom she paid to help with her delivery. On a night sixteen and a half years ago, she gave birth to twins.

During the delivery, she was stoned out of her mind, and the midwife took advantage of her condition. Marilyn didn't know she was carrying twins, and the midwife knew a couple who were desperate for a baby girl. She gave the boy to Marilyn along with a birth certificate and took the girl with her. The couple paid her a rather large sum of money, and she gave them the daughter and a birth certificate naming them the parents. They immediately moved to another city where they were not known and began raising the child.

Six months later, they attended a party, leaving the baby with a baby sitter. On the drive home, their car was struck by a drunk driver, and they were both killed. The baby ended up with child protective services. The woman had a sister whom she apparently spoke to infrequently. CPS located her through letters found in the deceased's home, and when they asked about the child, the woman apparently had enough of a family connection that she felt obligated to take the child, even though she didn't even know her sister had a daughter. Thus, Danielle ended up with the woman she thought was her mother.

This woman had a friend who could manufacture fake documents, and rather than go through the process of adopting the girl, she had a birth certificate created and inserted in public records showing her to be the mother. Her sister had kept her maiden name, so Danielle's last name never changed. The mess fell apart pretty easily under our investigation, but up until then, no one had any reason to examine any of the documents. If you would like, we are prepared to have a correct birth certificate issued and have the fake ones removed from public record. It will be as though the other two never existed."

Michelle croaked, "How did you find any of this if all of the fake parents were dead?" The man smiled. "We found the midwife. From there we found the neighbors of the man and woman who originally took Danielle, both before they moved, when the woman wasn't pregnant, and the new neighbors, when she appeared with a new baby.

We followed the trail to Danielle's home in New Orleans. Her neighbors knew she was the sister's daughter, but didn't know the birth certificate had been changed. No one thought it strange that Danielle called the woman mother, and with the transient nature of the neighborhood, few people were around who remembered the arrival of the baby. The woman next door who runs a boarding house knew but saw no reason to tell the little girl."

Robert and Michelle shared a look, and Robert asked, "When do we tell Jeff and Danielle? I think we have to do this in person." Michelle said, "As soon as possible, like this coming Saturday. We'll need to take Lizzie and the "sisters", if possible. I'll call Danielle and ask her to take care of the reservations." She laughed. "That won't make them curious at all." Robert laughed in agreement, still in shock from the story they had just been told. He told the man, "We'll let you know about fixing the birth certificates after we talk to them, but I assume Danielle will want them corrected."

Still in a daze, they said their goodbyes and made their way to Michelle's SUV. As Robert drove them home, Michelle called Cindy to ask if she could fly to Australia for a few days beginning Saturday. Cindy was delighted, but when she asked what the occasion was, Michelle just said it was a surprise for Jeff and Danielle. She repeated the call to Lily's mother and repeated the question. Lily could be heard in the background screaming with excitement at the news, especially after her mother said yes. As she ended the call, Robert glanced over and commented, "It's a good thing everyone is keeping their tourist visas up to date."

Once home, Elizabeth was told about the trip, which led to more jumping and screaming. She accepted the explanation of a surprise for Jeff and Danielle with some suspicion. "There's something you two aren't telling me," she said with a look. "Her mom just smiled and answered, "You'll know soon enough," and the girl had to be content with that mysterious statement.

Later that evening, when she knew the twins would be awake but not on their way to school, Michelle called Jeff. She reached him at the breakfast table, and he put his phone on speaker. "We're coming for a visit, if that will work for all of you." There were raised eyebrows around the table, and Danielle, after a nod from Sophie, said, "That would be super! What's the occasion? And who is we?" Elizabeth said, "Mom and Dad have news, but they won't tell me what it is. We is us and Cindy and Lily."

Jeff said, "Really? News important enough for a trip? Now I'm not curious at all. When do you want to come, and do you want us to make the reservations?" Robert answered, "Yes, please. If you can, set us up to arrive on Saturday. Lily will meet us in LA. We'll need hotel reservations for somewhere nearby. And a car?" This last was a question. Jake immediately said, "We'll take care of your transportation." Lucy added, "Acacia will be excited to see Lily again!" Elizabeth chimed in, "Lily has probably already told her."

The call ended amid speculation regarding the purpose of the visit, and Jeff and Danielle took their plates to the dining room where they could set up their laptops and make the necessary reservations before they left for school. In spite of the short lead time, Danielle was able to book all five of the travelers into first class for the long flight over the Pacific. The cost was high due to the short lead time, but really, it was a drop in the bucket compared to the twins' income. Lily would arrive in LA ahead of them by an hour or so and would be waiting at the gate when the rest of the group arrived. Jeff booked them into a couple of rooms at a nearby hotel between the Armstrong home and the airport. Their part was done. Now the waiting and anticipation began.

The next few days went by in a blur for Jeff and Danielle. They couldn't imagine what news their family thought was so important that they needed to fly to Australia to tell them. Surely Michelle wasn't expecting a baby. That would be exciting news, but they could have told them that over video chat. Only their discipline allowed them to pay attention at all to their classes, and finally, Saturday did arrive.

# Chapter 43

Jake, Jeff, and Danielle waited at the curb for the group from America. Danielle had ridden in the car with Jake while Jeff rode his motorcycle. They could have possibly crammed everyone in the vehicle, but their luggage would have been left on the curb. As it was, everyone held their carryon luggage in their laps, and the remainder was ingeniously stowed in the rear or tied on top. They had arrived on a cool, clear day in the last month of winter, and the jackets that had earned them strange looks in LA were very nice to have now.

After stopping at the hotel long enough to check in and drop off their luggage, the group proceeded to the Armstrong home where a late breakfast awaited them. There were a flurry of hugs and hellos followed by excited chatter and the clatter of flatware as the food was consumed. Then everyone sat back expectantly as they waited for Robert and Michelle to tell them why they had come. They asked everyone for their patience while they walked off with Jeff and Danielle to the backyard. Once there, they sat at the picnic table, and Michelle began.

"While the two of you were in the hospital the last time, I took some of your blood and sent it off for DNA analysis." The twins' faces immediately grew still and blank, and the adults could imagine the thoughts flying through their minds. It had always been a bit of a joke that they were related because their birth certificates both said unknown for the father. They didn't really want to know for certain that it wasn't true. But their mom and dad wouldn't fly all the way here just to tell them that, would they?

Michelle continued. "I know it was wrong, but it was on my mind, and I thought, just in case, it would be good for someone to know. Then, when the results came back, I didn't look at them for a year. Finally, I took a look. I don't know how, but you two do have the same father." The look of joy on Jeff and Danielle's faces was a sight to behold. It turned to shock when Michelle told them the next bit of information. "You also have the same mother. You really are twins."

Danielle stammered, "Who? How?" Robert told the story, explaining the situation with the two fake birth certificates. Jeff's face changed to ecstatic, but Danielle's went pale and angry. "Marilyn was my mom? And I lost all those years? She didn't even like me until Jeff gave her his baby seal charm." Now she was coldly furious, stalking around the table like an angry predator, clutching her head and crying.

She turned cold green eyes on Michelle and Robert. "Where is the midwife?" Robert answered calmly, "You can't go kill her." She said, "Yes, I can." Jeff told her, "Danielle, our mother didn't start to turn around until we turned fourteen. The midwife isn't the one who kept mom from us, and she isn't the one who took her from us at the end." Danielle dropped back into her seat at the table. "I know. I just want to hurt something."

Michelle wrapped her arms around the strong shoulders, and Danielle leaned into her. She opened her eyes and stared at Jeff. "Twins. Told you so." Jeff rolled his eyes. Robert asked him, "What about you? Are you okay?" "It didn't change anything for me. Mom was always mom, and Danielle was always my sister. DNA tests don't change any of that."

After a bit more time had passed, the four rose and moved to the lounge room where everyone was sitting around visiting. Silence immediately settled over the room as they entered, and the group waited expectantly for the announcement that had brought the group, Jeff and Danielle's immediate family, to Australia.

After the four had taken seats, the American twins on the floor, Jeff with Lucy in his arms after the small girl had climbed into his lap, Michelle told the story again, beginning with sending off the DNA samples. There were exclamations from the American girls when she told how they did indeed share the same father, but silence followed by an explosion of sound when she told how they also shared the same mother, followed again by shocked silence when she confirmed that mother was Marilyn.

Into the silence, Michelle poured the whole story. When she was finished, Sean proclaimed, "That's insane! It's like some incredible mystery story!" Elizabeth, Cindy, and Lily were all crying with happiness. Zoe asked, "What does it mean?" Jeff shrugged. "It just means that what we've been saying for years has been proven to be true." Cindy pronounced archly, "There is still a mystery man out there. Are you going to try to find him?" Danielle answered, waving at Robert and Michelle, "No. We have our parents and our family." Now Michelle swiped at the tears running down her cheeks, Robert rubbed his eyes, and Elizabeth beamed happily.

Jake said, "I think this calls for a celebration, mates." He named the family's favorite Italian restaurant on the harbor, and Lucy yelled, "Yaaay! Souffles!" Everyone else laughed. Suddenly, Jeff and Danielle shared a look and stood up, Jeff standing Lucy on her feet. He said, "We'll be right back. We have to make a phone call." They left the surprised group behind sharing puzzled looks as they returned to the back yard. Jeff slid his phone out of his pocket and pressed the speed dial number for Owen Morris' bodyguard. It was evening back home, and the phone was answered on the second ring with a curt, "Yeah?"

Jeff said, "Tell him to leave her alone. We're fine." Then he hung up. Alone with Owen in his home office, he told the crime boss the substance of the call. Owen gave a bark of laughter. "I should wait a bit before making any plans to see if I get a phone call, eh?" He had, in fact, already issued orders for the midwife to disappear and was reluctant to rescind them. On the other hand, he was, if not afraid of the twins, at least cautious, as he would be with anything dangerous. He was fairly certain that if they put their minds to it, they could eliminate him, no matter what his bodyguard did, and if they failed, God would pick up where they left off. He laughed again, and waved at the bodyguard, who made the call. The midwife never knew how close she came to ending her life in a shallow, unmarked grave.

The group spent the rest of the day until dinner catching up on news. They took both cars out to the children's ranch that was under construction. Foundations for the first buildings were in place, and the framework was going up. Cable fencing around the entire property was finished. Work on the training buildings had begun. Trenches had been dug everywhere for the various utilities.

The project was not without its difficulties, some of which had nothing to do with construction. As soon as word had gotten out that the ranch would be religious in nature, with the Bible and the gospel taught, opposition had arisen. The ranch did not and had no plans to receive any funding from the government, so their case was not as strong as it might have been. Plus, the twins were tenacious in fighting any negative publicity with positive information of their own and were more than willing to sue if any lies were propagated, which some organizations found out, to their dismay. This was not a barely surviving, live by the skin of their teeth operation.

Lucy had taken over the project as her own, and she was not shy about commending the workmen on jobs done well or telling them when she didn't like the quality of the work. Backed up by Jake and the twins, some people were replaced and the ones remaining as well as the ones replacing those banned from the site were very conscientious about their work. In time, everyone working on the site was either Christian, or, at a minimum, not hostile to Christianity. It wasn't a requirement; it just worked out that way.

Jeff and Danielle, the Armstrong family, and many in the church poured their prayer into the project. Various child services expressed interest in the ranch, and long before it was ready to accept its first children, the buildings were full, with a waiting list.

The next day in church, Lily hugged an excited Acacia hello. Although they had been in almost daily contact by video chat since they had met, this was their first face to face meeting in months. The two girls chatted non-stop as they skipped to their Sunday School class, now somewhat larger than when the two Camerons had joined the church. Jake and Sophie led Robert and Michelle up the steps of the white building next door to the church. They had known about Jeff and Danielle's purchase of the building for Sunday School rooms and the living quarters for the pastor and his family, but this was their first time inside the building.

Although the two families spoke often and the Americans knew the church was growing, this was their first time to actually witness it. The classroom was similar to the old one with posters on the wall, rows of chairs, and a coffee maker, but it was larger, with twice as many chairs as before. Sophie smiled as Robert and Michelle stared around the room. "This is largely thanks to Jeff and Danielle. It's funny, but it seemed to begin with the connect the dot pictures. And the binders they were part of." She waved around the room. Everyone either had a binder along with their Bible or there was a binder and Bible on a seat.

Robert shook his head. I saw it at our church, and I heard about it at their second church, but it's still pretty amazing. Are they writing any music for the church?" Jake answered, "Not a lot. They're pretty busy, you know, with schoolwork and exercise and their projects, especially the movie." Sophie added, "And Lucy. She takes up a great deal of Jeff's time, but he never seems to mind. We spend time almost every day at their gym. They are something to watch."

The members they had met on their first visit clustered around to greet the Americans, and they were introduced to the new members. Jake was scheduled to teach that day, an ongoing Bible study on the book of Jonah, and the class settled into their seats, opening their binders to the section for class notes. Robert and Michelle shared a thoughtful look as they gazed around the room, thinking about the influence Jeff and Danielle had once again shed on the people in their lives, some of whom they had never met or had very little contact with.

Robert and Michelle were observed from a nearby seat by Officer Victor Cameron. He had spent much more time with the twins than he would have liked in his official capacity, them and their lawyer. To him, it said a great deal about the twins that they needed a full-time lawyer. So far, they had not been totally at fault in any of the interactions, although a couple were maybe a bit sketchy. He thought they just shined very brightly in the world, and sometimes the people too near them received burns. He prayed almost daily that they would make it out of Australia without any serious run-ins with the Australian justice system.

Over in the youth classes, Lucy was telling all her friends that Jeff and Danielle's family were visiting and why. No one had told her not to, and she was an excited little chatterbox. In her classroom, Lily was doing the same. Elizabeth and Cindy had joined Jeff, Danielle, Zoe, and Sean, and they were all keeping quiet, not for any particular reason; it just never came up. However, the first Sunday School period was over, and as people moved around for the second service and Sunday School classes, the story about Jeff and Danielle's history began to spread. By the time the 11:00am service began, the sanctuary was buzzing, and people were craning their necks to catch a glimpse of the Americans.

From church, the story jumped to school. Some of the young

people in the church attended Jeff and Danielle's school, and the story was just too good to keep quiet. And, there was no particular reason to keep it quiet. Their friends congratulated them on the good news, some people tried to turn the information into an insult, but when they found it had no impact at all on the twins, they eventually gave up. The news was nice, but after the past several years, it was pretty anticlimactic.

The visit did give the four adults some additional face to face time to observe Jeff, Zoe, and Lucy and discuss the future. That Jeff and Lucy loved each other was a given. That Jeff and Zoe were falling in love with each other was also obvious. Jake and Sophie confirmed that the two still had not so much as hugged or held hands; well, seldom hugged. In fact, they seemed to work quite hard at avoiding touching each other at all, to Danielle and Sean's amusement, and Jake and Sophie's relief. Otherwise, the two living under the same roof would have been uncomfortable in a different way, one which might have led to Jeff and Danielle leaving.

Robert and Michelle were concerned because Jeff had already been through two girlfriends, three counting his crush on Beth. Not to mention that he was only seventeen, even if it was a very mature seventeen. They didn't want him making any long-term commitments for a while yet. Jake and Sophie felt the same way about Zoe, for the same and different reasons. She was only eighteen, although in some ways a mature eighteen. And a mother. A mother who had had no boyfriends over the years since Lucy was born.

That didn't even bring Lucy into the equation. None of the four had any idea how they would pry her away from Jeff if it came to that. Now they had to think about how to proceed. The idea that still seemed most likely to work was time spent attending school on both continents. Robert and Michelle liked this idea, especially since they had been without Jeff and Danielle for most of a year. Jake and Sophie did not look forward to the same situation in their own lives. Still, all four thought it was a good situation and would give Jeff, Zoe, and Lucy more time to spend together and determine if they would work as a family. Unspoken was that Danielle would be wherever Jeff was, and vice-versa. No one saw that changing anytime soon.

Jeff and Zoe had the same discussion, about the same time. One day after school, while Danielle and Lucy were in Lucy's room having a guitar lesson, Sean was out with friends, and the four adults were in the kitchen chatting over cups of coffee, Jeff sat with Zoe in the game room, showing her different ways to play a particular song on the keyboard.

He paused, and she raised her hand to lay her palm against his cheek, saying, "You know how much I care about you, yes?" He raised his hand to hers and said, "Yes. I care about you, too." She sighed and said, "What do we do? You'll be going home soon." Jeff shifted to face her. "You want to go to uni, yes?" Zoe nodded, and Jeff continued. "Mom and Dad suggested we spend a semester here and a semester in the US. In between we can travel and work on projects." She smiled. "What if we don't get accepted?" He shrugged. "Do you want a degree or knowledge or the uni experience: sorority, dorm, parties, and so on?"

Zoe laughed. "Knowledge first, then a degree. Maybe a bit of the experience, but no sorority, dorms, or parties." Jeff nodded. "We can always take classes for the knowledge, in night school or community college or whatever. And it isn't as though it has to be completed in a set amount of time. I know a man whose education was interrupted by war, and he finished his degree decades later." Their feelings out in the open, the beginnings of a plan in mind, they continued with the lesson.

No one thought to tell Lucy about the discussions.

# Chapter 44

On Saturday, the Americans flew home. The following weekend, the Armstrong group visited a hospital in Melbourne. In between, Ivy and her friends came calling. The group had begun to visit often since Jeff and Danielle arrived; much more often than before even though the performing arts school wasn't far from the Armstrong home.

They often showed up unannounced, just about dinner time, and whoever was responsible for the meal that day would shrug and throw in more of whatever they were preparing. Ivy seldom came alone, but her friends could number from just her boyfriend to the entire group of four that usually hung around together and sometimes included a girl who was sort of a friend, maybe a frenemy. Lucy was not fond of the frenemy and thought her stuck up and mean. She loved the two guys and would demand that they dance with her and watch as she showed them the latest dance or kata moves Jeff and Danielle had taught her or listen to her play her guitar. And she really liked the other girl in the group, a blond who was just fun to be around.

One of the two boys was from the outback, the back end of beyond as he liked to say, and had worked very hard to reach acceptance at the school, competing against dancers who had studied since they were small with big city dance instructors. He made up for his lack of training with sheer raw talent. He was also the one with the richest Australian accent, and a favorite joke was to create entire sentences to use on Jeff and Danielle made up of slang. The twins were quick learners, and he was only able to use each one once before they knew what it meant.

Danielle also paid him back on one of his visits. She and Jeff were cooking dinner that day, a meal of grilled chicken breasts and vegetables. As they cooked, the other young people gathered in the kitchen to talk and observe, and the young man contributed his usual collection of slang sentences. Danielle smiled sweetly and told him, "For every word you use that we don't know, I will be removing a bite of your dinner from your plate." He laughed until, when one sentence later he commented, "Oi, we should fang it to Maccas for brekkie," and she cut a slice off a chicken breast and slid aside a forkful of vegetable. "That sentence cost you a bite of each."

He stared uncertainly at the two bits of food and said, "You're joking, right, mate? Having me on a bit?" Danielle just said, "Nope. You are on a diet." Two sentences later as the group was discussing clothing, he commented, "You should see Ivy's new set of trackie daks," and she moved two more pieces of food aside, commenting, "Keep it up." Staring at the diminishing servings that were apparently his, he held up his hands and said, "I'm sorry. No more." Unfortunately, he finished the sentence by saying, "You're just so aggro," which cost him another slice. Now that he was trying not to, he couldn't stop, and words kept spilling out. By the time they were ready to eat, his portion was basically a bite of each. The others laughed at the expression on his face.

Danielle thought back to the first time they had really experienced the Aussie use of words. On their day at the beach that first week, Zoe had asked Elizabeth to hand her Lucy's thong from her bag. Elizabeth had stared at her, unsure if she had heard correctly. Surely Zoe wasn't asking for a skimpy swimsuit for the little girl. Zoe watched her in puzzlement, waiting, and finally waved a flipflop at Elizabeth and said in a questioning tone, "Thong?" Elizabeth looked in the bag, spotted a small shoe, pulled it out, and handed it to Zoe, who nodded and said, "Thanks, mate."

For the rest of the visit, Elizabeth and Lily were incorrigible. Whenever they passed a display of the beach shoes, one would ask something like, "Wouldn't these thongs look marvelous with Swarovski crystals on them?" Then both girls would collapse into giggles. Cindy and Danielle would roll their eyes, and Michelle would say sternly, "Girls!" but the two couldn't seem to stop. It never grew old for them.

Danielle finally showed leniency, and the boy smiled happily as the portions he had lost were returned to his plate. Soon everyone was seated around the dinner table, laughing over the story and coming up with their own examples. Jeff said, "How about when Sean looked in the freezer yesterday and said, "Oi, who ate all the red Zooper Doopers?" Lucy, knowing the red ice treats were Sean's favorite, made a point of eating them first.

Jeff and Danielle had picked up many words quickly, quite a few at the grocery store. Mince was ground beef; servo was the gas (petrol) station; ripper was really great. The Australians had as much trouble with the two Americans, and the household was developing a mishmash of the two forms of English. Lucy was also in the habit of throwing in bits of other languages such as the Japanese and elvish she was learning, and Zoe was beginning to think she might reach a point where no one outside the family could understand her.

After dinner, all the young people trooped to the back yard to practice dance moves. Zoe was an excellent dancer and could possibly have attended the dance academy if she were interested in it. Jeff and Danielle were also excellent dancers, but all their moves tended to, sooner or later, resemble Capoeira, the Brazilian martial art. They were, in fact, all dancing in the back yard to music with a Brazilian sort of beat. Lucy was demonstrating that she could throw a roundhouse kick while spinning with one hand on the ground. It caused her to fall over, but she just spun on the ground and rolled quickly to her feet, ready to continue, just as Jeff had taught her. The older kids all applauded her efforts.

Ivy and Zoe watched from the side of the yard, chatting. Ivy asked, "What are you going to do about Jeff and Danielle going home in December?" Zoe shrugged. "We don't know. I don't think it has occurred to Lucy yet. Hopefully we'll have something figured out by then. I am applying to the uni there. Jeff and Danielle are applying to the one here." Ivy raised an eyebrow. "Part of the time here, part of the time there? That's clever. Too clever for you. Who thought of it?" Zoe poked her. "Careful, or you won't get invited back again." Ivy laughed. "We weren't invited this time. Great dinner, by the way."

# Chapter 45

Jeff, Danielle, Henry, Zoe, and Lucy sat in various postures around the coffee table searching the internet for theaters playing a movie Lucy wanted very much to see. Henry had a two-day pass and was spending it with Danielle, starting with this evening. So far, they had been able to spend very little time together. One school holiday, Jeff and Danielle had flown to Africa. The second one, they and the entire Armstrong clan had flown to the US.

He had been busy as well, with various training exercises and the day to day of serving in the military. There had been moments together here and there such as the pig hunting expedition in Victoria or the birthday parties. Still, they had been alone exactly zero times, and it did not appear that would be changing anytime soon. This evening's adventure was the closest to a date they had had since the twin's arrival in Australia, and it would involve four teenagers and Lucy. He smiled ruefully to himself.

Looking up, he spotted Danielle watching him. Jeff was staring at him as well. It was like being stared at by two cats, except he was pretty sure these cats could read his mind. To his relief, the front door opened, and presently, Sean and his date passed through the doorway into the lounge room and joined them. He said, "Hey, guys, decided on a theater yet?" Everyone greeted them, and Lucy exclaimed, "We're going to walk to the one by the high school! Then we'll eat popcorn and candy and drink cokes until we explode!"

Jeff had explained to Lucy, much to Zoe's dismay, that all soft drinks were called cokes, and people had to tell you which flavor of coke they wanted. She had commented, "Of all the things you've taught her, that may be the one I don't forgive you for." His understanding smile had done nothing to relieve her exasperation. She wasn't really worried about the eating until they exploded part. Under Jeff's tutelage, Lucy was acquiring a very healthy palate, and even though she liked chocolate as much as the next kid, she was more likely to share a fruit snack with Jeff than eat a candy bar.

Sean said, "We were talking about it and decided that's what we want to see, too, so if it's okay, we'll tag along." Danielle said, "The more the merrier. Are you ready to go?" Shortly, Lucy had been bundled into her coat and the others had pulled on theirs, Danielle standing patiently as Henry assisted her, Zoe waiting on Jeff's help with much more gratitude.

On the walk over, the company broke into three groups that intermingled with the others, then split again, like amoebas. Lucy walked between Jeff and Zoe, holding both their hands, when she wasn't running to stare in shop windows. Danielle glided beside Henry, hands in her coat pockets, chatting about the training they shared in common unless one of the others pulled even for a different conversation. Sean and his girlfriend strolled along hand in hand, laughing softly about the tension between the others, wondering where it would lead.

Eventually, they found themselves sitting in a row of comfortable seats in the half-filled theater. Each of the three groups had a tub of popcorn and containers of soft drinks. Lucy had a cup of water, but Jeff and Zoe were sharing tiny sips of their drinks with her. The two were only willing to go so far with the small girl's sugar intake. Jeff, with Lucy on one side and Danielle on the other, was keeping half an eye on his sister and Henry.

He wasn't that concerned. Danielle could take care of herself and wasn't shy about protecting her space. He just wanted to make sure he could move Lucy out of the way in case Henry did something stupid and ended up flying toward the movie screen.

That was why he noticed, about 3/4's of the way through the movie, that Henry had laid his hand on Danielle's and rather than pulling it away or damaging him, she had turned her hand over and intertwined her fingers with his. Jeff turned his head to find Zoe watching him and nodded toward the pair of hands. Her eyes widened a bit, she smiled at him, then returned her gaze to the movie. Lucy, entranced by the activity on the screen, didn't notice anything.

After the movie ended and all the coats that had been tucked over the backs of seats were in place for the walk home, they started out. This time, Sean and his girlfriend were in front, and Danielle and Henry were behind, again holding hands. They were talking softly about staying in touch after the twins returned to the US, and Jeff glanced in alarm at Lucy, but she was chattering away animatedly about the movie she had just seen, paying no attention to those in front of or behind her.

Back at the house, they found Jake and Sophie had returned from their dinner out, and everyone sat in the lounge room telling them about the movie. Well, Lucy told them all about the movie, with appropriate gestures and movements, and the others chipped in to remind her of parts she had forgotten. Danielle and Henry were sitting together but not holding hands. Jeff and Zoe were sitting near each other but not so much as brushing shoulders or knees. Sean and his date were sitting side by side on one of the sofas, holding hands, bumping heads, acting like a normal couple, and watching the other four young people with amusement. Jeff knew they would talk about him and Zoe and probably Danielle and Henry when Jake took them home. What a mess.

Later, in their room, Zoe said, "So, you and Henry held hands, huh?" Danielle actually blushed, something she had never done before. She smiled and shrugged and said, "Yes. It was nice. Now I know what Jeff has been talking about." Then she added seriously, "It could get me killed if it's distracting at the wrong time." Zoe started and said, "Wait! What?!"

# Chapter 46

Jeff was flying north with his flight instructor on the first leg of his final flight test. Soon he would turn west and begin the second leg of the flight. This was the culmination of almost seventy hours of training time, ten of the hours solo. He and Danielle had more flight time than that, but most of it didn't count since it was with their jump pilots and not with an instructor who could observe competent planning and management of the flight as well as their navigation, radio work and airmanship and make sure they followed all procedures and rules.

Jeff and Danielle had signed up for training soon after their seventeenth birthdays. The time since had been hectic with the emergency flight to the US when Lily was sick, the two weeks in Africa, and the hours spent on the movie. They had at least been able to fly at the same time with two different instructors and two different planes; otherwise it would have taken twice as long. The aircraft they trained in was smaller than the jump plane they had the most hours with, and the control panel was much simpler. They enjoyed flying the jump plane even though it was a workhorse compared to this little sportscar of a plane.

Danielle had taken off behind him with a flight plan that called for heading south, then west; a mirror image of his own flight plan. It was a beautiful day for flying. Winter was apparently leaving quietly, the blue sky was cloud free, and the air on the ground was in the 60's. It wouldn't give the instructor much opportunity to see his skill handling inclement weather, but, as a beginner, Jeff wasn't really expected to either. That skill would come with time and flying experience.

As he looked below, always searching for a place to land in case of engine failure, Jeff noted the areas of houses and farms along the way, groups of houses making way for open areas of trees, pasture, and farmland, then more houses. The instructor commented, "Not a lot of places to set down in an emergency, mate." Jeff shrugged. "We could land on a street if we had to. Or even a swimming pool. The water would stop us pretty fast." The man stared at him, not sure if he was kidding or not. Jeff smiled. "It might be better than landing on a house. Or in a yard." The instructor shook his head.

At the designated point, he swung the plane's nose to the west and continued on. The houses were surprisingly dense. There were some open areas, probably parks, possibly fields. It would be disconcerting to attempt an emergency landing on an open area that appeared to be a pasture from several thousand feet only to turn out to be a field of twelve-foot sunflowers when it was too late to change directions. At least if that turned out to be the case, it wouldn't take long to stop.

The aircraft droned on. Jeff kept part of his mind on the instrument panel and the continuous search for an emergency landing spot and part of his mind on the visit earlier in the month by his family. What did it mean that Danielle was his real twin? Did it mean anything? Did it change anything? They had been brother and sister for all practical purposes for eleven years now. There might be some legal ramifications they hadn't considered, but he didn't know what they would be. It was something for their lawyer at home, and maybe Oliver, to investigate.

Then, as he pondered, he felt the instructor's eyes on him, specifically on his hands. He glanced over, and the man jerked his eyes up to meet Jeff's, startled at being discovered. "I was just noticing the scars on your hands. Interesting ones, mate." Jeff glanced at the marks. They had faded with time and were barely noticeable now, except by the wrong people at the wrong time, like when they made Sophie throw up. Jeff said, "It happened a long time ago." He considered who had given him the scars, and in relation to his earlier thoughts, he didn't know what the man was. Before, he was Danielle's stepdad, but since his wife wasn't really Danielle's mother, what did that make him? Still her stepfather? Just some random guy? A kidnapper? He shook his head. It didn't matter. He was just some murderous aberration who was now dead.

The plane reached its next turning point, and Jeff banked to the left, coming to a new heading of southeast; the hypotenuse of the triangle. According to the GPS and his dead reckoning, they were exactly where they should be and a few minutes off schedule. He had faced a slight headwind on the northern leg which had slowed him down. On the western leg it had pushed him slightly south of his course, and he had crabbed sideways occasionally to stay on his flight line. He could have waited until the end and flown northwest to his turning point but had chosen to correct along the way. Either choice seemed fine with his instructor who made notes now and then on his clipboard. Jeff would have the same problem on the last leg of the certification flight.

As they soared through the air, he wondered how Danielle was doing. Her test was not going as well. The instructor had been awake much of the night with a sick child and a sick wife. Calling in had not been an option for him as they needed the money to keep the lights and water on in the house. By the time he needed to leave, she was feeling well enough to take care of the child, and her mother was coming over as well to help out; to him, this was another reason to be out of the house. She wanted him to get a real job and give up the one he loved. Loved most of the time, anyway. This morning, giving the final test flight to a young American, he could have done without.

Danielle was waiting at the plane when he arrived, examining the outer surface inch by inch. He gave the plane his own examination when he arrived, then climbed into the cockpit to mark his clipboard as she ran through the preflight inspection. Soon enough, he gave the okay, she started the engine, and when it was ready, asked the tower for permission to takeoff, joined the queue, and lifted into the air.

Her first leg would be south by southwest, with the ocean to her left and national parks to her right. The wind that was pushing Jeff slightly south was doing the same to her, and she adjusted her course slightly as they went along. Her instructor nursed the carry cup of coffee in his hand, wondering if the caffeine would ever kick in. Grateful that Danielle wasn't chatting, he asked questions occasionally, testing her knowledge of the aircraft and procedures.

Occasionally he would ask, "Where would you set down now if the engine failed?" and she would answer with her current choice. He didn't always agree and would point out problems with her choice, mainly based on his knowledge of the area. At least she was looking and thinking about the issue. And to be fair, all her choices would probably have seen them down safely, even if the plane might not survive or the ordinances broken might be expensive and time consuming to navigate. Her only comment to his observations had been a quiet, "Any landing you can walk away from." Instead of irritating him, her comment had cheered him up and brightened his day.

On the final leg, she noticed him staring at her curiously. With a raised eyebrow, she asked, "What?" He said, "You look familiar, but I can't remember where I've seen you." Then his face lit up, and he said, "You're her. You and your brother were involved in all those rescues. Usually the two of you have on school uniforms, though. I bet your school principal loves that." Today, Danielle, like Jeff, was wearing cargo pants, long sleeved shirt, combat boots, her leather jacket, and Maui Jim aviator sunglasses. She gave him a lopsided smile. "No school clothes today. And he doesn't always appreciate what we do." He sat in thought for a moment, then broke into laughter. "I'll bet he didn't like the wet dishrag look after you rescued that family in the ocean." She snorted. "Yep. That was one of the rescues he didn't like."

From that point on, the instructor seemed more alert and cheerful. Maybe it was because they were reaching the end of the test. Maybe his coffee finally kicked in. Whatever it was, by the time Danielle landed and taxied the plane up beside Jeff's, he was in a positively good mood. Jeff and his instructor were still sitting in the cockpit, chatting as items were marked off on the clipboard. Danielle could tell from his posture that his flight had gone well. She turned her attention to her own instructor who began his final review. The gist of it was she had passed. He recommended that she review the terrain she would be flying over, unless she was familiar with it, to get some idea of possible emergency landing areas that would not only get the plane down safely but keep her out of trouble once the plane was down. Adding, "Of course, the primary concern is getting down alive."

Climbing out of the plane, they joined Jeff and his instructor on the short walk to the office. They were now too mature to perform a happy dance, but just barely. Maybe when the instructors were out of sight. They found all the Armstrong family waiting for them in the office, and their restraint broke. Lucy started it, and they found it impossible not to join in. The others didn't join the dance but did congratulate them on their latest achievement. Soon the family was in the car, driving to a celebratory dinner at their favorite Italian restaurant.

# Chapter 47

Officer Cameron waited for Jeff and Danielle to pass on their way to the swimming pool. It was his day off, and he sat on the hood of his car in the early morning hours, parked along the path he thought the twins might take on their way to a morning's swim. Although the season was heading into spring and the day would be sunny, the air temperature was still chilly. He didn't know how they could even think of getting into the water.

Ten-year-old Acacia would be getting herself ready and off to school, something the independent little girl was quite capable of doing on her own. The officer hated the idea that she had to do it alone on one of his days off, but he needed to speak with the twins, away from everyone else; he had a favor to ask. He also felt guilty about the favor, but he didn't know where else to turn.

His deceased wife's sister had married a loser. He and his wife had both tried to talk her out of the marriage; in fact, from dating the guy at all. But she had insisted, and had begun a life of quiet desperation, culminating in a vicious divorce. It hadn't ended there, though. He had begun stalking her, leading to a restraining order, which he customarily ignored. Violating the order should have landed him in jail, except the judge he repeatedly appeared before was of the firm opinion that couples should work out their differences outside of court, and, when the man said he was trying to resolve their differences, the judge released him.

Now, encouraged by the judge's attitude, his activity was approaching violence. So far, there had only been bruises, mainly from him grabbing her. But his sister-in-law had gone from exasperated to angry to scared. There was no way she could handle him on her own no matter how many self-defense courses she took. In desperation, she turned to Victor, but his hands were tied. He could arrest the man for violating the restraining order, which he had done more than once, but the man was always back on the street before Victor even finished the paperwork.

Which brought him to option two, Jeff and Danielle. He spotted them riding toward him on their bicycles, and as they drew even, they pulled to a stop. Jeff greeted him. "G'day, Officer Cameron. How's it going?" The officer laughed. "You have the G'day down. Has Lucy been working with you?" The twins laughed with him, and Danielle said, "She does use it a lot, doesn't she? It looks like you were waiting for us. What's up?" He sighed and explained the situation. Jeff cocked his head. "It sounds like you're asking us to deal with him." Victor said, "Can you? Without killing him. Or getting arrested."

They asked for more details, and he showed them pictures of his sister-in-law and her ex-husband. He told them her routine and where her ex typically confronted her. Eventually, they agreed to see what they could do and continued on to the pool while the officer returned home in time to see Acacia off to school. As they rode, Jeff and Danielle discussed the issue, planning out a strategy.

The first thing they considered was dealing with the man standing across the street from his ex-wife's house late at night, just staring. It was the least offensive thing he did, but one that bothered her the most, never knowing if he would stay there or break into her home. If she called the police, he wouldn't be there when they arrived, making her look like an idiot. If they did catch and arrest him for violating the restraining order, he would be back on the street shortly, across from her house again, except this time he would be angry.

Jeff and Danielle slipped out of the house that evening for a while and rode their bicycles to her house. They spotted the man staring at the curtained windows, watched for a bit, then returned home. The man regained consciousness in an ambulance on the way to the hospital. It appeared that he had been struck unconscious by something and found by a passerby returning home, who had called emergency services. Outside of the visit to the hospital and treatment, he was also arrested for violating the restraining order. Most of the police who patrolled the area knew about the situation and were as frustrated as Officer Cameron. They were happy to lock him up, for what it was worth. By happy coincidence, a quick investigation showed Officer Cameron had been on patrol with his partner, dealing with a wreck blocks away from the incident, and his sister-in-law was at a wedding party at the time.

A couple of days later, the ex was back in front of her house for a late-night vigil, and the scene repeated itself: hospital, arrest, release. Now he was growing angry, more unstable, but also just the least bit scared. A couple of days after this, on her regular shopping day, Jeff and Danielle ran into her. Her usual grocery store was the one the Armstrong family had shopped at briefly when the twins were banned from their regular one. It was a little farther from the Armstrong house and in the opposite direction.

They had a bit of trouble getting away alone. Zoe and Lucy both wanted to go, and all they could say was, "Not this time." Lucy pouted, but Zoe was immediately suspicious. Jeff smiled blandly and said, "Just something to check on." Zoe wasn't happy, but she took Lucy by the hand and said, "We'll go with them next time. Let's go help Mummum." It was also suspicious that they had changed out of their school uniforms and were wearing cargo pants and combat boots. As they strode toward the front door, Zoe murmured, "Please don't end up on the news again." Jeff nodded.

Once at the store, they browsed around until they spotted

the sister-in-law. They purchased a couple of items from the produce section, and were dawdling by the door when she exited, carrying a reusable shopping bag in her arms. They fell in behind her, arguing noisily over the best Australian musicians. Before the little group had traveled a block, she turned around and said, "Seriously? You really think that bloke is any good?" She walked on with them as the discussion continued.

Just as they reached the steps leading to her door, her ex stepped from behind a parked car and approached the group. Danielle, whose arms were empty, stepped between him and the woman and asked, "Can I help you, mate?" He tried to step around her, and when he found he couldn't, swung a vicious backhand at her head. There was a loud snap, and he was face down on the ground with a broken arm.

Eyes blazing, he shoved himself to his feet with his good arm and pulled a punch knife from his belt, a weapon illegal under any circumstances. While a chef might make a case for carrying his cooking knives between his place of business and his home, or a hunter could possibly justify a hunting knife in his car on the way to a hunting trip, no one could justify this type of weapon anywhere, home or car, and certainly not on their person. He thrust his fist at her, and it was all over except calling for the ambulance to carry him away. And ringing their lawyer.

The police arrived, then Oliver, then the ambulance. There were a few witnesses to the attack, and they all agreed on the order of events. No one seemed interested in asking any embarrassing questions, such as why Jeff and Danielle were with her in the first place. It seemed obvious that they were just walking along after having bought some groceries. No one asked why Danielle had stepped between the man and his ex-wife. It was enough that he had tried to hit Danielle and then had pulled a highly illegal knife and tried to stab her. The story was also only a blip on the news, buried in other crime stories from around the city.

The twins did not call their news contact about the story, and it quickly faded away.

The man would be in the hospital for some time recovering from his injuries, although all the witnesses agreed that after he tried to stab her, Danielle had only hit him three times. She stopped when he was on the ground again. From the hospital he would go to jail for weeks of rehab. Then to prison. No more judges calling for reconciliation. The trial took place shortly before the twins left for the US and did not last very long. His defense counsel didn't ask why the twins were shopping at that store or were walking with the woman. The two times the man was knocked unconscious near her home never came up. The twins and Officer Cameron never spoke of it.

They told Oliver everything. He listened to the story, shook his head, and said, "It will probably be best for everyone when you're out of this country." That's when they told him their plans for spending time in the US and Australia. He stared at them for a while, then said, "My life won't be boring, but my hair will probably turn prematurely gray."

The Armstrong family did not take it so quietly. Even though Jeff and Danielle did not tell anyone about Victor's request, they had a pretty good idea what had happened when the woman started coming to church and Victor introduced her as his sister-in-law. They did not think as highly of him after that, although it seemed a bit hypocritical after forgiving Harry for what he had used the twins to do, which in their opinion was much worse. Zoe told Jeff angrily in the back yard, "You are not responsible for everyone who needs help!" He gazed at her, and she thought of all the people he and Danielle had helped and what would have happened if they hadn't been there.

She put a hand on his arm and said, "I don't want to lose you to something like this." He shook his head and said, "We'll be here as long as God wants us here. It does help, though, when people pray for our protection." This was actually already happening, every day, by numerous people. Zoe and Lucy. The Freedmans. The Jacobs. The Averys. Mike and his family. Alice. Eunice. And dozens of young people and their families who had received patches. It would have been natural for interest to fade some over time, but instead it grew, fed by the stories of the things they were up to that filtered through the Baby SEAL website community. If there was one thing they had, it was prayer coverage. And a good thing, too. It didn't end there.

Owen Morris was still keeping an eye on the twins, and he went ballistic when he heard what had happened. Jeff and Danielle didn't think to call him since this incident wasn't about them, and in this case, it wouldn't have done any good if they had. He had let the kid go who had rammed them with his car even though it had put the entire Armstrong family at risk, not just Jeff and Danielle. He had also let the kid go who had driven his car into the pond. The twins had never really been at risk from that one. This attack, because of the knife, he took personally, and he made a phone call.

# Chapter 48

Speaking of Owen, not long after the movie date, Jeff and Danielle received a call from Robert that almost sent them home again, this time to deal with Owen. The family was sitting at breakfast, discussing the upcoming visit to a hospital in Sunshine Coast and the opening of the children's ranch in the not distant future when Jeff's phone rang. He glanced at it, prepared to send the call to voicemail since phones weren't allowed at mealtime, but when he read the caller ID, he said, "It's Robert," and answered.

The conversation was brief. Jeff listened, said a couple of, "Uhuh," and "I understand," finished with, "Goodbye," and hung up. He sat in silence for a moment, shared a look with Danielle, then faced the group and said, "That kid driving the car that ended up in the pond when we were all in the US?" When he received their nods of acknowledgement, he continued. "He died last night in a car accident. His car was traveling too fast and missed another curve. This time he hit a bridge instead of a pond. He died at the scene."

Jake asked, "Why did Robert think that deserved a special call?" Jeff answered, "Well, he HAS been trying to sue me and Danielle ever since that wreck." Indeed, the boy had tried a number of ways to sue, including wrongful injury and unnecessary damage to the car for Danielle breaking the car window. The insurance company had written the car off as totaled. One broken window on top of the other damage was laughable.

As they broke up to gather their backpacks for the walk to school, Zoe walked beside him and asked, "What's really going on?" She was getting very good at reading him, and she knew he was tense, even if the others hadn't noticed. He glanced at her, then said, "Nothing." She shook her head. "Don't tell me nothing. You and Danielle both have that look." He shot her a quick glance and asked with interest, "What look?"

Exasperated, she snapped, "Don't change the subject." He sighed. We're just a little suspicious that a problem on our plates has suddenly gone away in a violent manner." She said tentatively, "Maybe God took care of it?" He said, "I don't think God would have killed him for that; more like put him in jail to think about it or something. We're afraid something human may be at work." She stared at him. "You think someone killed him to stop him bothering you?" He shrugged. "Maybe. We'll check into it."

A little earlier, Owen had been carrying on a conversation with his bodyguard about the same topic. Owen asked, "Do you think Jeff and Danielle will think I did this?" Without looking up from the newspaper he was perusing, the man said, "You did ask me to deal with the kid who was copying their t-shirts. And the kid in Australia who rammed them with his car." Owen glanced at the man with annoyance, then asked, "We didn't do anything about this kid, right?" The bodyguard said, "No. You never asked." Owen stared at the ceiling, then said, "Think we should tell them it wasn't me?"

Now the bodyguard raised his head from the paper and said, half jokingly, "Maybe. I wouldn't be surprised if they're booking tickets right now to fly home and deal with you. They might be getting tired of having to call you off every time someone tries to do something to them." Owen didn't bite. "Nah. I would have heard if they were booking tickets home." The other man asked,

"What if they hired a private jet?" Now Owen looked at him and nodded. "Better make the call."

Which was why, on the walk to school, Danielle received a call from an unknown number. She answered it, and a voice she recognized said, "It wasn't us; the punk was just speeding again and lost control of his car," and hung up. She put the phone back in her pocket and told Jeff, "He says it wasn't him. Just an accident." Sean and Zoe watched her as they all continued to walk, seeking more information. Zoe noted that some tension seemed to flow out of both of them. Danielle elaborated a little for the Armstrong's benefit. "Just a little more information from home about the boy who was killed. Some confirmation that it was an accident."

Sean gave her a questioning look. "What else would it have been?" Jeff shrugged. "Right. What else would it have been." Back in the US, Owen was continuing the conversation with his bodyguard. "You know, my son works on their IT team. Sometimes he monitors security for their gym in Australia. He told me the other day that sometimes they'll be at the gym by themselves, and they'll just disappear. One minute they're there, next minute, gone. He'll look around at the different camera views because they haven't scanned themselves out, and suddenly, they'll be back. Like, standing by a weight machine or in that sword fighting ring or on that obstacle course. And, he doesn't know how they got there. Weird." The bodyguard agreed. "Weird." Both returned to their previous activities, reading the paper and staring at the ceiling.

# Chapter 49

Jeff held up the card[11], and Lucy pronounced, "What is sin? 'All wrongdoing is sin.' 1 John 5:17." Jeff laid the card on a stack of others on the floor, and Lucy beamed. The cards were color coded, and when she completed one color successfully, she received a reward. Or, she could combine rewards to receive a greater reward. So far, the most she had been able to combine was two, the extent of her self-discipline, and that had been more because she hadn't had an opportunity to claim the first reward than that she had waited to combine it with a second one.

Jeff had begun the memorization soon after arriving in Australia. Her Sunday School class had a similar program, but since they only met once a week, their goal was one verse a week. Jeff's goal was a verse a day, for this year anyway. Next year the goal would increase to memorizing chapters at a time. So far, Lucy had memorized verses covering Understanding Salvation, Knowing God, Growing As A Christian, Enjoying God, Building Character, and now she was memorizing her way through Great Bible Truths.

The cards were part of a small box he spotted at a garage sale shortly after he and Danielle became Christians at age seven. The box was in pristine condition as were the sets of multi-colored 3X5 cards and the small paperback book inside, unusual and sad since they were over twenty years old but had obviously seen little use. Jeff and Danielle memorized all the cards long before the day of the concert, and, without realizing it, the verses that had settled in their hearts and minds had helped them through the several years they spent mad at God.

It was Sunday afternoon, lunch was finished, and the entire family was gathered around the lounge room. Jake, Sophie, and Sean were studying and working on the day's inserts in their church binders. Zoe was helping Jeff with Lucy. Danielle was sitting tailor fashion on the floor, Bible open in her lap, memorizing, for reasons known only to her, the book of Zephaniah. When asked, she simply replied, "It's short." Jeff had his suspicions, but he kept them to himself.

Lucy's review began with earlier cards to make sure she could still remember them, the reason for the cards already on the floor. Zoe held up the next card, and Lucy recited from memory, "Forgiveness. But if we confess our sins to him, he is faithful and just to forgive us our sins and to cleanse us from all wickedness.' 1 John 1:9." Zoe smiled. "Very good. What does it mean?" Lucy answered happily, "It means when I do something wrong, I tell God, and He forgives me. Like when I broke Sean's footy trophy, I told God, and He forgave me."

Sean's head jerked up, and he exclaimed, "What?" Zoe asked, "When did you break the trophy?" and Lucy replied, "Yesterday." Sean scrambled to his feet and left the room, returning shortly with a trophy about one foot tall, wood on the bottom with a rugby player, ball tucked under his arm, mounted to the top. Except the top half of the rugby player was broken off. Sean was very proud of the trophy. His team had worked hard to earn it. He showed the broken pieces to Lucy and asked, "Why didn't you tell me you broke my trophy?" She replied calmly, as if to a very slow person, "I told God, and He forgave me."

Sean wasn't yelling, but his voice was definitely getting louder. "What about me? What about the trophy?" Lucy's lip began to tremble a bit. "But God forgave me!" Zoe shared a look with Jeff. Everyone else in the room was watching with interest as well to see how this little incident was handled. Apparently, Lucy had taken the verse to mean that if she did something wrong, all she had to do was ask God's forgiveness, and everything was okay.

Zoe said, "Lucy, God forgave you, but what about Sean's trophy? It's still broken. God didn't fix it. I think He left that for you." Tears were now running down the small girl's face. She turned to Sean and said, "I'm sorry, Uncle Sean. I don't know how to fix your trophy. I can give you my rewards for the Bible verses I've memorized and learn as many as I can to earn more rewards to give you." Now Sean was feeling pretty low. After all, it was just a piece of wood and metal, and when he went to uni next year, he probably wouldn't even think about it again. It had been the principle of the thing: she had invaded his room, broken something of his, and not told him.

Sighing, he said, "It's okay, sweetie. We'll see if we can fix it with superglue after you finish showing your mom and Jeff how much you've memorized, okay?" The girl sniffled and nodded. Zoe said, "Lucy, being forgiven doesn't fix what was done. Well, it fixes the feelings, maybe, but if something physically happened, it doesn't fix that. Like with Sean's trophy. God forgives you, and Uncle Sean forgives you, but the trophy is still broken." Lucy asked, "What if I break something that I can't afford to fix? Or what if I break something that can't be fixed?"

Jeff said, "Sometimes you have to ask someone for help to fix something. Or maybe they'll decide you don't need to fix it. Remember the story of the ruler who forgave his servant millions of dollars of debt? And you're right, sometimes it can't be fixed, and everyone just has to live with it. That happens, too." Lucy shook her head. "I hope I never do anything like that," not realizing she was sitting there as an example of that very sort of thing. Danielle, realizing what might be going through Zoe's mind, said, "God also said, 'And we know that God causes everything to work together for the good of those who love God and are called according to his purpose for them.' That means

234

that God can take something people thought was bad and turn it into something good."

With that, everyone returned to what they had been working on. Lucy continued reciting her way through the cards, and when she finished, she and Sean carried the trophy to the kitchen to see if it could be glued back together. As they left the room, Sophie called, "Put newspaper under it. Don't get glue on the kitchen table." She wiped her eyes again as she leaned into Jake. Zoe reached out and touched Jeff's hand. Then she, Jeff, and Danielle retreated to the kitchen to supervise the repair job. Another valuable lesson had been learned concerning love and forgiveness.

# Chapter 50

On the second Monday of October, the children's ranch was ready to receive its first occupants. Everyone had been hired, including the woman who would be running it, a former bank president who had switched to a non-profit three years earlier and would now be in charge of the ranch. At first appearance, she had reminded Jeff and Danielle of Amy, but after the first ten minutes of the video interview with Jake and the foundation board they sat in on, she reminded them more of Mike: tough, professional, and totally dedicated to the people she was responsible for, from the most responsible to the most vulnerable; exactly what they were looking for. She was also available to begin transitioning immediately and could go full time a month before the ranch was scheduled to open.

She was also very smart. It hadn't taken her long to figure out that Jeff and Danielle weren't just the foreign exchange students living with the Armstrong family. After a single visit with Jake at the ranch when the twins were present, she had noticed the attention he paid to their suggestions and simply asked what their role was. To her credit, when Jake explained that it was their project and they were on the board responsible for it, she hadn't immediately resigned in a huff, but asked them about their experience and expectations, performed her own research, and continued on. Part of her research was a phone call to Pastor

Marcus for some background, and that conversation might have contributed to her decision to remain.

With the help of Pastor Shane and the members of Victory Bible Church, plus her own list of contacts, staff had been hired for every position, supplies and teaching materials had been stocked, and every building and room made ready. Now, with the first students arriving, the ranch was as prepared as it could be for its shake-down cruise where every forgotten task or ill-conceived idea would be revealed.

By the time the Armstrong family arrived late in the afternoon, the students had finished unpacking and were enjoying some free time and snacks before dinner. Jake parked the SUV in front of the main building, and the group trouped inside the noisy building which contained kids at the Ping-Pong and foosball tables, two playing chess with another watching, and a couple of kids sitting on a sofa and chair reading. They had spotted a few walking around outside exploring with one of the dorm parents, and noticed a few more on the deck around the swimming pool. The weather was still a little cool for swimming, but in another month, they would be in the water and on the water slides.

Lucy had been convinced, barely, that her construction clothes were not needed for this particular visit. It had been a tough sell, and the clothes, hardhat, and tool belt were sitting in the SUV just in case. She greeted each of the new children with her trademark, "G'day, mate!" Some responded with a shy smile, some with a sarcastic one or a tough, "Hey." The children were a mixture of ages and personalities. The youngest were in some stage of shock or denial. The oldest didn't expect to be there long or for their lives to be any better than they were in the past.

They ranged from just wanting a place that was safe, to trying to be friends with everyone in hopes of finding a protector, to making sure everyone knew they weren't to be trifled with. Jeff and Danielle, with Lucy beside them, met everyone, and at least after speaking with the twins for a few minutes, one thing the children all agreed on was that they would be safe on the ranch. A couple knew about the twins, the rescues they had been part of so far, and one even knew about their work with the hospitals.

The Armstrong group joined them in the main building for dinner. Normally, each dorm building would serve their own meals; the main building was reserved for special occasions. Opening day was considered such. Jeff and Danielle prepared baked Alaska for everyone, and it was brought out by the adults with sparklers blazing on each platter. After a timid beginning, more robust applause developed, especially with Lucy standing on her chair leading the cheering.

Finally, just after dark and with many goodbye waves, the Armstrong SUV drove down the gravel road to the highway and headed home. Everyone agreed it was an excellent opening, although Lucy thought she should have at least been able to wear her construction hat. "Just to be more official, you know?" Sophie told Jeff and Danielle, "I can't believe you pulled it off in less than a year. And the next buildings are moving along as well." The second pair of buildings had already been framed, and the walls were going up. Those two buildings would be ready before Jeff and Danielle left for the US after graduation. Zoe reached across Lucy to touch Jeff's arm, saying, "You and Danielle did something amazing there." Jeff laughed. "Thank you, but your dad did this. We just wanted it." Lucy laid a hand on each of their arms and sighed happily.

On the drive home, the conversation was mostly about the ranch, a little about the progress on the movie, but nothing about uni. All four teenagers had submitted their letters to universities. Sean hoped to attend one nearby and live at home or possibly rent a flat with friends. Jeff, Danielle, and Zoe had submitted letters to universities both in Australia and the US, near their parents' homes. For Jeff and Danielle, it would just be continuing toward their degrees since they had already earned credits at home. They just had to work with a counselor on taking some courses there and some in Australia. Zoe was somewhat anxious about her admission letter from the US. Jeff had assured her everything would work out, one way or the other, but still. Time would tell. Meanwhile, they needed to get the movie finished.

# Chapter 51

One Friday late in October, the four young people returned home from school to find no Lucy greeting them and an exasperated Sophie sitting in the kitchen. They stopped in the entrance, and Zoe asked, "Where's Lucy?" Sophie looked up to say, "She's in her room having a meltdown. She overheard me on the phone telling a friend that Jeff and Danielle would be returning to the US after they graduated. It has been a very long afternoon."

It would appear that all their ideas to tell Lucy about the end of school plans later when they were more finalized might have been a bad idea. They dropped their backpacks off in their rooms and, after knocking on the closed door, Jeff, Zoe, and Danielle entered Lucy's room. The young girl was sitting on her bed, facing the door, hands in her lap, staring straight ahead with tears streaming down her face.

Sean leaned against the door frame, interested to see how the others would resolve this crisis. It also helped to know that there was a solution, and it would make Lucy very happy. He looked forward to watching her face light up; which would be a major change from the way it appeared now.

Jeff and Zoe sat on either side of the girl while Danielle sat tailor fashion on the floor in front of her. Jeff asked, "What's wrong, sweetie?" In a mournful voice, Lucy said, "You're going to leave me. I thought you loved me." Zoe asked, "What makes you think he's going to leave you?" The young girl sobbed, "I heard Mummum on the phone. He and Danielle are going back to the US after they graduate."

Jeff said, "We do have to go home. We miss our family and friends. And we need to check on our projects there. What makes you think we're leaving you behind?" The girl's head popped up. "What? What do you mean?" Zoe said, "We weren't going to tell you anything until we worked out the details, but when Jeff and Danielle fly home, we'll be going with them." Lucy's tears dried up as if by magic. "Really? Are you getting married? I knew it! Where will we live? Where will I go to school?"

Sean, from his observation spot in the door, was loving this conversation. It was everything he had hoped it would be. Jeff said, "No, we're not getting married. We'll live with my family. You'll attend the Shepherd homeschool while your mom and I and Danielle take classes at uni." Lucy pouted, but it was difficult since she was so ecstatic after finding out she would be going with Jeff. "I don't know why you and mom don't just get married so we can be a family."

Then she changed directions. "What about Mummum and Poppop? Are they coming, too?" Zoe took this one. "They'll fly over with us for a few weeks like they did earlier, and then they'll come home." Lucy pouted again. "Why can't they stay?" Zoe said, "Who will take care of the children's ranch and the other projects?" Since Lucy was one of the ranch's most ardent supporters, this was an acceptable response.

Jeff asked, "Are you okay now? You really worried Mummum." Lucy nodded, and the group walked back to the kitchen where the small girl ran over to hug Sophie and apologize. Sophie hugged her back and said, "I'm sorry we didn't tell you sooner." Life in the Armstrong household eventually returned to normal.

# Chapter 52

The movie opened in Australia over what would be the Thanksgiving weekend in the US. In Australia, the only national holiday in November was Melbourne Cup Day, but it had already come and gone. Completed a bit ahead of schedule and almost exactly on budget, Jeff and Danielle had discussed an opening date with Sebastian, but there didn't seem to be a particularly opportune time, and in the end, he said it was really up to them. So, they chose Thanksgiving weekend in the US, which was a big movie release season there.

The next item was where would it open, in a few select theaters or as many as possible. Jeff and Danielle were of the opinion it should be as many as possible. It wasn't as though they would have to produce a film copy for each of the more than two thousand theaters in the country. The movie was a file that would be downloaded to each of the theaters' servers. If the theater in question wasn't yet up to that standard, then they would skip it. This movie wouldn't be on any type of film.

Thirdly, would the movie be advertised on telly, radio, or internet. Telly and radio, no. Obviously, it was already present in some movie databases. A project as large as this one with so many actors and crew would have been impossible to keep a secret. Jeff and Danielle weren't all that concerned with the movie being kept secret; just their involvement in it. The twins wanted a word of mouth campaign only.

And to that end, first, members of their church were told about the movie, with links to movie sites with previews. Then, friends at school were told. From there, word spread to their friends and relatives, then to their friends and relatives, growing exponentially. By the time opening night arrived, churches in every city or town with a theater knew about the movie, and attendance promised to be high, at least at the first few showings. After that, it would make it or crash on its own merits.

Who would go to opening night, and to which theater? Or would it be several theaters? Did the actors want to go quietly or become part of the movie star world? After much prayer and discussion, the actors all decided to go; after all, they did want to be in movies. Otherwise, they wouldn't have tried in the first place. However, they were determined to be Christians in that world, even if it severely limited the roles they might be offered.

Lucy was outraged to discover she wouldn't be going, in disguise or otherwise. Jeff and Danielle discussed the rating issue with Sebastian, and settled on an M rating. The movie board might have downrated it to PG, but had no issue with the M rating if that's what the producer wanted. No one ever asked for a harsher rating for their movie since it would cut down on their potential audience. After rolling their eyes at the crazy Christians, they had assigned the rating. Why hadn't they just made a G movie or maybe a PG movie in the first place?

Jeff explained to Lucy that they had created a G version just for her. This did not make her happy if she still wouldn't be able to attend opening night. She had the perfect dress for it and everything. When Jeff said he and Danielle would stay home with her, she finally relented. And it was fine with them. They had watched the movie more than once, not counting all the individual segments they had reviewed. Opening night wasn't that big a deal to them. They were more interested in how the movie did as a whole.

In fact, the whole family, minus Lucy, had viewed the movie

at a private showing at the studio. The family declared themselves extremely satisfied with the way the movie had turned out. Everyone except Sean planned to stay home on opening night. He was taking his girlfriend to the opening. Perhaps, after the movie, he would explain to her that it was about Jeff and Danielle.

Jeff and Danielle sat in on a meeting where the young actors discussed what they would wear to the movie opening. The choices ranged from cargo pants and t-shirts to tuxes and party dresses. Except for the two youngest, all of their hair was military short. So, the discussion also included wigs or no wigs. In the end, there was a mix: dress with long wig, dress with no wig; cargo pants and wig, cargo pants and no wig. Some of the boys wore tuxes, some did not. None of them wore wigs. There was no red carpet or a big deal made of their entrance, and no one really recognized them until after the movie anyway when they stood in a group in the lobby and ended up signing a lot of autographs.

The movie was in fact two movies. After all the video was completed and edited, it made two moderately long movies, the first one ending on Jeff and Danielle's tenth birthday. After the credits rolled, previews for the second movie played, turning the unhappiness at the incompleteness of the ending into anticipation for the second movie, which was planned for release at the beginning of the next year. The second movie ended with a teaser showing the beginning of the shark attack in their twelfth year. This had taken stage work and special effects to create safe, murky water to work in, water not inhabited by crocodiles, especially saltwater ones.

Jeff and Danielle had written ten songs for the movie, then ten more when the decision was made to produce two movies instead of one. Sebastian had hired a composer who wrote the background music, and the songs written by the twins would be released as movie albums. Terry's band performed the music, and after some initial complaining about not using local talent, everyone accepted that Terry's band played all of the twins' music.

Using the film crew as extras in the movie and showing those sections of film with their names had gone over surprisingly well with the audiences. Very few people left as the credits section ran, and while the audience might not have paid that much attention to the names displayed, they still recognized where the scenes appeared in the movie.

There had actually been two groups of shots. As soon as the decision was made to create two movies instead of one, a search was performed to make sure the crew was present in both movies. A few additional scenes were videoed, adding little to the overall length of the movies, but providing a boost to the already great morale.

Time would tell, but from the results of opening night, it appeared the movies would probably pay for themselves. This was before they were even released in the US and the rest of the world. Profits from the Australia showings would all go toward the Australian branch of the foundation. The future was looking secure for the children's ranch and other projects.

Sitting at home on opening night, the family, minus Sean, sat in the lounge room, popcorn and drinks in hand as they viewed the G rated movie with Lucy, who was very vocal and demonstrative from beginning to end; another reason not to take her to a theater. She laughed when it opened with the scene of Jeff and Danielle's first meeting, exclaiming, "You were as young as me!" as though she hadn't seen the young actors being recorded during the scene. She cheered at the concert, cried at the hospital scene, was indignant at Marilyn, loved the young Cindy and Elizabeth. At an early scene involving Robert and Michelle, she hugged Jeff and said, "I'm glad they're your parents."

Word of mouth of the movie spread, and attendance grew, pushed in some cases as church Sunday School classes and home groups all went to a showing together and praised the movie to their friends, neighbors, relatives, and co-workers. The actors appeared on television talk shows and performed radio interviews.

Jeff and Danielle were not to be found. They would be leaving the country soon anyway. Word spread, though, that the two American foreign exchange students who appeared regularly in the news for one reason or another were the ones behind the movie, and reporters camped out at the home and at school. They discovered the twins' ability to disappear in plain sight. All of it added to a mystique. At one point Zoe said, "It's a good thing we're leaving soon."

Lucy learned to smile, wave, and say nothing anytime someone asked her a question about the twins, even when the question was mean or cruel. Frankly, Zoe was a bit astounded by her self-control. She personally found it difficult to not lash out in Jeff's defense when a reporter said something harsh, even though she knew that was the intention. Yes, she would be glad when they were on the plane and out of here for a while. Although the movie would be opening soon in the US, and the problems might follow them there. Time would tell. Surely they could hide in the middle of Texas.

# Chapter 53

The first Monday of December, Danielle was on video chat with Elizabeth, Cindy, and Lily as well as Sydney and Rachael. The conversation had progressed from the twins' eminent return to Jeff and Zoe. Rachael, who had spoken to the group the least, asked, "Has Jeff given Zoe a Baby SEALs charm yet?" Danielle sighed. "No. They spend so much time avoiding each other, he's never had a chance." A puzzled Rachael asked, "Why are they avoiding each other? I thought you said they really like each other."

Elizabeth said, "Because they like each other, but he's a guest in their house. It wouldn't be proper. They have never even held hands." Rachael said, "Ouch!" Lily chimed in, "It's so romantic. They're still coming to live with you while they go to college, right?" Elizabeth confirmed that that was still the plan. Sydney said, "So the hands off will continue? That's just cruel. Are the new rooms ready at the house?" referring to the additions Mike was making for Robert and Michelle so the two additions to the household could each have their own room.

Elizabeth smiled to herself, and Cindy laughed, saying, "Just about. One final coat of paint, and everything will be finished. Jeff and Zoe will be as far apart as it is possible to be in the house. I think Robert plans to put collars on both of them that will give them a shock if they get within ten feet of each other." Sydney broke in with, "Stop it, y'all! I think they've been really sweet during this whole year. You can tell they really care for each other, and it's impossible to miss how much Jeff loves Lucy. We should be supporting them every way we can."

Rachael said, "Back to my original question, what about the Baby SEAL charms?" Danielle said, "He hasn't given her one, but he's thinking about something. I'll ask him this evening what the plan is." The group disconnected shortly after that, and Danielle went in search of Jeff. She found him in the back yard tossing a frisbee with Lucy. Standing next to him and taking turns tossing the disc to the small girl, she asked, "Are we going to give Zoe Baby SEAL charms? Inquiring minds want to know." He gave her a quick glance as he caught the frisbee and sent it on its way. "You've been talking to the "sisters", haven't you?" She caught the frisbee and tossed it back. "And Sydney and Rachael."

Jeff sighed. "I have no chance, do I?" She laughed. "Not really. What's the plan?" He said, "I'm thinking of getting Ann to design a ring." Danielle's eyebrows went up. "What kind of ring?" He answered, "Platinum with white enamel seals, one with blue eyes, one with green eyes, if that's okay with you. Like the charms, except on a ring. Like a promise ring." Danielle was not surprised. She had supported him through Beth, Rachael, and Sydney, and while she liked all of them, she had never really considered any of them a forever relationship. Zoe was different. She could picture him, Zoe, and Lucy together in ten years, twenty years, sixty years. And not just the three of them. She could see them with more children.

She asked, "So, are you going to ask her to marry you?" He shook his head. "Not anytime soon. At least one of us has to be twenty-one, don't you think? But before Lucy gets too old. And I want to talk to mom and dad. And Jake and Sophie. But she could have the ring regardless. If it doesn't work out, I'm not sure I'd be open to any more relationships. I think I would assume that your analysis was correct, and it just isn't to be." This was in regards to the pronouncement Danielle had made that the things that happened to them were direct attacks to try to kill them.

The next evening, Jeff called Ann to describe what he wanted. As he described the ring, she exclaimed, "It's just like the charms, except on a ring! I love it!" She assured him it was totally doable and promised to have a sample ready when they arrived home. Then she asked a question that had confused men for centuries, "What size does it need to be?" Jeff, however, had already thought about this. Zoe had a few rings which she wore occasionally. Jeff borrowed a ring size stick from the nearby jewelry store to measure one of them. Actually, he had to rent it. They weren't keen to let him borrow one until he offered them a twenty-dollar deposit on the five-dollar item which the sales clerk cheerfully returned to him when he brought the stick back the next day. So, Ann's question received a prompt answer. He had even taken a picture with his phone which he texted her in case she had any question about his ability to measure the ring properly.

# Chapter 54

Flick. Lucy turned to glare at the boy standing behind her on the bleachers. He smiled happily at her as he sang lustily.

There would be a Christmas concert at church the day before the Armstrong family, Jeff, and Danielle flew to Texas. Jeff and Danielle had written a couple of the songs for the children and young adults to sing, and Lucy would perform a solo. Stage fright was a foreign concept to the little girl. She was happy to be in front of people at any time for any reason. The attitude had been present before but had accelerated since Zoe had become a real mother, totally involved with Lucy's life.

One problem, however, was a little boy Lucy's age who had a crush on her and no clue how to properly express his liking. As untrained boys had been wont to do for ages, he showed his affection by finding ways to annoy her. One of the most successful seemed to be flicking her ear when all the children were standing on two rows of bleachers practicing for the concert. There were only the two rows, and he was placed on the second row directly behind Lucy, a perfect location from which he could easily reach her ear.

The children's choir director was a lovely young woman, very proficient with music, but less skilled with children. She was astute enough to recognize what the boy was trying to accomplish, but not ingenious enough to deal with it properly. The solution would have been simple: move either Lucy or the boy farther along their row on the bleacher. Unfortunately, in the young choir director's ears, this would have been detrimental to the sound, so she tried to deal with it in other ways, solutions that might have worked with adults or more mature young people, but not in this case.

She tried simply telling him to stop. That didn't work. She tried telling him she would have to remove him from the concert, but as he had an excellent voice for his age, she was reluctant to apply this solution, and he knew it. The director told the boy's mother, who was almost as helpless. She explained to her son that his actions were in error, as though speaking to an adult, or to a computer. He ignored her as well.

The action continued through the three weeks of rehearsal. Lucy grew increasingly angry, at the boy, at the director, at the adults who were not dealing with it. She didn't tell Zoe or Jeff, or Danielle, or even her grandparents. The young people would not rehearse with the children until the dress rehearsal, at which time all of her family members would realize what was going on. Lucy didn't wait that long to deal with it.

On the night of the last practice before the dress rehearsal, as she felt the familiar pain on her ear, she spun and delivered a palm strike to the boy's diaphragm, which was located at just the right height. His eyes flew open, and he toppled off the riser he was standing on, landing with a loud thud on the carpeted floor of the platform. There was a mixture of expressions from the other children, ranging from laughs to gasps to a couple of shrieks. The choir director stood open-mouthed, her life flashing before her eyes, thoughts of things she should have done or said to address the situation occurring to her, now that it was too late.

Lucy, satisfied with her action, had turned back to face the director, ready to continue with the rehearsal. That wasn't going to happen. A group of mothers who were standing at the back of the sanctuary chatting rushed forward, unsure of anything except that a child had fallen and was lying on the floor gasping for breath. One was the boy's mother. She leaped on the stage and rushed over to her son, who was just beginning to recover his breath. He seemed unshaken by what had happened, smiling at his mother and wheezing out, "She likes me, too!"

His mother asked frantically, "What happened? What's wrong?" One of the other children answered helpfully, "Lucy hit him." Her visage of worry for her son became one of anger aimed at Lucy. She spat, "How dare you hit my boy!" She almost seemed ready to strike the little girl. The choir director interposed her body between the two and tried to calm the woman. "You know what has been going on. I didn't fix it. You didn't fix it. Remember who she is." The last statement didn't seem to have any meaning to the woman. Then Jeff, Danielle, and Zoe arrived, drawn by that sixth sense the twins seemed to have for trouble.

Jeff calmly asked Lucy, "What's up?" The exasperated girl said, "He kept thumping me on the ear, and no one would make him stop. So, I hit him." Jeff swung his head toward the choir director and asked, "Is that true?" She stammered yes and tried to explain how she had tried to stop it, but Jeff had turned his head toward the mother as he repeated the question. She, too, said yes as she also tried to explain how she told him to stop. Although his face didn't change, the temperature seemed to drop, and the woman shrank back against her son. Danielle murmured softly in elvish, "Don't kill her."

The boy, too, smug as he had been in his knowledge that neither the choir director nor his mother could make him stop, suddenly wished very much that they had, or that he had listened to them. For some reason, it had never crossed his mind who Lucy lived with, perhaps since he was only doing it because he liked her. Maybe she really hadn't hit him because she liked him. Jeff lifted the boy to his feet by his arm and said, "Let's go over there and talk," nodding toward a corner of the stage a few feet away.

The boy's mother was suddenly an angry mother bear whose

cub was in danger, but Danielle took her by the arm and held her in place. "Jeff won't hurt him, and they will be right there." Jeff reached his destination, turned the boy to face him, and knelt with his back toward the others so they couldn't see his face. Then he explained a few things about being a gentleman and the appropriate ways to let a girl know he likes her. It didn't take long, and even though every eye was on them, the boy kept his on Jeff's face. When Jeff stood, the two walked back over to the waiting group. The boy told Lucy, "I'm sorry. It won't happen again." Lucy started to say, "It had better not," but Jeff gave her a look, and it changed to a formal, "I accept your apology." The two took their places on the bleachers and appeared ready to continue the rehearsal.

Everything seemed to be resolved, but after rehearsal that evening around the kitchen table, Lucy received a scolding from her mother and her grandparents. She responded sullenly, "No one would make him stop." Zoe said, "Did you tell me?" This received a curt, "No." Sophie said, "Did you tell me or your grandfather?" Another curt, "No." Jeff asked, "Why not?" Tears started running down Lucy's cheeks. "Everyone knew! Why didn't you know, too?" Danielle asked, "Are we mind readers?" Lucy said, "Yes." That was a tough one to respond to since Jeff and Danielle did seem to often know things they shouldn't have been able to, such as showing up that evening after Lucy struck the boy in response to some unheard summoning.

Jeff sighed. "Our knowledge isn't perfect. We know what God wants us to know. We didn't know about this. Maybe God wanted to see if you would handle it properly by telling your mother or grandparents so they could deal with it." Lucy sniffed. "You fixed it tonight." Danielle said, "They could have fixed it the first time it happened. You could have hurt the boy badly, hitting him the way you did and knocking him off the bleacher. Boys can be silly if they aren't brought up properly, and he obviously hasn't been or he would have known a better way to tell you he liked you." Lucy scowled. "Stupid boys," and the others in the room tried hard not to laugh. Jeff added, "Maybe that's why things happened the way they did now. It could have been much worse if he didn't have a clue when he reached my age. Now he knows better." Talk turned to the upcoming trip to Texas, now less than two weeks away.

# Chapter 55

Friday evening was the Grade 12 formal. Two weeks earlier, on the Saturday after the movie release, Sophie, Zoe, and Lucy had dragged a reluctant Danielle and a cheerful Jeff on a shopping trip to buy clothes for the formal. They had consistently said no to a pant suit and only rolled their eyes when Danielle explained that she wouldn't wear something she couldn't fight in. It didn't help her mood when Jeff showed up half an hour into her ordeal, suit bag in one hand, shoe bag in the other, finished with his shopping.

She was only on the third dress chosen for her. The first two dresses had been a complete failure from the moment she first appeared in them, the low cut backs not only displaying her cross tattoo but her scars as well. They stopped bringing her that style of dress to try on. Zoe, also trying on dresses, was examining herself on the pedestal in the middle of the dressing room mirrors while Sophie and Lucy ooh'd and aahed. Danielle was trying to perform deep knee bends, and, finding she couldn't, rejected the dress over the other females' strenuous objections. Lucy exclaimed, "But you look amazing in it, mate!" The others agreed.

Jeff disappeared and reappeared carrying a green gown in the correct size that was slit on the right side to above the knee. He handed it to Danielle, who gave it a quick once over and disappeared with it into the changing room. Then he turned an admiring eye on Zoe, who spun for him. He smiled and said,

"Nice." She turned back to the front and agreed, "It is, isn't it? I think I'll take this one." Her mom and Lucy both clapped in agreement.

Danielle appeared a few minutes later wearing the green dress and stepped on the pedestal. Slowly she raised her right leg in a side kick, stopping and holding the poise when her right foot was even with the top of her head. The dress broke smoothly at the split and fell out of the way. She returned to a standing position and tried the same thing with her left leg, stopping when the dress began to rise up her leg and threatened to rip. The sales clerk who had stopped in to assist them put her hands out and said, "That isn't going to work. Wait here."

She left and came back with a gown in a slightly different color of green, although it matched Danielle's eyes even better. The style was also different, reaching almost to her neck front and back, with splits on both sides to just above the knee. Danielle smiled, took the dress from her hands, and glided back to the changing room. The sales clerk followed her exit with her eyes and asked, "Why exactly does she need to do that in a gown? Is the dress for some sort of dance competition?" Jeff and Lucy both nodded solemnly, and Jeff said, "Exactly."

Soon Danielle was back. The dress looked magnificent on her, and when she repeated the two, slow sidekicks, the dress slid away smoothly on both sides. This one also had long sleeves that covered the backs of her hands with an elastic loop that fit over her middle finger and held the sleeve in place. She nodded. "This is the one. Done!" Sophie, Zoe, and Lucy also said simultaneously, "Nu-uh! Shoes!" Jeff turned away and smiled as Danielle scowled and said, "I'll wear my boots." The sales clerk disappeared and returned with four boxes of shoes, two for Danielle and two for Zoe. She obviously had an excellent eye for foot size as all were correct. Zoe loved both pairs immediately and sat to try hers on, Jeff kneeling to assist her. Sophie smiled to herself at their innocent use of the moment for physical contact.

Danielle was surprised at the shoes offered her as both had low, one-inch heels. The wise sales clerk, assuming that someone who was concerned with being able to perform the moves Danielle had exhibited would not want to do them in three- or four-inch heels, opted for the lower ones. She could have brought flats but thought that surely she would want some extra height, even if it was only one inch. Although, at six feet, Danielle didn't really need any extra height. Danielle tried on both pairs of shoes, found both acceptable, and turned to the other women. They walked around her, examined the shoes from all angles, and finally agreed on one of the pairs. Danielle sighed. Done. Just before she turned back to the changing room to put on her street clothes, she pivoted her head to glare at Jeff, and he knew she was thinking, "I still hate you." He smiled blandly back, intoxicated by the time he had spent helping Zoe with her shoes.

Jeff and Zoe would be going to the formal as a couple. While this wouldn't surprise any of their close friends, it might be a shock to others, the rest of the school, especially the principal, and the church. They would be flying to the US soon and would be missing from sight for months, so any surprise would have abundant time to wear off.

Sean would be going with his latest girlfriend, Gloria. When Jeff and Danielle had first arrived, he was keen on a tall, dark haired, brown-eyed beauty who was very smart; possibly smarter than all the young people combined. She was socially clumsy and prone to answering honestly without thinking. Sean was attracted to her because she was pretty and smart, and she probably migrated to him because he was attentive, patient, and kind. They had little in common, and even though she could state every rule in all of the league rugby manuals, which she had memorized in passing to have a common interest for conversation, and even though she could explain the physics that were taking place during a game, she had no interest in the game itself or the players, their character, or history, and the two parted ways amiably before the State of

Origin games when she found someone who was patient, kind, and as smart and socially clumsy as she was.

His next attraction was to a short, athletic, red-haired fireball who played in a girl's rugby league. She was possibly stronger and more athletic than Sean, but she was somewhat in awe of Jeff and Danielle, especially after she and Sean stumbled into one of their training sessions in the back yard, with fists and feet flying freely, and Lucy keeping score, cheating a bit to make sure Jeff won. They discussed rugby happily, but they split within a month on the subject of the church. She was not a Christian and had no interest in anything regarding it, especially attending church or Sunday School. Jake and Sophie were glad to see her go.

Following rapidly were a poet who caused Zoe to put her finger down her throat in a gagging motion any time she saw her, a feminist who seemed to hate all men except Sean and made Zoe want to punch her in the face, and a whiner, who thankfully lasted less than a week. Danielle proclaimed that Sean only dated her to clear his palate after the last one. She said this out loud at the dinner table, causing more than one of those sitting there to choke on their drinks.

Then Sean met Gloria, so Australian she made Jeff and Danielle's eyes water. She had grown up deep in the outback and had only moved to the city with her family in the past year. Her hair was sandy blonde, her eyes were blue, and a line of freckles crossed from cheek to cheek across her nose. Her height was average, and her build was muscular. The words that came out of her mouth sounded to Jeff and Danielle like a foreign language. They thought they knew Australian slang from Ivy's friend, but Gloria taught them otherwise. Sometimes they just stared at her, parsing her latest sentence, trying to determine what she had said.

Gloria abbreviated everything, from arv for afternoon to rellies for relatives and avo for avocado. Then there was the rhyming slang such as Captain Hook for take a look. At least once they knew what the term meant, it didn't change. It wasn't as though someone could make up a new phrase each time; that would have made conversation impossible. If Gloria might not use them quite as much in her normal conversation, she made certain to use them with Jeff and Danielle. Sean and Lucy thought it was marvelous. Zoe was smilingly sympathetic.

She was a Christian, firm in her belief, strong in her memorization of verses, but unschooled in her apologetics. Her faith was unshakable, but she couldn't argue convincingly with the unchurched. That began changing rapidly when her family joined Victory Bible Church, which was where Sean met her. Soon she was spending time at the Armstrong home and learning about Jeff and Danielle, Zoe and Lucy.

Lucy adored her and thought she was the greatest thing since sliced bread. Or Milo. Or cherry Zooper Doopers. She called her Glo, and Gloria called her Luce. Gloria was impressed with Lucy's growing guitar playing skills, and proved that she could play an instrument as well: a handmade wooden flute. Lucy demanded that Jeff and Danielle write a song for her which made use of her musical skills, and they did. Gloria loved Sean's birthday song, and clapped appreciatively when Jeff, Danielle, Zoe, and Lucy played it for her.

Gloria also attended school with the family. Sean had seen her there but hadn't really paid attention until her family joined their church. Her education in the outback had been by correspondence, and she was well up on her courses. Her father had been a gold miner and had struck a rich vein which he sold to a large mining company. The amount he found before he sold the mine set the family up comfortably for the rest of their lives, and the percentage from the future take from the mine was just icing on the cake. Neither he nor his wife wanted to sit around doing nothing, so he was educating himself on web design and she was enrolled in cooking school with the hope of opening a catering business in the future. Gloria would attend uni, majoring in business and possibly run both their companies.

Jake, acting as chauffer, drove both couples to the hotel where the formal would be held. Lucy rode along, sitting between Zoe and Gloria in her booster seat. Sean rode shotgun; Jeff rode in the seat behind Zoe. Neither couple thought this was an ideal seating arrangement, musing that a limo where the couples could have sat together in seats that faced each other would have been nice, but they were good natured about the arrangement. Once they arrived at the hotel, Jake left the auto with the valet, telling him he and Lucy would be right back after they took some pictures of the ballroom for Sophie. His three young people had promised to take an abundance of pictures, as had Gloria to her parents, who already had numerous ones of Sean when he went to the door to pick up their daughter. Just as Sophie had of Jeff and Zoe.

Sophie had also taken pictures of Danielle, who would be going unabashedly alone. Plenty of their friends would be there, and she had also brought a sketch pad in her messenger bag; no tiny clutch purse for her. Inside the ballroom, Lucy twirled around, mesmerized. She grabbed Jake's arm and pointed excitedly at different decorations, exclaiming, "Take a picture of that, Poppop! Take a picture of that!" When she was satisfied that he had enough pictures, and after the four young people all hugged her goodbye, she allowed him to lead her back to the hotel entrance where the valet grinned at the tip, handed him his car keys, and pointed at the auto parked just a little way up the curve of the hotel drive-through. Soon they were home, and Lucy was explaining all the pictures to Mummum.

Meanwhile, all five of the party goers passed through the photo area and had their pictures taken. Then they searched for their friends and found them at a group of tables near the dance floor. Heads turned as they passed by, and more than one girl punched her date on the arm to bring his eyes back to her when the three girls slipped by. Soon the five were seated in the middle of their friends, laughing happily, and beginning the explanations of why Jeff and Zoe were together. The questions faded when everyone began eating and fled entirely when Danielle produced her first drawing. As had happened in the past, a line formed at their table when people realized what she was doing, and Jeff and Zoe, Sean and Gloria left her to it, leading their dates to the dance floor as the DJ began his set.

Some of her friends helped by writing numbers on green sticky notes and handing them out to the people standing in queue. This broke up the long line as people could move away and go about the business of enjoying the formal, dancing, and filling plates from the buffet. One of the friends would stand on a chair and hold up fingers indicating which number Danielle would be ready for next, and ten or fifteen young people would gather near the table. One laughingly commented that Danielle should charge for the drawings to raise money. She smiled politely, thinking, "Been there. Done that."

The DJ's first songs were lively. Some were even Reggae. The laughing crowd moved energetically about the dance floor, and Jeff and Zoe laughed as they danced near each other. Then the DJ threw in a slow song, and the two moved together, spinning slowly. Some fool tapped Jeff on the shoulder, asking if he could cut in, and both of them said emphatically, "No!" Nonplussed, he moved away to commiserate with his friends. Danielle, glancing up, spotted them and told two of their friends, a boy and a girl, to go rescue the two from themselves, and Jeff and Zoe soon found themselves dancing with someone else and smiling ruefully at each other. Jeff gave Danielle a look, and she gave him a cheerful thumbs up.

At the end of the song, Jeff, Zoe, and the two friends made their way to the buffet to fill some plates of their own. Jeff brought an extra plate for Danielle, who paused between drawings to grab a bite or two. As she ate, a girl with an angry, frustrated, and anxious look on her face appeared at her side with one of Danielle's drawings in her hand, dripping with what appeared to be soft drink. She said, "Would it be possible to get another drawing? My drongo boyfriend was mucking about with his mates and spilled my drink on it. Laughing, Danielle complied, saying, "Poor boy." The poor boy in question, hovering nearby, received glares from all the girls standing in line.

The formal continued with more food and drink, more conversation, and more dancing. Following Danielle's cue, Jeff and Zoe were not allowed to slow dance together until the very last one of the evening. Even then, they were aware that their friends were surrounding them, keeping an eye out that nothing got out of hand. Zoe whispered in Jeff's ear, "We have such good friends." His, "Yes, we do," was sincere and not sarcastic, as it could have been. Sean and Gloria were held to no such restrictions, and, while sympathetic to Jeff and Zoe's plight, still found humor in it.

Thanks to texting, Jake pulled up to the front of the hotel just as the five reached the end of the walkway. After a moment of silent conversation, Danielle sat in the front passenger seat while Sean, Gloria, and Zoe slid in behind them. Jeff climbed in the back row. All five regaled Jake with stories about the formal, and Gloria and Zoe both effusively praised Danielle for her drawings. Zoe exclaimed, "Everyone wanted one! You were probably the most popular person there." Gloria asked, "Have you created drawings like that before?" Danielle laughed. "Yes, several times. At formals just like that one. Since we were twelve."

This led to a clamor for stories about the previous times, and before anyone realized it, Jake pulled up in front of Gloria's home. Sean walked her to the front door. While he was gone, Jeff moved up a row and slid in beside Zoe, who immediately took his hand. Tales of the formal continued for the remainder of the drive to the Armstrong home, but Jeff and Zoe weren't paying as much attention as they had been before Gloria was dropped off.

Once home, the group settled in the lounge room with Sophie to tell her about the formal. Danielle jokingly told her how their friends had kept Jeff and Zoe separated until the very last slow dance. The older woman smiled with appreciation at Danielle and with sympathy at Jeff and Zoe. "Things are moving quickly enough for you two, I think. It's best not to test your self-control any more than necessary. There will be enough temptations in your path."

# Chapter 56

Friday. The last day of school, and a very busy one. First, there was a final visit, hopefully, to the principal's office. They appeared in front of his admin's desk, who waved them in without a second thought. Once seated in two of the not particularly comfortable chairs in front of his desk, they examined him. The school year had not been kind to the man. His hair had considerably more gray in it, and there were more wrinkles around his eyes and his mouth. They weren't smile wrinkles, either. His eyes had a harried glint that hadn't been there in January, and he glanced around the room anxiously, as though waiting for the other shoe to drop.

Jeff and Danielle shared a look. Surely it wasn't because of them. They had seldom visited the man's office more than once a month, and some of those had been to receive congratulations for the positive image they had given the school. Perhaps he really shouldn't be the head of a large high school.

He spoke for a few minutes, telling them how pleased he had been to have them in his school for their last year before uni and wishing them success in their future endeavors, wherever they might lead them. They told him how much they had enjoyed their final year of school and thanked him for everything he had done for them. When they found themselves in the hall with their friends a few minutes later, it was with the distinct feeling that they weren't quite sure what the meeting had been about. It seemed as though the man just couldn't bring himself to say what he really wanted to say; possibly something like, "I'm glad you're leaving. Please don't come back." Shrugging and receiving their friends eyerolls, they continued on with the day. Next was the talent show.

Sean was going to sing his birthday song, accompanied by Jeff, Danielle, Zoe, and two of their friends who would play bass and drums. Gloria would be joining them as well. Jeff and Danielle had added a flute solo for her, which made her and Sean both very happy. One person who was not happy at all was Lucy, who wanted to join the group on the stage to play her uncle's song. She was, after all, the one who had helped play it for his birthday. And Gloria got to play. Sometimes life just wasn't fair to six-year-olds.

The talent show began at 1:00pm, and the school auditorium was packed with students and their families. Sophie, Jake, and Lucy sat with Gloria's parents near the stage and watched as a variety of students from all the grades performed. Some were quite good, pianists and singers and dancers, many of whom would be going on to pursue more education or careers utilizing their talents. One young man quoted a famous 19th century Australian poem. He was destined for parliament.

There were humorous acts as well, a ventriloquist with her dummy, a standup comedian or two who had varied degrees of success, a magic act that wasn't necessarily supposed to be funny, but someone had apparently been at the props, and the bunny that was supposed to appear from the hat had been replaced with a Tasmanian Devil, thankfully stuffed. The young magician dropped it and screamed, then was chased off the stage by a small dog wearing a very realistic alligator costume. From their level, the audience could see the dog under the costume, but from his level, the alligator appeared quite genuine; and fast. The principal restored order, condemned the pranksters, and Jeff and Danielle, waiting their turn from the wings, began to have an inkling as to where his gray hair was coming from. At least it wasn't just them. He really needed to move on to a less stressful occupation.

Their turn arrived. While the curtains were drawn, the drum set was moved on its rolling stand to a position in the center of the stage. The others arranged themselves in prearranged positions, the curtains opened, and, at a nod from Jeff, the bass player began. He heard Lucy stage whisper to Sophie, "That's my part!" and shared a look with Zoe and Danielle, all three working hard to not laugh. Sean began singing the song, and the others joined in on cue. Lucy had started those around her snapping their fingers and clapping, probably having as much impact as Sean from the stage. Part of the audience was familiar with the song, most were not. When the song finished, however, it earned a standing ovation, much to Lucy's delight. Her Woohoos were clear to the band, and they all waved to her before the curtains closed to allow time to roll the drum set off the stage before the final few acts.

That evening, the auditorium was full again for the graduation ceremony. There were the usual speeches and the long line of graduating students striding across the stage and receiving their diplomas. Jeff and Danielle both thought they saw relief in the principal's eyes when they shook his hand. Finally, it was over, and everyone gathered at the Armstrong home for a graduation/goodbye party. It was a time to say goodbye to many of their high school friends who would be scattering to various schools to continue their education, starting full time jobs, or perhaps lazing around their parents' homes until they were kicked out. The greatest ambition of a couple was to spend as much time as possible surfing, following the waves and seasons around the world, doing only what was necessary to support that lifestyle.

Sean and Gloria would be starting at the uni in the fall semester. Jeff, Zoe, and Danielle would be back for the spring semester. They would reconnect with their friends then, those who were still around. Otherwise, there was still the internet, and they wouldn't be surprised to see friends dropping in from time to time to visit them in Texas. A few were attending university in the US. As always at times like these, there was anticipation and moments of bittersweet regret. Some would be friends for a lifetime, others would fade into memory, perhaps to resurface years down the road in unexpected places. Only time would tell.

# Chapter 57

Lucy, now on her second flight to the US and an old hand at first class, climbed into her window seat. As first-class passengers, they boarded first, stowing their carryon luggage in the overhead bins. Soon, those needing assistance and families with small children boarded, followed by all the other passengers in a steady flood. Eventually, all of the passengers were on board, the doors were closed, and the plane pulled away from the gate. Soon thereafter it lifted into the air, and the flight to the US began.

This trip was different than the previous flight. It was late spring in Australia and late fall in the US, but the temperatures at their destination would only be in the mid-sixties; mid-forties at night. Sweater weather during the day. Lucy was very unlikely to see any snow for Christmas. At least until they flew to Colorado to the ski slopes. A shopping trip was planned in the coming week to buy ski clothes and gear for everyone.

The flight departed Australia shortly after noon the day after the concert at church. They had eaten lunch at an airport restaurant and walked about afterwards, stretching their legs before the long flight ahead. Lucy scampered here and there and greeted the workers she remembered from the previous trip. She might not remember their names, but she remembered their faces, and they remembered her: the cheerful little dark-haired girl with the boisterous greeting, trailed by the young blond woman who was apparently her mother and the large young man and woman who might be brother and sister. They glided silently behind the girl and might even be her bodyguards. They certainly seemed very protective of her as they shielded her from being stepped on as she darted here and there like a hummingbird.

Once the flight reached its cruising altitude, the first-class attendants served drinks and snacks. Lucy began asking questions about the next few weeks. She wasn't particularly happy about the schedule. At home, she would be on summer break. Now, she would be starting school again after the first of the year, and felt terribly cheated. She asked about summer break in the US, counted the months until they would be returning to Australia, and turned an outraged face to Jeff. "I'll miss most of summer break in the US, too! School will still be going on when we go home." Now tears of rage began running down her cheeks. "It isn't fair!"

Jeff assured her that they would work it out so she didn't miss all the breaks. "Danielle and I pretty much went to school year-round once we started school. It will be fine. You'll see." Lucy wasn't convinced, but she trusted Jeff, and settled down to enjoy the flight, the tears disappearing as if by magic. She watched a movie on her personal airline screen, pausing occasionally to stare out the window at the ocean far below. When it ended, she pulled her church binder from her backpack and settled in to work on her Bible study.

Jeff, Zoe, and Danielle spent the time carrying on a lively conversation concerning Sean and the various girls he had dated since the twins had arrived in Australia. Since Sean was sitting directly behind Zoe, he could overhear snatches of the conversation although the air vents open to full and the engine noise prevented him hearing clearly, much to his chagrin. Then again, maybe not. Perhaps he was better off not knowing. He did occasionally lean over the back of her seat to say, "Sitting right here, mate," just to keep them honest. Jake and Sophie looked on in amusement.

Gloria hadn't wanted to spend the family's first Christmas in the city away from her parents; otherwise, she would be on this flight as well. It wasn't as though Sean hadn't asked her to come. It would be a long few weeks for him, and he almost hadn't made the journey himself. Only the thought that it would be the last time he saw Zoe and Lucy for months convinced him. Thank goodness for the internet and video chat.

The plane traveled on, time passed, dinner was served, Lucy watched another movie, Jeff and Danielle prepared the picture and the sheets for the church binders to be emailed home before the following Sunday. The group prepared for bed and drifted off to sleep about 10pm by their usual Australian time. The plane landed in Los Angeles at 9am local time, 4am by their internal clocks. By the time they cleared customs, it was almost time to board their flight for the next and final leg of their journey.

Soon enough they were in the air, and the friendly and efficient flight attendants were serving a late breakfast. This flight was much shorter, and it seemed like almost no time before they were landing at the airport. Robert, Michelle, Elizabeth, Cindy, and Lily greeted everyone with boisterous hugs and carried the group off to the Freedman ranch to unpack and relax before the barbeque planned for that evening. It wouldn't be a huge affair; just the addition of Mike, Ella, and Savannah, and Steve and Amy.

Since their visit earlier in the year, a new bedroom had been added for Lucy. Previously, there had been four bedrooms upstairs: a master bedroom for Robert and Michelle with a master bath, one for Elizabeth and one for Danielle with a bathroom in between, and a bedroom for Jeff with a bathroom across the hall. The rest of the second floor was made into a large game room. Now the game room had been divided in half and made into a bedroom for the small girl, very similar to her room back in

Australia, even down to the furniture and paint color. Zoe moved into Jeff's old bedroom, and she and Lucy shared a bathroom.

Part of the basement had been finished out as a bedroom for Jeff with a built-in closet, chest of drawers, two single beds, and desk with bookshelves. He and Sean would be staying here again, but this time it was an actual bedroom, with real beds, a door and everything. His bathroom would be the one off the kitchen, near the basement door. And, for the parents' peace of mind, Jeff's and Zoe's bedrooms were two floors apart. Not that they didn't trust the young people, but it was just a good idea to remove temptation where possible.

So, Lucy had her own room, Zoe had her own room, Danielle would stay in Elizabeth's room until Jake and Sophie flew home with Sean, and Jake and Sophie would stay in Danielle's room. And, of course, Robert and Michelle occupied the master suite. Easy-peasy. Jake and Sophie didn't even pretend to object to the arrangement. It made sense, it was convenient, and everyone was happy.

# Chapter 58

Soon after everyone, mainly Lucy and Zoe, had unpacked to their satisfaction, the guests arrived. It hadn't taken long. Lucy and Zoe had each brought two suitcases. Jeff and Jake both told them they could buy anything else they needed while they were here, so they had mainly brought underwear and their favorite clothes. Jeff and Danielle both tossed their backpacks at the foot of their beds, and they were done. The others would be returning to Australia in three weeks.

Mike's family was the first to arrive. Savannah, now nine, rushed up the steps to the wrap-around porch where Jeff and Danielle waited with the others and flung herself at Jeff, hugged him furiously, then did the same to Danielle. Lucy watched, a bit perplexed that someone else was hugging her Jeff like that. All she said, though, was a perhaps less than usually energetic, "G'day, mate," to the three. Jeff noticed and gave her a wink, which cheered her back up.

Steve, Amy, Cindy, and Lily were right behind them. These received a more enthusiastic welcome since Lucy knew these were basically family. The herd of people moved into the house, but Mike peeled off Jeff and Danielle with a jerk of his head, and the three disappeared to the back yard. Once there, he said, "Harry told me about using you against the bank robbers and why. I understand, but I wasn't happy, and I let him know. I get the feeling I wasn't the only one unhappy with him although the list of people who know it was you is very short. How are you two? And how did you target the men through the walls of the house?"

Jeff and Danielle shared a look. Danielle said, "Why did he tell you? We don't know for sure, but this could blow up in everyone's face. What if someone asks you what you know about it?" Mike shrugged. "He told me because I am the closest you have to a squad commander. Everyone who knows would lie through their teeth to protect you, even under oath. Why would anyone ask? It's over." Jeff said, "A reporter could dig, just out of curiosity, and figure it out through luck. You know we have forces working against us that aren't flesh and blood."

Mike shrugged again. "Tell me about the shots through the walls of the house." Danielle explained how the walls had seemed to become transparent, and they could see what they needed to inside the house." Mike grinned and shook his head. "Outside of the miracle you just described to me, that was excellent shooting. Two thousand yards on targets, some of which were moving. And speaking of the miracle, there may be forces working against you, but there are also forces working with you." He paused, then added, "Or, as I've always suspected, you're aliens." With that, the three returned to join the others who had been wondering where they were.

Robert had been keeping an eye on them from the grill where he was cooking steaks for the meal. Mike paused by him as Jeff and Danielle continued on into the house. Robert asked, "Did you get things straightened out?" Mike snorted. "As much as anything ever gets straightened out with those two." Robert continued, "You think they're okay?" Mike nodded. "Things that I think should bother them don't, and things that I never even think about bothering them do. What about Jeff and Zoe?" Now it was Robert's turn to shake his head. "I guess time will tell."

The evening went off as planned with good food, happy conversation, stories about the time in Australia and what had been happening while the twins were away. Around 10pm, those not staying said their goodbyes, and those staying went to bed, the ones from Australia trying to sleep at what would have been just after lunch back home.

# Chapter 59

On the weekend before Christmas, the two families took a quick road trip to Dallas to visit Holiday in the Park at Six Flags Over Texas and to attend the Christmas music service at a large local church. The two cars pulled out of the Freedman driveway at 10:00am on a cool, cloudy day. Lucy stared at the sky hopefully, searching for any sign of snowflakes, but Robert explained to her sadly that there was little chance of snow. The climate was just too warm in this part of the state in December.

The trip passed quickly, lively conversation in both vehicles filling them with laughter. Native Texans explained the passing scenery and its history to the visiting Australians. They arrived at their hotel and checked into the two suites reserved for them, carried their luggage to the rooms, and left again to find a restaurant. Lunch eaten, they returned to the hotel until it was time for the park to open and were among the first at the gate. Soon the group was strolling through the grounds, admiring the thousands of lights and decorations and deciding which rides should be first.

As they attended shows and were thrown here and there by the various rides, families began to find Jeff and Danielle. First there was a family of four with a twelve-year-old girl in a stocking cap; not too unusual for the cool weather except close inspection showed it was to cover a bald head. Robert, Michelle, and Elizabeth set up to shield them so passersby wouldn't think it was a sketching station, and the Armstrong family quickly joined them. This had not happened much in Australia, showing the difference between one year of notoriety and several years.

Lucy watched with interest. This was the first time she had seen Jeff and Danielle doing their thing outside of a hospital environment, and she found it fascinating. The group was clustered around the front of a building featuring a Christmas musical, sitting on benches in the outdoor waiting area. Fortunately, the next performance was an hour away, and no one was interested in queueing up that far in advance; they had the area to themselves. Fifteen minutes later, the group was on the move again, but that wasn't the only stop. Four more times during the evening, families recognized and approached Jeff and Danielle, who patiently stopped, drew sketches, and explained the website.

During one of the stops, they were approached by park security who wondered if they were freelancers, drawing sketches for a fee without approval from park management. Robert intercepted the pair and explained the situation. They listened with patient understanding, and one of the officers radioed in a message with Jeff and Danielle's description and the situation. Robert was startled to hear the exclamation that came over the radio and the orders to the two officers to escort the group wherever they wanted to go and make sure they weren't disturbed. Apparently, someone knew about them, and, from the radio messages, was on their way to meet the twins.

It was half an hour and two sections later before the man caught up to them, and Jeff and Danielle recognized him immediately: the father of one of the children they had met at the children's hospital on an earlier Dallas visit. His son, now two years older, was with him, and the young man rushed up to hug them, chattering rapidly about everything that had happened in his life since he received his patch, the new friends he had made, and the sports he was now able to participate in. A bemused

Sophie asked Michelle, "Does this happen a lot here in the states? I mean, this is a huge park. Does everyone recognize them? It wasn't like this in Australia, even after all publicity they received on the news."

Michelle laughed. "This is fairly normal. They're only popular with specific people, not everyone. I hope the movie doesn't change that. It shouldn't because they aren't in it personally. Danielle walked up and put her arm around Michelle. "Ready to carry on? There is a lot more to see." Jeff, Zoe, and Lucy were right behind her, the small girl holding Jeff's hand and bouncing on her toes. She had declared herself too big now to ride on Jeff's shoulders "unless absolutely necessary". She certainly had the energy to keep up, running or skipping as necessary to stay even with the longer legs of the adults.

The two families stayed until the park closed before returning to the hotel. After breakfast the next day, they checked out of their hotel and drove into Dallas to check into their new hotel and spend the day roaming the downtown area, visiting historic sites, and eating lunch in one of the local restaurants. They left in time to arrive at dusk for Holiday in the Park and enjoyed the various attractions until closing. There was only one thing left to do before they drove home the following day.

# Chapter 60

Bright and early the next morning, the two families were walking through the parking lot of the large Dallas area church. Even though they had arrived half an hour before the service was scheduled to begin, the parking lot was at least 75% full as parents, grandparents, and family filed into the sanctuary to hear the Christmas music service which would include not only the regular choir and orchestra but the older children as well.

The weather wasn't particularly cold, with temperatures in the mid-fifties although snow was possible by Christmas day. Lucy had heard this forecast that morning and was skipping across the parking lot in happy anticipation. Jeff and Zoe, holding her hands, were walking at a fast clip to keep up with her as the others followed more sedately behind. The people attending the service noticed the young girl from the moment she reached the front door which was held open by an older woman with white hair and a smiling face. Lucy greeted her with a loud, "Gooday, mate!" which earned her a, "Hello to you, too. Welcome!" in return.

Inside, Lucy stared around at the large foyer with its various kiosks for service projects and information and the large staircase leading upwards. Still gazing around, she allowed herself to be guided by Jeff and Zoe's hands to the doors leading into the sanctuary. She made another friend here when she greeted the lady handing out programs with a cheerful, "Gooday, mate!" and

"Thank you!" Those nearby turned to stare at the sound of the strong Australian accent.

Continuing into the large sanctuary, the group was met by an usher, who, when told there were ten in the group, led them to a mostly empty aisle several rows from the front and guided them in. Robert entered first, followed by Michelle, then Elizabeth, Zoe, Jeff, Lucy, Danielle, Sean, Sophie, and Jake. As they stared around at the people, the decorations, and the orchestra setting up, Danielle pulled her sketch pad from her messenger bag and began a connect-the-dots picture for Lucy. The girl divided her time between gazing around and gauging the progress of the picture.

The time passed quickly as families continued to file into the sanctuary, filling the seats around them, greeting their friends and welcoming visitors, including the Freedmans and the Armstrongs. The Australians soon became a center of activity as those around them heard the accents and made a special effort to speak to them. Jeff and Danielle, especially Danielle, also drew their share of attention as they removed their jackets and their muscles were on display, Jeff in his short-sleeved shirt and Danielle in her sleeveless one. Robert, Michelle, and Elizabeth were drawn in as well when Jeff called out with, "Mom," and asked her a question. A mystery to be solved, indeed!

The service began, announcements were made, and everyone stood to greet those around them. By this time, everyone around them knew the Armstrong and Freedman families, and much of the attention was focused on Lucy, who, supported by Jeff and Danielle, stood on her seat to be at the proper height to greet people. There was a lot of laughter at all the "Gooday, mates!" she threw out gaily. Eventually, everyone sat back down, and the program began.

Soon, Lucy was the center of attention in their area again because she was loud in her praise of the music, especially the soloists, be they vocal or musical. Her shouts of "Woohoo!" and "Good on you, mates!" at the ends of these numbers was met with laughter and cheers, as was her impromptu dance in front of her folded-up seat to a song that was described as a 15<sup>th</sup> century song that might have also been a dance tune. During the singalong portion of the program, Lucy again stood on her seat. And during much of the program, she sat in Jeff's lap where she could see better.

When the program ended, many people in the audience wanted to meet the little girl, and as the lights came back up, Jeff signed up and down the aisle, "Protect Lucy!" It was partially in jest, but partially serious as the small girl might get trampled by accident in the departing crowd. The exit from the sanctuary was not as swift as it might have been as people stopped by to greet Lucy and the others, but finally they made their way out of the building and toward their cars, with Lucy skipping and dancing all the way. Soon the two vehicles were on the freeway, starting on the four-hour drive home.

# Chapter 61

Christmas Eve night, Jeff and Zoe were sitting in the living room at the ranch. Jeff was on the floor leaning back against the sofa with Zoe also sitting on the floor, leaning back against him, his arms around her. Both were staring at the fire. Robert and Michelle were seated on the other sofa watching them unobtrusively as was Elizabeth who was curled up in one of the reclining chairs. Danielle was seated cross-legged on the floor, also staring into the fire. Jake and Sophie were seated in two other chairs, sipping hot chocolate. Lucy was asleep in bed; so was Sean.

Danielle handed Jeff a gift-wrapped shirt sized box. He took it and placed the box in Zoe's lap. "This is an early Christmas present for you from me." In addition to the time spent working with Ann to create the gift, a great deal of time was involved in discussion with Robert and Michelle, Jake and Sophie, and Danielle. In several video chats with his adoptive parents, he had told them how he felt about Zoe and Lucy. His feelings toward Lucy were obvious. Jeff had walked a very fine line between being her friend and acting as a parent because, well, he wasn't her parent. He never spoke with the voice of parental authority, but worked through suggestion, approval, and sometimes, outright bribes. He never spoke against or tried to undermine Zoe, even when he thought she was wrong. As Lucy's mother, she was the voice of absolute authority.

Fortunately, there had never been a major area of disagreement. Zoe had appreciated Jeff and Danielle teaching Lucy gun safety even if it was unlikely she would come across one by accident under Australia's restrictive gun laws. She indulged him teaching the little girl karate although she drew the line at the full-blown ABS technique. Who wanted to explain to another parent why their bully of a child was in the hospital with something broken, even if they did deserve it? She could hardly disapprove of Lucy's improved manners, and the jump in reading, verbal, and math skills was nothing short of amazing.

Elvish would have been another indulgence, except Zoe had learned it herself. The Japanese and Spanish were useful. Perhaps their greatest area of current agreement was in the area of God, Jesus, and the Bible. Lucy could present the gospel message plainly and in a manner simple enough for a child her age to grasp. She had spent the past year memorizing Bible verses, not in a haphazard way, but in a coherent flow, one verse leading to the next. Zoe had memorized right along with her, and her own faith had grown as well.

Robert and Michelle recognized that both young people were, perhaps sadly, mature beyond their years and had far too much life experience for their ages. They thought Baby SEAL charms in the form of a ring was an acceptable gift. Their main request was that at least one, preferably both young people, wait a while before they made any permanent decisions. They understood that Jeff didn't want to wait too long for Lucy's sake, but when he was twenty-one, Lucy would only be ten. They were also pretty sure that Lucy would be wishing for Jeff to be her dad on every birthday candle, every wishing well or fountain she came across, and in her prayers every night if she wasn't already.

Jake and Sophie were of the same mind. The past year had been spent observing the interaction among the three, and they had been touched and amused by the restraint Jeff and Zoe had shown as the obvious attraction between the two had grown.

Frustrating as it was to Lucy, they had resisted all her attempts to get them together, from seating them together at the table to unsubtle suggestions Jeff take Zoe for a walk or bicycle ride. The latter suggestions were usually self-defeating because Lucy also wanted to walk or ride bicycles with them, and they were relieved to take her along.

Now, Zoe sat for a moment with the box in her lap, staring at it. She couldn't imagine what it contained. It weighed practically nothing for its size, as though it was practically empty. Finally, she untied the bow and lifted off the lid. Inside, nestled in sheets of red and green tissue paper and secured by a thin ribbon to a blue velvet cushion was the ring Ann had created for Jeff, shining in all its platinum glory.

In a way, it wasn't a ring just from Jeff since it also bore Danielle's charm. In another way, it was all Jeff, with Danielle adding her approval. Zoe untied the ribbon securing it to the velvet and lifted it out to examine it closer. She whispered, "It's beautiful." Then she took Jeff's left hand and placed the ring in it, lifting up her left hand for him. He took the ring in his right hand and slid it onto the ring finger of her offered hand. Leaning her head back, she told him, "Turn your head." When he did, she kissed him on the cheek, murmuring, "Thank you." He hugged her while the others in the room smiled at them.

Jeff and Danielle shared a look, as did Robert and Michelle, Jake and Sophie, and Elizabeth. In all their minds was Danielle's assertion that the things that happened in the twins' lives were not accidents or coincidences but direct attacks on them. Now, they had brought Zoe and Lucy into the crosshairs as well, perhaps putting their lives in danger as a means of destroying Jeff and Danielle, or at least their faith. As always, all their lives were in God's hands, and they would live as long as He had determined.

# Chapter 62

Christmas dawned clear and mild; no snow on the ground, not a cloud in sight. Lucy was disappointed, but the Freedmans had promised to take everyone skiing in Colorado the following Saturday, and there would be plenty of snow then. The little girl was up at the crack of dawn, and the others found her sitting under the Christmas tree, shaking her presents. The others gathered around the living room as Michelle and Robert prepared coffee and hot tea, and Elizabeth, Jeff, and Danielle poured orange juice.

Soon everyone was seated in a comfortable spot with their favorite morning beverage, and Elizabeth was handing around presents. They group watched as Lucy ripped into her first package and squealed with delight when the box held a complete English riding outfit except for riding boots. Another box contained riding boots, another paddock boots, and still another, a riding helmet. Then there was a box with cowboy boots and a western shirt. Lucy thought all of this was so she would have the proper clothing for riding the two horses already present on the Freedman ranch. Until she tried on her English clothes, and the family took her out to the barn to show them to the horses.

There, saddled, bridled, and standing ready at her stall with Elizabeth holding the reins, was a pony. She was covered in a thick, winter coat of golden fur, her long flaxen mane draping gracefully along her neck. The equally full forelock was braided and secured out of her eyes with a rubber band, and her tail swished cheerfully as she watched the group approach. A nameplate on the stall in front of her read 'Scout'.

The evening before, after Lucy had finally been tucked in bed and after receiving a text, Jeff, Danielle, Elizabeth, and Zoe had walked to the gate near the house that opened into the children's ranch where they were met by the school's horse trainer, who was standing there with the pony. After a quick exchange of greetings and Merry Christmases, the four young people led the pony back to the Freedman property and tucked her securely into her home, the stall next to Elizabeth's horse, Cinnamon.

She had really been living there for a while. Robert and Elizabeth had begun the search at Jeff's request as soon as it was certain Zoe and Lucy would be coming to the US for an extended period. It had taken a couple of weeks and a lot of ponies to find just the right one: smart, gentle, and active enough for a six, soon to be seven-year-old girl. Scout fit the bill perfectly, trained in English, western, and even jumping. Now to see if Lucy liked her.

Jeff wasn't one hundred percent certain about this; maybe eighty percent. She had certainly been excited enough to ride behind him the little time they had had since they arrived, and she seemed thrilled when Elizabeth let her ride Cinnamon around the covered arena as she walked beside her. Now Lucy and Scout stared at each other, and she said, "Who's this, mate?" Jeff said, "This is your pony, Scout." Lucy froze. "My pony? For me? Really and truly?" She gazed from face to face: Jeff, Zoe, her grandparents. They all nodded yes.

Laughing and crying, she ran over to the pony and flung her arms around its neck, or as much of her neck as she could reach. Scout reached down and nuzzled her hair with a velvet nose. Lucy cried, "Can I ride her now?" Elizabeth said, "That's why we're here." Zoe handed the girl her helmet, which she quickly fastened on her head. Elizabeth led the pony outside, gave Lucy a leg up, and she was sitting proudly on her first horse. The group followed as Elizabeth led the way to the arena, and once inside, gave Lucy her first riding lesson on her new pony. Soon she was posting at a trot, and shortly after that, taking her first solo canter, whooping with glee. Elizabeth spared a glance for the onlookers. "Looks like we have another horse lover on our hands."

It was a test in parenting skills to get Lucy off her pony where Elizabeth continued her lesson with untacking, haltering, brushing, and cleaning of hooves. Finally, Scout was out in the pasture near the arena with Chester and Cinnamon, and the humans were inside preparing lunch. Lucy was babbling happily about her new pony. Then she spotted the ring on her mom's finger. Her horse comments immediately stopped as she grabbed Zoe's hand and stared at the ring. She asked excitedly, "Does this mean Jeff is my Dad?" Zoe smiled down at her daughter. "No, mate. But we are one step closer." Lucy rolled her eyes. "You two are taking forever!" Jeff said, "It's a forever kind of decision. We want to get it right. Besides, I'm only seventeen." He added teasingly, "I need to be at least twenty-five." Lucy did the math in her head and said with exasperation, "I'll be a hundred by then, mate!" Everyone laughed, and Zoe said, "I see we need to focus on your math more."

Lucy couldn't stay upset long. She had her own pony, and they would be flying to Colorado to ski for a week in just a few days, so she would see all the snow her heart could desire. On the downside, her grandparents and Uncle Sean would be returning to Australia soon after that, and she would start school. She didn't want to be greedy, but if they had stayed, and she didn't have to go to school, life would be perfect. Well, if Jeff was her Dad, anyway.

She forgot all this over the next couple of days as she spent time with Elizabeth learning to ride Scout. Two days after Christmas, Elizabeth demonstrated riding barrels on Cinnamon, and Lucy was hooked. Zoe couldn't believe it. Her daughter might as well have shown an uncommon interest in sky diving. How could riding a horse at insane speeds be fun? And it turned out, Scout had a knack for the sport, and even seemed to enjoy it immensely. And jumping. Scout loved jumping. So did Lucy. Zoe saw a lot of stress in her future. Unless she found some way to love all the danger as well and trust God with the results. It wasn't as though Jeff lived a safe life, either, although except for the sky diving, he didn't intentionally participate in something that put his life at risk. Except SCUBA diving, but since she loved that as well, it didn't count.

# Chapter 63

In the few days between Christmas and the weekend, a flurry of shopping took place; there were ski clothes to buy for the upcoming week in Colorado. Jeff and Danielle had bought a condo in a popular resort town. The unit consisted of three bedrooms and three bathrooms with a large kitchen, large dining room/living room combination, and a large patio with a view of the village's shopping district and the mountains in the background. Jake couldn't imagine what it cost. Most of the time, the twins left it in charge of a rental agency, but their friends could use it whenever they wanted. So far, there had been no conflicts, and no one abused the privileges. For this upcoming trip, they had also rented the unit across the hall for the Armstrong family and two more units farther along the hall for Steve, Amy, Cindy, and the Avery family.

The day after Christmas found the Freedman and Armstrong families in a popular ski shop not far from the Freedman home, busy trying on ski clothes and ski equipment. The Freedman family already owned everything they needed, but the Armstrongs had never been skiing and had nothing. The sales clerks were happily assisting them, visions of dollar signs shining in their eyes. The main items were chosen such as jackets and ski pants and turtle necks, ski boots and skies, gloves and goggles and ski hats. Then, to the pile were added thermal underwear and socks and glove liners.

All of the new skiers needed a week's worth of clothing. By now, the Armstrongs were familiar with Jeff and Danielle's generosity and just accepted everything they suggested, knowing it would be used one way or another. At one point, Zoe glared at Jeff. "I know all of this would not fit in your backpack." He smiled and said, "It's like SCUBA diving; ski gear gets its own duffle bag." She rolled her eyes and continued handing clothes to Lucy to try on. Finally, they were finished, with everything they could possibly need paid for and loaded in the two vehicles. They headed back to the ranch, stopping only long enough to eat Mexican food at a popular hole-in-the-wall restaurant as they neared home.

That evening Jeff received a call from Officer Cameron that put a bit of a chill on the upcoming ski trip. He was in his new basement room, taking a quick look at the Baby SEALs website when his phone rang. Checking the caller ID, he answered, "Hello, Officer Cameron." His voice had a bit of question in the tone. He couldn't imagine why the Australian officer would be calling, and he especially couldn't think of any good reason for a call.

The policeman's first words were, "That man who attacked Danielle? He died last night in jail. Stabbed. I thought you might want to know." Jeff felt a chill run up his spine, and the conversation ended quickly. He didn't know what to think or who he and Danielle could talk to about it. His first thought, of course, was, "Owen. We never told him to leave the guy alone." Climbing the stairs, he walked through the house in search of Danielle. Robert, seeing his face as he passed by, thought, "Uh-oh."

Danielle was in the living room with almost everyone else, discussing the upcoming trip. She was already watching for Jeff, having felt his change in mood during the phone call. He glanced at her as he passed through, and together they walked through the front door and out into the front yard. He told her what Victor had said. She sighed and repeated the thought that had passed through his mind, "We didn't call Owen." He said with some heat, "I'm getting tired of calling him telling him not to kill people who have something against us. We can't even talk to anyone about this." She snorted. "Maybe the priest in New York." He stared at her. "Think we could come up with an excuse to go visit him?" She said, "We could always go visit the hospital there." He considered it. "Maybe in January or February. Until then we just have to stay out of trouble." She laughed bitterly. "What could possibly go wrong with that plan?"

Robert and Michelle knew something was on their minds. So did Zoe. It slid past the rest of them. Zoe caught him in the kitchen later that evening and asked, "What's wrong?" He laid his forehead against hers and said, "I can't tell you." She pulled back. "Why not?" He said, "No one can know about this. It isn't safe. We're going to have to deal with this ourselves, somehow." She said, "You have a ton of friends including policemen and lawyers, not counting me. You shouldn't have to deal with it alone." He shook his head, "This one, I think we are. But not until next year. Right now, we have a ski trip to enjoy." They heard Sophie and Michelle chatting together as they walked down the hall and pulled apart, leaning back against the kitchen counter and still holding hands as the two women passed through the kitchen door and smiled at the two young people. Soon all four were deep in conversation about the upcoming trip.

Two days later, Mark landed on the ranch airstrip at 8am. It was really just a pasture that had been cleared of all foreign objects such as rocks or branches, leveled, and rolled smooth. The pasture was large enough to land in any direction, depending on the wind. An air sock on a pole showed wind direction. Mike and Robert had taken care of it as soon as Jeff and Danielle acquired their pilot certificates, knowing the twins would want it sooner or later. Mark would come along as the main pilot although Jeff and Danielle would perform most of the flying. Steve, Amy, and

Cindy would be joining them for the flight. The Averys would be flying in from Phoenix to be part of the fun.

Luggage and ski equipment loaded and pre-flight inspection complete, everyone strapped into their seats, and Jeff lifted the plane into the air for the first leg of the trip. They would refuel in Amarillo, and Danielle would take over the controls for the remainder of the flight. As everyone stretched their legs during the refueling, Danielle commented to Jeff, "We should get our jet certificates next." He nodded. "That would be fun. And faster." Mark shook his head. "You'll need a lot more hours first." Danielle nodded. "We should learn to fly helicopters, too." Robert overheard this and chuckled. "Maybe learn to fly the space shuttle?" Jeff shook his head seriously. "Too late for that. Maybe the next generation?"

The plane lifted into the air, and a few hours later, the group was dropping their luggage in their units with Lily hovering around to help, the Averys having arrived earlier in the day. All of the kitchens were stocked with food and snacks, mainly breakfast items, but a few dinners would be eaten at home as well. Lunches would all be on the slopes. The young people all set out to explore the tourist town while the adults gathered in the Freedman unit to catch up with Mia and Preston and relax from the flight. Mia asked how the trip had been with Jeff and Danielle at the controls. Michelle said, "As good as you would expect with those two. Smooth flying, no bounces on the landing. It was good to have Mark along in case of an emergency that they don't have the experience to handle, but I'd feel okay flying with them."

In the town, the young people were staring up at the mountain, watching as the last of the day's skiers rode the lift up the mountain. All of them knew how to ski except the Armstrongs, but the others promised them they would all be skiing by the end of the next day. The town was bright with Christmas lights and decorations, and they wandered around window shopping until the smells wafting from the various restaurants drove them back to the condos for dinner.

For this first meal, Jeff and Danielle decided to cook crepes. Everyone filled out a sticky note with their choice of filling, for their main meal and dessert, and the twins set to work. Cindy, Elizabeth, and Zoe prepared a spinach salad with a hot mustard dressing, and with two crepe pans cooking away along with an electric griddle to prepare the various meats, happy munching was soon underway. There was a pause after the main course while more crepes were cooked with an assortment of fillings, from fresh fruit to ice cream with a pecan praline or chocolate sauce, and eventually, everyone declared themselves full. Sophie commented to Michelle, "They can spoil you with their cooking, can't they?" Michelle agreed.

Early the next morning, the large group rode up the mountain and split up, some to ski, some to learn. Jeff, Danielle, and Cindy took the Armstrong family to a gentle slope to learn the basics. By noon, all of them were comfortable with their ability to stop and make turns. Lucy was exuberant and fearless, and after lunch, she swept off with Elizabeth and Amy to try some blue slopes. Sean tagged along with the other adults while Sophie and Jake followed Jeff, Danielle, and Cindy as they took them through tougher and tougher exercises including a slalom made by all the previous skiers, learning to first jump moguls, then ski through them. By the end of the day, they were exhausted but happy. And starving.

After everyone had showered and changed out of their ski clothes, they walked to a nearby Japanese restaurant for dinner. And that day set the tone for the remainder of the trip: up early enough to eat breakfast in the Freedman condo and catch the first lift as soon as it opened, ski until lunch which was eaten at one of the spots on the mountain, usually soup or a sandwich, ski until mid-afternoon when everyone took a hot chocolate break, then ski again until the lifts closed. Everyone would trek back to the condos, laughing and discussing the high points of the day, to hot showers and clean clothes and dinner at the condos or out at another restaurant: Italian or steak or seafood.

The new skiers worked their way through green beginner slopes to blue intermediate slopes. Some of the group stayed there. Cindy and Amy added black advanced skier slopes to their day as soon as the Armstrong family was up and running. Jeff and Danielle joined them for some of these, but mainly Jeff stayed with Zoe and Lucy. The small girl resembled the energizer bunny, always ready for another run and reluctant to stop even to eat or take loo breaks. She was sad when the week ended, not just because of the end of skiing but because her grandmother, grandfather, and uncle would be returning to Australia soon, and she would be attending the Shepherd homeschool. Jeff promised that they would come skiing again before the end of the season, and she reluctantly agreed.

Jeff sat in the pilot seat for the first leg of the return trip to Amarillo. Mark had spent the week with friends and showed up as the others were returning their rental cars. Greetings were exchanged, luggage and ski equipment were loaded as Jeff and Danielle walked the plane with Mark and completed the pre-flight check: before long, they were on the way home. Several of the passengers were soon sleeping; the week had been fun but tiring. Cindy and Amy were stilled wired and regaling each other with their high points. Lucy was dividing her time between watching Jeff at the controls and staring out the window at the ground far below.

Sunday was spent at church and packing, and Monday, the three Armstrongs boarded the plane to Australia, and an unenthusiastic Lucy, still upset at losing a month of freedom, started school.

# Chapter 64

L ife settled quickly into a routine. Michelle was working part time at the hospital to keep her skills current. Otherwise, she and Robert planned and executed projects for the foundation. Elizabeth attended homeschool with Lucy, although she was also taking a course at the university. Jeff, Danielle, and Zoe also started at the university, or, in the case of Jeff and Danielle, continued where they had left off.

On a cold, clear afternoon, Jeff, Danielle, and Zoe pulled away from the university campus and drove to the Shepherd homeschool to pick up Elizabeth and Lucy. Once the two girls were safely buckled in, Jeff drove the short distance to a nearby cemetery. Along the way, they passed apartments, homes, a small university, a state cemetery, a museum, and several strip shopping centers.

Entering the gates, he drove down well-kept drives until he reached their destination and pulled onto the grass verge to park. Lucy, who had been watching their progress on her tablet from the car's four cameras, asked, "Why are we here?" She was the only one who didn't know. Jeff, Danielle, and Elizabeth had visited occasionally before the twins left for Australia. Zoe had been told on the drive over from school and had agreed with sympathy and understanding. Peering over the seat at Lucy, Jeff said, "There are some people buried here we want to visit. Lucy shrugged and said, "Okay, mate."

With Jeff and Danielle leading the way, they trooped the short distance over the low, brown winter grass to a bronze plaque buried flush with the ground. A bronze flower vase was inserted in a socket at the head of the plaque. On the plaque was inscribed, "Marilyn Mitchell," her date of birth and date of death, and, "Child of God." The twins knelt by the grave, and Danielle removed the plastic wrapper from one of the bunches of flowers they had purchased on the way over. Carefully, she arranged them in the vase, added some flower preservative, and poured in water from a metal bottle to fill the vase.

After a bit, Lucy asked, "Who is this?" Jeff said, "This is our mom." Lucy, a puzzled expression on her face said, "I thought Michelle was your mom." Danielle smiled at her. Our mom died before we came to Australia. Robert and Michelle adopted us. Lucy sat and pondered for a bit. Then she asked, "Then who's your dad?" Jeff said, "We don't know." Lucy immediately said, "Like me!" Zoe gave Jeff a look, and he said, "Sort of like you," and Lucy said, "Huh! Weird!" After another moment, she added, "Why did she die?" Jeff said, "She had cancer." Lucy shook her head. "I don't like cancer. If God loves us, why does He allow cancer?" Zoe said, "This isn't the world He created. This is the world we live in because Adam sinned, and when he sinned, all sorts of bad things entered the world. One day, it will be perfect again, the way God intended." Lucy frowned. "I want it to be perfect now." The others all laughed, and Elizabeth said, "Don't we all."

They sat there for a while, telling stories about Marilyn, especially ones about her final year. Jeff said, "You know how we all went shopping for clothes for the formal?" Lucy giggled. "Danielle didn't want to go. She hates shopping for clothes." He continued. "When our mom was alive, she took her, and it was almost bearable. Danielle scowled at him. "Barely." The others laughed.

Lucy, noticing the other two bunches of flowers by Danielle's side, asked, "What are those for?" Jeff and Danielle gracefully rose to their feet and extended hands to help the others stand. Danielle said, "Come on; we'll show you." She and Jeff led the way to two more plaques located nearby. These were inscribed, "Tom McAdams" and "Audrey McAdams". They also showed birth dates and dates of death and "Child of God".

Zoe read the plaques and asked, "Who were they?" Danielle said, "My second foster parents, before Marilyn adopted me." Zoe shook her head. "I thought Marilyn was your mom." Jeff said, "Yes, but we didn't know that until Robert and Michelle came over last year to tell us." Zoe said, "Your childhood was really messed up." Jeff, Danielle, and Elizabeth all laughed, and Elizabeth said, "You have no idea."

Lucy performed the math in her head and said, "They weren't very old. They were Mummum and Poppop's age. Why did they die?" Jeff shared a look with Danielle and Elizabeth. Wow, how to answer that one. Lucy stared at one then the others of the three. Finally, Jeff said, "One bad day, things just went terribly wrong, and they were killed." Lucy seemed to accept that, but he could tell Zoe didn't. He would have to give her more complete details later.

Danielle repeated the process of removing the plastic wrapping, placing flowers in each bronze vase, and adding preservative and water. They bowed their heads in a moment of silent prayer and returned to the car. When everyone was safely buckled in, Jeff asked, "Would you like to drive by the school we attended for a week in first grade before we joined the Shepherd homeschool?" Zoe answered with an interested, "Yes," Lucy with an excited one.

Moments later, he was cruising past the front of a large school. Curious, Zoe asked, "Why did you only attend for a week?" Elizabeth laughingly said, "Because they beat up some kids and were expelled." A horrified Zoe exclaimed, "What? In your first year? What were you, six?" Elizabeth totally took over this story, and Jeff and Danielle could only listen in bemusement.

"At the end of the first week, some third graders attacked them in the restroom and tried to steal their lunch money. By the time a teacher could get in there, the older kids were beaten to a bloody pulp, and everyone involved was expelled. While they were walking home, they passed the Shepherd house, and when they told Mrs. Shepherd what had happened, she invited them to join their homeschool, and they did."

Zoe laid her hand on Jeff's shoulder. "Every day, it's like there's something new to learn. I can't even keep up with what happens when I'm with you. What happened before I met you is totally beyond me." He took one hand off the steering wheel and grasped hers long enough to say, "There's plenty of time to catch up," before returning his hand to a safe driving position. The drive home continued, with discussion about Marilyn and the grade school, followed by a rambling explanation from Lucy about everything she had learned that day in homeschool.

Arriving home, everyone scattered to their rooms. Except Zoe, who dragged Jeff to the living room and asked, "What really happened to the McAdams? Sighing, he explained that last day, the layoff, the drinking, how they had shot Danielle, he had killed Tom, been shot by Audrey, who had been killed by the police. It took a while, and Zoe passed through rage at them to understanding to sadness. "I thought my life was awful." Jeff smiled. "We've both had our ups and downs." She nodded. "I have Lucy to show for my life. What do you have?" Now his smile grew. "You. And Lucy." She gently rubbed his shoulder. "Good answer." They followed the others to their rooms.

# Chapter 65

On Sunday afternoon between church services, everyone was sitting around the living room, engaged in Bible study or typing up notes from the morning service. Zoe paused to gaze at the walls, specifically at the pictures on those walls. There were many, ranging from old black and whites to electronic frames that flowed between pictures.

One of these was specifically of Jeff and Danielle and moved through their ages from six to the present. This particular frame had an extra button that changed the picture files from general viewing, acceptable to everyone, to a more comprehensive file that displayed their more violent activities including war games at Stuart's ranch and the Padre Island shark fight when they were twelve. Only a few people knew about the button, and the frame would automatically reset to the general file after one run through the special file. There was a second button to turn sound off and on. This button stayed on until turned off. The electronic frames also acted like night lights in the room even though they dimmed to match the amount of ambient light available.

As Zoe's eyes moved from picture to picture, she noticed ones that seemed to be Robert's parents, both now dead, and Michelle's parents, whose father was dead but whose mother still lived near Michelle's old house. Since Jeff and Danielle didn't know who their father was, she didn't expect to see a picture of him or his parents. But while there were pictures of Marilyn, there didn't seem to be any of her parents. So, she said, "I don't see any pictures of Marilyn's parents." The room seemed to freeze, and she thought, "Uhoh. Now what have I done?"

Jeff said calmly, "They disowned mom when she got pregnant and kicked her out." Zoe asked, "But what about you? You're their grandchild. And do they even know Danielle is your real twin?" Danielle explained about the trip to Keely when they were thirteen. "Jeff met with them, and they told him they weren't interested in getting to know him. We haven't spoken with them since." Michelle added, "We discussed it when we learned the truth about Danielle, but after Jeff's experience, we decided to just let it go."

Zoe shook her head sadly. "My grandparents are all gone. At least Lucy has Mummum and Poppop." Jeff said, "We have other grandparent figures, like Pastor Marcus." Robert laughed. "You'd better not let him hear you say that. On the one hand, I'm sure he would appreciate the sentiment. On the other hand, he still thinks he's twenty-five." The others in the room laughed and agreed. All of this sailed over Lucy's head. She was buried in her church notebook, puzzling over her Bible study. Her head did pop up when she heard her grandparents' names mentioned, but when she determined the conversation wasn't about them, she returned to her study.

No mention was made of her biological father's parents, and so far, they had made no attempt to contact the Armstrong family. The two adults sat stonily through their son's trial, never making eye contact with any member of the Armstrong family, but not really supporting their son, either. They appeared to be deeply ashamed but caught up because he was their son and family. Jake and Sophie had discussed between themselves that they might even have been silently glad he had died in prison. They could just pretend that he never existed. Since they lived on the other coast, there was little chance the two families would ever run into each other after the trial. All the older Armstrongs sincerely hoped this would remain true. Lucy wasn't old enough yet to wonder about it, and besides, she had her sights set on her father of choice.

Things were about to change where Marilyn's parents were concerned. Life had not gone well for them since Jeff and Danielle's visit to Keely. The transformation began slowly because at first the only ones who knew of their rejection of Jeff were those in the café when he walked across the street to speak with them at their insurance office. This included Mike and his team, the café owner, one of her waitresses, and the police chief. Even though Danielle told them not to let anyone know, it's difficult to keep a secret like that for years, and word had slowly leaked out, always with the admonition not to tell anyone, which slowed the spread but didn't stop it.

The attitude in town began to alter toward Seth and Katherine Mitchell. It took a few years, not only because of the slow spread of the story, but also because they weren't the friendliest couple in town anyway. There was no long list of friends who suddenly didn't have time for them. Most of the members of their church were just like them and approved of the treatment of their daughter and grandson. Their insurance business was run well and honestly, and most of the town's inhabitants were willing to put aside their opinion of the couple when it came to doing business.

Little things became noticeable, though, and grew. The atmosphere at the local business meeting became chiller toward them. They weren't invited to some weddings and graduations they expected to receive cards for. When their clients stopped in to discuss their policies, they didn't chat about their families the way they had before. Seth and Katherine weren't averse to this lack of conversation; they weren't comfortable with personal talk anyway, but they noticed the difference. Over dinner some evenings, they would talk about the changes going on around them, wondering if they were being paranoid.

Finally, Katherine made a comment to one of their church members, who stared at her in surprise. "You don't know? It's because of your grandson. A lot of the people in town don't approve of the way you treated him when he visited with all those parachute people. Especially after he helped rescue Navid and Forough." Katherine was puzzled. "That was years ago. Why are people starting to act differently now? How do they even know what we said in the insurance office? Did he tell everyone?" The other woman shook her head. "Only Paige, Carmelita, and the police chief knew. They didn't tell anyone for the longest, but then I guess word slowly leaked out. Now I guess about everyone in town knows."

After church, Katherine told her husband what she had learned. They spoke about it off and on for days, then weeks. As time passed, the atmosphere in the town did not improve. There were other insurance agents, and while they didn't lose much of their existing business, a few people changed, and they weren't getting new business the way they had before. And it seemed every Bible verse they read, every sermon they heard on the radio, even their daily devotionals all pointed out that they were wrong. Eventually they reached the conclusion that perhaps they had made a mistake. It wasn't an emotional or heartfelt conclusion; more of a logical progression. The result was the same. They decided they should try to reconcile with Marilyn and Jeff.

This decision led to a new problem. They had no idea how to get in touch with them. They didn't even know what city they lived in. When Marilyn had sent her one letter, Katherine, with Seth's approval, had marked it in large letters, "Return to sender", and tossed it back in the mailbox without paying any attention to the return address except to note it had come from Marilyn. She and Seth had more discussions regarding how to proceed. One evening, Seth said, "Maybe the police chief knows. He spent a lot of time with them when they were here."

The next day, Seth crossed the street to the diner when he spotted the police chief enter. Pushing open the door, he walked to the table where the man sat alone, hat on the table in front of him. Carmelita was hurrying toward the kitchen having just taken his order. There was an exchange of the usual, "Chief Green." "Seth." Then Seth sat in the extra chair and asked, "Do you know where we can find my daughter?" The officer sat back, surprised by the question. "Why would you want to?" Whatever was on the man's mind, the chief wasn't going to make it easy for him.

Seth clasped his hands on the table and said, "Katherine and I have come to think we made a mistake, and we'd like to try to make it up to our daughter and our grandson if we can. But we don't have any idea where they live. We thought you might." The chief snorted. "Did people's attitudes toward you around town have anything to do with your change of heart?" The other man shrugged. "It's what brought it to our attention, but it isn't what changed our minds. Seems like everywhere we turn lately in our Bible reading or our daily devotionals, we keep running into verses about children being a blessing and what our role as parents is supposed to be. It seems pretty clear to us that we need to make this right if we can. They may not want anything to do with us, but we have to try."

Chief Green didn't know whether to put much stock in this sudden change of heart or not. The couple, seeing the direction the wind was blowing, might just want to cut their losses. Performing some quick math in his head, he decided Jeff was old enough to decide for himself what he wanted to do, and he said, "I'll make a phone call and see if I can get the information for you. I'll let you know. How's that?" Seth nodded. At least it put them a step farther along than they had been before. If the chief couldn't find the information, they would have to try something else.

That evening over dinner, the chief told his wife about the conversation. She was skeptical as well. "They're just starting to get the cold shoulder around town, it's costing them business, and they want to fix that. They don't care about their daughter or the boy." He frowned. "Maybe. They are a religious sort, in their own cold way. Maybe God finally got through to them." After dinner he pulled out his phone and dialed Mike's number. After a couple of rings, Mike answered, and the chief identified himself. Mike was surprised to hear from the man. They hadn't kept in touch over the years.

When Chief Green explained the reason for his call, Mike was dumbstruck. He hadn't seen this coming at all and was skeptical as well. In addition, since he had last spoken with the chief, Marilyn had died, and Danielle had proven to be Jeff's real twin. His grandparents were in for some shocks. And it would have to wait until after the twins' birthday. They had too much on their plate to worry about grandparents who had wanted nothing to do with them for years.

# Chapter 66

Unaware of the new grandparent drama, Jeff and Danielle studied, did homework, and carried on with their projects. They also focused on two additional items: a trip to New York to speak with Father Stephan, and planning the American release of their movie. The four sets of actors portraying Jeff and Danielle would be flying to the US for opening day, swinging by to visit the Freedman ranch on their way back to Australia. Father Stephan had agreed to a visit, and the date was set for the Monday after their birthday.

They were telling everyone they wanted to visit the hospital in New York again, but no one was buying it. Robert and Michelle had given up asking, trusting the almost eighteen-year-old twins to make the correct decision, whatever it was. Zoe was more persistent, especially with the Baby SEAL ring on her finger. Plus, she wanted to visit New York, as did Lucy. Jeff held firm. He couldn't go with Zoe without an adult chaperone, and that meant even more people. He promised that they would go again, making a sweep down the eastern seaboard as the family had done the previous year.

Zoe's main concern was not seeing the city; she wanted to know what was bothering Jeff so much and why he didn't want to talk to her about it. Finally, he sat down with her and tried to explain, beginning with how he and Danielle had hidden Anna White in a hotel and how the plan had blown up in their faces, involving people they had tried to keep out of it. "She'll probably be at our birthday party. You can meet her then. We've helped different people over the years, and some of the ways we did it weren't always legal. So, we try not to get our friends and family involved in our schemes. That way no one gets charged with conspiracy."

Her first question was, "And flying to New York is one of these schemes?" He answered, "This one is way more complicated than that." Her second question was, "Should you be involved in illegal things?" He shrugged. "Sometimes the only option is to say no to helping, and we can't do that." Zoe said, "Like with the woman just before we left." He nodded. "Something like that." She punched him in the shoulder; or, rather, she would have if he hadn't slid smoothly out of the way. It was hard to punch someone in the shoulder when they had the reflexes of a snake.

The dating situation had been resolved, more or less to everyone's satisfaction. Any dates would involve Danielle, of course, and Robert and Michelle or Steve and Amy or perhaps Mike and Ella, possibly with Savannah as well. And probably, but not necessarily, Lucy. Everyone already knew there would be no kissing. Holding hands was acceptable. As was hugging. Being alone together in a place where they could not be observed was not acceptable. Basically, Victorian era dating rules. All of the adults were happy. Jeff and Zoe were okay with the rules. The "sisters" thought the rules were hilarious.

Danielle was basically under the same rules, but since she would seldom have the opportunity to see Henry, the rules for her were pretty moot. She would, however, be back in Australia for six months or whatever schedule they ended up working out so Lucy wasn't going to school year-round, and she could fly Henry to the US whenever he had leave long enough to make it worth the trip.

Meanwhile, Jeff and Danielle's birthday approached, and planning was underway. Slated for Steve and Amy's house, the guest list included about forty people. The Avery family would be flying in from Phoenix. Many people who would have loved to attend lived in other cities and even other countries, and attending the party would not have been practical; otherwise they would have enjoyed being present.

The party fell on a Saturday and would be a lunchtime affair, commencing around 1pm. Jeff and Danielle were forbidden to cook anything, but were ordered to stand around and be available. By now, everyone was familiar with Zoe and Lucy. Zoe was immediately cornered by the "sisters", and Sydney and Rachael, and questioned about how things were going with Jeff and the "dating rules". She rolled her eyes and answered as obliquely as possible, which only led to more questions. Lucy held court in the kitchen until Amy banished her to the living room, where she entertained the guests with her Australian accent and her unedited version of life in the outback, which she had never seen. She did have thrilling stories about a funnel web spider in the backyard and a poisonous snake at the Australian children's ranch to keep her audience enthralled.

She also told them about the movie, which she had finally been allowed to view; the edited, more G rated version. Her audience was anxious for the movie to open in the US and had questions of their own as to whether there would be a third one. Jeff and Danielle had reviewed the results so far from the Australian theaters, and they were promising. Their initial investment had been recovered, and the future proceeds should be able to fund the children's ranch and possibly some women's shelters as well. A third movie would be much more hands off, however. They would turn their notes over to Sebastian and let him take over from there. As long as God would receive the glory, they would probably be happy with the results. The cast and crew knew what was expected.

Food was served, and Jeff and Danielle wandered through the various rooms, chatting with all their well-wishers. Jeff snatched the fork from Lucy just before she launched it into the atmosphere as she gestured wildly during one of her stories. He said, "Careful, little one," in elvish as he handed it back. She grinned, said, "Thanks, mate!" and carried on with her tale. Jeff mock glared at her audience and said, "Don't spoil her!" Mike and Ella smiled guilelessly at him, and both said, "Not a chance!" Jeff rolled his eyes and moved on.

Jeff found Zoe in the kitchen chatting with Sydney and Rachel. Their conversation cut off abruptly as he appeared, and his two ex-girlfriends moved away. Nothing suspicious about that. He asked, "Have you met everyone? Are you having a good time?" She laid a hand on his arm and said, "All of your friends are amazing. My friends all seem so ordinary. Yours all have stories to tell. You and Danielle have saved half of them, or they've saved you." She paused and added, "I wish you weren't going to New York. Or I was going with you. Will you ever tell me what it's about?" He shrugged. "Maybe someday. When it's safe for you to know."

They wandered together into the living room where everyone was gathering. It was time for Jeff and Danielle to open their presents. Their friends, knowing the twins' propensity to only keep what would fit in their backpacks, had given gifts of consumables, plants for the Freedman garden (from Alice), electronics, eBooks, and such. When all of the packages had been opened, nothing whatsoever would be added to the limited backpack space. Jeff and Danielle had to laugh at their friends' ingenuity. Even Mike and his family had given them new leather arm sheaths for their knives. This earned a slight frown from Zoe and the promise of a future discussion.

That evening after the party, as Jeff and Zoe listened to Lucy's prayers and tucked her in, Jeff thought about the year past, and the year ahead. He and Danielle had survived Australia and graduated. The children's ranch was up and running. The first movie had been released, with the second not far behind. The church there was growing. Danielle had a boyfriend; her first. He had met what seemed to be his forever love and a daughter. Ahead of them lay new challenges: release of the second movie and production of a third; dealing with Owen one way or another; uni. It was promising to be another busy and exciting year. And he didn't even know that Marilyn's parents were searching for him.

Lucy gave each of them a hug. She told Zoe, "Love you, Mom," to which Zoe replied, "Love you, too, Luce." When she hugged Jeff, she whispered in his ear, "I love you, Dad." He was stunned speechless for a moment before he smiled at her and said, "I love you, too, Lucy." She snuggled into her bed, eyes closed, a grin on her face. Everything was coming together as she had planned from the very first.

I will love the light for it shows me the way, yet I will endure the darkness because it shows me the stars. Og Mandino

# Cast of Characters

Introduced in

| | |
|---|---|
| Book 1 | Jeff Mitchell (Blue SEAL) |
| Book 1 | Danielle LeBeau (Green SEAL) |
| Book 1 | Robert Freedman (Jeff and Danielle's adoptive father. Police officer who rescued Jeff and Danielle when they were 7; on the foundation board) |
| Book 1 | Michelle Freedman (Jeff and Danielle's adoptive mother. ICU nurse; on the foundation board) |
| Book 1 | Elizabeth Freedman (Michelle's Daughter) |
| Book 1 | Cindy Rogers Jacobs (Danielle's first foster sister and one of the "sisters"; adopted by Steve and Amy Jacobs) |
| Book 1 | Amy Jacobs (Steve's wife; on the foundation board) |

| | |
|---|---|
| Book 1 | Steve Jacobs (met Jeff and Danielle when they were 6; first to invite them to church; on the foundation board) |
| Book 3 | Lily Avery (nickname Lily; the hidden "sister"; cancer patient) |
| Book 3 | Mia Avery (Lily's mother) |
| Book 3 | Preston Avery (Lily's father; in Phoenix) |
| Book 2 | Chloe Wilson (Rainbow) one of the "sisters" |
| Book 4 | Village Sunshine (eight-year-old girl in village of Izersteling. The African "sister".) |
| Book 6 | Jake Armstrong (Australia. Father; Lucy's Poppop. 2nd host family.) |
| Book 6 | Sophie Armstrong (Australia. Jake's wife. Lucy's Mummum. 2nd host family.) |
| Book 6 | Sean Armstrong (Australia. Son. 2nd host family.) |
| Book 6 | Zoe Armstrong (Australia. Daughter. 2nd host family.) |
| Book 6 | Lucy Armstrong (Australia. Zoe's daughter. 2nd host family.) |

| | |
|---|---|
| Book 6 | Captain Harry Webster (leader of Australian special forces team. Brother to Sophie Armstrong.) |
| Book 6 | Henry (Australian special forces team; sniper) |
| Book 6 | Ned (Australian special forces team; corpsman) |
| Book 6 | Lieutenant Lachlan Carter (2nd in command of Australian special forces team; lead diver) |
| Book 6 | Angus Campbell (Australian special forces team; lead scout) |
| Book 6 | Oliver McDonald (Jeff and Danielle's lawyer in Australia) |
| Book 6 | Ivy Henderson (Captain Webster's niece; attends performing arts high school) |
| Book 6 | Alfred Henderson (Ivy's father) |
| Book 6 | Adelaide Henderson (Ivy's mother) |
| Book 2 | Owen Morris (Anthony's father. Crime boss in US.) |
| Book 6 | Shane King (Pastor at Victory Bible Church in Australia) |
| Book 6 | Sheila King (Shane's wife) |

| Book 6 | Officer Victor Cameron (Australian police officer who keeps showing up at Jeff and Danielle's incidents) |
| --- | --- |
| Book 6 | Acacia Cameron (Kitty) (Officer Cameron's daughter) |
| Book 6 | Sebastian Strange (producer of Jeff and Danielle's movie) |
| Book 6 | Barb (employee at Skymasters in Australia) |
| Book 6 | JR (Jeff and Danielle's parachute instructor in Australia) |
| Book 7 | Moncrief family (Wedding where Zoe is attacked) |
| Book 7 | Gloria (Sean's girlfriend) |
| Book 7 | Linda (TV news reporter in Australia Jeff and Danielle give information to) |
| Book 7 | Gerald (11-year-old prodigy in Jeff and Danielle's senior class) |
| Book 7 | Bobbie Steinfield (Six-year-old Danielle for movie) |
| Book 7 | Merit Steinfield (Eight-year-old Danielle for movie) |

| | |
|---|---|
| Book 7 | Abigail Steinfield (Ten-year-old Danielle for movie) |
| Book 7 | Caroline Steinfield (Twelve-year-old Danielle for movie) |
| Book 7 | Alexander Leighton (Six-year-old Jeff for movie) |
| Book 7 | Ashton Leighton (Eight-year-old Jeff for movie) |
| Book 7 | Asa Leighton (Ten-year-old Jeff for movie) |
| Book 7 | Alec Leighton (Twelve-year-old Jeff for movie) |
| Book 7 | Akala Webb (Five-year-old Elizabeth for movie) |
| Book 7 | Alba Webb (Seven-year-old Elizabeth for movie) |
| Book 7 | Alinga Webb (Nine-year-old Elizabeth for movie) |
| Book 7 | Akina Webb (Eleven-year-old Elizabeth for movie) |
| Book 7 | Kiernan Allan (Ten-year-old Cindy for movie) |

| | |
|---|---|
| Book 7 | Eloise Allan (Twelve-year-old Cindy for movie) |
| Book 7 | Erica Allan (Fourteen-year-old Cindy for movie) |
| Book 7 | Odeya Allan (Sixteen-year-old Cindy for movie) |
| Book 7 | Hanna (Haimanot's assistant with clinic billing) |
| Book 4 | Ketema (Sgt. Etefu's brother; lives in Tsege Mariam) |
| Book 4 | Negat (Ketema's wife) |
| Book 4 | Sebhat (Ketema's son) |
| Book 5 | Bayissa (Abeba's husband) |
| Book 5 | Ezana (Abeba's oldest son) |
| Book 5 | Berhanu (Abeba's youngest son) |
| Book 4 | Girma (2nd in command of soldier escort; now chief of police at Izersteling) |
| Book 7 | Steven Colling (general contractor for children's ranch in Australia) |

| | |
|---|---|
| Book 6 | Dr. Juliana Gomez–Bello (permanent doctor for the region of Tsege Mariam and Izersteling) |
| Book 6 | Pastor Ezera Bello (pastor for the region of Tsege Mariam and Izersteling) |
| Book 5 | Dr. Braxton Flowers III (1st doctor sent to Africa. Sets up Hope Clinic in Izersteling.) |
| Book 7 | Dr. Carlos Munoz (first dentist at Hope Clinic in Africa) |
| Book 7 | Katie (cancer patient in Gold Coast) |
| Book 7 | Scout (Lucy's horse in Texas) |
| Book 1 | John Patton (Head pastor at 2nd Street Bible Church; on the foundation board) |
| Book 1 | Sam and Kathy Shepherd, Sam Jr., Bailey (homeschool Jeff and Danielle) |
| Book 1 | Marcus Hall (formerly associate pastor at 2nd Street Bible Church; now in charge of the children's ranch; on the foundation's board) |
| Book 1 | Marilyn Mitchell (Jeff's mother) |
| Book 1 | Beth (special needs kid on cruise; Jeff's first crush) |

| Book 1 | Alice Springley (Danielle's next-door neighbor when Danielle was six; on foundation board) |
| Book 1 | Eunice (Alice's sister) |
| Book 1 | Tom and Audrey McAdams (Danielle's 2nd foster parents) |
| Book 3 | Anna White (first homeless kid Jeff and Danielle help; 2nd artist to help Danielle with patches; lives with Jordan and Abbey Lee) |
| Book 3 | Paige (owns restaurant in Keely) |
| Book 3 | Carmelita (waitress at restaurant in Keely) |
| Book 3 | Chief Green (police chief in Keely, Colorado) |
| Book 4 | Ambassador Lemma (ambassador from the African nation where the water project is located) |
| Book 1 | Adeela (customer service at bank. Also on foundation board.) |
| Book 5 | Aidan (driving instructor) |
| Book 1 | Stuart (Ex-Navy SEAL; friend of Mike's. Owns land east of city with trees and underbrush and long shooting lanes. Likes to dive.) |

| | |
|---|---|
| Book 5 | Sydney Edwards (Olivia's middle daughter; Jeff's 2nd girlfriend) |
| Book 5 | Amber Edwards Frederick (Olivia's oldest daughter) |
| Book 5 | Jason Frederick (Amber's husband) |
| Book 5 | Kendall Frederick (Amber's youngest daughter) |
| Book 5 | Kylie Frederick nickname Dragon Rider (Amber's oldest daughter) afraid of flying |
| Book 5 | William Edwards (Olivia's oldest son) |
| Book 5 | Reagan Edwards (William's wife) |
| Book 5 | Levi Edwards (Bear) (William's son) |
| Book 5 | Mckenzie Edwards (William's daughter) |
| Book 5 | Christian Edwards (Olivia's youngest son) |
| Book 2 | Alexandria Walker (Rachael's mother) |
| Book 2 | Evan Walker (Rachael's father) |
| Book 2 | Katelyn Walker (Rachael's middle sister) |
| Book 2 | Makenna Walker (Rachael's oldest sister) |

| | |
|---|---|
| Book 5 | Sally (leader of the elementary age Sunday School class at the first church Jeff and Danielle visit in new town) |
| Book 5 | Taz (Charles) (young cancer patient at the resort pool) |
| Book 3 | Kayla Young (cave diver. Deaf. Saves Danielle at lake.) |
| Book 5 | Kaleb (boy at volleyball court on cruise) |
| Book 5 | Skylar (Kaleb's sister) |
| Book 5 | Marian (creates Dobbieball app for Baby SEALs website) |
| Book 5 | Heather (girl at school showing the videos on her tablet) |
| Book 5 | Cupcake (student at Jeff and Danielle's new public high school) |
| Book 5 | Simone (Michelle's friend at the hospital who wants a bodyguard for her patient) |
| Book 5 | Taylor (Simone's patient that Jeff and Danielle guard) |
| Book 3 | Aisha (Nabeel's youngest daughter, 14) |
| Book 3 | Ammara (Nabeel's oldest daughter, 18) |

| | |
|---|---|
| Book 1 | Andrew (Drummer in Terry's band) |
| Book 1 | Marcy (One of the keyboard players in Terry's band) |
| Book 2 | Anthony Morris (Badger) cancer patient |
| Book 2 | Ashley (Princess) cancer patient |
| Book 3 | Blake (cave diver) |
| Book 2 | Blizzard (cancer patient in Pensacola) |
| Book 3 | Brianna Phillips (Devin's wife; Haley's sister-in-law. Middle school math teacher) |
| Book 2 | Brook (Rose) cancer patient in hospital at Padre Island; one of the first patches) |
| Book 3 | Cody (cave diver) |
| Book 4 | Conner (Justin's brother) |
| Book 2 | Connor (Dingo) (12-year-old cancer patient in Jeff and Danielle's home town. Took Danielle to dance.) |
| Book 2 | Crusher (cancer patient in Pensacola) |
| Book 1 | Dan and Marla (members of 2nd Street Bible Church. In Jacobs Bible study group.) |

| | |
|---|---|
| Book 2 | Danny (Rocky) (cancer patient in hospital at Padre Island; one of the first patches) |
| Book 1 | Denise (1st grade Sunday School helper) |
| Book 3 | Devin Phillips (Haley's brother. Police detective) |
| Book 4 | Dr. Jennifer Donovan (vet at the clinic) |
| Book 4 | Dr. Kevin Donovan (vet at the clinic) |
| Book 2 | Dylan Wilson (Rainbow's little brother) |
| Book 2 | Hannah (Pepper) (cancer patient in Austin) |
| Book 4 | Ian and Jessica Decker (Husband and wife from Des Moines traveling with Mallory and Kyle to Africa) |
| Book 3 | Jamal (Nabeel's youngest son, 16) |
| Book 1 | Jamie (Beth's older sister) |
| Book 2 | Jenna (Dragonfly) (cancer patient in Pensacola) |
| Book 1 | Jim and Sherrie (members of 2nd Street Bible Church. In Jacobs Bible study group.) |
| Book 3 | Joseph Phillips (Son) |

| | |
|---|---|
| Book 3 | Dr. Romano (NYC friend of one of the doctor's in at East Side Memorial Hospital) |
| Book 1 | Eddie (works at the information counter at Jeff and Danielle's bank) |
| Book 1 | Elaine (night nurse at East Side Memorial Hospital; Michelle's best friend) |
| Book 1 | Elena and Tisha (friends of Jeff and Danielle at Viewpoint Apartments) |
| Book 1 | Emily Merrill (Boyd and Pam's youngest daughter) |
| Book 4 | Ethan Howard (Terrence's twelve-year-old son) |
| Book 3 | Faith Young (Kayla's mother) |
| Book 4 | Father Stephan (Priest at church near Central Park in NYC) |
| Book 3 | Firefly (Erin) (twelve-year-old cancer patient in Keely, Colorado) |
| Book 1 | Frank (one of first adults to give six-year-old Jeff and Danielle odd jobs; wants hoses moved) |
| Book 3 | Fred Robinson (mayor of Keely, Colorado) |

| | |
|---|---|
| Book 4 | Rylee Howard (Terrence's ten-year-old daughter) |
| Book 3 | Seth Mitchell (Marilyn's father) |
| Book 1 | Sgt. McKowsky (Robert's sergeant. First on the scene when Robert was shot) |
| Book 2 | Sparkle (NYC cancer patient) |
| Book 2 | Sparkle's mom. Friend of Megan. |
| Book 3 | Tanner (Cayenne's uncle; run's chop shop) |
| Book 4 | Terrence Howard (Nashville police officer at Tennessee civil war site) |
| Book 3 | Thomas Barlow (apartment manager in Kansas City) |
| Book 1 | Tom (one of first adults to give six-year-old Jeff and Danielle odd jobs; wants his front yard watered) |
| Book 1 | Tommy (runs the outdoor gun range where Jeff and Danielle fired guns for the first time) |
| Book 1 | Toni Patterson (one of first adults to give six-year-old Jeff and Danielle odd jobs; they watch her children for an hour twice a week) |

| Book 1 | Tony (works in a head shop; friend of Marilyn's) |
| Book 3 | Trevor (diver taking open water test with Rachael) |
| Book 4 | Wendy (attendant at gym in Boston) |

# Endnotes

1  https://www.tripadvisor.com/AttractionProductDetail-
   g255325-d14179849-Seascapes_to_Laneways_Walking_Tour-
   Newcastle_Greater_Newcastle_New_South_Wales.html
2  https://www.deinternational.nsw.edu.au/how-to-apply/
   brochures-and-forms
3  https://answersingenesis.org/blogs/ken-ham/2018/10/23/
   how-do-we-know-bible-true/
4  https://answersingenesis.org/kids/bible/
   where-did-the-bible-come-from/
5  https://answersingenesis.org/is-god-real/
   how-do-we-know-there-is-a-god/
6  https://answersingenesis.org/sin/god-and-sin-gibberish/
7  http://moringacommunity.org/OurWork/FoodPreservation.html
8  https://answersingenesis.org/what-is-science/
   deceitful-terms-historical-and-observational-science/
9  https://answersingenesis.org/kids/science/
   what-about-those-embryos/
10  https://www.army.gov.au/our-work/equipment-and-clothing/
   vehicles/g-wagon
11  Well-Versed Kids by Bill & Sue Tell